Foreword

The Misfits book series came about by accident. Having some time out from my normal career in marketing, I decided I wanted to write a short erotic leather story, just to see if I could. Leather wear and the use of it in the gay community has been a pivotal part of my own sexuality, so writing part one, The Chance Meeting, was the start. I shared the story with some like-minded men on social media and got some really positive feedback.

Despite my initial intention, thinking at first this would be a one off, I was asked by a couple of people to continue the story. So I wrote part two, Pain and Ecstasy. By the end of part two I really started to enjoy the writing process and particularly bringing the main characters to life. After part two I decided to map out three more stories to the series, taking my characters into new relationships and locations around the world.

In preparing this complete series edition, I have re-visited the text; correcting some errors and taking the opportunity to fine tune other passages, most notably the beginning of part two in order to improve the flow as a single book series.

All places mentioned in the book exist for real, from barber shops to restaurants, many of which I have been to on my travels with work. It's been a lot of fun to write this series and I hope you enjoy them as much as I have writing them.

I've welcomed all the feedback I've received. Some readers have asked if the story of Max, Bobby and Cole will continue. At the moment the series is complete for me, but who knows, I may bring them back. Never say never……

Nick

THE MISFITS

(the complete 5 part book series)

Part 1 – The Chance Meeting
Part 2 – Pain and Ecstasy
Part 3 – Opportunity Knocks
Part 4 – Passport to Leather Central
Part 5 – Tragödie in der Stadt

THE CHANCE MEETING
(Part 1 in 'The Misfits' Series)
NICK CHRISTIE

The Chance Meeting
(Part 1 in 'The Misfits' Series)
(Erotic Gay Fiction)

Nick Christie

Part 1 – The Chance Meeting

Chapter 1 - A Casual Acquaintance

Max Steadman is out on the town. It's a warm summer evening in Chicago. He's in a bar local to his apartment. He's in full leathers, jeans, shirt, boots and gloves. His jacket is neatly placed on the back of the bar stool next to him. Max sits facing the bar taking in his environment. He can see in the mirror opposite a young guy in the booth behind, checking him out. He's probably surprised at all this leather, Max smiled to himself, but he fucking likes it and that's all that matters. He's cute, but quite young, thought Max. Cute with a quiff of blonde hair. Probably mid-twenties. Max had just turned fifty, but was still in good shape and not bad looking. He had been very handsome in his youth.

Then, while studying the young man, Max notices another young guy walk into the bar. Strong build, toned, tanned and handsome. We are talking sexy, dirty handsome. Considering there are many other empty stools, Max is surprised that the new guy takes the stool next to him. Jeans, trainers and a white vest top. It's a very warm evening in Chicago, probably mid eighty degrees. Max acknowledges him and casually starts chatting to the young guy. He notices he's eyeing up his leathers. He seems quite interested and they chat about various stuff, you know small talk, the weather, cars and sports.

After a while, as he seemed interested, Max asked, "You wanna try my jacket on?"

The young man pauses, then does as suggested.

"Ok, looks like a good one," he says casually.

Max can tell the young guy is enjoying the feeling of it on his hard body. He sniffs the leather and can smell Max's smell on it. He looks so damn hot in my jacket, thought Max. It's tight on his bigger frame but the black leather looks awesome next to his dirty blonde hair, all messy and wavy. He's very handsome, boyish but with a 'square jawed' roughness. He looks Max in the eye and smiles. Max notices he's getting hard in his tight jeans. They talk some more over a beer.

The young man looks a bit of a tough guy and so Max asks him a question, "Have you ever roughed over anyone?"

"Yeah, plenty," he replied, "specially in my youth but now sadly it's harder to do. People sue you!" he laughed. He explained how he used to be a bit of a bully in school. Used to enjoy the domination, the power of the control and the fear in the eyes of the victims. Max agreed it felt great.

They talked some more about it, Cole explaining how the feeling of him and his mates screwing over other kids made him feel strong, and alive. The rush of adrenaline and enjoyment seeing others feeling small and worthless. The more they talked the more they both started to feel aroused.

"Do you want to do it again?" Max asked.

"How's that?" he asked.

"Let me show you...."

Chapter 2 - People Watching

Bobby Wilson was sitting in a booth in a local bar on his own. People watching was fun. He had a beer on the go, when he saw an older guy walk in and sit at the bar in front of him. He was tall, slim and had striking salt and pepper hair, cut short. But even more striking and unusual was that he was head to toe in black leather. Soft, shiny black leather. The man sat at the bar facing the mirror catches Bobby looking at him. Bobby turns away quickly, but struggling to resist, he looks back. The guy smiles and winks. The 'leather man' then orders a beer at the bar. An import. Bobby was even more intrigued. So he's sophisticated, he thought. The leather man then takes off his jacket and puts it on the chair next to him and neatly arranges it. In doing so, he reveals a leather short sleeve shirt and a wide belt on some amazing looking leather jeans. Did that zip go all the way round? He was wearing short cop style gloves too and didn't take them off to drink.

After a few minutes Bobby could smell that leather. So much of it. It was sweet and heady and really quite a horny smell. Not something he had thought about before. He knew bad boys wore leather, but he had never had any himself. But now Bobby could see the appeal. This older guy was quite hot and intriguing.

Then the door opened and in walked a face Bobby hadn't seen in a while.

"Fuck, it's Cole," he whispered under his breath.

Bobby hadn't seen him since high school. He was looking good. Fit and slim with a muscular build. He was in jeans with black Nike Shox and a wife-beater vest, the shirt really showed off his strong arms and shoulders. Impressive guns. His hair was short and he looked even more handsome than Bobby remembered.

Bobby forgot how much he dreaded and then missed his teasing at school. It was great to just get his attention then, even if it was with his fist. Bobby loathed Cole, but also used to beat off, imagining him fucking him hard. God he looked so hot now. Those old urges were starting to surge in Bobby's body, particularly his cock.

Strangely, Cole sat next to the leather man. Did he know him? After a while they started chatting. Cole even put on the leather man's jacket. It was tight. He looked amazing in it. Bobby had to put his hand on his crotch to cover his now showing boner in his jeans. Fortunately, Cole hadn't noticed Bobby, but then again, he never did....

Chapter 3 - A meeting of Minds

Cole turned to the Max and said, "I'm sorry, I haven't properly introduced myself. I'm Cole."

"I'm Max. I'm British, if you hadn't realised," he smiled. "I'm in the US for work."

"Cool," Cole said, "I kinda guessed the accent. Brits are cool. Cool Britannia and all that."

"Cheers, you're pretty cool too. Even cooler now you're in my jacket," Max grinned.

Cole interrupted the pleasantries and said, "So, you mentioned about re-igniting my domination and bully tendencies?"

"Oh yeah," Max said. "You fancy doubling up with me and playing with a victim?"

"Really? That sounds awesome. Is it legal?" asked Cole.

"It can be," Max replied.

"Ok only if I can wear your awesome jacket."

"Well I'm glad you said that. I have plenty more gear, if you're willing," smiled Max.

"Maybe," said Cole. "So, what's the plan?"

"Ok. Don't look too obvious. Look in the mirror opposite. You see that lad in the booth behind us? He's been checking us out since we got here and judging from the boner under the table, he would be perfect. Cute too. Ripe for a bit of destruction."

Cole took a look, grinned and then sniggered.

"Oh yes, he's perfect. And here's why: I know him! I used to beat on him at high school. Robert 'friggin' Wilson. Now he's older, this could be real fun. I'm sure he fancied me as well. What's the plan?"

Chapter 4 - Shox

Bobby couldn't keep his eyes off Cole and leather man. Both sitting at the bar. Their arses on the stools looked great. Nice tight denim on one and THAT all round zip on the leather of the other. Leather smell everywhere. Those Shox looked so hot on Cole. For some reason Bobby kept thinking of one of them on his throat as Cole stood over him. His perfect fantasy! 'Jeez you've gotta stop staring otherwise they are gonna come over for fucks sake,' he thought to himself. 'Oh, heck they are getting up and looking at me now. Shit. What should I do?'

Chapter 5 - The Booth Connection

Cole and Max stood up.

Max said, "Just follow my lead."

They turned round and looked at Robert in the booth and smiled. They walked over to him.

"You on your own? Would you like some company?" Max asked.

The young man went a bit red and smiled weakly and said, "Err ok."

Max nodded to the barman, "Can we have three more beers here please? This time we'll have Estrella."

"Hi. I'm Max and this is Cole, but I understand you know Cole. I couldn't help noticing you checking us out at the bar, which is fine. I'm flattered. You interested in having some fun tonight?"

"Errr, not sure maybe. What you thinking?" stuttered Bobby.

Cole butted in.

“Robert, you remember me right? Sorry I might have been a bit of an asshole in school but that’s ‘cos you kept checking me out. Judging by the boner in your pants you still want it.”

Max stepped back into the conversation, just as the beers arrived.

“I have an apartment round the corner and I’m feeling fucking horny at the moment. You fancy coming back with us for some fun. Noticed you checking my leathers out. You like them? My jacket looks great on Cole don’t you agree?”

Chapter 6 - Do dreams come true?

Bobby was nervous as they approached his booth and sat down. They ordered more beer, Spanish this time, and asked if he was interested in some fun. They both looked so hot opposite him. Cole was still as cute and fit as fuck. Slim waist with powerful thighs. Max introduced himself and was English, with a very sexy accent. Confident and had very attractive eyes. Bobby guessed he was about forty five but he was in good shape. Also slim, and wow all that leather. The smell now right up close. Bobby had never thought about leather before until now. The short gloves were so tight and well fitting. His cock was raging now in his pants. Max then asked if Bobby wanted to have some fun in his apartment. Bobby paused, but he was free and fuck, this may be his chance to get his dream fuck from Cole.

'Hell yeah' Bobby wanted some nasty fun with these two and Cole looked great in that leather too.

Chapter 7 - The Elevator

"Drink up," Max said and put down a fifty for the drinks. "These are on me. Let's go."

All three looked at each other and each checked out their boners. Robert had a great arse thought Max. He was in jeans and a t-shirt and some battered old brown ankle boots. They all walked out the bar into the warm night air.

Robert piped up as they walked, "By the way, I go by Bobby now. Robert is what my mother calls me when I'm in the dog-house."

Max and Cole both laughed.

"Ok, Bobby it is," Max said. It was getting dusk now. "Turn left and up this street," Max instructed.

They got to his apartment and into the lobby. They entered the elevator. The door closed on the mirrored lift and at that point Max grabbed Bobby and pushed him against the wall and put his leather gloved hand over his mouth and pushed his thigh against his crotch.

"Don't fight it boy or Cole will hit you hard. Just like he used to."

Chapter 8 - Down to Business

Bobby left the bar with Cole and Max and they strolled a few blocks, before reaching Max's apartment building, where they then all entered an elevator. Nice place Bobby thought. As the door closed, he was pushed up against the wall by Max. Gloved hand over his mouth and a strong thigh pinning him against the wall. Cole was grinning and clenching his fists. Max took the glove away and kissed him deeply. He tasted of beer and kissed aggressively. Bobby's dick reacted. His heart was racing. Fuck, these guys were gonna destroy him and deep down he wanted it.

Max instructed, "Don't fight it."

Bobby replied, "Oh no. Do your worst, I've wanted this all evening. Cole, just treat me like the piece of shit you used to think I was."

"Awesome. Fuck this is gonna be the best," Cole grinned widely and wildly.

Chapter 9 - So it begins

They all walked out the lift and came to Max's apartment. They went in. It was a good size. Lounge, two bedrooms and a dressing room. Cole and Bobby were thinking the same thing, Max had to be loaded.

"Grab him!" said Max to Cole.

Cole held Bobby's arms back with one hand and put his other over his mouth. Max got a kitchen chair and a roll of duct tape.

"Strap him to that."

And so it began. Once taped to the chair, Max signalled to Cole to follow him into his dressing room. He did so dutifully.

Chapter 10 - Dress Code

Cole was amazed when he saw the dressing room. It was huge and smelt of sex. One side was normal suits, clothes etc, but the other was another story. It was a wall of leather and denim and it smelt amazing. Cole, like Bobby, had never been that bothered by leather. He'd had a jacket in his youth. Made him look hard and tough. All the better to bully in. He walked over and touched the leathers. He was still wearing Max's jacket.

Max asked if he wanted to wear some more leather. "Cole you would look great in some jeans maybe. What waist size are you? Thirty two inch?"

"Umm I'm a thirty," Cole replied.

"Erm and with your thighs they ain't gonna fit," Max said staring at Cole's powerful athletic legs.

"No worries," said Cole.

"No, no, hang on. Try on my chaps. I wear these over jeans so they are a bit bigger and should fit. Hold up a second," Max said reaching for something on a shelf. "Take your trousers and boxers off first. And put this on." He threw over a leather jock with a detachable cod piece.

Cole looked up at Max, "Really?"

"Yeah give it a try. Once you feel leather against your cock you won't want anything else," laughed Max.

Cole paused, shrugged and then stripped. He got the jock on and over his growing boner.

"Wow," Cole said. He was struggling to clip the poppers of the codpiece on.

"Here," Max said with a huge smile on his face. "Let me help you with that."

Max got on his knees and clipped on the first two poppers and could smell the warmth of Cole's crotch. He couldn't resist he licked the side of Cole's shaft. Cole quickly pulled back.

"That sure tastes good," Max said. Cole wasn't sure. "Oh come on. You're gonna get that dick well and truly sucked when we get back to our victim. You're gonna be throat fucking him very shortly."

That sexy evil grin came back to Cole's face.

"Indulge me," said Max, "You are a really sexy looking guy."

Max finished getting the codpiece on and then got Cole to put on the chaps. "Take that wife-beater off. Sexy as it may be, I have something better for you." He pulled out a chest harness. "On that chest it's gonna look beautiful," Max said. "Slip the jacket back on and I think the Shox will give your leather a nice street look. My boots won't fit."

Max stood back.

"Fuck Cole, you look amazing. A real nasty looking bad boy. One final touch. Will these gloves fit you? They've gotta be tight." Cole force them on. Snug and tight. "Ok, let's go ruin this boy together," grinned Max.

Chapter 11 - Your God

Bobby sat strapped to the chair. Where had they gone? What were they doing? His heart was racing and his cock was throbbing. They were gone for around ten minutes when the door they went through re-opened.

Max appeared first, grinning from ear to ear. He said, "You are gonna be in for a real treat Bitch." Max was followed by Cole who was now head to foot in leather. Jacket, a harness revealing a beautiful chest with some nice chest hair and treasure trail. 'That's grown since school' Bobby thought. Leather chaps tight on his thighs which looked great with the Nikes. But then, wow. The crowning glory. A leather jock on his hairy crotch. Cole looked fucking evil in that gear. Hot and evil. Bobby knew he was in for some real trouble.

Chapter 12 - Adrenaline

"Ok," said Max, "Listen very carefully, I'm in charge and if you follow my instructions, we will all have a good evening. You Bobby will be referred to as Bitch from now on and will do as we say. The safe word is 'RED'. Be sure to use it at any point you want us to stop, and we will. But I really hope you don't have to use it. Do you understand, both of you?"

"Yes," said Bobby.

"Uh huh, whatever," said Cole.

"Ok Cole, over to you. Play with Bitch however you wish, while I get some beers for us two. Be sure to show your inner bully again. I want to see Bitch cry tonight."

Max got some beers and passed one to Cole who was still standing looking at Bitch. Max sat down opposite for a ring side view of tonight's action.

Cole took a swig and put the bottle down. He walked up to Bitch. He looked real nervous and excited and then scared. Cole laughed, and kicked the chair Bitch was taped to, backwards. Bitch just managed to brace himself as he careered backwards and crashed to the floor, just managing to not bash his head. Cole grinned, a look of pure evil. Cole then got his Nike and put it on Bitch's throat.

"Still fancy me boy?" smirked Cole.

"Yes," said Bitch.

"Perfect," Cole sneered, "You like my gear? You turned on?"

"Yes sir," said Bitch.

"Lick my Nike's boy. Show some appreciation to your old friend."

Cole then decided to sit on Bitch's chest, with his leather crotch right in his face. His bare arse on his T-shirt. Bitch could smell his crotch and arse. It was warm and musky. "You want my cock boy?"

"Yes sir," Bitch continued to reply.

Cole then shoved his gloved hand on Bitch's throat and the other he put in his mouth. "Taste the leather boy."

"Very good Cole," Max said from the sofa. "This is getting me nice and hard. Keep going but remember to leave some for me," he laughed. "Be real brutal though and don't hold back on Bitch. I think he can take it."

Cole slapped Bitch's face and then stood up. Both legs either side of his head.

"How hot am I?" Cole asked.

Bobby lay there seeing his dominant aggressor standing over him. Those powerful legs in leather, the musty stink of his well used Nike's either side. The wonderful arse and crotch above him and Cole's handsome cruel face looking down, laughing at Bobby's pathetic state. He was amazing. As amazing as Bobby remembered, but ten times more aggressive. Shit this was so hot and he could feel his heart beating hard, pumping blood towards his own cock in his jeans.

"You are amazing Cole. ....Sir," Bitch corrected himself.

Cole righted Bitch's chair and then pressed his crotch into his face.

"Lick the leather boy. Lick it. Use your teeth to release my cock."

Cole's cock was now hard as a rock and pushing against the pouch. Bitch did as he asked and was rewarded with the most beautiful hard cock. Cole pushed Bitch's face into it. "Smell it!"

Cole's cock smelt awesome he thought. Sweaty and pissy. Nice and ripe.

"Open wide Bitch and take it."

Cole thrust in all nine inches and grabbed Bitch's head. He fucked that face so hard. Tears were in Bitch's eyes. He was gagging and choking but doing the best he could. Cole asked if Bitch wanted a drink. Bitch nodded.

"Open up," Cole said, pulling his cock out of Bitch's mouth. Cole took a swig of his beer and then let it run out his mouth into Bitch's.

It tasted so good, thought Bitch. Cole then spat the last bit in his face and laughed. He raised his arm and then swung it and stopped just before he hit his face. Laughing again.

This was such great fun, thought Cole. Cole was getting harder by the second.

“I’m really enjoying this,” Cole said.

It was the best feeling. Cole couldn’t remember when he last got the chance to beat someone up. Years, and he missed it. The power and the adrenaline always got him hard. At school it was easier to get away with it. Not so much when you are an adult, until today. Fuck this is gonna be a great night, he thought.

Chapter 13 - Collar

Max said to stop.

"Untie him from the chair and bind his hands behind his back. Bring him next to me on the sofa. Tear off his t-shirt and get this Bitch naked."

Cole did as he was told. He was loving the violence. It had been too long. Too fucking long. It was fun and fucking sexy. He tore at that shirt, it came off in two rips. Then the boots, and the jeans were dragged off, revealing Bitch's boner in his briefs.

Cole sniggered, "Look at little Bitch, all turned on by his old bully." He soon then got those briefs off.

"Open that drawer," Max instructed, pointing to a small cabinet. "There is a leather collar in there. Put it on Bitch. Will make it easier to move 'it' around as we play with it." Bobby then realised he was now a thing. Not a person to them.

"Christ man. You have everything you need for this don't you?" said Cole.

"Yes I do. This is just the start," Max replied.

Cole dragged Bitch to Max's feet. Max instructed "Bitch, lick my boots now. Lick up my leg and my thighs. Can you taste the previous cum of other doms I've played with, and our victims on them? The sweat and tears?"

"Yes sir," Bitch replied.

"Then we shall continue…."

Part 1 – The Chance Meeting

Chapter 14 - Playing with the boy

Once Bitch was near the top of Max's thigh, Cole watched closely and was beating his own meat. He was finding this such a turn on. This gay doming is great, he thought. The fags love it and don't cry as much as the girls. This is awesome. Perfect world for bullies.

Max unzipped his full zip round fly. Something that had intrigued Bobby in the bar.

"Smell my balls and cock Bitch."

He dived in without hesitation. Max was is great shape. Flat stomach and nice hairy cock and balls. Seven and a half inches. Not bad. Hard as a rock too. Bitch got in and started licking.

"Smell it," Max instructed. It smelt awesome. Sweat leather and piss. Toxic. "Lick my dick!" Bitch did as he was told. Licking the full length of Max's veiny hard cock.

"Now take it to the hilt! No teeth or I'll fucking punch you," ordered Max. Bitch did as asked. Took it in one go. He'd done this before and loved cock from an early age. Sucked a boy in the local woods at the age of fourteen. Cock was his world.

"Keep sucking. Now Cole, prepare that boy's cunt," Max ordered. "Spit on your hand and lube him up."

Bobby moaned. He was gonna get it from both ends. Cole spat on the glove and started circling his hole, eventually ramming a couple of fingers in. Bitch jolted.

"Come on. More than two" Max said. "I wanna hear him squeal like a pig." Cole spat on his hand again and put all four in hard. Bitch squealed and bit Max by accident.

"You fucking cunt!!"

Max struck Bitch in the face with his gloved hand and then forced his head back on his cock. "Not again. Better not feel your teeth again. Now look at me."

Bitch looked up. Tears in his eyes. Max smirked back. To see the boy's vulnerability and pain made his cock tweak a little harder. He then forced Bitch back on his cock. Cole meanwhile was pushing his fingers in and out, spitting on the glove occasionally.

"Now Cole. Fuck him hard," Max said.

"Wondered when you were gonna let me at it," Cole said, just as he was about to take his jacket off.

"Keep those leathers on. The sensation of leather on your thighs and body as you fuck a boy cunt is a beautiful thing. The perfume that rises from the heat of arse and leather is magnificent. Plus, when I wear them again I will smell your man smell on them, which on leather, is nectar."

Cole did as instructed, crouched down and spread Bitch's arse cheeks. He spat on his cock and then drove all nine inches in at once. Bitch cried out but managed to not bite.

"Good boy. You're learning," Max said.

Both doms rammed into both Bitch's holes. Max was watching Cole's face. It was beautiful. He was loving destroying his schoolboy victim. This time really destroying him. The joy and intense excitement as he pumped Bitch was wonderful to watch. This was made all the more intense as Bitch was face deep on his own cock. Perfect combination.

Max pulled Bitch off and offered the collar to Cole. "Go on, fuck him raw. If you can, make him bleed. Grab his hair. Punch his back. Enjoy it, you've earned it Cole, all those years of waiting to really ruin him."

Cole was in heaven destroying the boy like a rag doll on his knees. He pumped harder and harder, his cock was almost getting sore, Christ knows how Bitch's hole felt, but he didn't care. Judging from the whimpers and cries, it was hurting, which made it all the better. He was ruining this boy and he was getting so much pleasure from it. Another punch and hair grab will help me get close, Cole thought.

"Fuck, I'm gonna cum real soon," he groaned.

Part 1 – The Chance Meeting

Chapter 15 - The Destruction

“Go on breed it. Breed his gut,” Max said. “Take him for the slut he is. Use his body for your pleasure, don’t have a care for him. He’s worthless, you are the master of him. You have the power and the control.”

Cole was so charged to hear Max’s words he grabbed Bitch back up by the collar, put his gloved hands round his throat and pulled open his mouth to get more traction. He drove his cock in and out harder and harder. Cole thought how he could hurt Bitch further. That’s what he liked and wanted to see and hear. It came to him in a flash. He took one gloved hand back looked down and shoved two gloved fingers into Bitch’s hole on top of his cock. No spit. Just dry leather.

With his powerful hands he drove them in and out repeatedly, tugging upwards as he finger fucked. Still fucking his nine inches deep, at the same time.

Bitch screamed, “Please stop!”

“No way boy, you’re truly gonna get it and I’m having too much fun back here.”

Cole kept going grinning as he punished that hole. Stretching it further. He noticed the fingers started to get easier going in and out. It was self lubing. He looked down and then realised where the lube was coming from. His fingers were covered in blood.

“YEAH!” he shouted. “I’ve made him fucking bleed,” he laughed out loud.

Max clapped a gloved clap, “Bravo young man, you’ve blooded him.”

This drove Cole on further. A second wind of thrill. He took the fingers out and punched Bitch in the back, repeating three or four times. Leaving his blood prints on his back and sides.

Bobby's legs were buckling but the strength of Cole's legs and arms had him just where he wanted him. No escape. He was being fucked hard by Cole. Finally, it was happening. He was crying in pain, but it was pleasure as well. He was now gurgling.

"Stop, stop!" then that became, "Harder Cole, ruin me, I'm fucking worthless!" he shouted.

Cole laughed and fucked him even harder if that was possible. This was the best he'd felt in years. This was the best sex he had ever experienced. So powerful.

Max was beating his meat at this fantastic spectacle. Two young lads. One more powerful, destroying his weaker prey. Beautiful.

"You are a true alpha master Cole, finish him off now," and with those words Cole grabbed Bitch's throat and buried his dick in as far as he could and dumped a huge load in Bitch's arse and roared loudly.

Cole then threw him down but then immediately yanked Bitch's head back to meet his face, gloved hand over mouth and throat again.

"You're forever mine, you are now marked by me," he then spat in Bitch's face and pushed him back down.

He pulled out with exhaustion. Cole stood up, grabbed Bitch and ordered him to turn around and suck him clean. His cum covered cock. Bitch did immediately as he was told. He did it because he wanted to service his old master. His handsome Cole. His fantasy world a few years back. Now he was here with him at last, owned, marked and doing his bidding, as he should.

Max was beating his dick watching the awesome action happening in front of him.

“Pass it to me,” he instructed Cole. “My turn.”

Part 1 – The Chance Meeting

Chapter 16 - Ownership

Max stood up and Bitch was dragged by his collar by Cole to Max's feet.

"Stand up," Max instructed.

Max also got up and stood behind Bitch and primed his arse with his finger. Max then put his gloved hand over Bitch's mouth and shoved his cock deep up his arse. Max used Cole's load inside as lube. It felt perfect. Max rutted that boy standing with his hands round his neck. Bitch moaned with pleasure. He was hard now also. Cole watched from the sofa stroking his newly hard dick. Again, he was grinning to see Max in action. Man, he was good. This British guy was awesome Cole thought. Bitch could see his old school bully in front of him smirking and stroking as his hole was being wrecked by the new British daddy bully. He was in fucking heaven.

Max lifted Bitch up and down on his dick by his neck, fortunately Bitch was reasonably light so easy to control. Max pounded his arse and said, "You are a worthless cunt boy for your two masters. Cole has bred you with his load and marked and blooded you. You are his and his cum is now lubing my cock in your hole. When I cum I will also have marked you as mine. You will serve us both won't you?"

"Yeeesss Maaasters," Bitch gurgled in some discomfort. That sound was the trigger for Max, his victim had submitted and with a final yank down and balls deep, impaled, he filled Bitch's gut with his load to mix with Cole's.

Slowly he lifted Bitch and withdrew his dick and then just dropped him. Bitch fell to the floor exhausted, but it wasn't over.

"Bend over," Max instructed, "and present your arse upwards." He then dug his full gloved hand into his arse to the knuckles. Bitch yelled. Max twisted it, and scooped out both loads on that gloved hand, which was now also blooded. Cole was wide mouthed at the sight, and then cracked up laughing when he saw Bitch's whimpering face.

"You've the man Max, fucking evil."

"I know," he winked.

Max sat down next to Cole and beckoned to Bitch to come over. "Now clean that glove. Clean our loads off that glove. Totally clean."

Cole laughed out loud again. Grinning as his old victim was shuffling towards them.

"Max," Cole said, "you are one real awesome guy. Wish we had been mates at school, we could have had such fun. You are so fucking nasty."

"Thanks," said Max, "we will have to make up for lost time," he winked again and smiled.

Bobby was looking exhausted, but he was rock hard. He was enjoying his new position at the bottom of the food chain of these two handsome Masters who now owned him. He licked that glove clean as Cole and Max drank more beer. Both were also hard and gently stroking their cocks. Max kept looking at Cole. He really was handsome and that evil streak was a real turn on. He grinned at Cole's dick and said.

"Can I?"

Cole was relaxing into this gay world now. "Yeah sure."

Max leaned over and started sucking Cole's cock. He tasted good. Spit, cum and arse. They got closer and so did Bitch. He was between their legs waiting on instructions. Max moved back and instructed Cole to untie Bitch's hands. Then they both sat back on the sofa.

"Bitch, pleasure us both. Wank us off," ordered Max.

Meanwhile Max leaned in and kissed Cole's handsome face. A deep kiss. He tasted so good too. Bitch did as he was told and pleasured both dicks with both hands. They both came, almost together, all over their leather thighs. Though more milk cum this time, as it was a second load for both. 'Now what to do with Bitch next....' Max thought.

Part 1 – The Chance Meeting

Chapter 17 - Fair's fair

Max decided it was Bitch's turn. "You wanna cum?"

"Yes please, sir," Bitch replied.

Max instructed Cole to stand in front of Bitch with his gloved hands on his mouth and throat. Now wank boy. Cole teased and pinched Bitch's tits as he pleasured himself. Bobby was looking into the eyes of his teenage tormenter who was now a handsome young man in his mid twenties, dressed in the sexiest gear he could have imagined. Cole was smirking and spitting in his face and mouth as Bitch wanked.

"Come closer. Wank over me," Max said. Cole turned Bitch round in one easy move. "Cover my leathers boy," Max ordered.

Max noticed that Bitch was also pretty cute. Nice lean body. In average shape. Sweet. He reached forward and took his cock in his gloved hand and started to wank Bitch for him. His cock was very hard, and a similar size to Cole's, possibly eight inches. Big for a small guy. Both were cut, unlike Max's British uncut dick.

"Hold him up higher," he instructed to Cole. He wanked at that cock so hard Bitch couldn't stop. He blew the biggest load all over Max's leathers. Five or six ropes of cum shot from his dick. He'd been holding in cum since the initial boner in the bar. He totalled Max's jeans, boots, shirt and his chin. Max smiled at the vision. "Nice load boy."

Cole let go of Bitch and sat back down next to Max. Bitch dropped to the floor again and crawled closer knowing what the next instruction was going to be.

Max then instructed Bitch to clean everyone up with his tongue. It took a while but it tasted so good. Bitch tentatively started on the chin. "May I?" he asked.

"Yes," said Max.

As Bitch moved in and licked Max's chin, Max grabbed his face and kissed him hard and deep. A long meaningful kiss. Something Bobby had never felt before. Finally, Max drew back still holding his face. Smiled and kissed him tenderly on the nose. "I like you boy. Once done cleaning me up, you are gonna rim us both," he whispered.

Ten minutes passed. "Rim us, now," ordered Max.

Cole asked, "What's that?"

"You never been rimmed?" Bobby said out of turn

"No," Cole angrily replied.

"Get on your knees on the sofa," said Bobby. Seemingly taking charge.

Max smiled and followed up and said, "Yes do as he says. You're gonna love this." Max also took position next to Cole leaning on the sofa both heads close.

"Now start."

Bobby dived into Cole's bare arse with his tongue and rimmed him so good. Cole looked shocked and then felt the pleasure.

"My God. This is amazing. You gays really know how to have sex. Straight sex is so fucking boring. Chaps make it even easier."

Bobby worked his magic, which gave Max the opportunity to kiss Cole again. Max so wanted to fuck Cole or be fucked by him, but that would have to wait. Tonight would be too soon. He needs to build his trust, but at some point Max would take Cole and have him his way and on his terms. Max kissed deeply, this time Cole didn't resist and kissed back instantly. Bobby then moved to Max's arse through that awesome zip. Max moaned as Bobby cleaned him up and teased his arse.

"Boy you are good at that. One of the best. I think we struck gold with you boy in many ways."

Part 1 – The Chance Meeting

Chapter 18 - The Deal

Exhausted they all sat in the sofa. Max asked Bitch, "You ok? Did you enjoy yourself?"

"It was a bit scary at times but it was amazing, I've never been fucked like that, or controlled, but it was awesome. But my arse is fucking killing me now," Bobby replied.

"Cole. How about you?" Max asked.

"Fuck man it was truly awesome. I wanna do it again. We need to find more fags to abuse. This is so good, way better than chicks."

Max raised an eyebrow and smiled, "You moving to the dark side Cole?" he laughed.

"Fuck can it get any darker," Cole sniggered.

Bobby said, "I know others like me who want this. I can get more victims. If I can join in on some of the fun."

"Then we shall. Bobby, you wanna wear some leather next time? I'd like that," asked Max, using his real name for the first time since they all arrived in the apartment.

"Yes, if it pleases you sir," Bobby replied

"Have a look in that room and choose some stuff that takes your fancy. You also Cole. But I may need to order some slightly different sizes for you."

Cole got up. "I need a pee."

Bobby stood up too. "Wait. I want that," he said.

"What?" said Cole.

"Feed me your piss," said Bobby.

"You're fucking crazy."

"No. I want it. Take me in the bathroom and give me that piss. Don't waste it." Bobby asked again. Cole was really learning a lot tonight. Max followed them to watch.

"Ok," said Cole, "I'm busting."

Bobby sat on the floor with his head in the shower stall. Cole grabbed his head still wearing the gloves and directed his cock at his face.

"Open wide Bitch."

An initial rope of cum that was still in his shaft, a nice bonus, fell on Bobby's tongue followed by glorious hot stream of piss covering his face and hair. The warm salty liquid was beautiful.

Max was laughing in the door way. Cole finished up and looked down at Bobby.

Bobby said, "I've wanted you for so long. Over twelve years of waiting to be humiliated fully and fucked over by my handsome nasty school bully. Thanks Cole. You were worth the wait."

Cole smiled, "You twisted fuck."

Max moved across. "You want mine also Bobby?"

"Yes sir."

Max put his cock in his mouth fully and started to piss. Choking Bobby as his stream of piss ran out his mouth. Splashing Max's leathers and the floor. The handsome Brit looked down at the piss boy, his urine everywhere and his happy face.

"Now clean this mess up."

Cole and Max walked out and sat on the sofa again. When Bobby was done. He joined them and sat between them.

"Let's start planning our next session," Cole said.

"Yes, so which friend of yours Bobby is going to be our next prey?" asked Max.

"Oh, I know so many we can choose from, but one particular springs to mind after tonight....."

by Nick Christie

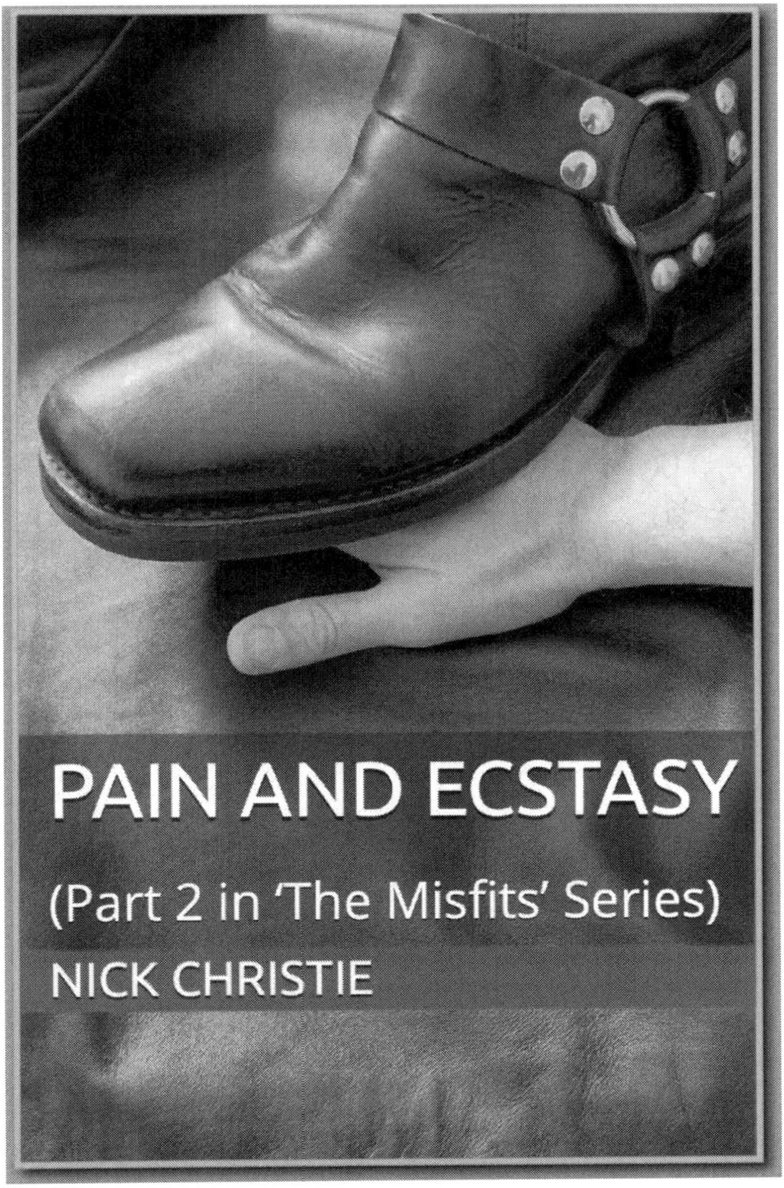
PAIN AND ECSTASY
(Part 2 in 'The Misfits' Series)
NICK CHRISTIE

Pain and Ecstasy
(Part 2 in 'The Misfits' Series)
(Erotic Gay Fiction)

Nick Christie

Chapter 1 - Our Heroes

Max, Cole and Bobby all met by chance a couple weeks ago in a bar and had a truly amazing sexual encounter together. A chance meeting that was now to start a new relationship between the three men.

Maxwell Steadman is a self-made English businessman. A fifty year old silver fox, hair cropped short, with a quiff, who looks great for his years. Sexy, slim, with a horny English accent and charismatic smile to match. He travels a lot and owns a large apartment in downtown Chicago, where he works six months of the year. The rest of his time is based in London and Berlin. His business is in real estate and his drive is making stupid amounts of money, buying leather gear, wearing leather gear and getting as much sex as humanly possible.

He is a master and controller of men, in work and play. He has been married to Peter for two years having been together for twelve, who lives in London. The fact they spend so much time apart and they both have a huge lust for sex, they both agreed to be in an open relationship. This works perfectly for them and when they are together they love to play with others too.

Bobby Wilson is a bright young man with light blonde hair, styled short back and sides but longer on top so that it falls to one side, perfect for grabbing. A twenty seven year old shop worker with the cutest face and smile, who came out as gay at school at the age of sixteen. He got a lot of grief from the jocks at school and was often the butt of their jokes and bullying. He hated them, but he also craved them, because they were so hot and masculine. He dreamed of being beaten and fucked over by his tormentors and since then has enjoyed rough sex. Bobby is willing to try anything and enjoys being 'enjoyed'. Since meeting Max, he is also interested in finding his inner dom. Max hopes to help him out on that.

This then leads nicely to Cole Peterson. Also twenty seven, Cole attended Bobby's high school and was one of his tormentors. A baseball jock, he is fit, strong, extremely masculine with a mop of dirty blonde curls but shorter round the back and sides framing a square jawed, real handsome face. A face with the devil behind his eyes. He's labelled as "straight", well he was until he met Max and reunited with Bobby two weeks ago.

Cole had a girlfriend but dumped her recently after sex with girls became less interesting. Cole learnt so much about gay sex that evening and fetish wear, that he hasn't looked back. Cole near destroyed Bobby on that night and enjoyed the experience of taking his school bullying to a new cruel level. Bobby enjoyed the night so much, he's wanted more.

They all have wanted more and agreed they would meet up to find a new 'project' to work over. Since that first meeting, Cole and Bobby have grown to "like/tolerate" each other, but the roles revert to type in the bedroom.

Bobby has been back round to Cole's digs a couple of times to service his handsome bully. He just can't get enough of that cock. Bobby has also serviced Max once since that first night. Bobby came round to collect his jacket he left behind. Max was dressed in only a towel having just come out the shower. The boner that greeted Bobby was too good to resist. Max had a soft spot for Bobby. He was a real cute lad and had a talented mouth and tongue! But Max's real aim was to bed Cole and take him hard; he wanted Cole to want it too. So that was going to take some time.

The two got on well, Cole was very impressed by Max's creativeness in cruelty and they often met for beers, but nothing had happened since that first meet.

Chapter 2 - The Plan

So as not to be overheard, they all met in Max's luxury apartment. Max started the planning.

"I have a plan to find a new victim we can all play with. Bobby, I'm going to describe a scenario and if you can think of one of your friends who would fit the bill, we can work on a plan to destroy that boy together."

Bobby had volunteered after the last meeting that he had lots of gay friends and associates who had many kinks. Many loved domination and some liked pain and would love to be worked over by handsome Cole and sexy daddy Max, and maybe he could get a bite too. Bobby would be perfect to bait these lads, looking so innocent.

Max continued, "I have been making some new purchases of gear for you both." They both smiled and sat up, excited.

"Leather?" Cole said.

"Of course," Max replied, "Cole you will be in some new leather jeans, zip round like mine for easy access. I also have a special harness to show off that chest and arms and a little something else, but you'll see those on the night. I want you to be excited, so it's good to have surprises. You will look beautiful, majestic and fucking strong and evil."

Cole smirked that awesome evil grin.

"Fuck I'm hard already," said Bobby.

Max continued, "You Bobby, I have something special. Do you know about football, or as you uneducated Americans call it, soccer? I have a black leather Adidas football shirt and short shorts hand made, with a red stripe detail. With it you will have some white and red long football socks, but the best part is a pair of black Adidas Predator X football boots, with special 'Bobby" engraved metal cleats."

"Fuck that sounds sexy and cute," said Bobby.

"This new gear is made to measure and will fit you perfectly, imported from Germany. You may look cute, but be aware you will be definitely taking part in the action this time, helping us dish out some pain," Max smiled.

Bobby grinned a little, "Awesome!"

"Pain, I'm liking the sound of this already, and football is a team sport. What you wearing Max?" Cole asked.

Max raised an eyebrow, "That will be my surprise for you on the night."

"So, we need someone who wants to be humiliated by three men and wants pain and doesn't mind getting hurt. We need someone who definitely is into it and not just saying it. A lot of planning is going into this," Max said looking straight at Bobby.

Bobby thought hard, "I know one guy at my work who has a few piercings and talks to me about the sadistic porn he watches. I have seen him a few times with bruises and black eyes, which he says he gets during sex. When do we want to do this?"

"Saturday night would be best, you will bring him to the apartment, Cole and I would be here already."

"Ok leave it with me. I'll let you know how I get on."

"What age and build is he," Max asked.

"Think he's older than me, about twenty nine, but shorter, say five foot eight and skinny build like all goths."

"Fucking perfect, he won't be able to punch back and mark my handsome face," laughed Cole. "He will be easy to throw around also."

So the plan was set.

Max smiled, "Bring Pain Boy to us at 9pm sharp."

Part 2 – Pain and Ecstasy

Chapter 3 - The Prey

Oliver Trent had been working in the Home Depot store with work friend Bobby for eight months. Both being gay they had been very honest with each other about just about everything. Oliver was skinny, always in black and had many tattoos, nose, lip and nipple (so he said) piercings. Over lunch, Bobby struck up a conversation.

"Ollie, you know how we discussed sex in the past and you like pain and humiliation, were you being truthful or just messing around?"

"Err, yeah I like it. Strange question. Why you into it too?" he replied.

"Yeah I've tried it a bit but not much. What have you done, you willing to share?"

"Yeah sure, I see a guy who likes to slap me, stamp on me, he has worked me over a couple of times, but he's a bit wet. He's not really strong enough, he's barely any bigger than me. I have wanted more, but there are some scary bat shit crazy people out there in this game, so you have to be very careful."

"I may have a perfect proposal for you. You've known me for eight months yeah, and you trust me right? I love sex and happy for it get a bit rough. Well I've met these two guys who are awesome alpha doms. One I knew at high school and one an older daddy. They are fit as fuck, strong sexy and into some real hot gear."

"They sound cool," Ollie interrupted.

Bobby continued "They worked me over and it was the best. I fucking loved it," Bobby detailed.

"Fuck! You lucky bastard," Ollie said.

“Well here’s the thing. We want to do more of this with different people. We want to do a pain and sex session with a new sub, and I thought of you.”

“Fuck,” said Ollie, “I’m not sure. Are they ok? Where do they do it?”

“In the daddy’s plush apartment. It’s beautiful. He’s loaded. I took a chance on them and they treated me fine. I was fucking ruined and my arse was suffering for a week but they were awesome. I had a safe word so was in control but I couldn’t get enough.”

“But I don’t know them from Adam,” Ollie said.

“Hey man, I’ll be there, I wouldn’t miss out on this, I’m part of the team now, so I would be there with you.”

Bobby decided at this point to keep back that he would probably also be subjecting Ollie to some of this pain under instruction from his masters.

“Well if you are there, then I suppose that would be ok. I have wanted some real punishment so bad, got into this when I got caned by my strict Dad. I don’t see him now. He was an arsehole, but after the second beating I started to enjoy it, fucking idiot never copped onto the fact I was breaking shit at home just to get a beating. I was hard as fuck after each one and would beat off straight after.”

“You free this Saturday?” Bobby asked.

“Err yes, on these shit wages of course I have a window in my diary,” Ollie laughed.

"I'll meet you for a beer in Cell Block bar at eight pm to loosen up and then we will go to his apartment at nine. Don't be late."

"It's a date," replied Ollie.

The plan was in motion, Bobby texted Max and Cole <Ollie is in.>

<Cool>, Cole instantly texted back.

Max texted back an hour later <Very good Bobby. Instruct Ollie to shower in the morning and scrub hard so his body is clean, but no deodorant or aftershave all day, I want his natural smell, but not BO. You guys do the same. You can deodorise a bit, but keep foreign smells to a minimum. I want the leather to take over the room. Cole, be here at 8.30. Bobby bring the victim at 9. No delays>.

Wow thought Bobby, he knows what he wants that Max. Next day Bobby relayed the message to Ollie, who seemed to understand, which was good. So the snare had been set.

Part 2 – Pain and Ecstasy

Part 2 – Pain and Ecstasy

Chapter 4 - Saturday Nights Alright

Saturday came round real quick. Ollie woke up in his bedsit and went to the bathroom. He took his morning shit and forced as much out as possible. He then jumped in the shower and scrubbed his body and washed his hair. He did as he was told and scrubbed all areas and cleaned his arsehole. He'd do that again and douche, just before he goes out.

Cole arrived at the apartment at 8.29pm and pressed the buzzer. The door unlocked with no comment from the tannoy. He arrived at the door and was greeted by Max who was naked. Cole was in tight jeans and an equally tight T-shirt and Nike Shox.

"Evening Stud," Max said and Cole walked into the apartment.

Fuck it was transformed. The sofas were moved back to reveal a larger space. The carpet in the centre was covered by a large black mat about twelve foot square. Hang on, that's made of leather, Cole thought. Thick black cow hide.

"Jesus Max! How many animals have died for your kinky lust over the years?"

"Hundreds I imagine and many more will die for my pleasure. It's the law of the jungle and as it should be."

The room smelt amazing Cole thought. The leather mat gave off a heady aroma and, judging by the marks and stains on it, it had seen some action.

To one side was a chair and a strong table bench. Funnily enough the length of an average man's body. Max opened a drawer showing rope, duck tape, wrist and neck collars and a small harness. He shut the drawer.

Part 2 – Pain and Ecstasy

"Man you have been busy."

"I have to live here, and who knows what bodily fluids are going to be flying around tonight."

"What will we be doing?" Cole enquired.

"That depends on how open you want to be Cole," Max stated as he walked into the dressing room that Cole remembered smelt of sex. He followed.

The neat room was set out perfectly. Hanging from the rail on the wall was the sexiest little leather football kit, ready for Bobby.

"Ahh cute," Cole said.

"Check out the boots," Max pointed. The Adidas size 9.5 Predator X were in shiny black leather looked real sexy. "Turn them over." Cole picked one up, the cleats (or studs) were bright silver metal, each engraved with "Bobby" but they also seemed more prominent.

"Fuck these seem quite heavy duty cleats. They can't be legal for the game," grinned Cole.

"They are not," Max replied. "So to your outfit Cole."

Max took out the wardrobe a pair of super soft shiny leather jeans size thirty two waist with a full double zip fly that can be fully detached, removing an hourglass shaped piece of leather.

"The removable piece is leather lined to ensure your dick balls and arse are always in contact with leather." Max handed him them and a pair of size eleven black army ankle boots with nice treads.

"You must tuck the jeans into the boots and leave the tops open," Max instructed.

Cole was looking excited.

"I have a leather cock and ball ring to keep your hard and comfortable throughout. No underwear."

Cole was then given the same gloves he'd worn last time, which still had some cum and blood on them. He smiled at the memory of Bobby's arse and his pain.

"Wear these and this," Max said. He handed Cole two leather wrist bands, a two inch wide double pronged belt and a what can only be described as a half gladiator style black leather harness with one shoulder cover plate. Cole started dressing and managed to get it all on with some help from Max.

Max smiled, "Go look in the mirror."

Cole did and his eyes widened.

"You look magnificent Cole, better than I imagined."

Cole smirked that sexy evil smile.

"And with that look you have made it even better. You are such a sexy bad boy Cole. I do have one other thing for you but that will be an extra surprise when we get into the action."

Cole couldn't stop admiring his gear and how powerful he looked. Like a film star. Everything fitted like a glove. Fucking made-to-measure. He'd never had anything made-to-measure. Fuck, tonight was gonna be awesome, he thought.

Part 2 – Pain and Ecstasy

Max then went into his bedroom to get changed. He came out of the room ten minutes later in a Dainese two-piece motorbike suit, tight fitting, with what looked like some extra modifications around the crotch and arse. Short cop gloves to finish the look.

"Fucking sexy Max," Cole said.

"This is a secondhand suit I purchased from a hot biker I met on Recon. He was my size; I wanted a well used one that had been worn by another hot guy. Knowing his body and cock had been rubbing in this, stressing it and making it supple, I demanded he didn't have it cleaned before sending it me. I was sure he would have jizzed on it too to help lubricate the leather. You should always christen new leathers with cum and regularly continue this ritual. You will do your's tonight. I then had my leathers altered for better sex access. Bike gear isn't that practical off the shelf."

Cole laughed, "When you got money this comes so easy."

"It does, but I've worked fucking hard for my money," Max snapped, taking the jacket off revealing his strong hairy chest and abs and some pretty toned guns.

Cole raised his hand to apologise. "You are fucking awesome man and thanks for doing all this. You look pretty hot too, with that haircut, it's very sharp." Max had had it trimmed. He had it done every three weeks.

"When the boys arrive I want you to go into the bedroom and wait. I want your entrance reveal to be impactful. When they arrive I will seat Ollie and make him feel comfortable and then Bobby and I will go get him kitted out in his new footie gear. This may take 10 minutes. This will give Ollie time to stew. When I call for you, I want you to enter calmly but with a look that draws heavily from your inner dom and cruellest bully. I want Ollie to feel nervous from the start. Tonight, I will be asking you to be the main destroyer under my instruction, which I know you enjoy so much. Maybe you will thank me later?"

Cole grinned, "That will be no problem at all. I won't let up on this little cunt. He likes pain, and I like dishing it out."

"Get us both a beer Cole while we wait for Bobby and the prey."

It was 8.55pm.

Chapter 5 - Where is he?

Bobby was in the bar at 7.55pm. His train got in early. Blue jeans, T-shirt and sneakers, plus a reversed baseball cap, a shock of his blonde hair sticking out the front. He had fifty dollars that Max had given him for drinks. Max was so generous he thought. Obviously rich but he didn't have to share it. Ok, he was getting some serious sex with some hot and cute lads half his age, but still, Bobby liked Max. He was kind as well as fucking awesomely nasty when it came to sex. A perfect older man in Bobby's eyes. Almost fatherly.

Ollie finally arrived at 8.30pm.

"Where the fuck have you been?" Bobby demanded.

"Soz. I got held up. You getting the beers in?"

"Hardly got time now," Bobby replied.

"Sure we have. Two more beers please," he yelled at the barman.

Ollie was wearing his skinny black ripped jeans, some battered Chelsea boots and a black Sisters of Mercy T-shirt. He was carrying a small black rucksack also. His hair was dyed black and shaved on one side and long on top. He was wearing some eyeliner and had his nose and lip piecing in. He was real skinny and had a delicate pretty face with an impish nose.

"You only washed this morning yeah? No scents," Bobby asked.

"Yeah, yeah. Bit freaky this guy Max," Ollie replied flippantly.

"Don't be an ass, he likes what he likes and you want this too, and by the way you're drinking his beer, so show some respect," Bobby snapped back defending his fatherly master. "Right we better go, we are already late."

They left the bar and arrived at the apartment and pressed the buzzer. It was 9.09pm.

Chapter 6 - Let's get ready

Nine o'clock came and went.

Max was annoyed, "Why are they late? If he does come he is gonna pay for this," Max stated.

Cole relished being able to be more fucking evil. They finished their beers as the buzzer rang.

"Right you go into the bedroom and make yourself comfortable. Close the door."

Cole got up and walked into the master bedroom. He closed the double doors behind him. Fuck this was nice. Huge bed with a mirror at the headboard and the ceiling. An en-suite as big as the main bathroom. The bed had crisp white cotton bedding and the carpet was thick and white also. A huge TV was opposite the bed, perfect for porn Cole thought. This guy had really made it. Cole decided to lie on the bed but was careful to not put his boots in the white bedding. He imagined what it would be like to sleep in such a bed, watching tv, fucking in the bed, maybe being in it with Max. It sure felt far better than his lumpy single bed in his bedsit with the non-matching faded bedding. He sighed. 'I need a self-made man' he thought, or did he mean to say, 'he needed to be a self-made man?'

"Sure is fucking nice," he muttered to himself.

Max opened the door after Bobby knocked. He greeted them with a big smile and a naked top half, his tight Dainese biker pants outlining his powerful thighs. He and gave them both a hug.

"Hello, I'm Max. Welcome to my home. Can I get you a beer Ollie? So good that you want this as much as us."

"Sorry we are late," Bobby apologised looking very sorry and down, Max lifted his chin and smiled at the young man.

"Have a seat Ollie. Here is your beer. You can hang your rucksack here. What's in there?"

"Thanks. Just a change of clothes, in case any of these get damaged," he laughed.

"Good thinking Ollie. Good preparation," Max smiled. "Right make yourself comfortable. I need to steal Bobby away to get him ready and myself appropriately dressed." They both walked into the dressing room and closed the door.

Bobby walked in and saw the football kit and smiled. The smile soon faded as he was grabbed by Max who snapped, "Why were you so late?"

"Ollie was late and dragged his heals. I tried to hurry him up but he was being a bit of an ass. I'm so sorry Max."

"Thank you Bobby. It's not you who should apologise. I noticed you did as you arrived and he said nothing. Ollie is going to pay for that tonight with some extra surprises. He's gonna need that change of clothes."

Bobby grinned and then looked back at the football kit.

"Is that for me?" he asked.

"Yes it is. This leather shirt and shorts are made of the finest and thinnest lambs' leather, double sided but still so thin that it hangs like a proper Adidas nylon T and shorts. Stripes and Adidas logos where they would be on the real thing," Bobby touched it. It felt cool and buttery soft.

Part 2 – Pain and Ecstasy

Max had previously taken full measurements of Cole and Bobby so he could order in clothing that would fit perfectly or had them made-to-measure.

“This kit is one of a kind and completely made for you. Get undressed and try it on.” Max watched as Bobby undressed naked. His body was perfect, not too toned but beautifully in proportion. His blond hair was going to look so good against the black kit with red piping.

“Here, put this cock ring on. This will support you throughout the evening and keep you hard,” said Max.

“Don’t think I’m gonna have a problem with that!” Bobby replied looking at his firming cock.

He put the kit on. It fitted beautifully. It felt amazing against his skin. The shorts being leather lined also felt amazing against his cock and balls.

“They should be roomy enough for you to pull your cock out one of the legs, if you need to and I have added two tiny popper studs on the gusset so you can open them for full access,” Max informed.

“Wow Max. You are the best.”

Max then passed him the cotton soccer knee length socks and the boots, indicating the cleats.

“Fucking hell,” said Bobby, “They could do some real damage.”

“Yes, that’s the general idea,” Max smirked. “Put them on.”

“And they have my name on each stud,” Bobby smiled.

Max grinned and then put his matching Dainese jacket on for his two piece bike suit, his gloves and bike boots. Bobby finished dressing and then turned around to Max. He looked the sexiest footballer he'd ever seen. That beautiful long mop of hair over the boyish handsome face and that gear really fit well. Bobby looked in the mirror and smiled.

"You look awesome," Max said. "But I have a finishing touch for you." He opened a drawer and pulled out a small, flat box. "Open it."

Bobby carefully opened the box and inside was a small pair of gloves. They were black, very short, with red piping around the cuff, matching his kit and the Adidas logo embroidered on the back of each hand in the same red.

"They are a 'version' of a goalie's gloves, but made of unlined lambs' leather; tight and short for a sexy look and they have an added detail. Put them on."

Bobby did. Max continued, "You will notice the palms are super soft and smooth, but the ends of the fingers are some tiny abrasive patches, just like a goalie's gloves. When you rub these on a nipple of cock they will feel nasty. You are gonna be handling a certain somebody's cock, balls and whatever with these goalie's gloves," he smirked.

Bobby grinned also and asked, "So am I gonna be doing Ollie some damage too? Not just Cole and you? Where is Cole by the way?"

"Cole is waiting in the master bedroom for his entrance. I wanted his arrival to be as exciting for you as it will be unnerving for Ollie, and yes Bobby you will be playing many key roles tonight. You are going to be our secret weapon where that Ollie is concerned. Let's go back out and start playing with our guest."

Chapter 7 - Disrespect

Ollie sat on the sofa and looked around him. Fucking swish place. Max has some money. Huge lounge kitchen/diner with what looked like two master bedrooms and a dressing room judging where Bobby and whatever his name went. Great view over Chicago he imagined, though the blinds were shut. He was on his own for a while and starting to get a little nervous but that also felt sexy too. The anticipation. How hard was he gonna get it. Ollie loved pain and if some fit dudes were doing it all the better. He looked at the leather floor mat and the table. Fuck they mean business. The table was more of a bench with places to attach "stuff" to on the legs and the top. Fuck I'm gonna be strapped on that. Cool, shall I get on now and wait? No better not, he thought and took another swig of beer.

At that point the door opened to where Max and Bobby had gone, Max came out first, now wearing his jacket boots and gloves. He was real handsome for an older guy Ollie thought. Then Bobby appeared. What is that? He thought. Is that leather also, a fucking leather soccer kit, and boots. Are we playing games? he thought. Then he saw the boots and the shining cleats and soon got the message. Ollie swallowed deeply. Bobby did look cute and quite sexy in that kit. It fit perfectly. Ollie had a bit of a crush on Bobby but they were just friends at work.

Max smiled, "Ok, Ollie. Shall we begin? Just some notes and ground rules. First do you have any concerns about this evening and have you any boundaries you wish to discuss?"

Ollie gulped, "Well please don't kill me if that's what you mean, or do me any unrecoverable damage. I like it hard and happy for you to try anything. Will I have a safe word?"

Max smiled, "Christ we don't want to kill you! Yes the safe word will be RED. Say that and I will stop everything. I might suggest you remove that nose and lip ring, as we don't want them getting badly snagged on something and doing some 'unrecoverable damage'. Any others?" Max asked.

"Nipples and a Prince Albert" he replied, taking out the face piercings.

"They are ok, we can have some fun with those. Ok tonight you will be taken to hell and back by me, a man called Cole and assisted by your work colleague Bobby. You can scream as much as you wish. The apartment is a corner plot and the side walls, floor and ceiling are sound proofed. I requested it in the build. I told them I was a musician and play my music loud. I am the main Master and will be controlling you and the events tonight, and you will also be subservient to Bobby. Take a seat next to Ollie, Bobby. But the one you really need to worry about is Cole. Are you ok with all this?" Max continued as he walked around the room and behind the sofa.

"Yes, that's ok, where is this Cole?" Ollie said nervously.

"Yes, let's introduce you to Cole. Cole!" Max shouted, "Ollie would like to meet you now."

After what seemed like a lifetime in Ollie's mind, the bedroom door facing him opened and a tall, very strong built young man stood in the frame. Ollie gulped again and his heart raced. Bobby had said Cole was handsome and looked mean and been his bully at school. Fuck! Ollie wished he'd been to that school. Cole was in army boots, leather jeans and wearing a strange half harness that made him look a bit like an evil superhero. Gloves and wristbands were a finishing detail. His face had a look of hate as he suddenly marched across the room to Ollie and grabbed him by the throat with both hands and lifted him clean off the sofa, in the air and right into his face. He stared into Ollie's eyes hard. Ollie's heart raced and his cock twitched. Fuck, Cole was beautiful.

Cole whispered, "I'm going to enjoy destroying you tonight. It's gonna be so easy."

Bobby was sat next to Ollie and saw the exact same thing. He hadn't seen Cole in his full gear. Max had kept some of the details to himself. Cole looked amazing. Bobby took a quick breath when he saw Cole, his eyes and mouth wide open, which pleased Max from his position behind them both, behind the sofa. Cole looked so powerful, those thighs, that gladiator style shoulder harness, the gloves, boots and that beautiful mop of hair framing his handsome but fucking scary looking face. Bobby was really fixated with Cole and falling in love with his tormentor.

"Put him down Cole," Max shouted. "We haven't started yet."

Cole threw Ollie, who was now rubbing his neck, back on the sofa, when suddenly, without warning, Max shouted, "We are starting now!!' and Max, from behind the sofa put his left arm around Ollie's neck and his gloved right hand over his mouth and with one quick twist, pulled Ollie straight back over the sofa. Sending him crashing to the floor. Ollie yelled and made a winded sound as he hit the carpet behind the sofa. Max threw him onto his front, pulled Ollie's left arm behind his back, put one knee on that hand and the other on the back of his head, while holding his right fingers in a crushing position in his own gloved hand. Ollie yelled again.

"That is for being fucking late to my party you fucking worthless piece of shit!"

Cole stood in amazement at the agility of Max. He was like a ninja. Both Cole and Bobby were kneeling on the sofa looking over at poor little Ollie in distress. Bobby was amazed too. He looked at Cole who looked at him, then they both laughed at Ollie. "Worthless fag," said Cole.

Max then directed Cole to come round the sofa.

Part 2 – Pain and Ecstasy

"Strip the cunt of all his clothes," Max ordered, getting up off of Ollie.

Cole stepped in and with one easy tug, tore the back of Ollie's t-shirt in half and cleanly off. Ollie rose and fell in the motion.

"Turn over and get those fucking jeans off," Cole ordered. Ollie did as he was told looked petrified at this point. This was all happening way faster than he was expecting. He kicked off his boots and tugged at his skinny jeans. They were too tight. Cole was getting impatient "Useless fag," he tugged at the ripped jeans and tore one leg off completely from the rip in the knee. He tugged at the rest and finally they were off. But now in three parts. Ollie was wearing a tatty pair of washed-out briefs which was hiding the start of a boner.

Max piped, "Well, you could have at least worn your best underwear you cunt, or is that them? Get them off and the socks and Cole get him on the mat."

Ollie had barely started getting the socks and undies off when Cole grabbed his hair and dragged him to the mat, giving him carpet burns on the way.

"Fuck we are gonna have some awesome fun with this tonight!" Cole shouted to the others.

"Right, let's all sit down and admire out new toy," Max said.

Cole sat next to Bobby and then Max sat next to him.

"Come here and sit in front of Cole." Ollie shuffled up and sat doggy style in front of Cole. "Lick our boots boy, all of us."

Ollie paused for too long, Cole moved in and slapped him so hard across the face. Ollie fell over.

"Too slow!" Cole shouted.

Max ordered, "Present yourself boy and do as I say immediately or who knows what Cole will do. Sometimes I really struggle to control him."

Bobby was amazed to be sitting next to Cole and seeing him again in action but this time not on him. It felt odd but real sexy too. He was so strong and mean and it was starting to get him aroused.

Ollie licked their boots. Each time he got up each one slapped him. Cole's was the hardest and for some reason, Bobby's stung the most. Cole got up and asked Ollie if he was thirsty. He nodded. Cole stood behind him and yanked his head back. "Open wide," he then dropped a long spit loogie into his mouth. Cole then put his hands around Ollie's face and put his gloved finger in his mouth and held his mouth open.

"Go on Max, feed him." Max leant forward and fired a loogie straight in. Ollie obediently swallowed. Cole then swivelled Ollie round to face Bobby. "Your turn Bobby boy," Cole cheekily said softly, looking kindly into Bobby's eyes.

Cole gave him a smile and a wink. Bobby's heart skipped a beat. For a few seconds Cole looked so cute and kind, that wasn't gonna last though he had Ollie to destroy. Bobby spat at Ollie and hit him in the eye. Cole looked down laughing, "No goal for the footie boy, but he just hit the post."

Ollie wiped his face and before he knew it was dragged and thrown on the leather mat. The cool leather against his back was quite stimulating.

"Right Cole, over to you as Master of Destruction. Make this bitch hurt. Tell us what you want us to do. Let's not hold back, he's up for it so is gonna get it. That ok with you Bitch?" Max said and stared at Ollie.

"Yes....sirs," Ollie replied.

Cole yanked Ollie's arms back flat and then stood on his hands with his full weight under his army boots. Ollie was positioned and could see right up Coles legs and could see his full width and strength. He was quite a man. He couldn't stop looking at Cole's leather crotch and the strange hourglass shaped double zip. The pain in his hands was bearable, nothing broken he thought, but he was writhing around.

"Grab his legs Max and kneel on his ankles, the bony part." Max did as asked. Ollie felt Max's gloved hands hold his knees in place as he climbed on his ankles and felt the full weight of his padded leather knees on his ankles and shins.

Ollie yelled and cried out, "Please stop."

Cole continued, "Now your turn Bobby. Stand either side of his body and face me."

"Gladly," Bobby said smiling.

"Now hold my hands." Their two leather gloves connected. Bobby's looked tiny compared to Cole's.

"Now let's see those cleats in action. Step up and walk on this Bitch." Bobby stood on Ollie's chest and the cleats did their magic. Ollie screamed. Cole laughed and pushed down on Ollie's hands, to double the pain.

Ollie yelled again, "Please sirs. Please sirs have mercy."

Bobby moved around on Ollie's stomach, which was less painful, he then noticed Ollie's hard-on.

"He's fucking loving it," Bobby said.

"Turn around Bobby, thighs now, this is really gonna hurt so make it count," Bobby looked at Cole and nodded, climbed off Ollie who breathed fast. Bobby turn around and Max raised one arm as support, to allow Bobby to climb back on Ollie's stomach. Ollie winced.

"Now thighs," Cole instructed. Bobby deliberately kicked Ollie's cock as he stepped onto the front of his right thigh. Ollie yelled twice and then the left leg was on the other thigh. The front of the thighs are tender areas with little skin and mainly muscle. The cleats sank in and made red marks as Bobby pretended to jog on the spot. Ollie cried out and screamed at every step. Bobby looked down at Max who was smiling up at him.

"You're enjoying this aren't you Bobby?" Max said.

Bobby grinned back, "Fuck yeah. What I'd also like is to suck and edge that dick," he replied to Max pointing at Ollie's now huge boner, at least eight inches.

"For one so skinny Ollie, you have a large and handsome cock," Max reported. Ollie couldn't acknowledge as he was now in so much pain, he was struggling to think straight. All he could do was look at Cole's crotch which was swelling with every yell and scream.

"This is so much fucking fun. I'm so fucking hard right now," Cole said. On hearing that, Bobby jumped off to take a look. Cole's outline of his handsome cock could be seen pressing against the butter soft leather of the double zip.

"Bobby, before you service his cock, you mind helping me with these zips? I can see Bitch boy Ollie here is getting real excited looking at my bulge and I think I have an idea that should make him very happy."

Bobby jumped on and then off Ollie, which made him scream, "I'll sort your cock out in a moment," Bobby said to Ollie, who was looking at him with tears in his eyes, "Cole's needs take priority over mine and yours."

Ollie watched as Bobby knelt behind Cole, who was still standing on his hands with some weight, (thank god for the leather cushioning of the floor), Max still holding his legs. Ollie tipped his head back and could see up Bobby's shorts at the beautiful boner he had growing. Ollie moved his head back to watch the perfect view of this God above him, about to be revealed to him. Bobby leant forward and licked Cole's arse and smelt it and the leather.

"Ummmm," he said.

He put both his hands through his legs and up onto Cole's crotch. Cole was staring down smiling. Bobby stroked and rubbed his hand along the now obvious shaft inside the trousers. Cole moaned a little.

"You are so naughty Bobby, release my tool!" he instructed.

Bobby took hold of the two zips and very slowly pulled them down, inch by inch together, Cole's cock pushed its way out when the zip was at the bottom and his balls fell loose, Cole grabbed his meat with the palm of his gloved hand and gave it a welcome stroke. "Oh that feels good," Cole moaned.

Ollie's cock was so hard witnessing this. He had never been so excited in all his life. These three bastards were the fucking best. Bobby finally got the zip fully round to the belt line and then detached the hourglass piece of leather. Bobby took the leather strip to his face and buried his nose and mouth into it, licking and smelling it.

"Jeez you smell good Cole," Bobby said. "Max you were so right about not using aftershave and stuff. Cole smells amazing," Bobby then grabbed Cole's thighs and forced his face into Cole's hairy arse and balls. Licking and sniffing. Cole reached behind and pulled Bobby out.

"Later sweetcheeks, our guest needs some of this and you have a dick to service," he grinned at Bobby.

Bobby got up and moved round to Ollie's now throbbing cock.

"Hold on," Cole said and everyone looked at Cole, especially Ollie. Cole got off Ollie's hands which had almost gone numb. He put his knees on Ollie's chest and then slowly lowered his crotch and arsehole onto Ollie's face.

"You've been admiring it while you've been down there, so now time for a closer look," he laughed.

"Fuck yes," said Ollie. Cole lowered down and then put his full weight on Ollie's face. Ollie's nose when straight into Cole's arsehole.

"Ooohh, bullseye," sniggered Cole. Cole then started to rub his undercarriage up and down on Ollie's face. Ollie groaned and moaned. Cole was stroking his cock as he rode Ollie. Max was watching from the other end laughing also. His two new associates were really mastering their craft well he thought. Cole it came naturally to; to destroy and be cruel was easy for him, he'd been doing it since childhood, picking on weaker kids. Now Bobby, previously a victim of Cole, showing his inner dom, was fun, and also his ability to convert bully Cole into his new friend had been enjoyable to see. Max knows Bobby is in love with Cole, but hell, so was he. That boy had it all, the body, looks, attitude, and that fucking awesome cock. Max thought 'I've got to have that boy!'

"Hey Max!" Cole shouted for the second time, "quit staring at my cock and give Bobby some assistance on edging this bitch."

Max was day dreaming and staring at that beautiful cock. He grinned and focussed. "Miles away. Is the bitch still breathing?" he laughed.

"Oh yeah, I can feel every breath up my arsehole." Cole lifted up to check for sure, and then placed his balls in Ollie's eyes sockets and rested for a while with his cock running up the length of his nose. He laughed as he looked down at Ollie. He couldn't see his eyes, for his nuts, but his nose and mouth were sniffing and trying to lick his dick.

"Right Bobby. Let's edge this cunt. Remember what I said about the gloves," Max said.

Bobby nodded and Cole looked questioningly at them both, mouthing, "What?"

Bobby held up on hand and showed the palm of this beautifully made football gloves and rubbed two finder tips together, there was a small abrasive sound like light Velcro.

"Gotcha," said Cole. "Max have I told you, you think of everything."

"Yes, countless times," Max replied.

Bobby lightly caressed Ollie's cock and took it in his mouth. It tasted great, a little pissy which was how Bobby liked cock. Not too clean, he wants to taste the guy. Ollie moaned as Bobby's tongue and mouth did its thing. Tenderly licking around his Prince Albert.

He then held the cock in the palm of his hand careful to not reveal the finger tips and started to run his hand up and down the shaft. Ollie moaned some more. While he was wanking gently, Max moved forward and stood up, biker boot to the ready, and placed it squarely on both Ollie's nuts. Not too hard but enough for Ollie to scream loudly. Cole put his arse back over his face to muffle the bitch. Max repeated up and down stamping on the ball sack while Bobby wanked his dick. He looked up at Max who nodded, Bobby changed his grip, and used his finger tips squeezing hard as he wanked Ollie's cock.

Cole knelt up to get a closer look, putting all his weight through his knees into Ollie's chest. Ollie was now repeatedly screaming in pain.

Max decided to check on things and said to Bobby to stop, "Ollie you want us to stop?"

"No sir, please give me more, you are all the best." Cole sat down again and Bobby and Max continued to apply the pressure for another thirty seconds.

Then Cole said, "Ok we obviously ain't being hard enough, time to go to the next level."

Cole, Bobby and Max all stood up, with Ollie still lying, flat, recoiling from his pains.

"What you thinking Cole?" said Max.

Cole clenched his fist, as he stood over Ollie and launched a huge punch downwards into Ollie's gut. Ollie yelled.

"I wanna do some boxing," Cole grinned.

Part 2 – Pain and Ecstasy

Chapter 8 - This is probably gonna hurt

Ollie now looked a little more worried.

Cole shouted “This has all been too nice. The boy obviously is enjoying this, which I don’t like. I’m not getting my kicks on people enjoying it, where’s the fun in that?”

Cole had really enjoyed his previous encounter beating on his fellow school pupil Bobby. It was great to really lay into him finally. Bobby looked so miserable as he beat on him and fucked him. Not to mention making him bleed. It was a fantastic experience. Cole wanted that again.

“Right, I wanna get him to the safe word,” said Cole, with red mist in his eyes.

Max leaned over to the nearby drawer, opened it and pulled out an item.

“Think you might want this.” It was a black leather eye mask. “Put this on and bring on your inner executioner.”

Cole put it on. Fuck he looked evil now thought Bobby, his cock tweaking in his shorts. Ollie looked far more concerned now.

“Please don’t kill me.”

“Let’s get him up, Max hold him facing me, with his arms around his back.”

Without any pause, Cole laid a massive punch in the side of Ollie’s face, so hard Max dropped him. Ollie yelled.

“Up again,” Cole said.

“Yes sir,” Max smiled and promptly got Ollie on his feet. This time he held him much tighter.

Cole punched his gut twice, “Yeah,” said Cole.

Ollie, winded by the blows, was yelling. Cole kept going; twice to the face, then the gut. Ollie’s face was getting real bruised and his nose started to bleed.

“Yeah blood!” cheered Cole.

“Keep to the body Cole,” said Max, “He has got to go to work Monday. Don’t want too many questions.”

Bobby was watching with amazement as his childhood bully was beating his work colleague. His handsome strong Cole was so hot in crushing Ollie, he was getting hard watching Cole in action remembering that look in his eyes, the enjoyment of destroying another. Fuck he really is sexy when he’s like this thought Bobby and now with an executioner mask. His boner was getting so hard, he pulled it through his shorts and started to stroke.

“Can I have a go?” Bobby said.

“Sure kid,” smirked Cole.

Bobby moved in, lifted Ollie’s chin who was looking a bit dazed, grabbed his neck and said, “You’re gonna need to take a sickie on Monday.” He kneed Ollie hard in the nuts. Ollie yelled and Max dropped him. Bobby then followed with a kick in the gut and then heeled his cleats in.

“Maybe the whole week by the time we are finished with you,” Bobby followed on. Max and Cole laughed.

"Well done kid," Max said. Cole was grinning and admiring the new blood on his gloves.

"Starting a collection of blood samples on these," he joked.

Max knelt down and grabbed Ollie's nipples and squeezed real hard. Ollie yelled the loudest yet. He squeezed again and a then a third time. Ollie screamed, "Stop Stop please!"

Cole stepped in and went for it on the forth squeeze.

His hands are bigger and much stronger. Ollie yelled, "NOOOOOO RED RED RED!"

Max shouted, "STOP EVERYONE!"

Max pushed Cole back who was too slow to stop to his command.

"I said stop!"

Ollie whimpered.

"That was the final straw, Christ my tits hurt." Ollie breathed and panted. "You guys are good though, fucking glad you stopped though, otherwise I think I would have lost a nipple."

Part 2 – Pain and Ecstasy

Chapter 9 - Team work

“You want to continue?” Max asked.

“Yeah, but only if he gets to fuck me hard,” Ollie said looking at Cole.

Cole was looking disappointed the fun had stopped but he did have a raging hardon. In fact all four had boners.

“Open that drawer Cole and get the wrist and ankle collars. Bobby get these onto Ollie.”

Ollie lay still as Bobby attached them.

“Right lay him on his back, on the table. Attach his arms to the connectors on the side of the table top and leave his legs hanging for now,” said Max.

Ollie’s head was hanging over the back of the table. his arms secured.

“Cole rape this Bitch’s throat, I’m gonna take his man cunt for a ride,” Max said.

Cole didn’t hesitate. He stroked his nine inch dick and walked up to Ollie, who looked excited and happy.

“Open wide I’m coming in fully,” Cole shoved his full nine inches in until his balls hit Ollie’s nose. Ollie gagged some but couldn’t move. Cole push in and out as Ollie gurgled. Bobby watched Cole’s yummy dick going in and out, expanding Ollie’s skinny neck. Fuck that was going in far. Of course, Bobby knew exactly how good that felt.

Max lifted Ollie's legs, unzipped his double fly, leaving the flap hanging, spat on his glove and cock and entered Ollie's arse pretty dry. Ollie yelped but fortunately didn't bite Cole. The both pumped that boy hard. Bobby decided to improvise and climbed on top of Ollie's chest and straddled him facing handsome Cole, who grinned at him as he pleasured himself in Ollie's throat.

Bobby started to jack off while looking at Cole. "Please kiss me Cole," Bobby asked.

Cole saw that little face longing for his lips and leaned in, he grabbed Bobby's face and neck and gave him a real deep kiss with tongues, long and sensual. It tasted amazing for both of them Bobby lifted his arm and pulled Cole's mask off, so he could properly see his eyes, and then continued to kiss.

Max watched the activity going on at the other end of Ollie, and decided to spice it up. He did what Cole did to Bobby two weeks previously and stuck two dry leather gloved fingers in his arse along with this cock and fucked hard, tugging at the hole. Ollie jolted, which broke up Bobby and Cole's kiss. Bobby continued to stroke his cock but was finding it difficult in the gloves. He leaned back and looked over his shoulder to Max.

"Can you help me out with this boner?"

"Sure kid," Max winked.

Bobby swivelled round on Ollie's body and then stood up, feet either side of Ollie's hips on the narrow table landing his rock hard cock in Max's face.

"Now that looks nice," Max said as he took it in his mouth. He pulled his fingers out Ollie's arse, continued to fuck him and grabbed Bobby's cute leather shorts covered arse and pulled him closer. Taking all eight inches. He blew that boy good, like he used to years ago in all the cottaging sites he visited in the eighties and nineties. Blowing strangers in the park. That young cock tasted so good.

After a while, he pulled out and grabbed Ollie's legs.

"I need to breed this bitch with a load. Bobby get ready as the clean-up boy between my legs."

Bobby jumped down and got between Max's legs. He helped by pulling the double zip fully round revealing Max's hairy, now very sweaty, hole and got full view of his handsome dick sliding in and out of Ollie's cunt. He couldn't resist, the smell of Max was awesome, fresh skin, sweat, used leather, and now with a hint of Ollie's arse. He dived into Max's hole with his face and tongue.

"Oh Bobby you are a good lad," said Max. That extra stimulation was all Max needed, watching the mighty Cole across from him mutilating this boy's throat and cute Bobby tickling his prostate Max shot his load hard into Ollie and roared at the same time. He could feel the ropes of cum jetting in, as could Ollie.

Max withdrew slowly to allow Bobby to fill the gap with his tongue.

"Suck that hole Bobby, felch my cum and prep him for Cole."

Cole smiled and said, "Hell Yeah." He withdrew from Ollie's throat, making him choke.

"Fuck, that's a nice cock," said Ollie.

"Don't worry," said Cole, "I'm coming for you at the other end."

"Let's turn him over and put him on the table, face down. Pin his legs and arms on each leg," Max instructed.

Bobby unlatched him. The connectors were so quick, which made life so much easier for your average bondage session. Cole, meanwhile, took off his belt and put it round Ollie's throat, then put the end over his shoulder and dragged Ollie off the table and down onto his back, like a sack of coal. He walked him around a bit laughing while Ollie was choking and gurgling, then let him down on his feet.

"Well it was the quickest way to get him to move," he joked.

"Strap on and have his arse and dick hanging over the edge of the table," said Max.

Cole left the belt on Ollie. Bobby connected Ollie's limbs and then Cole walked round and drove his cock in hard, using Max's cum as lube. Ollie moaned and Cole cheered. He pulled Ollie's head back up with the belt, riding him like a cowboy.

"Bobby, climb on the other end of the bench and fuck his face," ordered Max.

He didn't need to be asked twice, the little footballer climbed on the end of the table, as Cole pulled his head back with his belt. Ollie saw those soft leather shorts coming towards him, with Bobby's cock sticking out. The end had precum all over his helmet, and there was plenty of jizz on those shorts too.

"Give me that cock Bobby," Ollie shouted.

Bobby thrust it in and pushed his head down on it. "Choke on it you cunt," Bobby said and smashed his throat continually.

Grinning at handsome Cole who he rode the boy's arse, deep. Max could see Ollie's cock was hard as a rock under the table and decided to get under there and service that too. He deep throated that Prince Albert cock with ease. This man had been sucking dick for thirty four years, so had plenty of experience and had learnt many tricks. Ollie tasted good. A stranger's dick always did taste better, he said again in his head.

With all three now servicing Ollie's every sexual need, Cole shouted, "Take the load fag!" as he delivered his night's worth of cum deep into Ollie's hole.

The sight of Cole cumming was too much for Bobby, "Here's mine too," he pulled out and shot his load into Ollie's face, hitting his eye, nose, mouth and one rope of cum flew over his shoulder. Bobby beat the last pumps out of his cock on Ollie's cheek.

"Suck me clean!" he ordered Ollie.

Max came up for air and saw his two fellow comrades with huge smiles on their faces. Ollie looked exhausted, but contented. They had been destroying Ollie for almost three hours.

"Fuck I need to pee," said Cole.

"Me too," said Bobby. They looked at each other.

"I think we know what to do. Untie him," Cole said. They all quickly untied Ollie and carried him into the main bathroom. Ollie wasn't complaining; being manhandled by three leather doms was a dream come true.

"Put him in the tub," said Max.

Ollie was in the bath, still with a raging hard on. He looked up at his tormenters, who were now standing on the side of the bath, each getting their dicks into position.

"Give it to me," said Ollie, as he started to beat his raging hardon. He still hadn't cum tonight.

"Look at our poor pathetic victim, all bruised and battered, and now wanting our jizzy pee," said Cole mockingly.

He started to pee first and sprayed Ollie from side to side. Max then joined along with Bobby. All three were pissing hard onto Ollie. He was enjoying the warmth and the sight of these three handsome leather guys pissing all over him. He opened his mouth to get a taste too. It was all too much and he shot a huge load all over his skinny legs and belly.

"What a perfect end to a session," said Max as he turned the shower on over Ollie, who jumped at the initial cold water, that hit him.

"Let's all get cleaned up, showered, and out of this gear. Ollie shower here, towels are there. Lucky you bought that change of clothes. Bobby, use the separate shower here. Cole, there's one in the spare bedroom ensuite and I'll use mine," said Max.

Chapter 10 - Bruised and battered

They all got cleaned up and shower fresh. Ollie put on his change of clothes and came out the bathroom first. Bobby, cleaned up and wearing a bathrobe, took his football kit and hung it up carefully and put the boots in the box with the gloves carefully arranged on the top. Max came out of his room in a bathrobe also. Finally Cole appeared with just a towel around his waist, showing his magnificent torso and arms, his hair still all wet and curly. Max sighed at the amazing sight. Cole was also carrying his gear. He sauntered into the dressing room and slung the trousers and harness onto a chair with the boots kicked under.

Ollie was standing clothed and looking like a spare part. He had put his lip and nose ring back in and picked up his torn clothes. He had a real shiner to his left eye and a split lip and probably many bruises to his body.

"Thank you Ollie for allowing us to play with you," said Max.

"It was great, scary as fuck, but you guys are the best I've had," he replied.

"Thanks, how are you planning to get home its gone midnight?" Max asked.

"I live Southside so plan to get the L Train now. Hopefully won't miss the last one if I'm quick," grabbing for his stuff.

Max walked across the room and reached for his wallet.

"No, I'd rather you got home safely. Please get an Uber or cab. Here is $200 for that, and also to replace the clothing that Cole decided to make into a five piece shirt and trouser set," he smiled.

Cole sniggered.

“Really that’s too much,” Ollie said.

“No, take it. It’s the least we can do. Though I do suggest you take a sickie Monday and get something on that face.”

And with that Ollie said thanks and went out into the lobby and left.

“Good choice Bobby! He took a hell of a lot more than I thought he would,” Max said as he walked into the dressing room.

He stopped and sighed at the sight. Cole had thrown his gear on a chair, but then he looked right and saw Bobby’s football shirt neatly hanging up, the boots correctly in the box, and those cute gloves properly placed on top. He smiled at the contrast: good lad Bobby and sexy rascal Cole. He turned round and walked back in the room.

“Thanks Cole for hurling you clothes back in the dressing room. Bobby thank you for taking good care of them and putting them away properly,” he lightly commented. “By the way, where are the football shorts?” he added.

“Sorry I put them back on,” he raised his leg on his bathrobe. “They feel so fucking nice on, is that ok?”

“Sure, well they ain’t gonna fit either of us.”

“Now let’s have a proper drink.” Max said. “Do you guys drink wine?”

“Never tried it. Too fucking expensive,” said Cole.

“I’ve had some but its normally been a bit rubbish, so stick to beer,” said Bobby.

"Well for some reason wine in the USA is ridiculously expensive compared to home but tonight we deserve a treat and I would like you to try a good wine."

He walked across the open plan room to the kitchen area and pulled out a large wine cooler draw filled with dozens of bottles.

"Ummm this will do the trick. A nice bottle of Montrachet." He then took three beautiful fine wine glasses from the cupboard and placed them on the counter and opened the bottle. He sniffed the cork, smiled and then poured the light straw coloured wine into three glasses. Bobby was transfixed by Max's class and knowledge. He was worldly wise. Max passed the glasses and said, "Let's sit down."

They moved to the sofas. Cole and Bobby took the sofa and Max stood, raising his glass, "Cheers boys." He sat on the arm chair opposite them.

Bobby tasted first, "Wow that is good."

Cole tried his, he smirked, "Not bad."

"You know so much about stuff. This wine is amazing. Didn't know it really tasted like this," said Bobby.

"Well, it is a good wine, from the Burgundy region of France. Sadly it's not cheap, especially here in the US," Max said.

"You know so much. I feel I know fuck all. You Brits always seem be so intelligent," Bobby smiled.

"Hell, I'm nearly twice the age of you two. I've learnt a lot over the years. I can assure you at twenty seven I also knew jack shit about a lot of things. Also there are some fucking stupid Brits, most of them are at home and voted fucking Brexit, 'cos they preferred life like it was back in the friggin' 1950s. No don't get me started on that subject. Please tell me something about what you want to do with your lives. Cole you first," initiated Max, bringing Cole into the conversation.

Cole stuttered, "Oh I don't know. I wanted to be a baseball player but didn't cut it, so now I labour on the travel boats on the pier. The pay is shit and I have to be nice to wining kids. I live in shit digs, in two rooms. I got good grades at school, but it's so fucking hard to get a break, so guess I'll be on the pier for a while."

He had a sad vulnerable look in his eyes, for such a sexy looking guy. Max thought it looked adorable. His heart skipped. "Bobby, you," Max asked.

"I was a book worm at school, which was probably why Cole picked on me, and 'cos I was a fag."

Max jumped in, "Yes I want to say. I noticed the term 'fag' was used a few times and I've never liked it. We should all remember all three of us are fags. When we use this detrimental term, I feel it belittles the gay community and we shouldn't use it either. I'll get off my soap box now, sorry."

"I'm not a fag," said Cole.

"When you have your dick in another guy's arse, I'd beg to differ Cole," Max replied with a giggle.

"Fags are the weak fairies," Cole replied

"Thanks!" said Bobby.

"Oh I don't know," said Cole feeling a little outnumbered.

"See it's not great is it? We should stand united. Anyway back to you Bobby."

"Well, good grades at school, went to college, studied software development for three years, got a job in Home Depot stacking shelves," he laughed. "I'm hoping to work my way into management, but it's hard, I live in digs also. Not great, my Mum's downtown. Sadly lost my dad at the age of five. That's my life story," Bobby laughed.

"Yeah I don't see my parents," said Cole, "my Mum and Dad divorced when I was twelve and she had a succession of guys in the house. Fucking hated all of them. Was chucked out after College and not seen them since," Cole said.

"I'm sorry to hear that. What did you study Cole?" Max asked

"Sales and Marketing, for what it was worth."

"What a fucking waste. You both have such talents," Max said angrily as he raised his glass. "To your better futures."

"What about you Max? Tell us your story," asked Bobby.

"Christ! You don't want to hear about me," Max replied.

"I do. I really do," said Cole who had been quiet for a while. "You must have done something right to have all this."

"Ok. Well it wasn't always like this. I was born to working class parents in a small city called Leicester, which is about hundred miles north of London. My mother and father both worked in the town's shoe trade. In my early years, I was a keen learner and managed to get a scholarship to a public school. That's what you call a private school. It was an all-boys school so you can imagine I really got a taste for dick," he laughed, "but I also met a lot of other rich kids there and made some good contacts. I had to work harder, knowing I didn't have daddy's money to fall back on like lots of them. I started buying and selling just about anything. Some legal some not so. Then, I bought a property when the housing market crashed in the nineties and resold on the rise and made my first profit. This, then started something and my business grew and grew."

"I moved to London where it was easier to live out my fetishes. On a chance trip to Berlin's Folsom Weekend in 2006 I met the love of my life at the tender age of thirty nine. Peter, a forty three year old English visiting the event also. We met in a leather bar and he had the best arse in the bar, pushing through a pair of chaps. I was transfixed and couldn't stop staring at him. So much so he noticed and introduced himself. I thought he was German but he was from London. We spent the whole weekend together and went home after. We had moved in together within a month and started our own business in real estate two months later. He's the real brains. He has the knack of getting people to invest their money. He has real style. He runs the UK and Germany markets and I do the USA."

"Wow Max! He's smarter and more sophisticated than you?" Cole said.

"He sure is," replied Max.

"Does he know about us?" Bobby asked sheepishly.

"Yes, I've told him all about you. We are both open in our relationship. We started that when we were spending six months of the year apart. I can't go that long without my dick being sucked and neither can he."

"I want to thank you Max for being so kind and generous to us both. Paying Ollie to get home safe. You didn't have to do that, and all that gear you bought. Must have cost a mint," Bobby said.

"How much was that Max?" piped up Cole, "About $800?"

"More like $3000 bucks in total," Max answered.

"Fuck," said Bobby, mouth wide open.

"It was all custom made-to-measure with my own design features. They are all one of a kind. Half of the money was on your football kit, boots and gloves. That leather is very thin and expensive to produce."

Bobby stroked his crotch under his bathrobe feeling the buttery soft shorts underneath. "They feel a million bucks on."

They talked for a while about their ambitions. Max asked them both about their training and skills, taking in every detail. Bobby noticed how specific he was in his questioning and seemingly memorising all the information. But that was just Max, right? he thought. Bobby looked at the clock. It was 1.30 in the morning. Saturday was Sunday now. "I guess we better get out your way Max. It's quite late now." Bobby stated.

"It is late. If you like you can always stay here. I also have the spare room," Max said. Cole looked at Bobby who seemed keen. Cole also thought of those lovely white sheets, compared to his dingy bedsit.

"Ok I'm in, beats my place any day of the week," Cole said.

They all got up and Bobby said, "Should I clear up the place?" reverting to his sub role.

"No Tiger. I'll sort it all in the morning. You and Cole go to bed," as he walked to his room.

Bobby cleared his throat and paused, “Can I come with you please?” he said to Max.

“If you want to, but I would have thought you would prefer to cuddle up to that gorgeous hunk of man,” Max said staring at Cole.

“I’d like to cuddle up with both my gorgeous hunks, will you indulge me Cole..... please?”

Cole was at the spare room doorway. He paused, then grinned, tore off his towel and ran naked towards them both and burst through Max’s master bedroom door and threw himself on the huge bed like a giant star shouting, “Geronimo!”

Max and Bobby laughed and threw their robes on the floor and jumped on top of him.

“This bed can house six guys,” Bobby said.

“On many occasions, when Peter’s here, it has,” Max laughed.

Chapter 11 - It's so late

Max clapped twice and the lights dimmed to a lower level.

"So so cool. You are so smooth," said Cole.

They were all on the bed. Bobby lying on his front in the middle facing Cole and Cole and Max facing inwards on their sides looking at each other. Max had his hand on Bobby's leather football shorts. The only bit of clothing in the bed.

"They do feel good. Cop a feel Cole," Max said.

Cole felt the other buttock "Ummmm," moaned Bobby, "That feels even better. You know I really missed out tonight," Bobby said.

"What do you mean?" said Max.

"My arse didn't get a pounding from anyone tonight, and it's feeling really under appreciated," he replied with a giggle.

"Well Cole, do you think that's something we can sort out for the poor boy?" smiled Max.

"Yeah Cole, destroy me please," Bobby said.

"No," said Cole, "I don't want to."

Bobby looked puzzled as did Max at first but then he saw Cole's look at Bobby, a side we didn't often see. He looked softer. Could he look even more handsome?

Cole sat up on his elbow and looked at them both.

"I fucking loved destroying you when I thought you were the fa...the guy I bullied at school. It was hot. I didn't know you. I didn't give two shits how you felt. I wanted the kicks and to destroy you, that smart fucking kid who always got one grade better than me. Yeah I didn't care when I fucking made...... you.... you bleed," his eyes were all glassy. "I'm such an ass, and you are such a cool guy. I've really enjoyed your company these last few weeks and I know you like my cock, but I can't beat on someone I...." He paused. "I care about. There I said it. I care for you Bobby, so I can't."

He rolled on his back and put his hands over his face.

Max cleared his throat, "Err feeling like a third wheel here. Shall I go to the spare room."

"No," said Bobby. "I invited both of you into... your bed," he laughed and he pulled Cole's hands away from his face.

"You two are both awesome guys. I fancy the pants off the pair of you, says the only guy here wearing pants! I can see we have grown a bit of a bond and that you, Cole, don't look at me with the same contempt as you did. I noticed that at the end of our first encounter when I asked you all to piss in my mouth and how I told you that I had waited for you Cole to fuck me for twelve years and what did you say?"

"I can't recall?" said Cole.

"You called me a twisted fuck, but you said it with a smile from your eyes. I knew then that you had changed a little. Cole, you can care for me, and still fuck me hard. If I want you to fuck me hard, pull my hair even slap me....gently ideally, 'cos you are fucking strong, then we can."

Max piped in, "And of course Cole, you could sensually make love to Bobby instead. I'll be the first to say I fucking love rough sex, the harder the better, but I also love to have a passionate slow lingering deep kiss and a sensual hand running over my body. And to be slowly fucked."

Bobby turned to Max and grabbed his face and kissed him hard, "Like this…?"

After a long kiss, Bobby pulled away and said, "Now can we quit talking and somebody fuck me already."

"Ok Mr Boss. Turn around and face Cole. Look at that handsome face, that beautiful chest and arms, while I sort you out."

Max then wrapped his right arm under Bobby and held his chest firmly, moving his growing boner up against those leather shorts. With his left arm, he caressed Bobby's body, his arms, thighs, chest stomach and stroked Bobby's growing boner through those shorts. He was also kissing Bobby's neck, head and back. Bobby felt so wonderful held in Max's strong arms. So safe and warm. Cole watched Max in action, with even more admiration. 'Fuck, if I ever become half the man he is when I'm fifty I'll be so lucky,' he thought. Bobby was enjoying the attention and he was so aroused. Cole realised, he looked beautiful.

Max whispered, "Cole, open the draw and pass me the bottle, and Bobby I think it's time to un-pop those poppers"

"Please do Max."

Max ran his hand over Bobby's leather shorts and gently unclipped the poppers, opening up the way. Max then nodded to Cole to put some lube onto his fingers. Max gently lubed up Bobby's hole. Bobby was moaning at every gentle touch. The opening of his shorts, the lubing of his arse. Max then lubed his now raging hardon and separated Bobby's butt cheeks, resting his uncut cock against Bobby's hole.

Part 2 – Pain and Ecstasy

"You ready for me Bobby boy?"

"Oh I'm ready Daddy. Please breed me sir."

On that command Max gently eased his helmet into Bobby's hole, stopped, pulled back and then eased in again, a little further. Teasing Bobby. Bobby could feel Max's hands everywhere. His warm hairy body, freshly showered, his sweet breath on his neck, then the lubing of his hole, and finally the oh so gentle penetration. He could actually feel Max's foreskin rim on the edge of his hole when he first entered and hovered and then he pulled back and went in further. The guy was a master in so many ways Bobby thought. Age definitely gives you experience. Max was now fully inside Bobby and gently moving his shaft in and out of this beautiful young man's tight hole. He could smell his freshly washed blonde hair and his smooth soft skin. His longing moans of encouragement kept the rhythm going.

Cole was studying Max in action in complete awe. He had never seen sex like this. All the porn he saw was rough-banging screaming bitches. His experience until now had been with dumb girls who wanted to be with the jock. He never dated an intelligent girl. Most of the girls he fucked could only count to ten if they were able to use their phone. Even the new sex with men he had experienced had been real rough. Getting head meant you rammed your cock down their throat, right? Wrong, he thought. This guy can do both. This guy, Max, is the man.

He was watching his new friend Bobby being fucked in the most sexy awesome way and Bobby looked like he was in ecstasy, judging by the look on his face and his enormous hardon. Cole just released he was looking at Bobby as a friend now, not someone to bully. That change was significant for Cole, he thought and smiled. He looked at Bobby's face and then his hard cock. Cole decided to take hold of it and stroke it. Cole then put his other hand on Bobby's chest. He then moved in and kissed Bobby deeply. Bobby's eyes opened and then closed and he kissed back.

Max said, "Come on Cole, your turn now, but gently," and he withdrew his cock. "On your back Bobby, and let's remove those shorts."

Bobby moved on his back and lifted his legs and whipped those shorts off.

Cole lubed up his raging hardon, then moved over and crouched on top of Bobby between his legs, not putting his full body weight on just yet. Bobby wrapped his legs around his handsome jock. Cole wrapped his arms around Bobby and kissed him slowly and sensually. Bobby responded well to the kiss and put his hands and fingers through the jocks curly hair. Cole lowered and rested his cock against Bobby's hole. Remembering what Max did, Cole controlled his natural urge to ram it home, and slowly entered Bobby. Bobby smiled and moaned. Cole was bigger than Max and he could tell the difference. Cole lowered his weight onto Bobby and they were now chest to chest kissing and he was driving his dick deeper.

"A little faster," Bobby urged and Cole obliged.

Cole fucked Bobby for good five minutes. Bobby admired the view in the mirrored ceiling, Cole's arse pumping into him, his broad back was so sexy. He even had a handsome back for fuck's sake Bobby thought. Max lay on his side and watched these two beautiful young men enjoying themselves and each other. Bobby, so cute and sexy, with an intelligent and inquisitive mind. Cole, a perfect physical specimen of a mid twenties man, handsome cocky and mysterious. Max studied them. Cole may not be as intelligent as Bobby, but he was clever and had a charisma that could achieve greatness. Both could, if given the chance he kept thinking.

Remembering back to his early years and the struggle he had to get a break. Somehow, it seemed easier back in the eighties and in the UK. The USA is the land of dreams, but in the 21st century it's fucking hard to break out into the world, especially without money. Max broke away from his thoughts and noticed Bobby smiling at him, while Cole was necking him on the other side. Max sat up to get a better view of Cole's arse driving into Bobby's.

"Cole your arse if one of the best I've seen. Pert and slim and....oh fuck it I'm going in"

Max jumped to the end of the bed and put his nose right into the action, with both hands gripping his cheeks, he tongued that boys hole, getting deeper and deeper. Cole moaned, and looked back.

"Fuck Max, I'm kinda busy here," he said grinning like a Cheshire cat.

Bobby grabbed his face back and said, "Oh just fucking enjoy the attention. You know you love being the centre of it," and pulled him in for more kisses.

Max continued working Cole's arse with his tongue, then changed it for a lubed finger. Really carefully he started to finger Cole's virgin arse. Cole had never been fucked. He was "straight" up until two weeks ago. He'd allowed the occasional 'fag' to suck him off. He'd fucked a couple, but he had never been fucked. Max decided he wanted to be his first and was being very careful not to let this opportunity go.

Cole reacted to the finger abruptly, and said "Wooh, hang on, I ain't done that before and from what I've seen it fucking hurts. Well it does when I've fucked arse."

"Cole," Max said. "I'm going to introduce you to your prostate, I'm going to stimulate it with my finger. I'll be gentle."

Part 2 – Pain and Ecstasy

"You're gonna love this," said Bobby. Cole wasn't sure.

"Cole, I'm not going to harm you. You do know that? At first it will seem tight and a little painful, but if you can relax that hole, you will unlock so much pleasure, I promise. Do you trust me?" Max asked.

Cole paused fucking Bobby and waited a while. Everything else he had been introduced to in the world of gay sex had been amazing he thought.

"Ok, but please go easy."

Max giggled, "Like you did on Bobby and Ollie?"

"Yeah Ok, that's different. They seemed to like it," Cole replied.

"I fucking did," piped up Bobby.

"Ok Cole, carry on enjoying Bobby and relax, but I am going to need you to stop fucking him, I will do the rest."

Cole pulled his cock out and its full beauty hung there in front of Max. He couldn't resist and took Cole's cock in his mouth to taste him and Bobby together. After a full length suck he withdrew, "Fuck you both taste good."

Max then put lots of lube on his fingers to be sure he didn't fuck up this chance. Gently he circled Cole's ring and inserted the first finger. Cole moaned and Max could hear Bobby as he whispered to Cole, "Relax sexy." In and out he went and then a second finger. A bit deeper to start to find the edge of the prostate. Max was on it and gently he put pressure on it and teased it. Cole clenched Max's fingers.

"Relax," Max said.

He continued for a couple of minutes and his patience paid off. He felt Cole start to really relax and he could get a third finger in. Now was the time.

“Cole, move to the end of the bed, with your legs over the edge to get more comfortable on your stomach.”

Cole moved down saying, “This is starting feel pretty good.”

Once in position, Max again inserted two fingers and then three to get the motion going again. Bobby was sitting up watching this master in action. Max was so cool he thought. He has such authority and tenderness at the same time. ‘If my Dad was still alive, I hoped he’d be like Max’ he thought, then realising that wouldn’t be quite right considering what they had been doing together. Correcting his thoughts, Bobby just loved that he was such a fine English gent, but sexy as hell with it.

Reaching for more lube, Max gave his now hard cock a good coating, with an extra bit on the helmet. He moved up to Cole and their legs touched. His fingers still massaging his hole, he slowly took them out, while his cock was pressed ready to replace them. With great timing, he replaced the fingers with the head of his cock. He stroked Cole’s lower back. Cole moaned and made a squeak sound.

“Relax boy,” and Max entered another half inch, and then another.

He pulled back a little and then back in. Small rhythmic pumps, each one getting a little deeper. Cole was now moaning, as Max started to pump his hole and his prostate. Cole felt a mixture of being uncomfortable and aroused. His arse felt like it was in his throat. He couldn’t explain the feeling in his head. But as Max worked his way in and the rhythm started, Cole relaxed even more and started to feel the amazing sensations. Max felt Cole’s signal, and picked up the pace. He moved closer and lay on top of Cole, kissing his back as he pumped this beautiful man.

"I've wanted you so much Cole, since that first day you put my jacket on in that bar, you sexy boy." He pumped deeper and wrapping his arms around Cole who was moaning and whining but in a good way. Cole was in ecstasy. That handsome older man, who had been so generous to him, was now fucking him hard, and he loved it. Bobby was watching intently, beating his dick at the sight of his two handsome doms fucking each other, on this beautiful bed and in the amazing room and apartment.

Max was close and decided he had to finish in Cole's arse. He pumped and pumped first watching himself in the mirrored headboard and then looking across at Bobby's handsome dick getting a beating also. He then released his load into Cole's gut. Five deep pumps of fresh British spunk end their journey in Cole's perfect arse. Max collapsed on Cole with a groan. Then kissed his back and gently withdrew. Bobby sprang up and was straight into Cole's arse with his tongue.

"Feed me Cole," he instructed.

"Push back, give him my spunk from your arse," Max clarified.

Cole attempted to let the spunk out, a little unsuccessfully, but Bobby got some of it.

"Umm cum and arse," he grinned.

Cole rolled over and pushed himself up the bed and lay prostrate on it, his huge boner in the air.

"That was fucking amazing Max, you were so careful. I trusted you. I really think I'd trust you with my life."

Max was standing at the end of the bed, admiring Cole's body and that dick.

"I'm gonna finish you off then," Max said as he leant on the end of the bed and deep throated Cole's cock in one almost seamless move.

"Fuck, go baby," Cole said, now holding Max's head and pumping his cock in deep.

The old Cole was back and wanted to take back some of that control. Bobby wasn't going to miss out on the action, not with Max's arse hole right in front of him begging to be filled. He lubed his cock and Max's hole and took no mercy as he drove in fully in one push. Max gurgled and moaned and opened his legs wider. Bobby pumped Max as hard as his lighter frame would allow for a good couple of minutes, while Max noshed on Cole's glorious dick. It wasn't long before Bobby shouted, "Take it like a man Max!" as he pumped his youthful cum into his hole.

Exhausted he pulled out and flopped on the bed beside Max and Cole. Cole was sitting up now and lifted Max's head up.

"I wanna cum in your face Max," Max rolled over as Cole got on his knees. Max wanked Cole's nine inch cock until he could feel the change and then allowed the pumps to hit his face, throat, neck and chest. The warm ropes of Cole's cum felt glorious. Cole leant down and kissed Max deep and Bobby moved in to hoover up all the jizz on Max.

They all collapsed on the bed exhausted. It was just before three in the morning,

"What a fucking brilliant evening guys," Max said as he pulled up the covers. Bobby moved in between Max and Cole grinning from ear to ear. They lay flat breathing heavily as Max clapped three times and the lights went out.

"Too fucking cool," said Cole, as they all went to sleep.

by Nick Christie

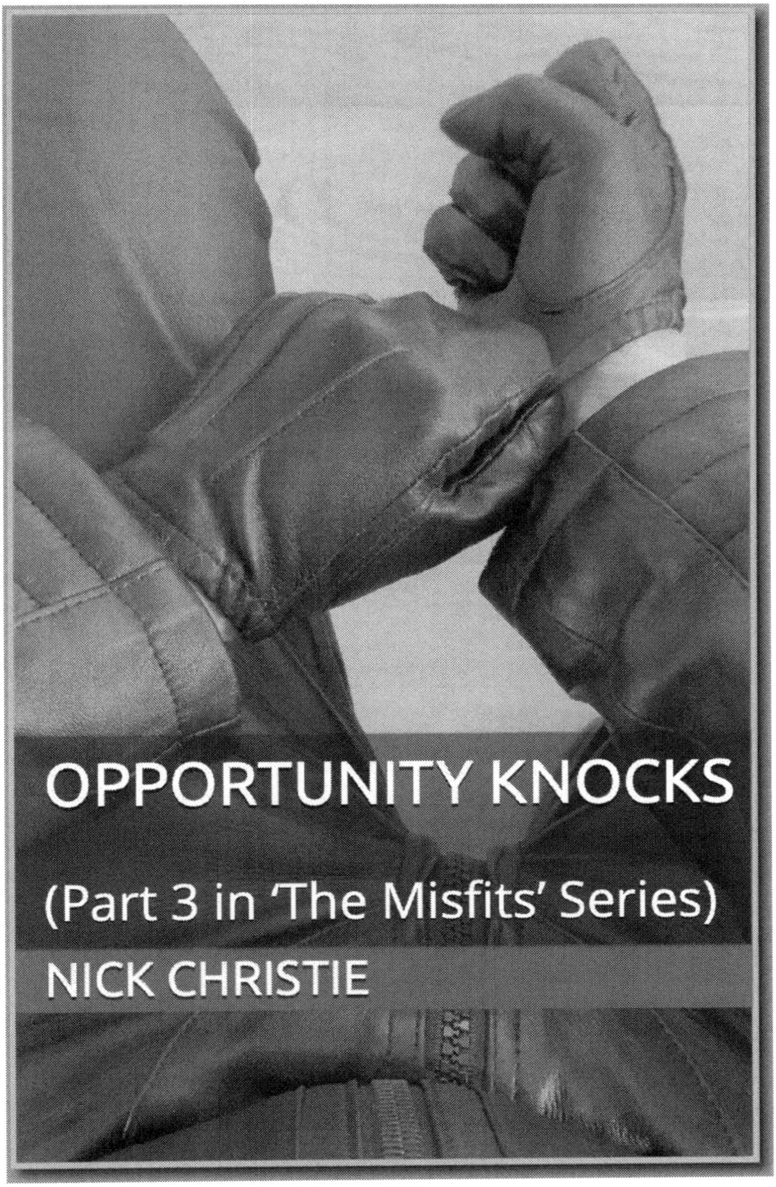
OPPORTUNITY KNOCKS
(Part 3 in 'The Misfits' Series)
NICK CHRISTIE

Opportunity Knocks

(Part 3 in 'The Misfits' Series)

(Erotic Gay Fiction)

Nick Christie

Chapter 1 - Lazy Sunday

Max woke up to find Bobby's head and arm resting on his chest. Fast asleep, his little angelic face breathing lightly on his chest hair. Max smiled at the sight and looked over to see handsome Cole, also fast asleep behind Bobby, his toned, muscular arm wrapped around the young lad. They both looked so cute and innocent when fast asleep. So different from when they are awake and their hormones are raging Max thought. He looked over his shoulder to catch the time, and saw it was 6.27am on the bedside clock. 6.27am on a Sunday morning after one hell of a Saturday night.

Max felt the urge to pee, so gently he unravelled himself from Bobby's clutches and gently put him on the pillow so as not to wake him. He crept into the en-suite. He shortly returned, picked up a bath robe, plus Bobby's leather football shorts, and slipped out of the room into the main apartment, leaving the sleeping beauties to rest. He looked at the room and decided he needed to get things straight. Max hated mess and liked things back into order. He got to work with some cleaner and wiped down the 'Fuck table' and cleaned up any signs of bodily fluids off the leather mat. Then he collapsed the table and put it away in the far corner of the dressing room, rolled up the leather mat, repositioned the furniture and put the mat under the largest sofa, in the special strap housing, so it was out of sight. He then went into the main bathroom, cleared all the towels about the place, that Ollie and Bobby had used the night before and replaced them with fresh.

The dressing room got a tidy up too. All items neatly hung up and stored correctly. He put Cole and Bobby's gear in a special end of the cupboard, so they wouldn't get mixed up with his huge array of gear. Max couldn't resist holding Cole's leather jeans to his face and breathing in the aroma of that beautiful young man and the leather. The crotch area aroma bought back the memories of the night before, with Cole in charge of Ollie's destruction. Max was getting a boner at the thought. He needed to crack on and get this apartment back in order. He took a final sniff of Bobby's football shorts, which also smelt equally good, before putting them all away.

Finally, he checked the en-suite in the guest room that Cole had used and collected the towel Cole dropped as he ran across the room. Max giggled at the memory. The apartment was now pretty much ship shape and he put the towels on to wash. Max kept thinking about Bobby and Cole and their shit start in life. Both in dead end jobs but seeming to have so much more to offer. Max had built his business from scratch in the UK and expanded it when he met his clever husband Peter 12 years ago. Max had managed to break out of his poor situation with a scholarship for a good school and then having the advantage of meeting well-connected people. It is so often a case of who you know, not what you know, to get on in life.

Max was always grateful of that and to this end, had always tried to give people a chance in his business. The employees within Max and Peter's business were very diverse. A vibrant mix of diversity, from race to sexual orientation. All were welcome as long as you worked hard, brought some skill to the party and were also open to working with others. No bigotry in any form allowed.

Max had met a few of his employees as hook-ups. If he had seen they were struggling, if he felt a connection and could really see a drive in that person, he would try and help. Others he met in restaurants or doing really low paid work but he could see they had potential. He had a great instinct with people. At least ninety percent of the people he found this way did cut it and worked out. Those who didn't had to go. Max was kind and willing to help but he wouldn't carry people, no matter how fit they might be. His business mattered, and it mattered to his team. If they saw him giving anyone slacking special treatment it would upset the balance. The team were a real bunch of misfits from the norm, but together they were a force to be reckoned with. Max continued to think about Bobby and Cole while he cleaned up the wine glasses and made some fresh coffee and a pot of tea. He would call Peter later to discuss his thinking.

Bobby woke up to find himself in a strange huge bed surrounded by soft cotton sheets and, more importantly, in the arms of a strong man. The night before came rushing back to him and he smiled. He could feel the strength of Cole's hard body surrounding and spooning him in bed. Oh, this was wonderful. Then he wondered where Max was. He could hear some general movement in the main apartment. He looked at the clock. It was 8.02am and a Sunday. Bobby felt down to find Cole's powerful thighs and shuddered at the size of them compared to his tender frame. He could also feel something else. Cole had a huge morning glory that was resting in the crack of Bobby's arse. It felt awesome. Cole was still sleeping gently. Bobby carefully turned around trying so hard to not wake him. There he was, his handsome Cole, looking so sweet asleep. That boyish mop of curly hair framing that strong featured face. Bobby needed that cock. He reached down and gently touched it and then started to stroke it. Cole slept on.

Bobby slowly moved under the duvet and got down to Cole's cock. Under the covers it was so warm that the aroma coming from Cole's crotch was intensified by the heat. Bobby gently worked his magic mouth on Cole's cock and it tasted good. He could taste a combination of Cole's load from last night, his own arse from when he made tender love to him and Max's cum and spit from fucking him also, but then blowing Cole. The combination of tastes and smells with the warmth of the bedding was intoxicating. Cole started to stir as Bobby got to work.

Cole woke up to the best feeling ever. He was in Max's huge bed with someone under the covers blowing him. He smiled to himself and lifted the covers to see Bobby noshing him hard. Bobby looked back at him, took his cock out is mouth and sang, "Morning!" before deep throating him again.

"Good morning to you. Fuck that feels good. Keep going and you'll get a breakfast treat," Cole said.

Bobby continued and very shortly Cole grabbed the covers and moaned as he shot his load deep into Bobby's throat. Bobby kept sucking until he got every drop of Cole's cum. Once done, Bobby emerged from under the duvet and gave Cole a deep kiss.

"You taste of me," said Cole.

"How would you know?" Bobby replied with a wink.

Bobby then jumped out of bed and found his bathrobe and said, "I'm going to find out how our host is."

He left the room, leaving Cole on his back looking down at his softening cock. He gave it a rub and a scratch and rolled over pulling the duvet back over himself.

Bobby entered the lounge to find Max sitting at the table drinking coffee and reading his iPad. Max looked up and smiled "You want some tea or a coffee young man?"

"Ooo, a coffee please. Black, no sugar thanks."

Max got up, made him a coffee and beckoned to Bobby to sit at the table with him. He drew up a chair and could see Max was reading the Sunday Times on his iPad, a British newspaper.

"Do you always read The Times?" he asked.

"I read the New York Times and the Chicago Tribune to keep myself abreast of US news. And I read The Sunday Times and watch BBC to get an idea of what is going on back home and the rest of the world. You?"

"Well I'll pick up a paper at work if someone has left it behind, but not really got the money to regularly buy or subscribe," Bobby said. "I don't earn much. I take home about $420 a week and rent and bills takes about $250 of that, so I have to be very careful. Plus I like to give some to my Mom each week. I try and put aside $20 or $25 a week to help her out. She's not in the best of health."

"I'm really sorry to hear that," Max said.

They continued chatting, when the bedroom door opened and a sleepy naked Cole came through the door.

"Any coffee left in the pot?"

Even when he wakes up with bedhead hair he looks amazing thought Max. Some guys just have great genes.

"Yes, help yourself. Mugs are in the cupboard above the coffee machine. Are you guys hungry?"

"Yes," they both replied.

"You fancy a proper bacon butty?"

"What the fucks a butty?" asked Cole.

"Bacon sandwich, proper Danish bacon, not that terrible crispy greasy streaky shit you guys always serve up. Bacon with HP sauce," replied Max.

"By the way you gonna put some clothes on?" Max added.

"Nah. Don't you like the view?" said Cole as he sat down.

Max set to making breakfast. Fresh white bread he cut into thick slices. The bacon was thick and smelt good as it fried. Served with butter and good dollop of brown sauce. They all tucked in.

"These are real good," said Bobby.

Cole added, "Yeah thanks for this. I needed.....oh fuck," a big dollop of brown sauce fell out the sandwich and landed in his lap and particularly on his cock.

Bobby laughed and leaned over, "I'll soon clean that up for you."

Cole pushed him back, "Ah ah, you ate my cock this morning."

"Oh, did you now," Max smiled.

Cole looked at Max and said, "Do you want to help me out here?"

Max looked at Cole's face, he had that dirty glint in his eye. "If you insist Cole. Seems a shame to waste such good sauce."

Max got up and moved round to where Cole was sitting and knelt down. He licked the sauce off Cole's thigh first and then lifted his limp dick up with his hand and put it fully in his mouth to clean off the sauce. He sucked it clean back and forth a few times. Max looked up at Cole grinning at him. He hadn't noticed Bobby applying brown sauce to end of his now erect cock.

"Oh no," said Bobby.

Max looked across and saw his beaming face and stroking his cock. Max moved across and blew Bobby hard. Both their cocks tasted better than the bacon sandwich. Bobby was moaning at his Master at work. Max was so experienced at blowing cock, Bobby was normally the one doing the sucking as a sub, so relished the chance when a handsome guy would suck him off. Cole would need some teaching. Max was a pro. It felt so good. Bobby could feel he was close.

"I'm close Max," he said.

Max placed his hands around his balls and massaged gently which made Bobby release. Max felt the warm seed lace the back of his throat and tongue. 'Fuck I love cock,' he thought to himself and he loved these two young cocks very much.

Max then got up and collected the plates.

"Ok, lads that's enough fun for today, time to jump in the shower and fuck off for now," he laughed.

"I've got some work to be getting on with and I'm sure you don't want to waste your Sunday here."

Bobby and Cole looked at each other and then around the plush surroundings.

"I mean it guy's. I have work to do."

They both got up and went to the shower. Max watched their pert arses as they went in the bathroom. So cute.

Bobby and Cole got dressed, grabbed their things and headed to the door.

"Max when will we see you again?" Bobby asked.

"I'll be in touch in the next couple of days," Max replied.

"Thanks Max for everything. You are the best," smiled Cole as he left through the door with Bobby.

Chapter 2 - Facetime

Finally, Max had the place back to himself. He loved those lads but he loved his own space even more. Last night was the first time Max had ever let a trick stay overnight, unless he counted the one tied up in a box all night. But Bobby and Cole weren't really a trick. They were on the first time they met, but they meant more to him now. Max preferred his own company on the whole. The arrangement with Peter was perfect for both of them. They loved each other's company but also valued the time apart and to play with others.

Max thought some more about Bobby and Cole's position. If Bobby was earning that little at Home Depot, Cole must be on similar at the Pier Boats. Even Max's intern execs were earning four times that. Within Max's business, he offered the same wage levels and benefits as his UK/EU employees. Good wages and good vacation benefits including healthcare. He believed in really looking after his team, so they worked the hardest for him. When the business had a success they all got a slice of the profits. He needed to help Bobby and Cole get on this team. Bobby was an obvious fit in IT and technical, they were stretched in that area, but Cole was a harder fit. 'I need to call Peter,' he thought.

He picked up his phone and looked at the time. 11am, so 5pm in London. Perfect. He facetimed Peter.

"Good morning sexy. Still in your dressing gown you lazy bastard?" said Peter as he answered the call with a beautiful English accent.

They chatted a while and then Max got down to business talking about Bobby and Cole.

"Max you can't just keep employing people because you like fucking them. Look what happened with Tyler."

"These guys are different. Yes, Tyler was a mistake, but all the other people I have employed have been stars. And for the record, I haven't fucked all of them," Max sharply replied.

"No, not all of them, just the men," Peter laughed back.

"Look, I'm sure you'd really like them when you meet them," Max continued.

"I'm sure I will, in our bed, but will they really bring anything to the business Max?" Peter replied.

"Yes, they will. I'm sure of it."

"Well it's your call Max. You run Chicago and I'm sorry to challenge, but you know that's what you value from me, along with my charm, connections and huge cock," he smiled down the phone. They talked some more on how and what areas Cole and Bobby could fit into the business and agreed that a trial would be a good plan, rather than taking them on instantly. Also, the team would have a say on whether they fitted in or not.

After twenty minutes Max ended the call and decided to go for a run and clear his head. Max thought and remembered Tyler. He was a thirty five year old handsome guy he picked up in a bar about four years ago. He was educated and recently been made redundant. Max took a chance on him but he was lazy and harassed a lot of the guys in the business for sex. He had to go and was gone within a month of starting. Hard work and respect for all team members were his main rule to abide by. You fuck either one of them up and you're out.

Chapter 3 – Bartholomew Steadman

Max arrived at the office at 8am on Monday to be greeted by Gina Garcia, his Office Manager. She smiled and said, "Good Morning. Your flat white is waiting on your desk."

"Thank you, but you didn't have to, but I'm glad you did. Good weekend Gina?" Max asked.

"Yeah, a nice quiet one, just me and the dogs, you?" she replied.

"Oh, me too. Real quiet one. Catching up on work," he lied thinking about holding Ollie by his arms as handsome Cole beat seven bells out of him, both head to toe in black leather. The thought made him smile and his groin stir.

Gina wheeled herself over to his desk and passed him a folder.

"Last week's numbers. Not looking bad," she turned and wheeled back to her desk. Gina, was a thirty eight year old, strikingly beautiful single women, of Spanish decent. She had been in a traffic accident eight years ago and was wheelchair bound from then. She had been forced out of her position within an accountant's firm due to ill health and their inability to manage a disabled person's needs. Terrible situation. She met Max by accident. She ran over his foot at a cinema and he dropped his drink in her lap. They got talking and she joined the firm three weeks later. That was about six years ago.

She ran the office like clockwork and put up with no shit from anyone. Formidable, but lovely with it, she was bloody smart and could easily run rings round the sales and marketing guys, so Max loves her being at his side. He knows he can leave the office in her capable hands if he was out or home to the UK for long periods.

Slowly the rest of the team filed in one by one, all at their desks by 8.30am. Max wasn't strict on time. If people needed time out they could come in late or leave early. As long as the jobs got done he didn't care. The office was also relaxed. He hated the cubicle systems he'd seen in so many American businesses. So anti-social and non-productive. The offices of Bartholomew Steadman, named after Peter Bartholomew and Maxwell Steadman, were on one floor and fully open plan. Max and Gina sat at desks in the middle of the room with the whole team around them. His desk and chair was no grander than anyone else's. Three meeting rooms were available and a kitchen, store room and two break out areas.

The Chicago branch employed twenty one people, half of whom were in sales. The rest made up, accounting, IT, marketing and communications and office support. The office was bright and with windows all around, and lots of plants. Max loved to see lots of plants and living things in the office. It made the place feel welcoming and bright.

Max called all his key heads for an impromptu meeting. Gina, Brad Regent, Head of Sales, Freddie Michaels, Head of IT and Technical and Dimitri Lopez, Communications Manager. He sat them down and discussed his idea to take on some new support. The team had all been here before with Max. At first, they didn't like this way of recruiting new members, but they all had to remember that this was how they started, so it was hard to complain. But with so many being successful, you couldn't argue with it. Not everyone was employed this way, in some cases normal interviews and job ads were sent out. Max didn't find people that easily just on the street.

Max described Bobby and Cole, omitting the detail of the weekends sexploits, and their areas of expertise. Bobby was an easy fit but Cole less obvious. They discussed a trial and how it would work. A plan was agreed and Max said he would come back to them all with precise timings giving enough time for preparation.

The rest of the team watched them come back to their seats.

Max smiled at them all, “Don’t worry, it’s all good. We may be getting some extra support in the team. Ok so let’s all sell some buildings to help pay for it,” and he sat down.

Part 3 – Opportunity Knocks

Chapter 4 – Things can only get better, right?

Bobby and Cole left Max's building and discussed the weekend's events.

"God I'd love to live in a place like that. What do you reckon the rental is on that?" asked Cole.

"I suspect it's bought and paid for. Remember him say he instructed sound proofing in the build cost. I imagine if it was rented it would be about $5k a month," Bobby replied.

"Shit, that's not far off what I'm earning all fucking year," Cole worked out. "Jeez Bobby why are we in such shit jobs. All that education to push kids out on boats and it's getting harder now to get a proper job once they know you've taken a shit one. I've seen them look down at me in interviews, if I'm lucky to get one."

"I know. Home Depot isn't much better. I keep being told I may get on the management programme, but they never seem to finally offer it."

"Max made it. I'm sure we could if we put our minds to it," said Cole positively. "Surely between the two of us we can think of something."

They both parted company to head back to their own bedsits. Both sat down in their separate dingy rooms and sighed. There had to be more.

Monday, they both headed to work separately. Bobby arrived for his shift at Home Depot at 7am. His supervisor Chris, an arsehole of the first order, called him over.

Part 3 – Opportunity Knocks

"We need you to work double handed today. Ollie called in sick. The pussy says he has a bad stomach or something."

"Oh, that's just great," Bobby rolled his eyes, thinking about how he was kneeing Ollie in the balls thirty six hours earlier and how Cole made light work of his face with his fists. 'Fuck, that boy is sexy when he's angry,' thought Bobby.

Ollie finally turned up for work on Wednesday with a shiner and a smile. They took lunch together and discussed the weekend's session. Ollie was still buzzing, which pleased Bobby as he was a little concerned they had gone too far and that might have affected their work friendship. But far from it, Ollie kept talking about the evening, the gear his tormenters were wearing and the thrill he got. He was also pleased to get some new jeans and other clothes, thanks to Max's generosity, after his got ripped off him during the evening's events. Ollie was one satisfied pain sub and was keen for more. Bobby said he'd ask but Max was in charge.

It was Thursday of that week before either Bobby or Cole heard from Max. He texted both of them and asked what evening they would be available for a catch up. He said he had a proposal for them. Bobby called Cole straight away.

"Wonder what the proposal is. More deviant sex I hope," sniggered Bobby. "I'm free Friday evening, are you Cole?"

"Yeah, I've got no plans and no money to have plans," he replied.

"Ok I'll message him back," said Bobby.

<Hi Max, nice to hear from you. Hope all is good. Cole and I are free Friday evening if that works for you, but we can be reasonably flexible. Just need to work around my shifts. Sorry>.

Half an hour later Max replied and said <Perfect, meet me at Wollensky's Grill at 8pm Friday. Meet in the bar area. Booking is in my name Max Steadman>.

Bobby paused, that place is on the river front. Lovely posh place and flaming pricy. He text back, <Ok Max. But I'll just stop by for a drink, I'm a bit short this week. Sorry.> His phone rang. It was Max.

"Dear Bobby, it's an invitation from me. I wouldn't dream of expecting you to pay and it was very kind of you to not just assume that either. But yes, I should be more mindful in future. Let Cole know also and I look forward to seeing you tomorrow."

Bobby called Cole straight away with the details, "You know where that is? It's pretty nice in there so I think we better smarten up for this one. Get your best clothes out. It will be casual, but we should be smart. I wanna give Max a good impression of us. He says he has a proposition, and I don't think it's just about cock."

"Ok, I need to get some laundry on tonight then," replied Cole as he hung up.

Part 3 – Opportunity Knocks

Chapter 5 - The Proposition

Bobby and Cole met outside on the waterfront. It was a hot June evening. Bobby was wearing a red shirt, black smart slim jeans with a black belt and black Chelsea boots. The red and black contrasted with his beautiful blond hair perfectly. He stood and watched Cole approach. He was in tight dark blue jeans, brown boots and belt, with a tight white shirt. His hair was tamed and smart. He looked so sexy thought Bobby and he noticed most of the women he passed crossing the bridge were all looking round at him checking out the rear view too. Cole was a real stunning looking guy. He greeted Bobby with a manly hug, still not totally comfortable with being fully out just yet.

"You look handsome," he said to Bobby.

"Thanks, you scrub up nice too." They grinned. "It's ten to, shall we go in?"

They arrived at the restaurant and Bobby said to the attractive lady at the desk, "Mr Max Steadman has a reservation and we are to join him at the bar."

"Yes, thank you sirs," she replied batting her eyes at Cole, "Let me take you to the bar, Mr Steadman hasn't arrived yet."

The two men took places on bar stools and looked around. Nice place looking out over the river waterfront. Everyone looked smart and loaded.

Cole sighed, "How the other half live."

"What can I get for you gentleman?" said a rather sexy dark haired barman.

He stared into Bobby's eyes a moment longer than required, a clear sign he liked what he saw.

"Oh, I don't know, we are waiting for someone else," Bobby said in a bit of a fluster, grabbing the drinks menu.

"What's the cheapest beer you got?" said Cole.

"Coors, Miller or Bud are the cheapest, but we have some international beers," said the barman.

"Two Millers please," replied Cole.

"Shall I put this on Mr Steadman's tab?" the barman replied.

"No, I'll pay for these now," said Cole.

Bobby said, "Max said this was on him tonight?"

Cole replied, "That may be true, but I don't think we should assume everything. He's spent a lot on us."

As the beers arrived, he handed over a twenty dollar bill, just as Max entered the room and walked over to them.

"I'll get those," he interrupted.

Cole put his hand up, "You're good. You can get the next one, what are you having?"

"The usual please. A dirty martini, extra dirty," he winked at the sexy barman.

"Yes Mr Steadman," he smiled back.

Bobby watched Max sweep into the room. Bold, confident and sexy. Tight, slim fit jeans, black harness ankle boots, red and blue paisley shirt and butter soft black leather jacket. So thin and soft it almost hung like a shirt. 'That's got to be a thousand bucks worth of jacket there,' thought Bobby. He also smelt awesome too.

The barman pushed the Martini on a coaster towards Max, and looked at Cole, "That's a total of twenty nine dollars."

Max was about to speak but Cole put his hand on his arm and looked him in the eye. Max stood down seeing this was a matter of principle for Cole. Cole put his hand in his pocket and found another ten dollar bill to go with the twenty he had out.

"Thank you, sir," said the barman, giving Cole the eye.

"Cheers Boys. To an interesting evening," said Max. "Love the views in here, outside the windows, as well as inside," he winked, eyeing up all the male waiters.

Bobby looked around, they were all pretty hot.

"Maybe if we are lucky, we can take one of these home with us tonight," Max laughed and they all took a sip from their drinks.

"Mr Steadman, your usual table is ready for you now," said the pretty girl who was on the desk.

"Thank you so much Stephanie."

She led them to what had to be the best table in the place. Window view, in a corner, so two aspects and quiet. Bobby was impressed. Max only booked this yesterday as they only confirmed to meet then. Max gets a table like this, on a Friday, with less than twenty four hours' notice. He had real style Bobby thought.

They all sat down, and Max took off his beautiful jacket and placed it on the back of his chair. His paisley shirt looked striking and fitted well. Not too tight and gaped a little for Bobby to see that lovely hairy daddy chest through the gap.

"Hello Mr Steadman and guests. My name is Paul and I'm your waiter for this evening."

They all looked at Paul. Paul was mixed race, medium build, probably mid twenties, with beautiful neat features, like an older Jayden Smith. They all smiled at him.

"Here are the menus and the wine list, I'll bring you some water."

"Fuck, he's easy on the eye," said Bobby as Paul walked away.

Paul returned with the water and then said he would return shortly for their order.

"Order what you want. I'm having a starter and a main," said Max.

They all ordered food with Paul, all struggling to stop staring at the handsome waiter. They all checked out his crotch as he went around the table. Looking at how his apron stretched over it, he could be packing a dangerous weapon they thought. Max ordered some wine also for them all.

"So, I suspect you are wondering what I dragged you out on a Friday night to talk about," said Max.

"We did wonder," said Bobby.

"Well, I hate to see good talent go to waste," Max continued.

He told them both about his business and what he did in greater detail, and how he had taken different people on to give then a step up and a lift. They both listened intently.

“I would like to give you a chance also.”

“What, we would come and work for you?” asked Cole.

“Yes, ultimately, if it works out for all parties,” confirmed Max. “I want to give you a week’s trial to come and work in the business alongside the team and see if you fit in with them. Also to see the roles are right for you.”

Cole and Bobby looked at each other and then back to Max.

“Can you take vacation from your present jobs? I don’t want you to jack them in, in case you need to fall back on them. You would need five days,” Max stated.

“I’ve got six of my annual ten days left, so I could take five but that pretty much wipes me out,” said Bobby.

“My hours are flexible, so don’t really have paid holiday. So I could try for some time out, I’d need to save up, as I’d have no income during that week, but I’m definitely interested,” said Cole.

“Good,” said Max, “My idea is for you Bobby to work with our technical and IT team. We need some help on social media and our internal system programs. You’ll be working with a guy called Freddie, my Head of IT. Real nice guy. Now you Cole. I think Marketing and Communications would be a good starting point, would you both be happy with that?”

“Yes sir,” said Bobby.

“Yes, I’ll give it a go. Hope I’m good enough,” said Cole.

"Sure, you will. I have faith in you both," said Max. "Now for this week's trial I will pay you what you are earning, to ensure you are not out of pocket. If the trial is successful, I will confirm the package via a proper job offer. You ok with that?"

"Yes sir," they both responded.

"Right enough business. Let's eat and enjoy the many 'views'" laughed Max. They ate dinner and chatted some more about their interests and what they hoped to achieve, giving Max more of a picture of the two.

Paul, the waiter was very attentive smiling at Cole a lot.

"He fucking wants you," said Bobby.

"I'm not surprised Bobby. I want both of you. You are both looking exceptionally sexy tonight. What do you say about some extra fun tonight? Let's see if we can get Paul involved," Max suggested.

"Sounds like a great idea," said Cole.

Max got up and said, "I need a pee," and winked.

He walked past Paul and whispered something and went to the restroom. Paul waited for about thirty seconds and then followed. Max was waiting for him in the lobby.

"Paul, I'm assuming you have gathered that my guests and I are of a similar persuasion. Would you be interested in a liaison when you knock off this evening?" Max said in his best English accent.

Paul smiled, "Would all three of you be there?"

"Yes, which do you like the most?" Max asked.

"I've always had a soft spot for you Mr Steadman, but that big guy with you is to die for," Paul said.

"Ah yes, Cole. He can be a bit rough, but I can control him," Max added.

"Oh, don't worry about that, I can handle most stuff. Anything but scat," Paul added.

Max smiled. "Ok, understood."

"I knock off at eleven. Here's my number. I'd better get back to work. See you later."

Paul walked off and Max checked out his arse. He pulled out his phone and called the Wyndham Grand hotel which was situated opposite the restaurant.

"I need a suite for this evening with your largest bed. Ideally with en-suite and separate bathroom." He paused, "Perfect, can you ensure there is a bottle of Laurent Perrier on ice in the room with four glasses. My guests and I will be arriving around eleven. My name is Mr Steadman, you should have my details on account," He paused. "Perfect, thank you and see you shortly."

Max never disguised to hotels what he was up to. It was pointless. They had seen it all before and he hated having to try and smuggle people in. He was paying big money and they didn't care.

Max went back to Bobby and Cole. "Paul is up for some fun when his shift ends at eleven."

Bobby looked at his watch. It was 9.30pm, "Cool."

Paul came over with their mains and smiled even wider.

"We are going to have fun with you tonight," said Cole.

"I do hope so," replied Paul with a wink and turned and left to get their sides.

"Are we going back to your apartment?" asked Bobby.

"No, I don't like to bring too many strangers to my place. You guys were the exception. I've just booked a suite in there," Max pointed out the window at the large hotel across the water from them.

"Ahhh, you are the man Max. Smooth," said Cole.

They ate their dinner and decided to have a few extra drinks at the Bar until eleven. Max paid the bill, said thank you to all who had served them, including Paul and then they all left for the lobby downstairs. Bobby, watched Max in the lift. This man had loads of money, yet he treated every member of staff with such respect. Unlike many he noticed in the restaurant. Some barely looked up at their waiters. He was gracious with all of them, which is probably why they also got exceptional service. It's a simple concept, shame so many others don't think like that.

It was still very warm outside, but with a nice breeze in the windy city. Paul appeared in the lobby and joined them.

"So, where are we going?" he asked.

Cole pointed up at the Wyndham as they crossed the bridge.

"Cool," Paul said.

Chapter 6 - Suites for my sweet

They crossed the water and walked into the lobby of the Wyndham. Max strode to the desk and got checked in. A handsome bellboy appeared, probably nineteen, dark short hair and cute thought Max. He smiled and they all followed the young man to the suite on the nineteenth floor.

While in the lift Max enquired, "Beautiful evening young man, and your name is?"

"Karl sir. Yes it is. You having a meeting this evening?" he asked.

"You could say that," Max winked back. The lad opened the room and showed them the space. Max gave him a twenty dollar tip and the young man smiled.

"If you need anything and I mean anything, please call me on the front desk. I finish at 1am," Karl detailed.

"Thank you. Of course when you are finished and fancy a night cap, give us all a knock, I'm sure we will still be busy then," Max replied. "I may do that," Karl smiled as he left the room.

"You shameless fucking flirt," Cole said. "Is he even legal?"

Bobby added, "I'd play with him any night of the week."

"Ok, let's get comfortable, and have some champagne," Max spotted.

He poured four glasses and toasted them all. Then Max grabbed Paul and kissed him hard. "I've been wanting to do that all evening."

Paul was then grabbed by Cole, who did the same and then Bobby got a turn. They were all standing together kissing each other.

Paul pulled back and said, "Do you mind if I take a shower, I stink of kitchen and fried steak."

"Umm tasty," said Bobby. Paul was taking his clothes off.

"Only on one condition," said Max, "that we all join you."

They all started to strip and watched each other. The large suite had a huge bathroom with a very large walk in shower. Paul walked in and Cole, Max and Bobby studied his slim pert arse and followed. Then Paul turned around as he switched on the shower.

"Yowsers," said Bobby. Paul was huge. Even limp that had to be eight or nine inches. "Fuck how big are you when you get excited?" he continued.

Paul looked back and smiled.

"Suppose you had better find out," and he got under the water and started to lather himself up. Bobby joined him under the water first and Max and Cole watched as the two slim lads circled the soap over their young hard bodies. Bobby's almost milk white skin contrasting with Paul's mid brown skin, both covered in suds. Bobby was helping Paul wash. His hands were everywhere, both were getting hard now. Max and Cole looked at each other.

Max said, "We better get some cock," and they both got in and started lathering up.

Bobby started kissing Paul and rubbing both their cocks. Paul was big. Could he be bigger than ten inches hard? Fuck they all thought looking down at him. Max turned Paul around to face him and started kissing him hard, feeling his warm wet body. Bobby stood behind and rested his cock in between Paul's arse cheeks and wet humped him. While Cole moved round and did the same to Bobby. Max had that huge tool in his hands. The soap was rinsing away now and Max decided he needed to taste that cock. He knelt down in the hot running water and took about eight inches in his mouth. Fuck. He couldn't take any more. He was gagging slightly on that. Paul held his head and tried to offer more, but Max pulled out.

"Too big for my throat. Bobby you give it a try," Max said, turning Paul round to face Bobby.

Paul laughed and presented his huge cock to Bobby.

"I'm always up for a challenge," Bobby replied as he opened up.

Bobby carefully took in inch by inch, breathing expertly as Paul's manhood went further and further in. Cole watched in amazement, stoking his own nine incher. Max and Cole watched as Bobby gradually took all of Paul in, and even managed to lick his balls for good measure.

"Fuck man. You are talented," said Paul. "That is a first. How about you sexy?" Paul said to Cole.

"No man, I'm new to all this. I've not had the training but I'll be the first to fuck you raw," said Cole.

"Let's get to it then," said Paul, grabbing Cole's arm and taking him out of the bathroom and into the suite to the huge bed.

Cole grabbed Paul and took back control. He held his face, kissed him hard, then threw Paul onto the bed on his back. Paul lifted his legs to present his arse. Cole decided, tonight was old Cole's night, brutal Cole, not sensitive Cole. He spat on his dick and lubed it up and took Paul's hole in a couple of pumps. Paul winced at first, but then started to enjoy this handsome rough boy, fucking him hard.

His handsome face with venom in his eyes, added to the thrill. Cole put his hand to Paul's throat for purchase and the other over his mouth, then a couple of fingers were pushed in. Paul moaned with pleasure.

Max and Bobby were watching, stroking their dicks at the action on the bed.

"Room for two more?" said Max as he grabbed Bobby and put him in the same position next to Paul and spat on his dick and entered Bobby.

Bobby watched as Max pumped into him, his handsome hairy daddy in direct view and his handsome friend, Cole, next to him fucking a stranger hard.

Paul and Bobby were both stoking their cocks at the sight of these two alphas in action.

Paul said, "Mr Steadman, all the gay waiters and some of the ladies in the restaurant wondered what you looked like under those good clothes. You really surpassed what I expected."

With that Cole said, "You better have some of Mr Steadman then," withdrawing quickly, and swapping places with Max, without hesitation, drove his cock into Paul. Cole did the same to Bobby. It was like synchronised fucking. Bobby was more than pleased to also be on the receiving end of his handsome Cole. He arched his back and added to the rhythm as they both fucked harder and harder.

Four men all in their prime were enjoying their bodies with relish. Max was fucking Paul real hard now. He had his left leg on the bed and had turned Paul on his side to get his cock even deeper into Paul's gut. Max was grabbing his hair to help drive harder in.

"Fuck Mr Steadman, you fuck so good. Harder sir, harder. Destroy my hole sir. God it's so good," Paul wined.

Cole was watching Max in action and looked at Bobby.

"Destroy my hole Cole, bully me like you used to. Hurt me Cole, be the hard man I fucking worship," said Bobby.

This was all Cole needed. He pulled out and grabbed Bobby by the throat with both hands and held him to his face. His strength was immense.

"You want me to destroy you Bobby?"

"I can't stop you Cole. You are too strong. I'm yours," Bobby replied.

Cole smiled that controlling smirk and threw Bobby back on the bed and grabbed his legs to flip him over on his front. Cole jumped on his legs and entered Bobby with force and rutted that boy relentlessly. He grabbed Bobby's long top hair and pulled him back and held his throat as he fucked him. Bobby yelled, but a yell of joy.

"Ruin me Cole, you sexy jock. Fuck I love your cock in me. Harder! Harder!"

After a couple of minutes, Max said to Cole, "Let's fuck 'em face to face."

He pulled out and dragged Paul round on the large bed and Cole did the same with Bobby.

"On your knees and face each other," then Cole and Max moved in behind them and re-entered their dicks into the lads holes, holding their chests as they fucked in deeper. Paul and Bobby were face to face and leaned in and started to kiss, but it was difficult with the rough alphas destroying their holes.

After a few minutes, Max said, "I gotta cum."

"Let's cream them together, on your backs bitch boys," said Cole.

Paul and Bobby laid down, Cole stood over Bobby and then Max copied the young master's idea. They wanked facing each other. Max could see how beautiful Cole looked, but Cole also really noticed, how handsome Max was. This man was just perfect. So handsome and in control.

"I'm cumming," said Cole. Bobby and Paul sat up to receive the gift from their gods. Cole shot a load that hit Max's abs, and both Bobby and Paul's faces. Long pumps released with force. The sight was enough for Max to reciprocate. He aimed his load at Paul and hit his target perfectly in his mouth and face. Paul smiled and grinned at the experience.

The doorbell to the room rang.

"Who the fuck's that?" said Bobby.

"I bet I know," said Max. He walked naked with a huge boner and cum dripping from his cock." He looked through the spy hole. It was Karl.

Max open the door fully naked to greet Karl. Karl smiled at the sight.

"You want some room service on that?" he said pointing at Max's cock.

"It does need a clean," Max replied.

Karl entered, shut the door fell to his knees and took Max's dripping dick in his mouth and cleaned him up thoroughly.

"You like dick? Three others need your services," Max pointed at the bed. Karl got up and started to undress as he went across to the bed. Bobby, Cole and Paul sat on the end of the bed and lined up for a blow job. Karl went to Cole first, as he could also see the cum on Cole's dick. His cock tasted hot, of arse and cum, the best. He cleaned him up and then moved to Paul. Paul was fucking big. He could only take seven of Paul's ten inches but he used his hands to give the feeling of a full suck and he wanked Paul. Paul was ready after an evening of action to lose a load. Without warning he shot his load into Karl's throat. So much cum. It came dribbling out of Karl's mouth like a fountain. Karl caught what he could with his tongue and hands and scooped the load back into his mouth.

Smiling he said, "Not wasting any of that."

Then he crawled to Bobby and took his cock deeply. But Bobby wanted more, he grabbed Karl's head and forced him on.

"Take my dick, cunt," he pumped his head up and down on his cock. "Fucking take my load boy." Bobby lifted his head up and let his cum pump out all over Karl's face and shoulders.

"Yes sir," said Karl. Karl was now hard from all the excitement, and Paul got on his knees behind him, and started to jerk Karl's cock with his hand.

Paul then moved Karl around and started taking his six inch boner in his mouth with ease, pleasuring his nipples as he sucked and played. Grabbing Karl's small buttocks, he took him fully in his throat. Karl was now close and within seconds delivered his youthful sweet load into Paul's willing throat. Paul swallowed every drop, no dribbles. A perfect finish.

They rested a while and finished the champagne, and then Max said, "Right, time for me to leave. Thank you, Paul, for your time tonight, and Karl, your service was impeccable."

Paul said, "I better get off. I have an early shift in the morning."

"Me too," said Karl.

With that they all got dressed. Karl and Paul left together, no doubt to carry on elsewhere. Then Max said to Bobby and Cole, who were still naked. "You guys stay. Enjoy the room. Its paid for the night, so you may as well enjoy it."

"Why you going?" said Bobby.

"I like my own bed and tonight was fun. I'll let you know about the timings for the work trial lads. Enjoy your night." He grabbed his leather jacket, and swaggered out the room, and blew them a kiss as he left.

Cole and Bobby stared at each other.

"Fuck that was fun and this is awesome," said Cole as he threw himself back on the bed.

"Come here Bobby," he said with his arms open.

Bobby crawled up to Cole's chest and fell into his handsome jock's arms. He was under his protection and it felt good.

Chapter 7 - Trials and Tribulations

Max had called Bobby and Cole and confirmed a start date of their work trials within his business in late July. It gave them a month to take time out from their present jobs and get themselves prepared for their roles. Max wired them both $600 to pay for their week, which was way over what they were paid, but Max wanted them to feel comfortable, and if they needed to get some clothes, they could. Both took the opportunity to get some new clothes. Bobby got a suit, Cole some new shirts and both got new shoes. Max asked them to report for work at 9.30am on the Monday.

Bobby and Cole agreed to arrive together and to be early to give the right impression. They arrived in the lobby of office block that Max's business was in at 8.30am. That was a bit too keen they thought as they sat in the lobby. Bobby looked around and watched the people coming and going. He smiled at a guy, slim but well-built all American guy who sailed through the lobby with confidence. Sharp brown hair and wearing a nice suit that showed off his toned physique perfectly. The guy smiled back and winked. 'Fuck!' thought Bobby.

Max was already at his desk at 8am along with Gina. At 8.35am Brad, Head of Sales, arrived followed shortly by Freddie, IT and Technology Manager and Dimitri, Head of Communications. Brad said to Max, "I think your new recruits are downstairs in the lobby."

Max looked at his Rolex, "Christ they are keen I said 9.30. Good start suppose. Let's make them sweat a bit."

They had their morning team meeting and discussed the week ahead. They discussed Bobby and Cole. Bobby would spend the week with Freddie and the IT and Technical tea. Cole would be with Dimitri and his Communications and Marketing team.

At 9.10am Bobby said, “I think we should say we are here.” Cole agreed, and they got up and walked over to the lobby reception. Bobby spoke to the lady on the desk.

“We have an appointment with Max Steadman at Bartholomew Steadman.”

“May I have your names?”

“Robert Wilson and Cole Peterson,” replied Bobby. She smiled while writing their names down, picked up the phone and called someone.

Gina Garcia, Office Manager, answered the phone, “Hi Stacy. Yes, we are expecting them. May as well send them up now.”

Stacy looked back at the two handsome guys in front of her. She couldn’t keep her eyes off Cole.

“Ok, you can go right up. Take the elevator on the right to the 16th floor and then turn left out the doors.”

“Thank you,” said Bobby.

“Yes, thank you,” followed Cole, smiling his best smile at her.

“You’re very welcome,” Stacy smiled back.

She watched them both as they headed for the elevator. Both had great arses she thought.

Cole and Bobby arrived at the door of Bartholomew Steadman and pressed the buzzer. A lady answered, “Come in guys,” and buzzed the door open. As they walked into the open plan space, Gina wheeled herself out from her desk towards them. Cole was a bit surprised to see a lady in a wheelchair, but then thought to himself, why should he be surprised. He was actually annoyed he'd thought the slightly prejudiced thought. They both walked up to her and smiled.

"Welcome to Bartholomew Steadman, I'm Gina," she said. Max was sat at the desk near her and stood up also and smiled at them both. He was impressed they had been prompt and made a great effort on their appearance. Nice fitting suits, and tidy hair and shoes. Cole's arse looked great in those suit pants he thought.

Bobby and Cole looked round to see everyone staring at them. They smiled and then Max said, "Let's all go in the Conference room and get settled. Tea or coffee?"

"Coffee," they both replied.

Gina took them through some basic HR details and paperwork and talked about general office protocol. She then beckoned through the glass to three guys in the office. All looked like they were in their thirties. One quite casual in style, and mixed race, the other much sharper dressed Spanish looking hipster with a beard, and the third Bobby recognised from the lobby, the all American white guy. They entered the room with big smiles.

Max introduced the casual guy, "This is Freddie Michaels, our Head of IT, and Bobby you will be working closely with him. And this is Dimitri Lopez, Head of Communications and Marketing, Cole he will be your mentor and finally Brad Regent is our Head of Sales."

They introduced and shook hands with each other.

"Ok we are going to leave you guys to it and I'll catch up with you at lunch time. Have a good day," said Max as he left with Gina and Brad.

“Yes sir,” Bobby and Cole replied. The subservience of the reply raised a smile from both Freddie and Dimitri.

“Ok Bobby, come with me. We can meet Troy, who is also in my small team, then we can get started on what you know,” said Freddie, leading Bobby from the room. Cole was left with Dimitri. Dimitri asked Cole about his education and training, how he met Max and tried to get a better picture on how Cole could work in communications. Cole was vague about how he met Max. He could hardly say it was over BDSM sex and fucking over his new buddy Bobby, by making him bleed and laughing about it. That’s hardly a way to start a working relationship. He said they met in a bar and got chatting. Seemed to work. Dimitri told Cole his story.

A Spanish boy brought up by immigrant parents in a poor part of town, he got his grades and worked in a few junior roles in Marketing, always hitting a glass ceiling because of his background. Two years ago he applied for a Job with Bartholomew Steadman and was surprised to get in. He worked hard and received promotion. Dimitri talked about how welcome he felt at the interview, not being slighted, no prejudice. He had never worked for a business like this. He loved the fact that everyone was different and nobody cared. The benefits were second to none too.

“Don’t get me wrong,” Dimitri continued, “Max is a task master and wants the best and for everyone to work hard. You don’t, you’re out. But he’s fair and gives back to you. When I needed time off because my child was sick and my wife couldn’t get time off from her crazy employer, Max let me take a week off, paid. Not out of holiday. Compassionate leave he called it. Never asked me to work the time back, but I’d do anything for him now and I’ll never forget that kindness. He even came to visit me, Rosa and Christian to check how my son was doing. Cole this is a great opportunity for you.”

Cole met Dimitri's assistant Gemma and then he shadowed them both on the planning for the next real estate sales promotion. Gemma couldn't keep her eyes off Cole. He was so handsome and had a fantastic body in those close fitting clothes. He smiled at her and she blushed. Cole knew that look. If he wanted he could bang her any or everyday of the week. She wanted him and he knew it. But he would need to be cool, this is work now, not some old slapper down the clubs and bars.

Bobby was introduced to Troy, a twenty two year old geeky kid who wore glasses. He looked like a real nerd, but one of those cute ones. The ones that could be quite hot when they take their specs off and had a good haircut. Bobby noticed he had a cute arse too, better not stare he thought. Freddie talked about the role of the IT team and how they supported the whole business. They were also connected to the UK and German office and the accounts were all connected for finance. Support of the company platform was number one priority then managing communications with technical support on social media and web platforms. Freddie talked about his way into Bartholomew Steadman.

"I was actually saved by Max. I was twenty five and begging outside Grand Central Station in New York, not the best time of my life I can tell you. I hadn't eaten in days and it was winter. So cold. Just me and my dog Stella. I was thin and in a terrible way. When this man knelt down and offered me his hand. No one does that. I looked up and saw this handsome middle aged man looking at me with a smile. He asked if I'd like some dinner? I said yes, and he took me and Stella to a diner nearby. The owner wouldn't let Stella in and wasn't keen on me either. Max put a $100 bill on the counter and said this was his if he let us ALL in. It was great to be in the warm and little Stella needed that too. Max fed us both and asked me about my situation."

Freddie paused and then continued, "My mother died in my teens and after I left school my Dad threw me out. We never got along. I struggled to get work; a gay mixed race in IT is hard for white America to comprehend. One thing led to another and I was on the streets, which is where I met Stella, a stray. We became inseparable. That night Max saved my life. He paid for me to stay in a small hotel for a week and bought me some clothes. He bought me a train ticket to Chicago and said to meet him there in a week. That was the test. Would I come to Chicago? I wasn't sure. But I did and haven't looked back. He gave me a job five years ago and I've worked up to my position. Max is a legend. We all love him, he's sexy too, but I shouldn't say that about my boss."

Freddie laughed. Bobby knew exactly what he meant.

Even Troy laughed, "He could be my Daddy any day."

Bobby was surprised by Troy.

"So, the whole IT team is gay?" said Bobby smiling. He told a simple story of how he met Max, again, like Cole, leaving out some of the details.

"Have you still got Stella?" asked Bobby.

"Sadly not, she came to Chicago with me, but she was getting older. I wasn't sure how old she was when I found her but I lost her two years ago. She was happy, warm and ended her life with me in our cosy flat. I do miss her. Right!" he said changing the subject, "Let's crack on with understanding systems."

They set to work.

Bobby and Cole met at lunchtime and compared notes. Both were surprised to hear most people's stories: probably half the team, Max had found and dragged from the gutter in some way. Others had come for jobs, having previously been overlooked or not acknowledged as any good. Faces that didn't fit. Everyone's face fit here. Bobby mentioned Troy and his cute arse and Cole said Gemma was keen. Bobby felt a bit annoyed that Cole still liked the idea of a woman but then he had to consider, not everything is black and white. Everyone is different, like Max's whole team of *misfits*.

Part 3 – Opportunity Knocks

Chapter 8 - D Day

The week past so fast and soon it was Friday. Max had been keeping abreast of the boys' progress. On the Friday he met with the two department heads, Freddie and Dimitri. Gina sat in the meeting also.

"Ok, what's the verdict guys?" asked Max.

"Well," Freddie started, "Bobby is very smart and sharp. He has been a great asset this week. His knowledge of programming and systems has been really useful and man he is fast. Troy likes him and we are working well together. I could really use a guy like this if we have the funds to take him on. I reckon he has the ability to save us money on all the outsourced resources we use. The fees from external support are high and he could save us circa $60k a year potentially and there could be savings in UK and Germany, if we put our heads together."

"Great!" said Max, "And Cole?" he asked Dimitri.

"Cole is a difficult one. He has some good ideas but is struggling to put them into practice. His written skills are poor I've noticed, so that needs improving. He does have the gift of the gab and Gemma really likes him. Probably too much. That handsome boy is proving a bit of a distraction. I'm willing to progress with him, but he needs some work," Dimitri detailed.

"Are you sure we can afford to carry someone?" asked Gina.

Max replied, "You may have a point Gina, what do you think Freddie?"

"I haven't worked closely with him, but Cole does have a dynamic personality and a presence. We are all here because we were given a chance, and five days is still early. I say we give him a longer trial. He's also damn easy on the eye as well," laughed Freddie.

"He sure is," purred Gina, "but that's not a good enough reason. I take your point on him having something though. I can't put my finger on it. He does have a charm."

"That was my gut feeling. They both had something. My gut is rarely wrong," Max replied. "We will employ them on a six month trial as we would with anyone else. Full pay and perks. I'll call them in at 4pm with Gina."

Bobby was loving his role this week. The team were fun and cute. The office was amazing and the work finally taxing his brain. Cole on the other hand was struggling. He confided in Bobby.

"I like the place and the work, but I'm struggling with getting my ideas down in writing. English was never my strong point. Math was better, I'm good with numbers. I'm not sure they are gonna want to keep me on Bobby," Cole said looking sad.

"If they don't take you I won't stay," said Bobby.

"You can't do that. You'd be cutting your nose off. If you get a job and I don't you can support me with my shit job on the boats," he tried to laugh. "No, you must stay, to not take this opportunity would be madness. Something else will come along for me."

Max told them to come to the conference room at 4pm for a summary of the week. They both felt nervous at the thought and the clock seemed to move so slowly that afternoon. At 3.58pm they both got up and went to the conference room. Max followed them along with Gina.

"Ok guys, I'll cut to the chase. You both have roles here," the relief on their faces was noticeable. Bobby thought how kind of Max to not string out the suspense.

"Ok Cole, can you wait at your desk while I take through Bobby his role, and then I'll do the same with you," Cole smiled and left.

"Ok Bobby. You have excelled this week and Freddie is really pleased with you. We are offering you a permanent position as IT Programmer on a salary of $58k per annum to start with, full health benefits and twenty days paid leave per annum. This will be a six months trial. If at any point, we feel this isn't working we will be able to terminate the contract with a week's notice. We will expect you to work hard, but we will be fair. Hours are 8.30 'til 5pm Monday to Friday, but there may be some occasional weekend or evening work. But that is quite rare. Are you happy with that?" Max asked.

Bobby was beaming his gorgeous, cute smile.

"My God Max. Thank you, thank you, thank you. That is better than I could ever have hoped. Yes, I want this job please."

"Good. I'm pleased you said yes. What notice do you have to give Home Depot?" asked Max.

"Oh, I'll work the weekend and give notice tomorrow. I can be back here Monday," Bobby replied.

"Perfect. Gina will get the paperwork done for you to take home with you tonight and if you can bring the contract signed with you on Monday we can start. Anything else you want to ask?" Max said.

"No. Just thank you again," Bobby smiled.

"Ok, can you send Cole in please," Max asked, as Bobby got up to leave.

Cole was watching Bobby in the conference room. He was smiling so much, Cole hoped the same was going to happen for him. Bobby came out of the room grinning and beckoned to Cole to come to the room. Cole took a deep breath and walked across the office to the room. All eyes were on him.

"Cole, please take a seat," Max smiled. "Now, we have a role for you, but I think you will understand that there are some development needs in the area you are working."

Cole sat with his head lowered a little.

"We are going to give you a chance to shine. We all believe in you. You have talent young man. We just need to find your true vocation and Bartholomew Steadman is the ideal place to do that. You will be employed at a Marketing Assistant on a salary of $40k per annum to start with full health benefits and twenty days paid leave per annum." Max took Cole through the same employment details as Bobby, emphasising he was still on trial.

"Cole, are you happy with that?"

"Yes sir," Cole smiled.

Max's heart fluttered at the sight of Cole's smile. God that boy was sexy as fuck. He was imagining tearing that tight fitting shirt and suit trousers off and fucking him hard over this table, in front of Gina if needs be. He could feel his bulge growing in his pants.

"Now, I know you and Bobby are close and you are going to talk, 'cos that's what young people do. No secrets. I will tell you, you are being paid less than Bobby, but you need to know this: Bobby has excelled this week and has some very in demand programming skills and the role demands a higher salary. Your role is equally important and is matched to the market salary levels, but still with a premium. Do you understand that?" Max asked.

"Yes, that's fair. The salary you are paying me is beyond my expectations, so thank you Max," Cole replied.

Max continued, "Now if you find your mojo and develop further, then salary packages will be adjusted accordingly. If you work hard for us, we will reward you accordingly. What notice do you need to give the Boat team?" asked Max.

"None. They fired me Wednesday. They were short and asked me back, I said I couldn't, so they laid me off permanent. So I can start straight away," Cole replied.

"God some employers are such arses," sighed Max, "Ok, Gina will sort out the paperwork for you to take home and bring back on Monday please. Ok, any questions?" Max asked.

Cole paused and said quietly, "Do you really want me, or are you being kind and 'cos you want Bobby? He's the intelligent one, I need to know?"

Max looked at Cole.

"Thanks Gina, if you could start on that paperwork for the gentlemen that would be great."

Max stood up as she wheeled herself out the room and left them together.

Max stared down hard at Cole with his knuckles on the table.

"Cole Peterson, you have only known me for a short time. You know that I'm a driven man who only does what I want, or think is right. If I did not think you had potential you would be out of here today, no question. There would be no sentimental reason to keep you. Even though I find you sexy as fuck and want you right now. It wouldn't be a reason to employ you in my business. I don't need to employ you to fuck you or Bobby. Business and pleasure are separate. You are being given a chance because I think and more importantly my team think, you have potential. So, remember that. If you hadn't that potential I would have dropped you in a heartbeat and still employed Bobby. No 'one for all, all for one' bollocks here. You prove me right is all I ask Cole Peterson. Now stop feeling sorry for yourself and show me the Cole I met in the bar a month ago."

Cole smiled. "You are the man Max. I could so suck you off right now sir, you are the boss. My boss."

"Maybe another time Cole," Max smiled. "I have calls and money to make before the weekend. Now off you go back to your desk."

Cole left the conference room with a semi in his pants and in those pants, it was hard to cover up. Bobby noticed it, as did Troy, as they watched him cross the room. Troy was transfixed. This alpha God walking across the office. That toned, slim, hard body under those perfectly fitting tight clothes. That beautiful, wavy, highlighted dirty blond hair and square jaw. He was perfect. And those hands, thought Troy, those powerful handsome hands. Yes, he had great hands, strong and in perfect proportion as was everything. For a second Troy imagined those hands at his throat and over his mouth. He then looked down as he realised he was staring.

Gemma was equally transfixed by Cole and smiling at him, hoping he would see her. But Cole was thinking of Max, and his cock. Cole hadn't sucked cock yet, always the dominant one getting head, but Max was the true alpha here and Cole was happy to be subservient. Cole imagined taking his boss's cock in his mouth and worshipping it. This was the first time Cole had wanted cock and now he wanted Max's badly.

He snapped out of his thoughts as Gemma said, "Penny for them....?"

"Oh err... nothing you'd wanna know," he laughed nervously.

5pm came around soon enough and people started packing up. Max got up from his chair and wolf whistled.

"Ok everyone, thanks for another great week, all have a fantastic weekend and we'll do it all again from Monday. I'm also pleased to say that Bobby and Cole will be joining us as IT Programmer and Marketing Assistant on Monday too, so please give them a round of applause."

The whole team stood up and clapped and cheered the two, who both looked very red faced. People came up to them and hugged them and the ladies gave them kisses on the cheek.

"Welcome aboard," one said. Then everyone slowly packed up and left. Bobby and Cole hung back and went over to Max and Gina's desks and again said, "Thank you," to them both.

"You've very welcome," said Max and Gina gave them both their contracts in envelopes.

"See you Monday."

They both walked to the elevators together and started their weekend with huge smiles.

Part 3 – Opportunity Knocks

Chapter 9 – Moving in

A month had passed and Bobby and Cole were starting to settle into their roles. Bobby excelling further and really adding value. Cole trying hard and achieving some good results, with support from Dimitri and Gemma. With their first salaries hitting the bank, Bobby and Cole decided it was time to find a new apartment and that they would rent together. Pooling resources meant they could get something nicer and bigger, with enough space to allow them to have independence as well. With Bartholomew Steadman's contacts they were able to get access to some good deals. They had seen a two bed furnished apartment advertised downtown which would be ideal for work and nightlife. They had arranged a viewing with a sales person called Jamie for Saturday. They arrived at the lobby and waited. A young guy in his twenties with dark brown, sharply cut hair arrived.

"Is one of you Robert Wilson?" he said looking longingly at Cole.

"I'm Bobby Wilson, and this is my partner Cole," Bobby interrupted Jamie's stare.

"Oh... cool. Come this way," Jamie said.

"I'm your partner, am I?" whispered Cole to Bobby.

They all got in the elevator. Bobby noted that Jamie smelt good. Nice cologne under his navy suit and Jamie looked like he worked out a little. Jamie noticed Bobby studying him and thought him cute also. Cole was handsome; Bobby was pretty and cute. They were lucky to have each other. Jamie hadn't been that lucky to find a partner in his years on the scene, he thought. Too many bitches. He liked these two and hoped he would get the sale as he needed the bonus this month.

Jamie showed them around the nicely furnished two bed apartment. It had a lounge with a kitchen diner and large bathroom. It was clean, spacious and had a nice view of the city, or the parts they could see from the window. After a good look around, Jamie sat at the table.

"Would you like a moment to discuss?"

Bobby and Cole went to the bedroom to talk it through.

"I like it," said Cole.

"Me too, and he likes us too. You seen the boner he's covering?" said Bobby.

"You're terrible, but yes I did. He's quite fit too," said Cole.

Bobby replied, "I think we can negotiate on the rent a bit, and also have him now, I'm horny and wanna blow him. You wanna fuck him Cole? Please say yes, 'cos I wanna watch you fuck him," grinned Bobby.

"For you partner, anything. So, I take it this relationship we have is an open one?" Cole laughed.

"Yep," said Bobby, "Now let's milk this salesman. Literally."

They got up and left the room to find Jamie standing looking out the window.

"Nice view," said Bobby.

"Yes, it's not bad," said Jamie. "No, I mean your arse Mr," Bobby added. "We want to negotiate on the rent. What's the best you can do Jamie?" Bobby smile angelically.

Jamie was blushing but quite excited as the two stood in front of him.

"Well it's on for $2100 a month plus fees. Not sure we can go any lower than that." Jamie was trying to play hard ball but needed this sale.

Cole stepped forward and stood real close to Jamie and said, "Let's see if this will help you loosen up the negotiation." He held Jamie's face in his hands and went in for a deep kiss. His tongue probed back and forth. Cole moved his left hand around the back of Jamie's neck and then moved his right hand down to feel Jamie's bulge. Jamie groaned.

Cole stepped back and said, "Has that loosened you up?" with his best boyish smile. Jamie was lost for words.

"You do a good deal for us and we can have some real fun to celebrate. You like Cole don't you? He's fucking awesome in bed and I'm a legend with a cock in my mouth. So what do you think?" Bobby asked.

Jamie regained some composure and said, "Ok sexy boys. The best I can do is $1800 and 10% off the fee. Plus, I want you to blow me wonder boy and the big guy to fuck me hard now. I have a forty five minute window 'til I have to be at my next viewing."

"Make that 25% off the fees and I'll rim you after to make sure your clean for your next appointment," said Bobby.

"Deal," said Jamie, unzipping his pants taking out a shapely sized six inch cut cock.

"That will be no problem," said Bobby as he got on his knees and expertly edged his mouth onto Jamie's cock. While Bobby was blowing him, Jamie took off his jacket shirt and tie to reveal a pretty good body with some nice fur on it. He was watching Cole as he got undressed in front him. Cole was magical to watch as he undressed. Wow what a body Jamie thought and fuck, that dick is huge.

Bobby pulled back and quickly pulled his own clothes off while Jamie took off his pants and socks.

"Let's christen one of the beds."

Cole grabbed Jamie's arm and took control of him, moving him into the bedroom. They stood by the bed and Cole turned Jamie round to face Bobby. He held Jamie from behind with his strong arms. Bobby kissed Jamie while slowly stroking both their dicks. Cole rested his huge hard on in Jamie's arse crack, gently moving it up and down between the cheeks. Jamie was moaning now.

"Time for you to feel Cole's strength Jamie," said Bobby.

"Fuck yes," gasped Jamie.

Cole pulled back and spat on his cock a couple of times, lubing it up and Jamie's willing hole. Then Cole grabbed Jamie around the mouth with his large left hand and, with his right, directed his cock into Jamie's hole as they stood. He pushed in carefully for Cole, not his usual style, but he wanted that deal to stick. Jamie moaned under his hand. With the second drive he was in. He then held him by the neck and pumped him hard. The sheer strength of Cole was amazing to see.

"Fuck your hole is tight and feels awesome boy. You gonna keep to this special deal I hope," asked Cole.

"Fuck, yes sir," replied Jamie.

Bobby was now stroking Jamie's hardon, simultaneously licking and gently biting Jamie's nipples. Finally, Cole moved them both towards the bed and push Jamie down on it, his legs still on the floor, Jamie's cock resting down the side of the bed between his legs. Cole got some new purchase and drove in again and again. Bobby got down between their two pairs of legs and put Jamie's cock back in his mouth, stroking his balls as he sucked.

"Oh fuck, I wanna cum!" said Jamie, and shot a warm creamy load into Bobby's mouth.

Bobby took it all. He loved the taste of cum. Even his own, would never waste a drop when he had a private wank. He loved how each person tasted slightly different. Jamie's was thick. This boy had not cum in a while. He needed today, Bobby thought. Bobby got up to watch Cole in action. God he was hot. Cole was driving his cock hard into Jamie. Cole had that look of total dominance. Jamie was moaning now and starting to move like a rag doll under Cole's strength. Bobby was so hard watching Cole in action. He started to wank himself watching the glorious sight. He was close himself now. He climbed on the bed and crouched down under Jamie's face and pulled his head up.

"Take my fucking load as a down payment boy," said Bobby, and he pushed Jamie's head on his glowing cock. With two thrusts he shot his load deep in Jamie's throat. Three pumps of Bobby spunk coated Jamie's mouth and some dripped out. He pulled out. At that point, Cole roared and shot his load deep in Jamie's gut.

"Fuck yeah," said Cole, pumping his mess into his hole deeper. "Fuck that felt good."

Cole pulled out and flopped on the bed. "Fucking clean my cock Jamie," he ordered.

Jamie was on it in a flash. Giving Bobby full access to Jamie's hole.

"I promised I'd clean you up," and he dived into Jamie's, rosy hole with his tongue. "Go on push back, I want Cole's load too," Bobby added. Jamie's sphincter pouted and twitched, then delivered a stream of glorious hot cum. Bobby lapped it up. The taste of Cole and stranger's arse. Perfect he thought. When they had all finished cleaning up their holes, they stood up and adjusted the bed, checking for stains. Bobby had been good to ensure all loads were recovered. They then all got dressed.

"Fuck that was awesome. If we make this a regular thing I'll knock 100% off the fees," Jamie joked. "But my boss would question that. Ok, sign these papers and we are good to go. The apartment is available from a week Monday. You can pick up the keys then.

"Sweet," said Bobby. As they all got dressed. He kissed Jamie and said, "Thank you for being so amenable."

"Thank you for an awesome fuck, I friggin' needed that. I've been going through a dry patch lately. You've given me a taste for anonymous sex again. Better get that Grindr app reloaded, fucking loved it. Cheers," smiled Jamie.

They all then left the apartment and Jamie left them in the lobby.

"He's got a spring in his step now," said Cole.

"I'm not surprised having had your rocket up his arse," grinned Bobby. "You are fucking sexy to watch in action Cole."

Chapter 10 - Perfect Pete

It was mid week in late September. Bobby and Cole had settled into their apartment now and were enjoying their routines. Great work, money to go out and party, picking up guys together and having huge amounts of meaningless filthy sex. Life was good. They were also growing closer as a couple, saving the rough sex for the hook-ups. They shared a bed in the apartment and started to enjoy making love to each other, rather than just fucking. In fact, the spare room became known as the dungeon and was used to ride which ever victim or victims they happened upon. Their room was kept for them. No three ways happened in their room.

Due to the amount of sex and the fact they were now earning some good money, they both decided to get tested for HIV before exploring PrEP. They realised they had been risking a lot and fortunately were both clear, now they needed to ensure they stayed that way. This was all new to Cole, but he valued Bobby's advice, it was good to have someone who cared enough to worry about him. Something he'd never really had growing up.

It was a usual week at the office, busy with targets, when a tall handsome man in his fifties came into the office. Bobby and Cole looked up. He was smartly dressed with a cropped beard and grey hair. He was wearing a beautiful navy three piece suit, with some tight short leather gloves and everyone stood up to greet him.

"Hey Peter!" many of the team shouted and whooped. Max stood up and went across to Peter and kissed him fully on the lips in front of everyone and gave him a hug. Bobby and Cole looked at each other. So, this must be Peter Bartholomew, Max's husband, over from the UK.

"Afternoon everyone," Peter said in a beautiful rich English accent. Even sexier than Max's, Bobby thought.

He was very handsome for an older guy. These Brits are so stylish and don't let themselves go like some Americans he thought.

"It's great to see you all again. I hope life has been good to you all these past three months since I was last here. Judging by the numbers you have been working extremely hard and we all thank you for that, I will catch up with you all individually over the next couple of days, but first I must steal my husband away for a chat."

Max took Peter to the conference room and they had a good catch up on the company and performances. Peter was over to meet with some contacts in Atlanta, but thought he'd have some time with Max. He would leave for Atlanta on Saturday. After business talk was done, Peter moved to lighter subjects.

"Well I spotted the two gorgeous new boys in the office as soon as I came in. Max darling are you sure you haven't employed them with your dick in mind. They are very easy on the eye," Peter smiled.

Max replied, "Yes, I'm sure. They are hot as fuck and very talented sexually, but they have real potential for the business. Bobby the little one with the blond hair is pulling up trees IT wise. He has streamlined a number of our systems and reducing the need for contractor work massively. He's very bright and can help the whole group in my opinion."

"He could help me with some relief right now. You know he's just my type and after that tedious flight, him sitting on my dick would be a perfect pick me up," Peter smiled.

"You know we don't take advantage of the staff like that Peter, dear boy," replied Max. "If Bobby wants to fuck you that's ok, but don't pressurise him Peter, that's not how we run Chicago."

"I know. I'm kidding, but he would be perfect. What about the strapping other young man? How's he doing? Apart from looking God like in a suit that is," Peter asked.

"Well, he's got loads of charm and charisma but is struggling a little in his role in Marketing. His written skills aren't the best," said Max.

"Then why is he still here? We don't carry deadwood, even if they do look like that." Peter tilted his head to one side.

"I'm not giving up on him. He has something, I can feel it," Max replied.

"I bet you can feel it…. How big is his cock? I know he's your type, macho and brutish," teased Peter.

"A good nine inches and he uses it like a weapon. But seriously though he has potential, so let's leave it there." Max closed Peter down.

"Well, I hope I get to meet the new recruits properly. Maybe dinner on Friday. I particularly want to get to know Bobby," Peter said. "Let's make Friday happen," he asserted.

All Wednesday night Bobby and Cole discussed Peter and Max sitting on their sofa in their new apartment.

"Peter is really sexy," said Bobby. "I thought Max was the perfect daddy, but Peter trumps him. Don't get me wrong Max is hot, but there is something so distinguished about Peter," Bobby added. "God, what's the chances of us getting into bed with both of them?" he wondered out loud.

"Probably pretty good if you and Max have anything to do with planning it. You are such a tart Bobby," Cole laughed. "Max is still the main man for me. I like his rougher build. He has strength and a brutal side I can relate to. I may one day christen my mouth with his cock. I've been thinking about that since he gave us these jobs."

"What, you won't suck mine, but you'll suck his?" Bobby retorted. "Well you don't want to come across as an amateur you better practice on mine," he said, pulling his limp dick out of his fly.

Cole looked at his friend's limp cock, "Maybe I will, but it will need to be in better shape than that. More like this," as he pulled back his sweatpants and eased out his monster tool that was now very erect after thinking about Max again. Bobby couldn't resist, and nose dived onto Cole's cock, slowly pleasuring him, licking his shaft and then downing it to the hilt, occasionally licking Cole's balls. He worked his magic until Cole finally held his head and shouted.

"Take my fucking load boy!" and delivered his warm creamy load into Bobby's throat.

Bobby took it with relish, licking every drop up. Fuck he loved Cole's cock and cum.

"Ok, now suck me," Bobby ordered, licking his lips.

"Maybe later, I'm hungry let's get some food. My turn to cook."

"Thanks. Leave me with this," looking at his hard on.

Cole looked back.

"I'll cook naked and you can wank watching me," Cole said as he got food out the fridge.

"Deal," Bobby replied.

Cole pulled off his sweatpants, top and undies and walked around naked. Bobby started beating his meat looking at his wonderful jock bully making dinner. Cole noticed and so did Bobby, a string of jizz hanging from his cock.

"Looks like you missed a bit."

Cole scooped it up in his fingers facing Bobby and stroked his cock to get the last pumps of cum from his flaccid cock. He then brought the jizzed fingers to his mouth and sucked them clean. That was enough for Bobby. He stood up and he blew a load in his hand and over the coffee table in the vain hope of saving his clothes and carpet from an unnecessary cleaning bill. Five beautiful ropes of cum hit his cupped hand and one hit the table. Bobby sighed and raised his hand to his mouth and ate his load as he always did.

"You're a fucking animal Bobby Wilson," said Cole. "And that's why I fucking love ya, you sexy little cunt." Cole surprised himself with the 'Love' word. Bobby was his childhood intellectual nemesis he had loved to taunt and wanted to destroy. Now he was, well perhaps, his boyfriend.

Bobby smiled back with a mouth full of cum then swallowed. He licked up the coffee table and then cleaned up.

"If we had CSI in here with one of those glow torches to show up spunk and bodily fluid, this apartment would look fucking crazy," Cole laughed.

"So you love me do you Cole?" smiled Bobby raising an eyebrow.

Cole froze, and then turned back to look at Bobby.

"Kinda," Cole said in a non-committal way. "But I do reckon we probably are a couple now, don't you think?"

"Yeah, sure. Boyfriend," smiled Bobby, "I like the idea of that." Bobby walked over to Cole and kissed him on the cheek.

****

Thursday. Peter spent the day in the office hot desking with the sales guys. He was happiest in Sales. He took the opportunity to go around and speak to everyone personally, asking them about their jobs and home lives, family, anything. This was their real strength. Peter and Max were so good with people. Even though Peter was a classy chap who obviously came from good stock, he was a kind hearted man like Max who really showed an interest in his team and the people's lives. The team really appreciated that and worked all the harder for them. The beauty of their success was having good people, treating them well, but being clear and firm on their rules. Most importantly Peter and Max were very clear on their strategies and direction. They never wavered on making decisions, tough ones or risky ones. This gave the team complete clarity on what was happening, which in turn meant they were also clear on what their role was and how they had to play their part. Peter and Max both knew that customers didn't come first. Employees come first. If you look after them, they will look after their customers.

Once he had been around the established staff, he made a beeline for Cole and particularly Bobby. As with all new recruits, it was tradition that Peter and Max meet them all and take them out to dinner as a welcome to the company. They normally tried to do this together when they were both in each region. So, no one blinked an eye when Peter asked Cole and Bobby to chat with him in the conference room one at a time. Peter started with Cole.

Peter took full advantage of watching Cole's tight arse walk into the conference room in front of him. He smelt good too. He could see what Max saw in him. Tall, young, handsome and well built, just Max's type. When they went looking for sex together in the clubs Max always liked strong fit guys, whilst Peter preferred smaller cute guys he could play and control more easily. Peter shook himself mentally, he wasn't here to cruise these lads, well not now anyway. He was here to welcome them to the business. Cole gave Peter a firm handshake and sat opposite him. Peter examined his amazing eyes and jawline. He was a handsome specimen. He asked about Cole's background and history, his interests and ultimately what he hoped to achieve at Bartholomew Steadman.

"I know how you Bobby and Max met, so no need to tell me about that, though it sounds like you had a very interesting couple of evenings a few weeks back," Peter followed on.

In all the conversation not once did Cole talk about marketing, surprisingly Cole declared he wanted to close the biggest read estate deal for the business and make everyone proud. This thought stuck with Peter. He asked Cole to leave and get Bobby to come in.

Bobby was watching his handsome boyfriend, talking to his really hot daddy boss. Peter was tall, slim frame, classy and elegant. He was very handsome for a guy in his mid fifties. Bobby hadn't had a father figure since the age of five and so he loved the idea of having one. Sexually the dominant handsome older man really got his juices going. He was getting a semi thinking of what it would be like to be taken by Peter Bartholomew. Then he saw Cole get up and leave the room beckoning him in.

"Your turn buddy," said Cole.

Peter watched the very cute lad with a shock of striking blond hair get up and walk around the desks. In a slim shirt and tight trousers, Peter could see the outline of Bobby's semi-erect cock pressing against his zipper. Peter knew he had to have him riding his dick. Fuck he's beautiful he thought. Peter could feel his own cock twitching in his pants. 'Come on Peter, be professional for Christ sake,' he thought. He stood up as Bobby entered the room and smiled.

He also quizzed Bobby about his ambitions career wise, and also praised him on the wonderful work he was doing to date. After they had had a fifteen minute chat, Bobby noticed Peter couldn't stop staring deeply in his eyes.

"Thank you Bobby," Peter said, "Very interesting. Can you ask Cole to join us please,"

Bobby got up and leaned out the glass walled room and beckoned Cole back in. Peter studied Bobby's crotch and arse and sighed.

"Ok I don't know if Max has told you or if any of the team has said, but it is standard practice for Max and I to take new recruits out for a meal when they join the business," Peter explained.

"Oh, that's nice. No we hadn't been told yet by Max, but some of the others said something like this might happen," responded Bobby.

"I know it's short notice, but I have to fly to Atlanta on Saturday, so tomorrow night, Friday, is really my only opportunity. Does that work for you?" asked Peter.

Bobby and Cole looked at each other, "You're the boss," said Cole.

"No," said Peter, "That's not how it works here, we are inviting you out, but if you have other plans I wouldn't expect those to change. We can do it another time. This is your time and not for Max or I to dictate."

Bobby looked at him and sighed. What a kind awesome man.

"We would be more than happy for tomorrow," said Bobby. "No plans, but we do now. Any requirements dress wise?" he added.

"Got any leather?" Peter joked forgetting himself. "I'm joking. It will be smart, will have to get something booked asap."

Bobby smiled, he knew Peter and Max met at Folsom Berlin Fetish Festival and that Peter, like Max, had a big passion for leather. This got Bobby thinking.

They all left the conference room and Peter walked over to Gina.

"Can you possibly get us a table for four somewhere damn nice for tomorrow evening, please Gina? Around 7.30? For the new recruits."

"Already sorted. Max asked me this morning. You have a reservation under Max's name at The Palm. It's a steak and fish house overlooking the river," Gina stated.

"Perfect, did you get that gentlemen? 7.30 at the Palm. Let's meet in the bar at seven."

"Yes Sir," the boys replied in unison.

That evening, Bobby and Cole got talking about Peter and Max. "I want to be fucked by Peter," said Bobby. "He's so classy but he has a dirty streak, I know. That leather joke wasn't a joke. Remember Max and him met at Folsom week in Berlin. He's mad for leather like Max. I think we should try and oblige, I could do with a good fuck session with both Peter and Max. It's been a while since I felt and tasted Max's awesome crotch and arse."

"You're unbelievable Bobby. We have to be careful. We don't want to fuck these jobs up just for sex," said Cole, being the sensible one for the change.

"Well, let's see how the night goes. If they are up for it, I'm in. We need to show willing and wear some leather. I have a small bomber jacket somewhere and I think you have the perfect thing. The leather waistcoat we got a few weeks back in the sales. Just enough to tantalise, but not too OTT," said Bobby.

They planned their outfits and got them ready for the next night. Bobby ironed their shirts while Cole cooked dinner.

Chapter 11 - Good to be Home from Home

Peter loved staying in Max's apartment when he came over. He was so tidy, and it was huge. All the rooms were at least twice the size of his apartment in London, which Peter owned, but the London place was worth a mint because of its location in Chelsea. Probably four times the value of Max's.

Peter and Max entered the apartment and Peter put his bags in the dressing room and took in a deep breath. The smell of sex and leather.

"I fucking love this room," he shouted.

Peter ran his hands through the gear. Mainly Max's but some additional items. The larger gear and boots, he heard about Cole wearing, were at one end. He smelt the crotch.

"Beautiful," he said.

Then the custom made leather football kit. He pulled the hanger down and held the shorts to his face and smelled.

"God so horny."

He opened the shorts to see the inside, he was in luck, residue of old jizz. Bobby's jizz. Just knowing his cock had been inside these shorts made Peter hard. He licked the shorts and held his crotch.

"I've got to have him," he said quietly.

Max came into the room.

"Ok perv, stop sniffing the merchandise," Max laughed.

Part 3 – Opportunity Knocks

"I need some leather action Max and, if they are up for it, I need to fuck Bobby hard with you. We gotta make it happen tomorrow and I want to see him in this gear," demanded Peter.

"We will have to see. If they are willing fine, but we are not pushing them. They are employees now Peter, so control your dick," replied Max.

"Let's fuck, now," said Peter.

He started to take his suit and shirt off, revealing he was wearing a leather jock under his suit. Max smiled at his cock straining against the soft leather. Peter was 6'3", slender but toned.

"Fucking take me now Max. Here in the leathers."

"Ok big Boss," Max undressed quickly. He was now naked with a raging boner. He picked up some gloves.

"Oh yes Max," said Peter.

Max walked up to his husband and kissed him hard and grabbed his bulge and pulled off the codpiece of the jock to reveal Peter's eight inch uncut British cock. Whilst he kissed Peter, he worked his cock in his leather gloved palm. Max then suddenly turned Peter round and shoved him into the hanging leather jackets and jeans. His face and chest buried in the leather clothing. Max grabbed some lube and dropped it on the tip of his cock, worked it around Peter's hole, so not to lube up his gloves. Then he pushed in, whilst grabbing Peter's neck.

"Fuck it's been too long," said Peter. "Fuck me Master."

Max drove in and out, putting his fingers in Peter's mouth and pushing him in and out of the leather gear. Peter moaned, feeling and grabbing as much leather as he could to spread it over his body.

The cold texture, the awesome smell, the smell of leather, sweat and cum. Peter was working his own cock now and loving every minute. Max was close and after several more pumps, shot his load deep inside Peter, his husband, his partner, his friend, his cruising fuck buddy, his equal, but his subordinate sexually.

Max pulled out and turned Peter round, then fell to his knees to take Peters cock in his mouth.

"Give Master your load," said Max. Peter wanked and Max sucked the bell end and shaft, grabbing Peter's buttocks hard.

"I'm cumming," said Peter and pumped a healthy load into Max's mouth and on his cheek. Max lapped it up and swallowed it all, scooping the jizz from cheek into his mouth and licking the gloved fingers.

"God Max, I do love you. You are a truly wonderful man," said Peter, still leaning into the leather jackets, but resting.

"Well, if you love me, you'll straighten up this room, looks like I've just dragged a whore through it," he laughed. "I'll go make dinner," grabbing a robe as he left.

Peter smiled as his sexy man walked out the room, he looked at his dripping cock, and squeezed out the last bit of cum, brought it to his lips.

"Umm," he said, then felt Max's load moving down his gut. "Better clean that up," he muttered.

They sat and had dinner in their robes. Max was an excellent cook. An amazing fish dish with fresh vegetables and a bottle of Italian white.

"Life is good Maxi. We are so damn lucky," said Peter, relaxing back.

"We made our own luck and now we are rightfully giving back to all our team and they are making us even wealthier. It will be good to see at year end, what the profit share scheme divvies up," said Max.

Max and Peter owned 80% of the business. The remaining 20% is shared amongst the employees while they work for the business. 20% of the annual profits is shared equally amongst the team, based on salary banding and responsibility.

Peter said, "I'm looking forward to tomorrow night. I like those two boys. Yes, they are sexy as hell but they are interesting devils. You were right. I thought at first you just liked them to look at and that's not hard to see why, but they do have a certain something. Bobby, already showing that. Not sure we have Cole in the right place if I'm honest, but your call Max."

"I think we need to give them some time," replied Max. "I'm sure, you're probably right."

"So tomorrow, I need to get geared up," said Peter.

"It's a fine dining restaurant, not the Blue Oyster Club," Max replied.

"I know, I have some new Armani leather jeans and a matching cafe racer jacket. Butter soft lamb's leather. I'm going to wear it with a crisp white shirt and tie," said Peter.

"I'll look forward to seeing you in that. Perhaps I should wear similar. Not exactly the same. I'll have a think when I see yours," Max replied.

"I think the leather will give the boys a clue as to what we would like. Would be good to see if they bite," smiled Peter.

"I imagine the whole restaurant will be thinking the same," Max laughed.

Peter and Max had never worried about wearing leather in public. They looked good in it, whether it was full bike gear or smart jeans. They had a style, something a lot of American and British men don't understand or have. In Germany it was fine. No one bothered to look there, but at home and in America, people would stare a little, with some whispering. That didn't worry them at all. They liked it and it made them feel good.

The following day, Friday, everyone got on with their business and worked hard. At 4pm, Max asked, "Unless anyone has a burning need to stay, I'm heading off for the weekend, I encourage you to do the same and see your loved ones, and I'll see you all next Monday."

Then he whispered to Bobby and Cole who were staring at him "And I'll see you guys later tonight," he winked.

Peter had been out the office all day, meeting some other contacts he knew, taking Brad Regent along. Peter wanted to introduce him to some important contacts who may help them all in the future. Peter's contacts ran far and wide and had helped the business no end. Peter loved sales. The thrill of the chase and he also liked Brad.

Brad was an all American boy, 5' 10", thirty one, unmarried and strapping but toned. He would look great in a cowboy outfit, Peter dreamed. He was poached by Max from a rival company two years ago, because he was such a charming sales man and got great results. The ladies loved him and he used all his resources. He knew Max was gay and flirted with Max during the interview. Brad would sleep with anyone male or female. He enjoyed sex and he enjoyed beautiful people. In his old firm he was held back by his boss, an ugly fucker who resented Brad's charm and ability to sell, but liked the results, but wanted to keep him in his place also. More fool him. Max snapped him up. No glass ceiling here.

Peter introduced Brad to some great contacts that day and he charmed them lightly as a starter and offered to keep in touch. He always played the long game. He would keep in touch via email and ensure the conversation gently continued with them until the time was right to ask for a proper business meeting.

By 4.45, the office was empty and closed for the weekend.

Chapter 12 – A pleasurable evening

Bobby and Cole showered together and had a kiss and a cuddle as they lathered each other. Cole got hard in the process and looked at Bobby.

"Down boy, we need to save ourselves for our hot bosses tonight," said Bobby, rinsing himself of soap and pushing Cole to one side as he got out the shower cubical.

Cole was jaw dropped. This was the first time Bobby had rejected his cock.

He smiled, "Ok little boss."

They got ready. It was still a warm night in September. Cole wore some black ankle army boots with tight jeans, tight white shirt and the black leather waistcoat. It was one that was designed to be worn open, like a cut away waistcoat. It showed his pecs under his shirt and his guns perfectly. His hair was washed, wet dried. He looked awesome as usual. Bobby wore skinny black jeans, a black tight shirt and Chelsea boots. He looked a bit goth like, but the fabulous blonde hair corrected that and shone brightly. He slipped on the leather bomber jacket and the look was complete. They both decided to go commando tonight. They loved the feel of denim on their tackle and it also meant easy access if any opportunities arose. These boys were learning and getting dirtier each week. Sex was available to them and they took it at every chance.

"I'm not sure about this jacket Cole, it looks a bit tatty and its quite worn out, but I don't have any other leather for them and I want to show willing," sighed Bobby.

"Umm you are right and you look so sexy showing off that new physique in the jeans and shirt," said Cole. Since moving into the new apartment, they had joined the gym in the basement of the building and the pair worked out together. Cole had a perfect body, strong and ripped, the jock body from school. He kept in shape regularly. Bobby, when they met, had a slim frame that was in proportion, but not toned. Cole helped Bobby in the gym with a programme to improve his core strength and the improvements could be seen. Bobby toned his abs, pecs, shoulders and arms. He was beginning to show a nice little T-shape to his body. It looked good. His slim frame was now nicely toned. With his cute boyish pretty face and the mop of blonde hair, tonight styled in a relaxed look, he was looking hot.

"Hold on, I have something for you. Was going to give them to you when the time was right. Now seems a good idea," said Cole. He went into their bedroom and returned with a small box.

"Open it."

Bobby opened the box to find some small black leather gloves and a couple of leather wrist cuffs. Bobby smiled. He quickly tried them on. Cole helped adjust the cuffs to fit his slim wrists and rolled back the shirt sleeves casually, to show the cuffs off perfectly. They looked great.

"Thanks Cole, these are perfect," he grinned.

"It's quite warm, so I'd put the gloves in your back pocket, so the fingers are sticking out," said Cole.

Bobby did that and pushed them into the back pocket of his tight black jeans.

"Perfect," said Cole as he knelt down and pushed his face into Bobby's pert little arse.

"Could you look any hotter or cuter my Bobby?" Cole said.

"Perhaps, when you see me later riding our bosses. Now let's get a move on or we will be late my sexy jock," Bobby laughed.

They both headed for the elevators.

Max watched Peter getting dressed. The Armani leather jeans and jacket were beautiful. Worn over a leather open jock.

"The leather of the jeans against my cock feels divine," said Peter.

The Ozwald Boateng white shirt fitted him perfectly. Max decided on a similar look. He opted for dark blue/black leather jeans and jacket he had purchased in Berlin a few years back. He wore it with black suede dessert boots and a tight short sleeve shirt in white that showed off his arm muscles perfectly. The smooth lamb's leather caressed Max's powerful thighs as he walked out of the dressing room to greet Peter.

"My God you look great in that. I forgot you bought that in Berlin," said Peter.

"Thanks, that Armani leather looks beautiful. I need to touch it," Max said as he grabbed hold of his husband and kissed him hard, groping his tight leather clad arse as he did so.

Peter returned the gesture and felt Max's hard body through the leather.

"God you are making me hard and the evening has barely begun," said Peter.

“Slow down tiger. Tonight we have some new recruits to play with, and they I’m sure will be up for it. I warn you, they can be real nasty if you want it,” said Max.

“Well, you’ve changed your tune, ‘Employer of the Year’. Fucking the recruits is now ok?” laughed Peter.

“These two are different. I met them for sex and they love it. They enjoy just about anything, hard, rough and sensual. These boys are real special,” Max confirmed.

“Well what are we waiting for? I need a hard fuck from some young blood. Rough is fine with me my dear,” Peter grinned.

“The Uber is outside. Let’s go,” said Max checking his phone.

Max and Peter arrived at the restaurant first and headed to the bar after giving their names at reception. These two men confidently walked to the bar head to toe in leather. The sight turned a few heads. The expressions were mixed. Some of surprise, some had a look of admiration and some of the male waiters checked out their arses in the wonderful leather. They sat at the bar and ordered cocktails. Peter studied the room.

“We have been noticed Maxi.”

“Some locals here but some tourists too I reckon. Judging from some of the bad hair on show. Amazing they are let in with hair like that,” Max laughed.

As they checked out the clientele further they noticed Cole and Bobby entering the restaurant.

“Oh my,” said Peter. “They took notice of my flippant comment to wear some leather. Subtle but sweet and very sexy.”

Part 3 – Opportunity Knocks

“They are so up for action tonight. Good lads. Cole looks magnificent as usual, but do I spy that Bobby has been working out. He seems, broader, not noticed it so much at work, but in that shirt.... ummm,” Max whispered to Peter.

“Hands off he’s mine. You can play with Cole,” Peter smiled back at Max as he got up to greet the young men at the bar.

Bobby and Cole walked in and instantly saw Peter and Max at the bar. Who else would be wearing total leather? They acknowledged them across the room from the check-in desk and the lady greeted them and then passed them through. She checked out Cole’s arse as he walked past her. He noticed and winked back at her, which made her blush.

Bobby led the way over to the bar. He was staring at Peter. He looked very cool in what looked like the softest leather. Max was looking awesome too, at first, he thought he was also in black leather, but it was dark blue. So cool these two and they looked great together. Two handsome daddies who, if he a guessed correctly, would be up for more than just dinner.

Bobby raised his hand to shake with Peter and Max. All four men shook hands and gave each other a gentle hug. Peter noticed the gloves in Bobby tight jeans and smiled widely. ‘That arse looks so perfect, I need my cock inside him very soon,’ he thought feeling his cock twitching against his leather jeans.

“What will you have to drink lads? We are on cocktails,” Max asked.

“Beers will be fine,” said Cole.

“Two beers please, something European ideally,” Max asked the barman.

"We have Estrella Damm, Kronenbourg or Grolsch," he replied.

"Two Grolsch. Is it flip top?" Max asked.

"Yes Sir."

"You really know your beers Max," said Cole.

Peter jumped in, "Oh yes, you see he came from a background of beer money, but now has champagne tastes."

"Err thanks Peter. I'm very proud of my background and upbringing. Not all of us are fortunate to be born with a silver spoon in their mouth," Max replied with a laugh.

"I'm only jesting Max. You boys, I'll have you know that Max's parents are wonderful. So welcoming and accepting of us and even me. They are very proud of their son and what he has achieved. My parents, on the other hand rarely talk to me. They don't agree with my 'lifestyle' as they call it. Fuck 'em. I knew I wasn't likely to see much of their inheritance, so decided I needed to build my own and then Max came along at just the right time. Swept me off my feet with his northern charm," Peter smiled.

"Hardly a northerner, Leicester is in the midlands," Max replied.

"It's north of Watford, so that's the north to us Londoners," Peter joked.

Bobby and Cole smiled, they hadn't a clue where Leicester or Watford was. Only London resonated. 'Maybe one day Cole and I will go visit England,' Bobby thought.

The receptionist walked over and asked if they would like to go to their table.

"Lead the way, please," said Max.

They were sat at a table, next to one of the tourist couples with a bad perm. The men all smiled at them. The tourists didn't crack a smile at all.

"They seem happy," whispered Peter with a smile. Peter and Max took off their jackets.

"Shall I take those for you sirs," the receptionist asked. They smiled and gave her their jackets. She walked off with them, gently feeling how soft they were.

They ordered their food and Peter chose some wine and the conversation was flowing. Max was chatting to Cole. Peter was sat next to Bobby and admiring the leather cuffs he was wearing.

"They look pretty hot," he said.

"I wore them for you sir," he whispered back smiling.

He then rubbed his leg against Peter's thigh. His forwardness excited Peter, who smiled back.

"What are you two chatting about?" said Max. "Work I hope," knowing full well it wasn't.

"We are admiring each other's leather," Peter replied.

The starters arrived and they all tucked in while carrying on their conversations, when they were interrupted.

"You guys make me sick," the woman with the perm said scowling at them. "I'm trying to eat and your shoving your fag lifestyle down my throat."

Cole and Bobby were quite shocked, but Peter had a look of steel, he turned around and said in his clearest and most authoritative English accent,

"I beg your pardon. What did you just say?"

Cole was about to stand up, when Max put his hand on his arm.

"Watch and learn," he smiled.

The tourist husband chipped in, "We are trying to enjoy our meal and you sit next to us, gaying up the place. It's not right. You chose that life. You should do it behind closed doors if at all."

Peter stood up and faced them with all his height and took one step forward.

"May I ask you a question?"

"Suppose."

"At what age did you choose to be straight may I ask?" Peter questioned.

People were looking round from other tables, and the manager was hovering in the wings.

"What you mean? I didn't choose to be straight you idiot. You don't choose to be straight you just are," said the out of towner.

"Neither did I choose or any of my friends. If you don't understand that, you really have so much to learn," Peter replied.

"Get...get out my face queer. People are sick of you guys ramming it down our throats," he stuttered.

"Interesting choice of words," Peter laughed. The restaurant were all listening now and some laughed at Peter's charm and joke.

Another man then shouted from the opposite table, "Hey bigot! Why don't you fuck off and crawl back under the stone age rock you came from?"

"Now now, thank you sir for your support, but let's not stoop to this man's level," Peter replied.

"You're damn lowlife," said the stone age wife.

"And you my dear have a terrible perm and it's not even Halloween. We all have our cross to bear. I'm done with you now, please don't address me again, unless you want a legal injunction slapped on you," said Peter as he returned to his table to a round of applause from the restaurant clientele.

As he sat down, the Manager came over to the couple and quietly said, "I'm sorry you don't like some of our customers and they are making you feel uncomfortable, so we would kindly ask YOU to leave."

"What, we have to leave?" she said.

"Oh yes, please leave quietly or I will call security. We don't allow any form of intolerance or abuse."

They got up begrudgingly.

"Too many fucking liberals in this city," he said. As they were walked off, the tables around clapped and cheered.

"Wow Mr Bartholomew, you were so cool," said Bobby.

"So calm with it. Total style," said Cole.

"A calm approach and an aloof English accent works wonders I find," he laughed.

The Manager returned to apologise to them all for the abuse.

"Please have the cost of your meal on us."

"No," said Peter, "That's very kind but you should not be penalised for bigots. Sadly they don't wear a badge to make them easy to identify. It's bad enough you have had to lose the value of their food they had their trotters in. No, we will pay, thank you."

The manager smiled and nodded and left.

The four finished their starters and their mains then arrived. The continued discussing the situation with the tourists for a while and then moved onto the subject of work. The young men talked about how much they enjoyed the business and the opportunity they had been given.

Once the main food was cleared and over dessert the topic of sex appeared. Well, Bobby brought it up.

"I have a question," said Bobby. "Would I be damaging my work prospects and respect, if I offered myself to you and Max tonight? I have to say, I've thought about nothing else since you arrived Mr Bartholomew."

"Please, call me Peter, well at least tonight," he laughed. "We try not to screw the staff, but you two are an exception. You are both extremely cute and handsome and Max has had you both already, so it's a little different. As long as you don't feel we are taking advantage, that is important."

"That's cool with me," said Cole. "Just don't want to ruin our chances in your business by being a laughing stock or the company fucks and, for the record, you both are extremely hot. I feel we could have some real fun tonight."

"I'm delighted to hear it," said Peter. "Shall we skip coffee and get back to the apartment? I have a boner growing that needs some attention."

They all laughed. Max beckoned for the bill. He paid and they all made their way to the door, picking up Max and Peter's jackets and hailing a cab on the street to Max's apartment.

In the elevator, Peter moved in on Bobby and grabbed his hair and kissed him hard, feeling his hard little body with his other hand. Max decided to do the same with Cole but kissed while groping his arse and pulling their crotches together. Bulges rubbing together. Once in the apartment, they calmed down a bit and got some drinks on the go.

"Now I have a request," Peter asked. "Bobby, I really need to see you in the football strip. It looks so hot. I've been thinking about it for days. Would you indulge me?"

"Yeah sure, I'll go change now."

Cole said, "You want me to change?"

Max replied. "You look perfect. How about losing the shirt and putting the waistcoat back on that beautiful body?"

The waistcoat drew the eye to his lovely treasure trail and chest hair.

Bobby came out the dressing room in the shirt and shorts, along with the new gloves he got from Cole. The look was perfect with the cuffs as well. The shirt was now even tighter over his new frame. He hadn't found the socks and boots, but he looked great with his newly developed legs and body. He found Cole shirtless in his jeans and waistcoat and both Max and Peter had removed their shirts. Just in their leather jeans. Peter's slender frame was beautifully toned for a man of his age, with a nice level of salt and pepper fur.

Peter stood up.

"Beautiful," he said looking at Bobby, "Come closer."

He grabbed Bobby and picked him up. Bobby wrapped his legs around him.

"I'm having him in here," as he walked to the master bedroom. "Feel free to join us in twenty." Peter carried Bobby through the door and slammed it shut behind him. Max grabbed Cole and took him to the spare room.

Peter dropped Bobby on the bed and looked down on him.

"You are so fucking cute, boy."

"Fuck me hard please, use me, own me, breed me sir. I want you inside me," said Bobby.

Peter climbed onto Bobby and kissed him. He kissed his neck and ears, under his arms. He felt the leather over his chest and took in the aroma deeply.

"Remove the shirt. Keep the shorts on," Peter commanded. Bobby obliged, revealing his new toned body. Smooth and firm, with perfectly formed chest and the start of abs. Peter dived into his arm pits sniffing and licking, down to his nipples and gently biting. Bobby and Peter were rubbing hard cocks through leather on each other. Peter reached down and unzipped his jeans to reveal his hard on.

“Lay back. Let me at that sir,” said Bobby.

Peter rolled back and Bobby straddled him, with his arse in Peter’s face as he devoured his throbbing cock. Driving it into his throat, in and out. Licking the shaft and enjoying it so. it tasted of leather and piss, the best. Bobby worked his tongue round Peter’s foreskin, he liked uncut cocks. Peter moaned as Bobby worked his magic. Meanwhile he was enjoying smelling and licking Bobby’s arse through the soft leather shorts. His perfect pert buns yielding a hole that smelt awesome. Peter noticed the small poppers. Max thinks of everything he thought. He undid them and revealed the prize. His tongue was in Bobby’s hole straight away. Bobby bucked and moaned at the feeling of Peter’s stubble. They both noshed each other for a few minutes, then Peter grabbed Bobby and said.

“Turn around and ride me, Boy. I wanna see your pretty face as I fuck you.”

Bobby turned around. He leaned over into the bedside draw and found Max’s lube. Lubed up Peter’s dick and his own hole and then lowered himself on. Peter watched as this beautiful lad, performed on his cock. His lovely face, his body writhing and moaning as he pleasured himself on his dick. Bobby’s own was now hard and lifting the shorts up.

“My, you are big for a small boy,” said Peter grabbing Bobby’s cock and stroking it gently to increase the sensation and intensity of the fucking. Peter couldn’t be happier.

Max and Cole lay on the bed snogging with their flies open frottaging each other. Their swords doing battle as the masters kissed. Max was tasting every part of Cole’s hard body, navigating the sexy waistcoat and working his way down his hard chest and licking his abs and treasure trail, until he found the treasure. He took Cole's thick cock gently and licked the shaft up and down. Then he took it in his throat. Down to the hilt. Cole, lay back and groaned at the feeling. Max could taste Cole's evening sweat and a hint of fabric conditioner and the precum that was now appearing with abundant.

Max looked up and said, "I need you to fuck me Cole, get those jeans off. I'll be back," Max rushed out the room and was back in a flash, with a leather muir cap and gloves in his hand.

"Wear this as you fuck me Master Cole," Max said.

Max lay back on the bed, pulled off his jeans and presented his arse with his legs in the air.

"I wanna see evil Cole, no mercy."

Cole pulled on the tight gloves, he looked at them, and they still had cum and blood on them from previous sessions. He grinned his evil grin and he gently put the Muir cap on. Fuck he looked so hot thought Max. Such authority.

Cole clenched his hands and punched them together flexing his fingers. He spat on both gloves and lubed up his cock. He pushed Max's legs up.

"Higher cunt," he grunted and rested his cock on Max's hole.

Without warning, he grabbed Max's throat and forced his cock in. Max yelled and then moaned and Cole pumped his boss.

He then started various levels of verbal as he bred his boss. Hand over mouth and slapping his face.

Part 3 – Opportunity Knocks

"You fucking want me yeah?... Want my young cock in your arse?... Submit to my power you cumdump.... Yeah you just want my cum and my power to control you, don't you?.... You fucking pathetic lowlife scum.... Take my fucking dick and shut your moaning."

Max was watching Cole intently. He looked beautiful in his waistcoat gloves and cap. A true leather dom. A nasty evil dom. The look in his eyes was amazing. Pure evil. Max was now so hard listening to his cruel words.

Cole pulled out and threw him over and took him from behind. Driving in, he grabbed his head back and put his hands on his throat and got more purchase as he raped his arse hard. Max gurgled and moaned. His arse was glowing in pain and pleasure, then suddenly Cole stopped.

"We need to get back in there and fuck our men, like the true masters we are Max," said Cole.

They got up and marched across the apartment to the master bed room, and burst in. Peter had Bobby still riding on top of him as they burst in.

"Don't you knock?" said Peter.

"Masters don't need to knock," said Cole as he climbed on the bed and stood over Peter facing Bobby. He drove his cock into Bobby's throat, holding his head with no mercy.

Meanwhile, Max smiled.

"Yeah you bitches are in for a surprise."

He climbed on and stood back to back with Cole looking down on Peter. He lowered and sat on Peter's chest and forced his cock in his husbands throat. Masters Cole and Max were now fully in control. This four way intensified with more commanding and degrading verbal from Cole and now Max.

"Let's swap," said Max and they changed places.

Peter finally getting the benefit of Cole's cock in his throat. Looking up at this leather god, made him pump harder into Bobby's cunt.

"I have an idea," Cole said standing up, "Bobby climb off and Max sit on Peter's cock facing him with your legs over the top of his chest." He did with some initial difficulty.

"Now lean back carefully, and Bobby climb on Max's cock facing him. Now find a rhythm."

All three gently grinded together. Peter needed to sit up.

"Careful to not tear your cocks off," Cole laughed. Cole moved around rested his thighs under Max's head and rested his cock on his forehead, grinning down at him. Then looking at Bobby, who was really enjoying the action.

Peter was close and shouted, "Feel the load Maxi!" as he pumped his cum deep in his hole. Peter was exhausted.

"Wanna take over Cole?" he said. He withdrew and moved out the way and lay beside Max and Bobby who were still pumping and riding in a more traditional position now.

Cole moved round the back and lubed up, and Max lifted his legs. Cole looked over Bobby's shoulder shaking his head towards Max with a gloved finger over his lips. "You want me Bobby?" Cole said.

"Always Cole," he replied.

Lubing his cock, Cole said, "How about both Max and I?"

"Fuck I don't know," Bobby said a little worried, "I've not done that and you are big Cole."

Peter was watching, with a level of concern and excitement. Would these two hurt this boy, his husband and Bobby's boyfriend. It would be exciting to see.

Cole gently approached Bobby's hole, Max eased out a little to make some room.

"Relax Bobby," said Peter. "Go easy Cole," he added.

Cole eased in.

"Fuck that's tight, slower.... slower for fuck's sakes!" Bobby cried. Max eased out a bit more to let Cole in another inch. Bobby was blowing now and crying.

"Come on Bobby let me in," Cole said impatiently thrusting too hard. "FUCK NO!" Bobby fell forward and pulled off, "I can't."

"Ok," said Cole, his tone changing to concern as he hugged and held Bobby warmly from behind. "Sorry, really sorry."

Bobby reassured Cole by holding his hands and arms that were wrapped around him.

"Come fuck me, Bobby," said Peter, "I know you're a master with your tongue and hole. Let's see how good you are as a top."

Bobby smiled, Cole released his boyfriend and Bobby moved over to Peter.

"I wanna rim you first," he said and down he went, Peter on his back and holding his legs up.

"Fuck he is good Max. You were right, Jeez," said Peter as Bobby used his tongue expertly, face deep in Peter's arse.

Cole looked a little sad at what he had done.

"Lay back Cole. I'll take care of that hard on," said Max, who then climbed onboard and sat on Cole's cock. Bobby came up for air, saw Max and Cole and decided to join the fuck fest, entering Peter with his dick, just on spit. Peter winced as he entered then sighed and moaned as he watched this beautiful boy, still in those open shorts, fucking him hard.

"Play with my nipples boy," Peter demanded. Bobby obliged.

Cole thrust up into Max's cunt and watched his boyfriend pounding his other boss. Cole pulled off the muir cap and passed it to Bobby.

"Go Master Bobby."

Bobby put the cap on.

"Fuck, you're so fucking cute and hot. Ummm drill me leather boy. Breed me hard, faster, faster," Peter demanded.

"I'm close," said Bobby.

"Cum over me Bobby," said Peter.

Bobby withdrew and wanked his cock in his gloved hand. After about ten or so seconds he shot his load right across Peter, reaching his face chest and stomach. Seven or eight ropes of cum left Bobby, as he yelled loudly.

"Fucking beautiful. Awesome load," said Peter.

"I wanna cum Max," said Cole after seeing Bobby.

"Give it to me too, I want more cum," said Peter.

Max jumped off Cole and then they both knelt next to Peter and wanked their dynamic loads over Peter, multiple ropes joining Bobby's on his chest and stomach. Peter started to smear the loads together and then licked his hand and fingers. Bobby moved in and started hoovering up the loads all over Peter's body and, with a mouthful, went into to kiss Peter, grinning his cum filled mouth. Peter gladly opened wide and took delivery of the cum kiss. It was a long kiss and it tasted amazing.

When Bobby pulled back Peter said, "Fuck you are a hot dirty bastard, so hot fella." Bobby smiled at the compliment.

They all fell back exhausted. All breathing heavily after the massive session.

"Wow!" said Peter, breaking the silence. "Thanks for a wonderful evening. I really enjoyed our conversation and the sex was some of the best. You guys have many talents."

"Thanks for the meal tonight and a great evening. I hope we get to see more of you Peter," said Bobby.

"I'm sure you will, but I'm off to Atlanta in the morning and then need to be back in London on Monday, so won't be for a while."

"We better get off," said Cole, "Can we clean up before we go?"

"Sure," said Max.

The young men left the room and went and cleaned up in the main bathroom. Bobby called an Uber and then they said goodbyes and left for their own apartment.

Max saw them out as Peter hit the showers. Max then joined him and they went to bed.

"Those two are very interesting," said Peter. "But I do feel Cole is not in the best role for him. I think you should let him spend some time with Brad, Sales would seem to fit his abilities I'm feeling, but you would need to see that."

"Umm you may be right, I'll have a think on it over the coming weeks." Max clapped his hands three times and the lights went out.

"You and your bloody gadgets," sniggered Peter as he cuddled in.

Chapter 13 - Where do we go from here

Peter kissed Max goodbye and got his flight to Atlanta. He was going to be there until Monday and then he was heading back to London. Max missed not having his man around so much, but it made it all the closer when they were together. Their open relationship worked really well for them. They loved each other and were always confident about that, but they also loved sex with others and with strangers. The thrill and taste of another body was a craving they both had and they often compared stories of men they fucked. No strings was what they needed, so that intimacy and love would remain their own.

The weeks passed on and it was now mid-October and the autumn was fully setting in. The weather in Chicago was starting to chill, and the impending cold winter was on its way. Max loved Chicago, but he didn't like the winter. Minus twenty degrees centigrade during the day with biting winds was not his idea of fun. But he had a few weeks to not worry about that. His more pressing concern was Cole's performance.

Dimitri had discussed Cole's work and he wasn't cutting it. Gemma was running rings around him and had been promoted to Senior Marketing Manager, much to Cole's sadness and annoyance. Cole knew he was in trouble, and even Bobby couldn't help him. Marketing wasn't his field of expertise either.

Cole was pretty down and that wasn't helping his situation. Bobby tried his best to cheer him up, but he had no mojo. Even sex was getting less, as he felt so low. His boyfriend Bobby was excelling which only made it worse. He was happy for him, but it really rubbed salt in the wound. He had had a lot of help and support from the team, but nothing really improved. Cole knew it wouldn't be long before Max decided he had to go. Cole knew the drill he signed up for. Max and Peter were good people, but they wouldn't carry guys who couldn't deliver for them. Even if they were as sexy as him, he thought. Then again, he hadn't felt very sexy lately. Not being good at work, made him feel less as a person and less as a man. His confidence was well and truly shot.

At the end of the week, Max called Cole into the conference room. He had a stern look. Cole knew this was it. He took a deep breath, and went and saw Max. Bobby watched intently, with a massive knot in his stomach.

"Afternoon Cole," Max smiled. "I've called you in because we both know this situation isn't working for you or the business. The fit isn't right and I can see you have been miserable this last month."

Cole looked sad and acknowledged Max's words.

"Thank you Max for giving me this chance, I'm real sorry I wasn't good enough. It saddens me greatly, as I feel I've let you, Peter and Bobby down. The whole team."

Tears were welling in his eyes.

"So," Max continued, "it has taken me a while, but I have had to come to this decision Cole. I think it's the best for all……"

by Nick Christie

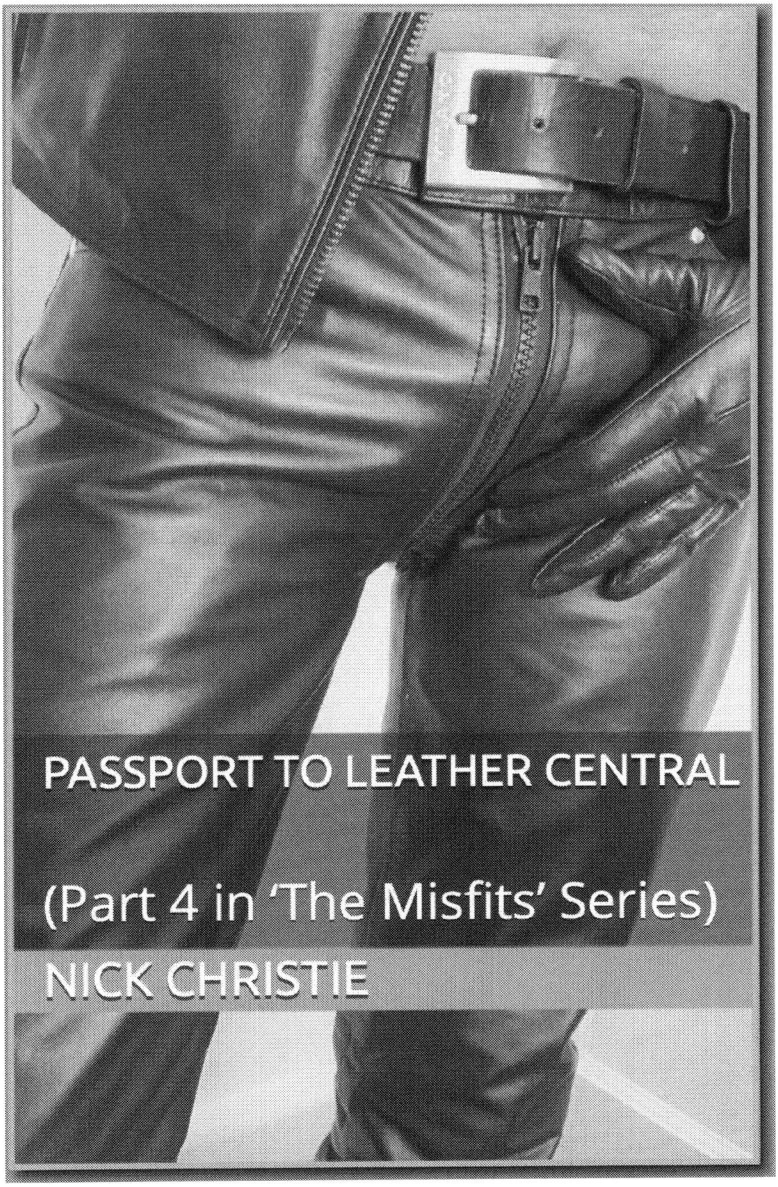
PASSPORT TO LEATHER CENTRAL
(Part 4 in 'The Misfits' Series)
NICK CHRISTIE

Passport to Leather Central

(Part 4 in 'The Misfits' Series)

(Erotic Gay Fiction)

Nick Christie

Chapter 1 - The End

Bobby watched Cole sitting, head down, opposite Max in the glass walled conference room. He felt so sad for his boyfriend, who was struggling in his role in Marketing. Bobby had been excelling in IT and that made it all the harder for Cole, and for Bobby. Bobby knew Cole was going to lose his job, it was always clear that Max could not carry people, he had given Cole all the help and chances to improve and sadly, he wasn't cutting it. Bobby felt he needed to look away.

Cole sat opposite Max in the room, staring deeply into the handsome man's eyes. Max had been so helpful to him, Bobby and all the team. He was excellent in bed too and Cole knew Max fancied him a lot, but he also knew that wasn't going to be enough to keep his job. He thought to himself, when I am fired, I must go gracefully, and thank Max. He wanted to keep in touch and also still have fun with him and Peter. He must not burn any bridges, he may be able to help in getting another job, who knows. He blinked out of the thought as Max started to speak.

"Afternoon Cole," Max smiled, "I've called you in because we both know this situation isn't working for you or the business. The fit isn't right and I can see you have been miserable this last month."

Cole looked sad and acknowledged Max's words. Max continued "So, it has taken me a while, but I have come to this decision Cole, I think it's best for all, you can't stay in marketing. You are miserable there and you aren't cutting it. That said I'm not giving up on you young man."

"What...?" said Cole.

"Cole, I want to try a new approach. I want to move you to sales, to work with Brad." Max paused, so Cole could digest what he had just said.

Max continued, "You would need two weeks intensive training, where you will spend a lot of time with him, shadowing his meetings. You must watch and learn and not interrupt in the early stages. Brad is very experienced and you could learn so much. Peter clocked the sales link well before me. He said from the beginning I had you in the wrong job. Let's try and prove him right. What do you say?" Max asked.

"Oh my God! I fucking love you! You are the best," Cole blurted out.

"Less of the love fella," Max laughed.

"I won't let you down, I promise. I want to help land loads more business for you and Peter and all the team. I want you all to be proud of me," Cole smiled. His posture more bold now.

Bobby could see through the glass something dramatic was happening. Cole was looking strong and majestic. He can't be fired he thought. What the fuck's happening?

"Now Cole, you will start as a Junior Sales Exec, which is lower paid, base wise, but you have commissions on sales to work for. Your basic will be $30k, you will have access to a pool car for meetings out of town and with commission, you could be making double base salary if you are good. So, two weeks training and then we will trial you in field for a month. If that doesn't work, it WILL be the end of the road Cole, you understand?" Max stated firmly.

"Yes sir. This time I'm not going to fuck up," Cole said.

He stood up and shook Max's hand. They both left the office and Cole strode out across the room towards Bobby. Troy looked up also and smiled at Cole. He was wonderful to see, 'The Majestic Cole'. It had been a while, with him being so down. That was the

Cole he missed seeing. The one he dreamed about one day fucking him hard, he knew he was with Bobby, but he could dream.

"Hey Bobby, I'm not going. I'm being transferred to sales for a final trial. Junior Sales Exec. It pays less basic, but I could get commission on top." Cole beamed.

"That's great news Cole, I'm so happy for you," he smiled and jumped up to give him a hug and a kiss. Bobby also whispered, "There's no 'could' get some commission, it's 'will', because no commission means no sale and no sale will mean no job I suspect."

"Yes, two weeks training and a month's trial. Make or break," Cole said.

Gina interrupted, "Cole, can you come over here please?" She waited for him to come to her desk. "Here is your new contract, read it and sign it by the end of the day. You start with Brad on Monday."

"Thanks Gina," Cole smiled.

Cole spent what was left of his last day in marketing with Dimitri and Gemma. They were kind and showed sadness that it hadn't worked out, but Dimitri knew he would be better in Brad's team. Gemma was sad to see her eye candy go as well, but Dimitri wasn't and was going to expect a 25% increase in output without Goldilocks as a distraction.

At the end of the day, everyone was starting to leave.

"Who's up for a quick drink in the bar on the corner?" said Cole.

"I'm in," said Bobby of course, but most people had plans and apologised.

“What about you Troy?” said Bobby to Troy.

“Me?” Troy said surprised. Being rather geeky and quiet he didn’t get much interaction with lots of the office team. “You want me to come?”

“Errr yes, that’s why he asked,” piped up Cole rolling his eyes.

“I’ve no plans, and never go out, so yes please,” he smiled.

They grabbed their jackets and headed for the door. In the elevator, Troy kept smiling at Cole, he smiled back.

“What you mean you never go out?” asked Cole.

Troy paused, “I don’t really have any friends in Chicago. I moved here for University and then got a job here. Being gay and geeky is not exactly a ticket to making friends, well not what I’ve found,” said Troy meekly.

“Man, that’s too bad. I’m sorry I should have asked you sooner, but you are real cute, I’m sure there would be plenty into a guy like you,” said Bobby.

“Cute?” said Troy.

“Yeah, I think with a cool haircut you would look awesome, I’m getting mine tidied up tomorrow. You wanna come with me and discuss a new look with our guy, Tony?”

“Errrr…yeah, ok, but I’ll need to understand fully what he plans to do,” said Troy reservedly.

The three walked out the building and down to the bar on the corner. They found a booth and ordered three beers and started chatting more about their lives and their backgrounds, including coming out. Bobby even touched on the previous relationship with Cole, which Cole sat through nervously, though Bobby skipped over how much of a bully he was to him and the night with Max earlier that year. Just implied he was gay and Cole the handsome jock, which of course wasn't lying. Cole was late to coming out.

Troy Jamison told them about himself.

"I was born in Idaho and have two proud, bookish parents. They helped put me through college and onto University. They don't know I'm gay, unless they guessed it, which they probably have. I came out at University, much good it did me never had a boyfriend. I'm twenty two, and I've never had a boyfriend," he sighed.

"Are you a virgin?" asked Cole.

"Hell no. I have loads of hook ups for sex, but no proper relationship. Dare I say it, I like it a bit rough and can be a bit kinky," Troy was getting more relaxed now chatting to his new work friends. He ordered more beers.

Cole got up, "I need a pee, that last one went straight through," he headed to the restrooms at the back.

"Sorry to say this, but I'd drink your boyfriend's piss all day," said Troy.

"I have on occasion," laughed Bobby.

"Christ, how did you manage to bag him? No disrespect you are fucking cute too, but he's such a sexy guy. I've been dreaming about him ever since you two joined," Troy replied.

"I got lucky and we made a connection. We are different which is why I think it works," said Bobby.

"I fucking love his hands. I could imagine his whole hand in my arse," Troy giggled. The beer was getting to him.

"You into fisting?" Bobby asked.

"Fuck yeah, and big cocks, dildos. When you are home alone at University, mail order cocks is all you can get for practice and they get bigger and bigger," he laughed.

Cole returned and they drank up, celebrating his job. After a third beer they decided to call it and night and go their separate ways.

"I'll be at Merchant & Rhoades, 900 North Michigan Ave at around 10.30 hope to see you there," said Bobby.

"Maybe," said Troy.

"Actually, I might get a tidy up ready for Brad on Monday. Yeah I'll be there too," said Cole.

Troy smiled and said goodbye.

Troy started walking and pulled out his phone and opened Grindr.

"I need to be fucked right now," he said out loud. The notification chimes started as he opened the app. "Oh hello Mr Yummy," he smiled.

Cole and Bobby walked home and picked up some groceries on the way, for their evening meal. Cole looked hot and frisky when they got in the apartment.

He put the groceries down and unzipped his flies.

"I got a new job, I'm horny, fucking blow me, 'cos I'm the Man!" he sang.

Bobby didn't need to be told twice, it had been so long since Cole was happy and in a good place. Sex had been non-existent this last month, except a few charity fucks that lacked any energy or connection. Bobby pulled off his jacket and got on his knees and took Cole's cock in one. He worked that bad boy with all the energy that had been missing this last month. Cole tasted awesome, he loved the taste of a man with a day's sweat and grime on him. He tasted real, manly, sexy, dirty and earthy. Cole's hands holding his head were strong and smelt of beer and grime also. Bobby, pull back and grabbed one and started licking it, his palms and his fingers. He stood up and pulled down own his pants.

"Finger me with those powerful hands," thinking of what Troy said, Bobby leant over the kitchen island counter. Cole spat on his fingers and did as he was told.

"Three fingers in," he said.

"Keep going," said Bobby, but he could only get 4 in up to his knuckles before Bobby said to stop.

Cole then pulled out and drove his dick in.

"That's more like it," Cole said.

He pounded Bobby on the counter, holding his head by his long fringe, his arse crack tasting fingers in Bobby's mouth. It wasn't long before Cole shot his load. A load that was a long time coming. It was big, thick and creamy, two weeks' worth possibly, all shooting up Bobby's rectum. Cole was still in his jacket and shirt, his trousers around his ankles.

He pulled out and groaned. Bobby turned around with a ranging hard on.

"Fucking blow me now. Let's get you in training. Start sucking and see how far you get," Bobby ordered.

Cole hadn't sucked cock yet, but he had wanted to suck Max's and yes, he needed some training. Now was as good a time as any. He stripped off his jacket and pants and got on his knees. He was eye level with Bobby's huge cock. It seemed even bigger at this angle. He held it at the base of the shaft and put the head in his mouth. It was dripping precum and tasted good. Yeah, it really did taste good. Fuck he knew how good being blown felt, but he never imagined cock would taste so good. He pulled back.

"Fuck that tastes awesome. What have I been missing?" he grinned.

"Yeah, so get back on it. Take it an inch at a time and relax the throat. It's hard to not gag without lots of practice and we are going get you in training. You may be training in sales for the next two weeks, but I'm gonna train you also in those two weeks. Train you in the art of sucking cock boy. Now keep going and pleasure my shaft with your hands. That's a good way to cover up that fact you can't fully down me yet."

Cole kept working but could only manage about three inches. But that was enough for Bobby. Seeing his jock school bully sucking his cock was amazing and made him wanna shoot.

"I'm cumin' Cole and you are gonna take it. Open wide and close your lips round. No wastage."

Bobby shot his load into Cole's throat and Cole could feel the spunk hitting the roof of his mouth, covering his tongue. It tasted good, similar to his own he had often eaten, but warm, straight from the tap. Bobby arched back as he shot his load and pulled out after. He looked down and saw Cole with cum dribbling from his mouth. He crouched down and kissed away the cum and licked his face.

"Think we better get washed up. I can feel that two week load moving down my arse," declared Bobby.

"You're such a dirty cunt Bobby, why did I wait so long to properly get to know you? I was such an ass."

"Hell, we found each other now right. Let's not forget, your nasty side was what attracted me to you, so without you treating me like shit, I wouldn't have been wanking myself to sleep each night dreaming of you fucking me hard and slapping me around," he stated as he ran to the bathroom.

"Fuck, Bobby, that's so fucked up," laughed Cole in a concerned way.

"Yep, we sure are," he replied.

Part 4 – Passport to Leather Central

Chapter 2 - Short back and sides

The following day, Bobby and Cole got up, showered and had a quick breakfast and then headed out to the barber to get their hair cut. They were just arriving, walking up the street, when Bobby said, "Good, he did come," seeing Troy standing outside. "I knew he would, when you said you were coming, Cole."

"Why, does he like me or something?" said Cole.

"Yes, dumbass. Are you blind? He can't keep his eyes off you. Told me last night, while you were in the bathroom, that he dreams of you fisting him. He's well kinky. Surely you've seen him staring at you?" Bobby said.

"Not really. He's so quiet, you hardly notice him."

"Well I plan to change that. I want to help Troy Jamison get more action."

"Hi Troy, how's you?" said Bobby.

"Ok. Hoped to get some cock last night but had two no shows. There are some real assholes out there. All talk and no fucking action. Anyway, let's go in."

They all went in and the place was quiet, which was useful seeing as all three were looking for haircuts. Bobby saw Tony.

"This is our friend Troy. I think he needs a makeover. What do you suggest?"

"Err makeover. I thought it was a trim," said Troy.

"Let's see what Tony thinks. Troy's a little shy, but I think under that mop is a good looking face and with a sharp new 'do' he could be real cute. What you think?" said Bobby to Tony.

Troy was 5'8" very slim with brown hair that looked like it was cut by his mother. Standard bowl cut, over the ears. Tony, moved in and felt his hair, lifted over his ears to check he wasn't having to disguise sticking out ears.

"I reckon you would look good with a short back and sides. Layered on top with a sharp side parting and keeping the length on top sweeping round," said Tony.

"I'm not sure," said Troy.

"I think that sounds real cool," said Cole, then he went in and whispered something in his ear.

"Ok let's do it," said Troy. He headed to the chair and Tony started cutting.

Cole and Bobby sat down and Bobby asked, "What did you say to him? He seemed very happy to have his hair cut after you spoke to him."

"I said, I reckon with a sharp haircut like that, I'd probably want to fuck him real hard," Cole laughed.

"Cheeky, don't tease him like that, unless you plan to," said Bobby.

"If he looks as hot as you, I might," Cole replied. He then got up as the next barber called for the next customer. "You want to have Tony, don't you?" he said to Bobby, "I'll go now."

Cole had a tidy up, noting that next time he would need to get his highlights redone, it could wait until then. He was finished at the same time as Troy, who was smiling.

"You've transformed me! Do I look stupid? Can I carry it off?" Troy asked.

Bobby smiled.

"That looks amazing. Your face is so cute, I knew you were good looking behind that hair and specs. The hair is perfect."

Cole grinned, "Who's the new hot boy in the office? It ain't me or Bobby. Way to go Troy. I may wanna give what I said a try."

Troy blushed feeling guilty. Bobby got in the chair and had his hair cut. Tony knew what to do without asking.

Cole said, "I'm gonna buy some new threads to look all salesman like. I'll see you later in the gym at 4pm," Cole kissed Bobby on the head, then regretted it after getting some stray hairs caught between his lips. They smiled.

"See ya sexy boy," he said to Troy, as he went through the door.

Bobby watched Troy through the mirror, watching Cole's arse and sighing and following him with his gaze down the street.

"I'll wait for you if that's ok?" said Troy.

"Sure," Bobby replied.

Bobby's hair was nicely cut. Real short back and sides and his floppy blonde mop fringe carefully trimmed. He liked the hair on top. It looked cool, but was equally perfect for being grabbed in rough sex. If there is a lot to grab it's easier to get purchase and because whoever grabs a lot, he doesn't end up with hair getting pulled out.

It was almost lunchtime.

"Wanna go down town and grab a bite? Also, are you a member of a gym?" asked Bobby.

"Yeah, that's why I look like this," Troy laughed, arms open showing his skinny wares.

"Why don't you come and have a visitor pass at ours? Cole and I are working out at 4pm. He could help you with a plan if you're interested, or you could just sit and watch Cole work out. He wears very tight shorts. That's how he got me started," he laughed.

"You don't mind that I fancy Cole, do you?" said Troy.

"No, who wouldn't. I have to expect that, he is beautiful. We are in an open relationship and we do play with others. We have a cool arrangement and it works," said Bobby.

"I'd love to see him in action and get some tips. I've noticed your body change since being at Bartholomew Steadman. I assume that was Cole?" asked Troy.

"Yeah, he worked out a plan for me and helps me with the heavy stuff," said Bobby

"Ok. Let's get some lunch and then I'll head back home and get some gym gear, or something that resembles it," said Troy.

"Well I have shorts and tops you can borrow. Just bring some sneakers."

They smiled and headed into town.

Chapter 3 - Gym buddies

Troy arrived at Bobby and Cole's apartment as arranged and rang the buzzer. Bobby answered and buzzed him up. He arrived at their door, which was ajar, and knocked on it as he made his way in. Troy was wearing jeans and sweatshirt as it was too cold to travel in shorts from his place. Bobby greeted him wearing satin shorts and a vest, which really showed his improving shape.

"You got any shorts I can wear?" Troy asked.

"Yes," said Bobby. "Cole, can you bring a spare pair of my shorts out with you?"

Cole came out of the main bedroom in the tightest shorts and vest showing every muscle and bulge he had, carrying a small pair of shorts for Troy. Troy couldn't stop staring at Cole as he passed the shorts. Troy pulled his jeans down and got changed.

"The gym is in the basement and we can come back here to shower later, saves taking towels and stuff to the gym showers," said Bobby.

"Ok gym buddies. Let's go work out," Cole announced heading for the door. The other two followed.

Cole discussed with Troy what he wanted to achieve.

"A body like yours," Troy laughed. "Or maybe like Bobby's."

"Mine will take years. I was training from a young age, but it is possible, done correctly without steroids but it will take some time. Bobby's level we could definitely start on. He developed that body in two months," Cole replied.

They entered the gym. Bobby went off doing his routine with his headphones on and Cole developed a set of reps for Troy and demonstrated them to him. Cole was a bit naughty and let Troy touch his muscles showing which ones would be working and then did the same back to Troy when he tried the exercise. Troy was mesmerised by Cole's body.

They all worked on their set programmes, sharing apparatus and helped each other. Troy was so happy to have found some new friends. Ones who had asked him to be friends, rather than him having to ask them. That was significant for Troy. So often he felt at school, he made the first move and then people were friends with him because they were sorry for him. Bobby and Cole asked him, he hoped this would last. He hadn't felt this good in a long time.

Troy spent much of the time doing his exercises watching Cole.

"You like what you see?" said Cole. Troy looked away and blushed.

"Hey, I wasn't mocking. Sorry."

"I do, very much. Your Bobby is very lucky," Troy added.

"I'm very lucky to have Bobby, he's helped me no end, I was a real ass to him at school," said Cole. "I'm just about done here," he added after finishing some final reps. They had worked out for an hour.

All three were glowing from the session. "Let's get upstairs and hit the showers and maybe we can do something about that boner of yours Troy," Cole laughed.

Troy looked down at the bulge in the shorts he borrowed from Bobby. He even had a precum stain showing.

"Oh shit," he put his hands over it.

"Let's go," said Bobby.

They got in the lift and Cole put his hand on Troy's bulge.

"Umm you are happy to see me," said Cole. Bobby laughed too.

"I think we can have a little fun if you're up for it Troy?"

"Yes, fucking please," said Troy as they burst out the elevator and down the hall to the boys apartment.

"Can I smell you Cole? Your sweat?" asked Troy once inside the apartment.

"Sure, go for it boy," Cole stood legs apart, pulled off his vest and then put his hands up behind his head, giving full access to himself. Troy felt his hard body and smelt his left armpit, then started to lick them. Cole grinned to Bobby. He moved to the other armpit and then down his chest, licking the beads of sweat off Cole. He knelt down and kissed his treasure trail, then buried his nose into Cole's shorts and crotch and inhaled his manly smell.

"Fuck you taste and smell amazing," Troy said. He moved over and held Cole's left hand and sucked the fingers. "Fuck I love your hands, I wanna be held down by those hands and fucked by them," he declared.

"Strip boy and we can see what we can do about that," said Cole. "I think we are gonna need the lube Bobby." Bobby grinned and went into the spare bedroom and came out with the tube. Troy was now naked and standing in front of Cole looking into his eyes. Cole moved in and grabbed him and threw him over his left shoulder in a fireman's lift. He was so light, thought Cole.

"You want my hands do you Troy?" said Cole.

"Oh please," Troy replied.

Cole grabbed and massaged Troy's buttocks whilst he was over his shoulder, feeling Troy's hard cock resting on his chest and oozing precum on his chest hair. Cole lightly stroked Troy's balls and the shaft of his cock, milking a few more drops of precum from Troy.

"Jesus, that feels awesome," moaned Troy over Cole's shoulder.

"Lube me up Bobby," Cole said, holding out his right hand. He ran the lube between his fingers and then brought his hand to Troy's expectant hole. He circled it. His hole was quite big already, Cole thought. This boy liked big things up here. Cole entered his four fingers with ease, slipping his hand in up to his thumb. Troy moaned with delight as Cole put his thumb in and then started a motion of feeling Troy's insides. He was starting a rhythm and Troy was groaning but a pleasurable groan. His cock was so hard now.

Cole walked around the apartment fisting this boy and laughing to Bobby.

"He feels amazing."

After a few minutes, Troy groaned loudly and Cole felt Troy's hot jizz pump down his chest.

"Bingo," Cole announced, gently pulling his hand out and letting Troy down to stand. Bobby wasted no time and licked the cum off Cole's body.

"Fuck that was amazing," said Troy. "You're so strong and just damn perfect."

"Let's get cleaned up in the shower," suggested Bobby.

The boys' apartment had a large bathroom with a shower over a good sized bath. Bobby got the water flowing and there was room for all to get in, just about. They lathered up and cleaned up. Bobby and Cole both getting hard and Troy took the chance to stroke them both.

"Wank us off," said Bobby. "Together."

They stood under the raining water and Troy knelt in the bath and wanked both at eye level, occasionally sucking the ends of both their cocks. Troy was impressed by the size of both of them. Both much bigger than his six inches. His technique was good and soon Bobby shot his load right into Troy's face and left eye.

"Bullseye," said Cole laughing.

He then took control and pushed his cock into Troy's throat and skull fucked him hard.

"Yeah boy you wanted it all afternoon, now you get it all."

Troy gurgled, but he was loving it. Being deep throated by this God was all he'd wished for this last few months. Cole pumped Troy's face and finally delivered his package, 'on time and in full', into the back of Troy's throat with his usual roar.

"Fuck yeah. Take that shit boy," he said pumping two last times, before pulling out and lifting Troy back up to his face. He then gave him a deep kiss, then turned round to Bobby, with some transferred cum in his mouth and kissed Bobby.

"Two for the price of one. Fuck!" said Cole smiling at Bobby, then reaching for the soap to finish his cock and balls.

Troy washed himself and they all got out the tub and dried off. The got dressed and sat in the lounge area. It was now 6.30pm.

"Fuck that was good," said Troy. "Thanks so much for that and sharing yourselves. You wanna go for a beer and a bite, my treat?"

"Yes let's. I'm hungry now," said Bobby.

"Me too," said Cole. They grabbed some coats and headed into town.

Chapter 4 - Manic Monday

Troy arrived at work to lots of whooping at his new hair and look. He'd bought some new clothes also. He was on cloud nine and was starting to love the positive attention.

Cole was starting his new job today and walked in the office with a real spring in his step. He had had an excellent weekend with Bobby and Troy. Now he was to starting his new role in sales. I really needed to make this a success he thought.

Brad met him as he arrived and showed him to his new desk position. The hot desks were used by sales as they were rarely in the office. Brad started to explain what was what.

"Ok Cole, you are going to be shadowing me for these two weeks and I also have you set to do a two day training course in sales, up State. That will be starting a week tomorrow. So this week you will have my company, ok?" he smiled.

"Yes sir. Teach me everything you know please," said Cole.

"I'll try," he laughed. "Now at Bartholomew Steadman, we deal in real estate a number of ways. We have smaller residential developments that we have built, housing estates and the like, which we sell direct to homebuyers. This will be where we start you after the training. Selling houses to families and couples. We also sell houses for other developers in a similar way. Finally we broker business properties and blocks. This is where the real money is. Working as a broker to sell high rises to large conglomerates. We take a percentage of the deal. That's the area I concentrate on and the sales team work on the smaller properties."

Brad said, "Let's get out there and see what's what," and they left and took the elevator to the car park in the basement. They headed past some silver Audi S3s.

"These are the pool cars you will have access to use when required. There are five within the team, if you perform well and need a car often, you could be offered a car permanently," he smiled. "This is mine," he said pressing the key fob and the lights flashed on a black Audi RS7.

"Fuck that looks awesome, like something out of Batman," said Cole.

The Audi had tinted glass and grey alloys. The car did look slick.

"Let's go see selling at work," Brad added, getting in the car and starting her up. The engine roared and purred as Cole got in the passenger seat. Red and black leather seats, Brad was obviously a bit of a lad, he thought. They drove out the parking lot and out into the crisp November air.

Cole spent that week watching and learning, questioning whys and whats with the team, getting a feel for the role. He noticed the best sales guys talked in a relaxed way with clients and didn't push too hard. Some used a harder approach and maybe got the sale, but the client looked less comfortable.

Brad detailed that, "It's important that the client feels he has got a win with the sale also. Win win. Make them feel as good about the sale as you will."

Cole completed his two weeks plus the training course and got good feedback on his performance. Brad sat down with Max and shared Cole's achievements. Both were happy for Cole to start selling homes on the Riverfield development, just north of Chicago. A selection of family homes and couples abodes. Cole started the following Monday. He worked with one of the other sales team but from Tuesday was on his own. There were thirty houses to shift, twenty four still remained. They had started selling these last week. They ideally wanted them all sold within three months.

Cole started receiving calls and arranged meetings with couples and families. His charm was notable. The ladies liked him and the men wanted to look like him. He had a knack of not making the boyfriends or husbands jealous that their partners liked him. He would sweet talk them about how good they looked together etc…. Within a fortnight he had sold eight of the properties, which was good going, and his discounts weren't generous. He was getting just shy of top dollar for these. They worked on a discount of up to fifteen percent off list if needed, but Cole never went lower than five, which was getting noticed at Head Office.

Two weeks in Cole could feel leads slowing. He called Gemma and asked about a social media push on the estate. "Aim it at newlyweds and offer ten percent discount on new houses on the first five customers to show they have just been married in the last six months. Run it to hit the newsfeeds on Sunday morning in the local area. Hit them while having a leisurely breakfast, looking at their phones," he requested.

It paid off. The phone was ringing again on Sunday afternoon and he took eighteen appointments for the next week. The first five got their discount and another eight he sold at a higher rate, emphasising they missed the promotion, but he could offer them a special extra deal of five percent. He even offered a Black Friday deal at the same rate just after Thanksgiving. By the end of the following two weeks he had cleared all twenty four houses.

This was a record, twenty four houses in a month. He came in the office on the Friday, with the completed sales paperwork for Gina and her team and Max came over and congratulated him.

“Well done Cole. You sold the lot and at an average of four point eight percent discount overall. Very impressive and so quickly. I liked the promotion too.”

“Thanks, the promotion gave people a sense of urgency, in case they were missing out to get in fast,” He said. “I also kept people informed at all times. Good communication, I feel, is important,” Cole smiled.

Bobby and Cole invited Bobby’s mother to join them in the apartment for Thanksgiving. She remembered Cole, but wasn’t aware he bullied her boy. He kept that quiet at the time. They had a lovely day and Cole cooked for them all. She was happy to see her son with someone and someone who was so handsome. She was also pleased that they had landed good jobs. It was a good day for all and Bobby was now able to help her with her rent and was using his money to pay her Medicare fees. This was something she had never had before and it worried Bobby. He was pleased he could now do that for her, in case she ever got sick.

Troy went to his family and Max stayed at home on his own. He didn’t really celebrate it as it was an American thing. He just enjoyed the time out to chill and listen to music. Christmas was his real celebration and he would be with Peter.

Cole was moved onto another housing estate sale with some of the other team, who were struggling. It was early Dec and a hard time to sell houses. Out of the blue, Brad called Cole and said, “I need you to come with me to a meeting at Trinity Enterprises in two days time. Meet me at the office later today at 4pm, I want to take you through the details.”

Brad and Cole met up and talked through the meeting. Trinity Enterprises was one of the groups Peter had introduced to Brad. Peter knew the acting CEO Cliff Boswell and Brad had been working with him to get a contract to be the Broker for them on all their property deals. This was huge and could deliver an annual income to Bartholomew Steadman of circa $15m. Brad had been working hard on this and they were in a tender with two other companies. The meeting was crucial. Max was to attend as well. Trinity Enterprises was owned by a man called Edmond Christy, who nobody ever got to see. He left his day to day business now to Cliff and his team and enjoyed the quieter life. Max had tried to get in contact with him, but never got past his personal assistant. He even wondered if he existed.

"So, wear your best suit on Thursday and clean your shoes. This is a watch and learn only," said Brad.

Thursday came, and Cole put on his best suit and shirt. Bobby had cleaned his shoes. He could almost see his reflection in them as he looked down. They got to the office early together. Max and Brad were ready to go at 9.30.

"Let's go Cole," said Max and the headed for the elevator. They walked to Brad's car.

Brad said, "Cole you drive, I want to discuss tactics."

Cole was surprised but loved the idea of driving the RS7.

Once they arrived at the offices, Max said, "Pull up outside and drop us off, and then go park under their offices."

Brad replied, "Yes, there is an elevator. Come meet us in the lobby."

They got out and went in the main entrance. Cole carefully drove the car into the underground parking lot. It was pretty full and he and one other were circling for a space.

Cole noticed the car because it was so old, an old Buick, but in great condition. It had to be about forty years old. The driver was a small old guy, who reminded Cole of Mr. Magoo, the cartoon character. He giggled. Cole noticed a space but felt sorry for the old guy. He had some time. I'll let him have that space. Cole wound down the window and beckoned the old guy into the space. He smiled and waved. Cole circled, and found a second space also. I'm sure the old boy must have passed this one, Cole thought.

Cole got out and locked up and headed to the elevator. He had to pass the old guy, who was struggling with some papers and a brief case from his trunk. Cole's hands were free, so he said, "Can I help you sir?"

"Oh yes," said the softly spoken man. He was quite short and hard to age. He could have been late seventies Cole thought.

"That is so kind. I do carry a lot of paper. I'm a bit old school. I like looking at numbers overnight, so take so much home. My wife goes mad if I leave papers at home."

He passed Cole his two cases and a large folder and carried two himself. He then locked the car with the key, the old fashion way. They both stood at the elevator waiting for the car.

"What are you here for?" the old man asked. "I'm coming with my Bosses to a meeting with Trinity Enterprises. We are hoping to close a deal. It would be great for us, as we are a small business and I'm new too," Cole replied.

"You like it at your company, what was it called?" He asked.

"Bartholomew Steadman, and yes I love it. Amazing company. The team really care for their employees, they really helped me get my first proper job when no one else would," the elevator finally arrived.

“I’m on twelve,” said the old guy. Cole pushed the buttons for the lobby and twelve.

“I’m Cole by the way.”

“Eddie. Very pleased to make your acquaintance young man.” The door opened at the Lobby.

Cole turned and said, “Are you going to be ok, you want me to come up to twelve and help you with those?” pointing at the cases.

“No, I’ll find some help up there, be sure of that, very kind though. I hope your meeting goes well,” and door shut.

“Thank you Eddie,” Cole shouted just as the door closed.

He met up with Max and Brad. “You took a while,” said Brad.

“Parking was difficult to find,” he replied.

“Right we are on,” said Max handing Cole a badge. “We are on the eleventh floor.”

They were greeted at the elevator and taken to a large glass walled board room and they set up for their pitch. Cliff Boswell arrived with three others. A gentleman and two ladies.

“Ok Brad, good to see you again.” They did their introductions. “You are the last to pitch and it’s all to play for,” said Cliff.

Brad lead the pitch, only supported by Max when asked, to keep consistency. Cole was in awe watching them both in action, absolutely in tune and slick, but not impersonal. After about thirty minutes, questions started, and Brad had all the answers. Bigger questions Max chipped in on. He looked like it was going well. Out the corner of his eye, Cole saw a small figure. It was the old guy walking past. He must be one of the accountants here. 'Ahh that's nice', he thought. The pitch was drawing to a close and the old guy was hovering outside and beckoned to Cliff.

"Excuse me gents," He left and went to chat with the old guy.

He returned in about three minutes.

"Can I introduce you to someone, he wants to meet you. This is Mr Christy our owner."

"Please call me Eddie," he said with a smile. It was the old guy. Edmond Christy shook hands with Max and Brad who introduced themselves and then he shook Cole's hand.

"Ahh we have already met, excellent asset to your business I imagine," Edmond said to Max and Brad's surprise.

Cliff continued, "Mr Christy and I are pleased to say you have won the tender, you were a close call with one other, but Mr Christy has swung it your way. He said he likes your business and team."

Eddie butted in, "I met this charming gentleman in the parking lot, who not only gave me his parking space, but helped me with all my papers and briefcases. He was very kind and thoughtful and sang the praises of the business he worked at. I then looked you up and liked what I saw. I also noticed I hadn't returned any of your calls, Mr Steadman, I do apologise for that. But this young man's kindness and vibrancy reminded me of many things. I hope you will look after him. He tipped the balance today, not wanting to take anything away as I understand the pitch was very good also. I'm glad we can do business together."

He smiled and shook hands again and left. Max, Brad and Cole said thank you to him and looked at each other.

Cliff said, "I'll get the contracts drawn up and over to you Brad tomorrow, and to get hold of Mr Christy is impressive." They said their goodbyes and headed for the lift to the parking lot.

"My god we did it," Max said. "Brad you did it, and Cole, well thank god you met him in the parking lot," Max laughed.

"I didn't know it was him, I thought he was an old guy in finance. He drove a forty year old Buick," said Cole.

"You didn't know it was him?" said Brad.

"No, he was just a sweet old man I wanted to help out," replied Cole.

"Fantastic work. You clinched this deal Cole, it could have gone easily to the other company," said Brad.

Brad drove them back to the office. They arrived and Max asked everyone to stop working. He announced the achievement and told the story. He praised Brad for all is work on getting to the tender and told Cole's part, to a round of applause. Bobby's clapping was the loudest and he was beaming.

Max asked Cole to the conference room once the celebrations died down.

"Cole I'm so pleased. You have excelled in sales. You have become our number one house seller and clinched the biggest deal for us, which is going to make us millions. Thank you, young man, for having good manners and respect."

"Thank you for not giving up on me and it really was Brad's deal, we must not take that from him," said Cole.

"Oh, he will be bonused handsomely and get all the credit, but you were the extra two percent that got us the deal. It's a great lesson, you can never be sure who you are talking too. Some people's appearances are not your expectations. I never thought Edmond Christy would look like him either," Max laughed.

The following day everyone was on a high. Max had delivered four cases of champagne to give to everyone to take home to share with their loved ones to celebrate over the weekend. This was a group win and would show in the coming year's share scheme. Max loved that everyone shared in the success, the juniors, everyone. Peter was told the news by Max on the day and was jumping around the room with excitement. He was also pleased Cole played a part and his recommendation to move him to sales was paying off.

Christmas was going to be awesome this year they thought and the office party was just around the corner. Gina organised the event. All the Chicago team were invited, along with partners. If you didn't have a partner you could bring a friend. It was six days before the party, which was to be held in the Howl at the Moon music venue. They were taking it over for the night on a Thursday and it was a meal and music, dancing and late night drinking. It was going to get messy, so Max agreed that the Friday would be a write off, and told people to not worry about coming in.

"It's a sleep it off day," he laughed. No meetings were booked for the afternoon of the Thursday or the Friday.

Troy was a little down as he had no one to take.

"You can come with us. A threesome," Bobby laughed. Then he thought. "What if I got you a blind date?" he said.

"Hell no, on a works event? That could be a disaster," said Troy.

"Or fantastic. We know a guy who rented us our apartment. Real cute guy called Jamie. He's a similar build to Cole, bit smaller. Sexy. How about you meet him before if he's interested?"

"Oh, Ok. Let's see if he's interested," Troy smiled, being around Bobby made him more willing to be bolder.

Bobby got on the phone.

"Hi Jamie, it's Bobby. You remember us, Bobby and Cole, you rented us an apartment? Yes, THAT Bobby and Cole. You still looking for love?" he laughed. "Uh huh... yeah.... time wasters the lot of them. Yeah.... I know.... fuck wits. Well how about going old school? No apps, a proper blind date. I have a good friend, who's real cute and is looking for a lovely guy and I thought of you instantly. I think you'd be perfect for each other, what do you say? Uh huh.... Yeah.... no no, he's real cool. Yeah..... uh huh."

Troy was listening rolling his eyes thinking this was now a bad idea.

"Cool, you won't regret it. We will see you in Cell Block at 7pm tomorrow evening. A double date. Cheers Jamie. Bye." Bobby hung up. "Done. You'll be with us and you can see how it goes."

"Flaming hell, that was all a bit quick. I hope he's nice. Got any pics?" asked Troy.

"No," said Bobby, "But you can try stalking him on facebook. Jamie Stewart, works at Hendry Properties. He may be on their website." Troy swivelled round and started typing at his keyboard.

"Later lover boy," said Freddie who had been listening in. Let's get on with some proper work. You can fix up your love life later."

Part 4 – Passport to Leather Central

Chapter 5 - Date Night

The following Saturday evening, Cole and Bobby arrived at Cell Block to find Troy already waiting for his date. Troy was looking pretty sharp in a nice pair of dark blue jeans, pointed brown boots, a check blue shirt and a smart blue fitted sports jacket. His hair was on point and he was smelling good too.

"Look at you Mr," said Bobby. "Hot to trot."

Bobby did actually think Troy looked very cute. The handsome young face he had noticed on day one, was now on show under a great haircut. His twinkling eyes behind the bookish glasses added to the appeal. A real sexy nerd, who wasn't actually a nerd, but a real dirty fucker.

"You are looking smart, I think it should be an awesome date," Cole backed up.

"I hope you're right. Been pretty nervous. I'm never like this on a hookup, but this seems different," Troy said.

"Let's get some beers," said Cole.

He went to the bar, returning with three Buds. As he did, the door opened and in walked Jamie, wearing army cargo pants, boots, a tight T-shirt and a leather alpha industries bomber jacket. He looked around and saw Cole and smiled and waved. Cole pointed to the beers.

"Yes please," said Jamie. Cole asked for another.

Troy watched as a handsome army type guy walked in. Not too tall, but solidly built.

"I hope this is him," he joked with Bobby wishful thinking. Bobby looked round to see.

"Hi Jamie, over here," said Bobby grinning.

"Fucking Hell! Really? He's so hot, he won't be interested in me," protested Troy.

"Trust me. Just be your fun self and don't try and be someone you're not," said Bobby.

Jamie came to the table and instantly approached Troy.

"Hello, you must be my blind date, I'm Jamie and I have to say, you are very easy on the eye," he was smiling broadly.

Troy beamed with the fact that Jamie seemed to like him and complimented him on his looks. Something people rarely did.

"Hello, I'm Troy and I'm very pleased to see you too."

They all sat down, Jamie opposite Troy, Bobby next to Jamie and Cole opposite. They started to chat and drink their beers. Cole and Bobby instantly noticed Troy and Jamie couldn't stop looking at each other. They also decided to keep their conversation to a minimum, only adding to it when needed to keep the momentum going. After a while they decided they were not needed. Troy and Jamie were so into each other, Cole and Bobby looked at each other and nodded.

"Ok you guys we are going to leave you to it, if that's ok. We have dinner booked," said Bobby.

"Err ok," Troy smiled. "You ok with it being just us two," he said to Jamie.

"Perfect. Glad to see the back of them," he laughed. "I'm joking, but thanks."

Cole and Bobby got up and left. They both looked back as they went through the door. Neither Troy or Jamie looked at them, they were too busy chatting.

"How cool was that," said Cole. "I didn't think they would fit."

"Yeah, just like us," said Bobby.

"Ummm you have a point. Hope it goes well," said Cole.

Bobby and Cole went for some dinner and discussed finalising their outfits for the Christmas party next week.

The following Monday, Troy came in the office, practically bouncing. He sat down quickly next to Bobby and told him everything.

"Oh my God, he's wonderful, so interesting and fucking sexy too. We had another beer and then got some food. We chatted all night and we have so much in common. At the end of Saturday night, he held me and kissed me, so good. I wanted to have him then, but we didn't fuck on the first date. I thought he was so sweet and I didn't want to ruin it or something. We met for a walk in Millennium Park on the Sunday which was lovely. I've asked him to be my plus one on Thursday and he's said yes. I'm going round to his tomorrow night for some dinner. He cooks for fuck's sake. My God I've got to have him in me tomorrow. I can't wait any longer."

"Wow that sounds so good. I'm so pleased Troy," said Bobby.

"Thanks Bobby. Dare I say it, but I think I'm in love?" Troy laughed.

"Don't scare him off with that," laughed Bobby.

The working week passed quickly and it was soon the morning of Thursday, the day of the party. Everyone was buzzing with excitement for the night's events. Those that had been before spoke highly of Max's parties and they were real fun and not stilted, which made the new people even more excited. Bobby and Cole were two of those excited newbies.

That morning Max got a call from Peter. It initially started with pleasantries then Max went quite silent, listening and then responding. He transferred the call to one of the meeting rooms, for some privacy. He was in there for about fifteen minutes. When he came out he called Gina and Freddie into the office.

He sat them down and said, "Ok, that was Peter. London have encountered a major IT error. They are having to run off the mirrored system in Berlin, but it's terribly slow. They had some patches done by the company they usually use but the main programmer they always relied on is on long term sick and it would appear someone else has fucked it up. They are struggling to sort this. We need to get someone over there to help them Freddie."

"Well, I'll give Brian a call in London and get an idea of the situation and come back with a recommendation in an hour," said Freddie and he got up and left the room.

"Gina, can you look at some flights for Friday or Saturday to London. I'll go with whoever needs to go. It would be nice to see Peter and see what the real damage is. I may even stay through to Christmas as it's only ten days away. I was flying out the following Thursday, so will need to adjust my flights to, please."

Freddie got off the phone and asked Bobby, "Have you got a passport Bobby?" So many Americans don't have passports as they tend to rarely travel abroad.

"Yes, I have. Why?" he replied.

"Let me chat to Max and then I'll let you know."

Freddie got up and headed over to Max's desk. "Ok, Max, I've spoken to Brian in London and they have got a real problem with the coding in the programming. Seems someone made changes and they are struggling to get them back to how they were without affecting other elements. I suggest that Bobby goes to London with you, he is the best coder here and he understands the systems well. He has a passport, I asked." said Freddie.

"Ok, let him know, we will get the next flight out," said Max.

Gina added, "Saturday is the best I can get you."

Freddie went back to Bobby.

"I need you to fly to London with Max on Saturday."

Freddie explained the coding issues and what had happened. Bobby was very excited at the thought of going to London. He couldn't wait to tell Cole. He was out selling and would meet him later when they got ready for the party.

"Ok Bobby's fine and happy to go," said Freddie to Max. "We will hold the fort here."

It was now mid afternoon and people were finishing up to go home to get ready for this evening. Max called Peter and said he and Bobby would be coming over on Saturday to help sort him out.

Peter remarked, "That Bobby can sort me out alright, shall we put him up in the spare room?"

"Yes, but normally you don't like others staying?" said Max.

"I'll make an exception for that one. Is he still up for playing? If yes, bring some gear in his size. I need a good hard fuck from both of you handsome men. It's been a bit dry over here."

"I'll find out, but he's pretty loved up with Cole," said Max.

"Shame he can't come with you," said Peter.

"Can't justify it and it's supposed to be a business trip to sort out the problems at the office. Or have you forgotten?" said Max curtly. "Gina will send the flight details. Can you get a car to pick us up?"

After some further small talk Max hung up.

"Ok," he shouted out to the office. "Why are you lot still here? Go home, get your glad rags on and get ready to party. Those that feel they must come in tomorrow do, but I really don't expect it and if you do, try and only crawl in in the afternoon. Ok I'm off, see you all later with your significant others and/or friends, or both."

Max grabbed his coat and headed for the door.

Chapter 6 - Let's get this party started

Bobby was in the shower when Cole arrived home. He stripped off and decided to join Bobby.

"Hello sexy. Did I catch you stroking your dick? Let me give you a hand with that."

Cole climbed into the shower and kissed Bobby, while holding his semi hard cock. They kissed hard under the running water and Bobby got harder. Cole then knelt down and took Bobby in his mouth and gradually sucked deeper and harder.

He had been practicing more with Bobby and getting good, learning to deep throat without gagging too much and enjoying the taste of cock more and more. Cole had hidden his real desires away for many years and struggled with being gay, acting macho and dating girls to put the thoughts behind him. Often beating up 'fags' to prove he wasn't one. Something he was pretty ashamed of now. What he had done to Bobby in the past. Even on their reunion, he was mean and nasty. But, in a crazy way, Bobby enjoyed Cole's dominant bully side. He found him so sexy when he was like that Cole only did it with permission, he hated hurting Bobby now. Bobby had been the best thing to happen to him in years. In his life for that matter. That and meeting Max on that strange violent sexy night. Now he was in a relationship, with a great job and enjoying so much cock, as much as he could get, Bobby's or others.

Cole was thinking of all this, with Bobby's cock in his throat, when suddenly he felt five belts of cum hit the back of his throat. He looked up at Bobby covered in water, smiling with pleasure. Bobby tasted good. The salty spunk was now held in his mouth. He stood up and kissed Bobby with the full load in his mouth, a spunk kiss. Bobby's favourite. They kissed hard, passing the load from mouth to mouth and then finally swallowing a share each.

"So, fucking hot," said Bobby, as he started to soap Cole's body.

Cole was now hard from the kissing and Bobby started to kiss and wank him, rubbing soap all over his body. Bobby turned Cole round and started fingering Cole's arse, with the soap as lube, while wanking him off.

As he fingered his prostate, Cole erupted and shot his load all up the tiles of the shower, roaring with pleasure as his cock spilled its load. He turned around and then kissed Bobby sensually, the water streaming down on them as they held each other.

Cole showered his spunk off the wall and they giggled and smiled at each other.

"Come on lover let's get dry and start getting ready, I also have some news," said Bobby.

As they were drying off Bobby said, "I've gotta go to London on Saturday for business."

"What? How and why?" said Cole.

"They have an IT fuck up in London and are struggling with the code. I have to go Saturday to help sort it out. Max is coming too, so I won't be alone."

"How long Bobby? Can I come?"

"Max is staying and I hope to be back mid-week. I'll be home for Christmas. It's not a holiday, but gotta say I am excited. It's lucky I had a passport, but I will miss you. It would be great to travel with you," replied Bobby.

"Yeah, damn I don't have a passport. That's not good is it for short notice trips? Will you miss me?" Cole asked.

"Of course. Traveling with you would be awesome. I think you should get a passport sorted asap, so you will be ready for any future opportunities and we also should think about holidays. Hell, we get plenty of days with Bartholomew Steadman, so we could go abroad," said Bobby.

"Yeah, you're right, I'll get on it. You're gonna have so much fun fucking all those cute British boys. I want details when you get back, and during. Show them we American boys fuck best," said Cole.

Bobby was pleased how Cole had taken the news. He was concerned that he would be upset. He was equally glad he was happy for him to fuck while away too, which he assumed also meant he was likely to do the same.

"I also want chapter and verse on who you plough while I'm away," smiled Bobby.

"Maybe we should find some fun tonight at the party. Bet there are some bar staff up for some action," said Cole grinning. "Let's get ready."

The boys had planned their outfits well. They both were wearing a stylised dinner suit, with a twist. They had white dress shirts with black satin dinner jackets, but their trousers were leather jeans, slim, black and tight. No underwear, to feel the leather, and make it easier for any action later. They had matching leather ties and belts too. Both were also wearing white vans sneakers with the leather jeans. The combination looked awesome. Both had recently had their hair refreshed colour wise. Bobby's blond hair was white blond, and Cole had had his highlights redone and trimmed. They both looked spectacular.

They wore matching scent, CK1. Though they were wearing the same outfits, their size and shape difference really worked, and they looked original in them.

"Let's get to that party," said Cole kissing Bobby on the nose.

They got an Uber to Howl at the Moon and were welcomed at the door of the venue by Max who was greeting every arrival. Making everyone feel special, that's what Max did so well. He even memorised all the names of people's guests. That was a great touch, saying hello to Gemma and Vince, her new boyfriend as they arrived, just in front of Bobby and Cole. She smiled at Cole and grinned at their jeans.

"You boys look adorable and very sexy. Hey Vince, can I convince you to get some leather pants?" she laughed.

Vince, who was medium build, wearing an off the peg slightly ill-fitting suit, grinned nervously and looked away without answering.

They all went inside and looked like they were among the last to arrive. The bar was buzzing and decorated like a winter wonderland. Bobby and Cole got drinks and started working the room to say hello to everyone.

Troy and Jamie were at a table, looking adorable, both in black suits. Soon it was time to eat and find tables. Gemma dragged Vince in their direction.

"Can we sit with you four. That would be cool," she said.

"Yeah sure, but don't be shocked by the conversation, you are now on a table with four queers and we don't tend to hold back," said Bobby with a grin.

"Oh, that's fine with me. Vince you Ok?" she said.

“Of course,” Vince said nervously, under his mop of hair.

The tables were set for eight and the six sat down. They weren’t sure who else would join them. Max and Gina sat with Freddie, and some of the admin team. Dimitri sat with some of the sales guys.

“Where’s Brad?” said Cole. His boss wasn’t in the room.

The door suddenly opened and Brad rushed in. Hands up in apologetic stance. He looked so different out of a suit. He was wearing dark jeans, square toed cowboy boots and a blue shirt, with a neat brown leather jacket on. Cole couldn’t stop staring at his boss. He looked really hot, something he hadn’t properly noticed before. He knew Brad was handsome, but tonight, he saw him a new light.

Cole whispered to Bobby, “Damn he looks fine.”

Bobby whispered back, “Remember he’s your boss and I’m not sure if he’s straight or not, but yes he does look friggin’ hot.”

Brad was on his own and was looking around the tables for a space. He glanced at Cole and smiled and then saw the space.

He walked over, “Is this a spare space?”

“Yeah sure,” said Cole. Brad smiled and noticed the leather jeans on Cole and looked him back in the eye and then winked.

“Thanks. Hello to you all. Have you all been introduced? I’m Brad, by the way,” he shook hands with Vince and Jamie as the guests.

“No plus one?” said Gemma.

“Nah, I’m young free and single, just how I like it,” he laughed.

They all started to chat as the food came around along with wine and anything they wanted to drink.

Halfway through the meal the Christmas music stopped, and two guys got up on the stage in the middle of the venue and started playing the two pianos. They were joined by a drummer and two singers. They started taking requests and playing some great tunes. It was like duelling pianos at some points.

Between courses people started to get up and dance. One of the piano players was really cute and kept looking over at Brad and then Cole and those jeans. Bobby and Cole danced together and looked so fit in their tight leathers.

Max came up to Bobby and whispered in his ear, "Be sure to pack those jeans, Peter would love to see you in those."

Bobby thought and smiled. Wow, he would see Peter again. Man, this London trip keeps getting better.

Brad sat down for a rest as did Cole. Bobby headed to the bar.

Brad pointed and said to Cole, "That piano guy is very cute. I wonder if he's gay."

"Judging by the way he's been staring at yours and my arse, I'd say yes. Why? Are you interested?" said Cole.

"Yeah I am," he smiled back.

Cole was only joking and hadn't realised Brad was gay. "Oh, I didn't know you were gay," he stammered.

"Technically I'm Bi. I like women too. But guys are easier for casual flings, which is what I like. I'm not into commitment at the moment, if you weren't spoken for, I'd be hitting on you, my sexy star seller," he laughed.

Cole put his hand on Brad's thigh, "Just name a time boss. We are open and you are making me hard. As long as it doesn't make work messy. But while Bobby's in London and if you are at a loose end, I'd be up for some fun."

Brad put his hand on Cole's strong leather thigh, "I may take you up on that." He then got up, and said, "Gotta pee."

Brad winked at the piano man as he got up and he winked back. He was in. He filled in a song request form. It said, "When are you on a break? I need to blow you."

He wrote his cell number on the paper too, and then pushed it onto the piano in front of him. The guy grabbed it before it got taken into the real requests pile.

Brad stood at the urinal and pulled out his semi hard cock and started to pee. He heard someone come in and Cole stood next to him, unzipped and took out his large cock to pee. Cole looked over and smiled at Brad who was looking at his beauty. Cole had deliberately pulled his cock and balls out of the zip, to present all his finery. And it looked so handsome in those leathers. Brad looked around, no one was in sight, he moved closer and held it.

"Man, that's tidy. You lucky, handsome fuck."

Someone entered the restroom. It was Vince. He moved into a space and started to pee. Brad and Cole both tried to subtly get a look, but Vince was self-conscious and slightly turned away. Brad and Cole forced they growing dicks back in their pants and washed up and left.

"Having seen that beast, I'm may take you up on your offer," said Brad as they moved into the noise of the room.

The musicians finished a song and announced they were off for a thirty minute interval, as the DJ started. Brad felt a buzz in his pocket. Text message <You have 20 minutes. Come via the staff door now.>

"I'm in with piano man," Brad nudged Cole, "See you later." Cole watched Brad head for the staff door.

Brad walked through and followed the corridor round to find a door open with people chatting. He stood at the door and saw the piano man with the others. He got up, approached and grabbed Brad and took him to a side room. He shut the door on what seemed to be a cleaning cupboard. Piano man unzipped his jeans and started stroking his cock.

"Get to it cowboy."

Brad wasted no time and grabbed his cock and stroked it. He then knelt down and took him fully. He was six inches hard and easy to blow. He tasted good. Hot crotch, sweat and a hint of piss. Nice and salty. Brad was grabbing his arse to get deeper and piano man held his head. Brad pulled at his zip to allow him to get his hand under his balls and to finger his arse as he serviced his dick. He was groaning with pleasure. Brad pulled off and stood up and started to wank him hard, kissing him on his neck. Piano man started to groan louder and Brad concentrated on jerking him hard and then watched as six ropes of cum shot out over the floor and onto some floor cleaning bottles.

Brad then unzipped his jeans and pushed him down on his released cock. With no mercy, he forced himself into his throat. He pumped that skull hard, holding his head. Piano man grabbed his arse and took it. Brad didn't take long, he filled that man's throat with cum almost instantly and piano man swallowed it all.

He gasped, coming up for air, "Fuck that was nice. I've been watching you and the guy in the leather pants. So hot the pair of you. Any chance of being sandwiched between you two any time soon?" he asked.

"We'll have to see. What's ya name piano man?" Brad asked.

"Josh," he replied.

"Well Josh, that was great and I have your number."

As they got up, Brad smeared the spunk on the floor with his cowboy boot, to try and disguise it. Brad leant in and licked some spunk off Josh's chin.

"You missed a bit. Don't want you to go out doing a second half with cum dribbling down your face," he laughed as he left the room.

Brad was always in control and left the proceedings without a blink of an eye. Cole had been watching the staff door for ten minutes when it opened and Brad strode out with a real swagger. 'He's fucking had him. So cool,' he thought.

"Any good was he?" said Cole smiling.

"Not bad. But he'd like to be spit roasted by both of us," Brad replied, leaving for the bar to get a drink.

"What you planning Cole Peterson?" said Bobby smiling. He had been watching the body language of the situation in the noisy bar. Cole told him everything and they both looked at Josh when he came out for the second half of their performance.

"Just be careful while I'm away Cole. He is your Boss. Don't make it complicated. I know we have done stuff with Max and Peter, but they are very clear on the boundaries. Be sure of them before you get involved."

"You're right Bobby, I'll have a think."

Cole thought for a while. Bobby was right to be careful. Work and sex could make matters complicated. But they had done so much already. Max, Peter, Troy and Jamie. He'd have to check that Brad was gonna be cool with no strings, inside or outside work.

By midnight, everyone was pretty drunk. Troy and Jamie were snogging in the booth. As was Gemma and Vince. Cole and Bobby were separately circulating and chatting with everyone. People kept stroking their leathers. They fascinated so many straight people. Bobby thought, they should just embrace leather jeans. They looked so hot on people with confidence to wear them.

By 1.30am people were starting to leave. Bobby found Cole, almost asleep, pulled him up and said goodbyes to the people he passed. He waved at Max, who was drinking with Gina, and took Cole outside. He found the Uber he called and folded Cole into the back seat.

Somehow, he managed to get Cole back to the apartment and into the bedroom and lay him on the bed. He took his jacket and shirt off and revealed that beautiful hairy torso. He pulled off his vans and then unzipped the fly of his leathers. Out popped a nice boner. Cole was almost asleep now, but Bobby couldn't resist. That cock surrounded by leather, he pulled his own clothes off except his jeans and lay on Cole. Leather on leather. His thighs on Cole's shins as he swallowed that awesome cock. It tasted of leather and precum. He pleasured Cole, who was out for the count now. Bobby enjoyed it and pumped him, until he came in his sleep. His second load tonight was thinner and more bitter, but still fucking yummy thought Bobby. Oh, how he loved cum, especially Cole's cum.

He rested and then stripped Cole and himself and got into bed beside him and turned out the light.

Chapter 7 - London Calling

The day after the party, Max woke with a sore head at around 8am. He got in, he recalled, at about 3am, after the last of his team had left. It had been a good night, but he had drunk too many cocktails. Max headed towards the en-suite and took a piss. A good long piss. He looked down at his semi hard cock and gave it a stroke. 'I love my cock' he thought. He reached into the cabinet and got some pills for his head. He drank them down and strolled back to bed holding his cock, which was getting harder by the minute. 'A good wank is what I need' he thought. Losing a load was a great way to release the tension of a headache. Max had done it many times. Any excuse for a wank.

He pleasured his cock pulling the foreskin back and forth. He spat on his hand and lubed up the head and thought about last night. The young guys he would love to have fucked. So many but all out of bounds really. The exception being Cole and Bobby, he'd enjoyed them many times. They both looked hot in their matching outfits and those leather pants. Bobby's new body was also looking very good. He imagined Bobby in just his leather pants standing over him on the bed. Stroking his cock above him. Yeah milking his own cock all over Max. That's what he was thinking, as he released a good load all over his stomach and chest. Fuck yeah, I wanna play with Bobby in London for sure. This is going to be a good trip Max smiled.

Cole awoke with a pounding head. Bobby was awake next to him staring at him.

"What you doing?" Cole asked with one eye barely open.

"Watching my sleeping beauty," he replied.

"Fuck I don't feel beautiful," Cole said and rubbed his body and crotch, to find some sticky remnants of cum in his pubes.

"What the fuck. What happened last night? I don't recall getting off with anyone," he enquired.

"YOU didn't, but you were barely conscious, with a huge boner, so I took advantage of you," smiled Bobby.

"Naughty boy. Was I good in the sack even unconscious?" Cole checked.

"You can still cum, but that's all you did, I did all the real work," Bobby laughed. "Drink this," Bobby was holding a glassed of fizzing clear liquid. "That should help. No work today and I need to think about what to take to London."

It was a lazy day for all. Everyone stayed at home. Max took some calls and made some calls. Gina directed the office calls to her mobile, so not to miss anything and Cole stayed in bed and watched TV, while Bobby paraded around the room trying on different gear.

"I've gotta take the leather pants, Max asked me to," said Bobby.

"You're so gonna get spit roasted by Max and Peter. You know that don't you," said Cole.

"I'm fucking counting on it," he laughed.

"We got so much attention in those pants last night. It's crazy. Leather pants do feel so sexy on. The feel on your legs, then when you place your hand on them that feeling is awesome too. And the smell that rises. I can see why Max is so into it. I get it now. At some point we should save up and get some more, I'd love a cool jacket, a good one," Bobby added.

"I agree. The feeling is immense. I had a boner most of last night. Just a shame I wasn't conscious to get the benefit of the happy ending," Cole giggled.

Max sent a text to Bobby with the details of the flight and said to be ready at 4pm the next day. The car would pick him up then. Bobby sent a text back <Ok, can't wait>. He then sent <Bring any gear you wish me to wear, I'm up for it> after he pressed send, he shook his head. I shouldn't have sent that he thought. He sent another. <Sorry, that was inappropriate I do understand this is a business trip> send.

Max replied. <It is business, but we can have some fun. See you tomorrow.> Phew thought Bobby.

After getting Bobby's text Max went to his walk in wardrobe of gear and had a rummage for half an hour selecting some choice items. He was going to need two cases he thought.

Saturday morning, Bobby started to sort his clothing for the trip. He packed a suit, in case he needed one, shoes and ankle boots. Jeans shirts and casual jackets. By mid afternoon he was set. At 3.45 he got a text from Max who said he was on his way. Bobby decided to be a tease and wore his leather jeans, with Adidas hi top trainers, long sleeve T-shirt and his fleece lined Levi denim jacket. He also wore his tight leather gloves, that Cole gave him, to complete the outfit. He had his work bag, laptop and passport. He decided he best wait downstairs in the lobby of the building to be ready. Cole smiled at him.

"You look cute and sexy. I'm gonna miss you buddy. I'll come down with you and see you off."

He carried Bobby's case for him and followed him to the elevator in his sweatpants and T-shirt. Inside the elevator, he kissed Bobby tenderly with his strong hands cupping his pretty face.

"I really will miss you. You have been such a wonderful boyfriend. I can't believe how lucky I am and how differently I feel about you."

"Christ Cole! I'm not leaving forever. I'm only going for four days! You be good, or if you can't be good, be careful," said Bobby kissing him on the nose.

"You too and bring me something nice back from London," Cole replied.

They waited at the window. The cold outside looked biting and Cole could feel the draught coming from under the door, only having a T-shirt on. A black Mercedes pulled up.

"This must be him. I'll text you when I arrive," said Bobby.

He kissed Cole again and opened the door to the biting wind. The driver got out and opened the trunk and put his case in. Bobby got in the back and waved at Cole.

Max saw them both standing at the window as he pulled up. Nice and prompt, he thought. Good lad. He watched him walk out, in his leather jeans and smiled, looking down at his own pair he had on. Bobby got in the car.

"Afternoon Boss, jeez it's cold," he grinned.

They both waved goodbye to Cole as they pulled away.

"Great minds," said Max, putting his hand on Bobby's thigh. Bobby grinned, putting his leather gloved hand on Max's thigh.

"You told me too sir and I always do what my boss tells me to."

Max was wearing smart ankle boots and a black suit style jacket with his leather jeans. A real cool look Bobby thought.

The drive took about forty minutes to the airport, which gave Max time to discuss the plans for the next few days. They would arrive Sunday morning and, depending on how they were feeling, they could go to Peter's office on Sunday. Brian was there round the clock trying to fix or patch stuff. Depending on how things worked the times would have to be flexible. Bobby said, "I'll do whatever it takes to sort the problem."

So once that was discussed, Max said, "Ok 'til we get to London, we can stop thinking about work and enjoy whatever we find at the airport or on the plane."

"Meaning?"

"Oh, there are lots of men travelling alone who are up for fun at the airport or on the plane. You with your looks will have your pick, I can tell you and leather jeans I find are the best signal to all the closeted gay men out there that you are available for fun. Peter and I always travel in leather jeans, works every time," Max smiled.

The driver pulled up and got the three bags out the trunk. Max thanked him and smiled.

"Two bags?" said Bobby.

"Well I'm staying for Christmas and I've also bought you some gear for any downtime. You did ask," Max smiled.

They headed for the check-in desk. Max asked for Bobby's passport and they headed to the fast track aisle. Bobby looked at the queue to his right. He felt a bit strange getting fast track treatment.

A male attendant was on the desk.

"Hello Mr Steadman," he said looking at his passport. "We have you booked on the 19.15 to London and we have you in Club World Business. As a Gold customer and frequent flyer, I would like to upgrade you to First. Is that Ok?"

"And my colleague too?" Max said passing Bobby's passport.

"Oh, let me see," said the attendant, "Unfortunately, we only have one spare seat in First"

Max sighed, "So why did you suggest it? You can see I am travelling with someone."

"I'm sorry sir, my mistake. You are right," said the attendant red faced.

Bobby said, "You take it Max. I'll be fine in Club. Believe me," Bobby smiled.

"No, we will stay in Club together. We have a duo, yes? We have lots to discuss," said Max.

"Yes, at the back, as booked," said the attendant.

"Perfect, my colleague is flying back on Thursday. Can we see that he gets the benefit of this mishap on his return journey?" Max asked.

"Will he not be with you?"

"No, I assume that won't be a problem, as it is purchased on my account," said Max forcefully.

"It's not normal sir."

"No, it's not normal, but also dangling First class to only take it away isn't normal either."

"Sorry, no that's not normal. There is space, and I have changed Mr Wilson's reservation to First."

"Thank you, that is very much appreciated. We have three bags to check in," finalised Max.

Bobby was amazed at the authority Max had and how he handled himself. Firm but always fair and calm. He could learn so much from him. Max thanked the attendant again, and smiled, again leaving a 'situation' on a high.

"Never get too nasty with airline staff. They all talk and they can make future flights difficult for you, even on other airlines. Now let's get to the lounge and get a drink. Anyway First is great for travelling alone, but the seats are not great for couples or pairs. There is too much equipment between you making it so difficult to get up to no good," Max laughed.

They arrived at the Executive Lounge and checked in. Max headed for the wine counter and poured a white for both. He then scanned the half empty room and found four unoccupied chairs. Perfect. They sat down leaving two spare chairs opposite them and looked around.

Max pulled out his phone and opened his Grindr app.

"Always a good start to see who's available and also who to avoid," he laughed. Bobby leaned in and started looking through the people in the vicinity on the app. There were a few cute guys but they appeared to be too far away. Probably somewhere else in the airport. Then they saw a torso that was supposedly ten metres away. He was broad, hairy and mid thirties. Judging from the body hair he was dark brown or black haired. They looked around. Max's profile pic was also his torso, so he wouldn't be approached by someone undesirable.

"Let's find out who this guy is," said Max.

He messaged. <Hello, are you in the BA exec lounge?>
<Yep> came the reply.
<What are you wearing or where are you sitting>
<By the water fridge, blue suit>

Max signalled to Bobby to go take a look. Bobby casually walked over to the area and past an average looking businessman in a blue suit. Stocky guy. He noticed Bobby in those jeans and smiled at him. Bobby smiled back and carried on walking and then doubled back.

"Not sure, he looks a bit boring to be honest," said Bobby.

"Nobody else is showing who's close," said Max, as he closed the app. The guy in the suit was looking around the room, hoping to find them, but they carried on with their drinks.

After about ten minutes, a man came and sat opposite them in the spare seats. Odd considering there were plenty of other seats available, that he chose the ones close to them. He was mid to late thirties, with long shoulder length brown hair, about 5' 7" and medium build. He was wearing sweatpants, Nikes and a hoodie. Unusual for BA lounge. Then so were leather jeans.

The guy at first didn't acknowledge them, rummaging through his bag to find his phone. He looked up, "Do either of you know the WIFI password?" he asked in a British accent.

"Err no," said Bobby smiling.

"It's usually Vancouver all lower case. Try that or you may need to check at the desk," Max interjected.

"Thanks," he said and typed in his phone. "Bingo, you were right," he smiled, checking out their jeans.

"You heading home for Christmas?" asked Max.

"Yes, back to my wife and family, over here on business for a month, gonna be back 10th of Jan. We sell beer in the USA." he answered still looking at both of them and their crotches, Max noticed.

"Me too, heading back to my husband, with my work colleague. We work in London and Chicago, so I'm heading back to London for Christmas and Bobby here is coming to help fix some programming issues and then heading straight back, aren't you?" Max said looking at Bobby.

"Yes, first time to the UK for me."

Bobby and Max looked at each other and smiled and nodded. They knew there was something about this guy. He may be married, but the bulge in his sweatpants said otherwise. He was kind of cute too.

After some more small talk they were starting to get quite friendly, his name was John and he asked quite a bit about Bobby and Max, especially Max's husband and then asking about if Bobby had a lady. Too obvious a question thought Max.

"You say you are married with a family, but the bulge and signals you are giving off says you would be interested in some fun," Max said abruptly, forcing the conversation to where they all wanted it to go.

John paused and smiled and said, "Yeah. What you got in mind?"

"You tell us, what you'd like. Being married must mean you have to grab these golden opportunities," said Max.

"I wanna blow you," he said to Bobby. "With you watching," he said to Max.

"I suggest we find somewhere a little more private. They headed to the restrooms, which fortunately in Exec lounges are large rooms, to allow people to wash up, so they have a toilet and a sink and a reasonable amount of room. They headed off to the restrooms, Bobby entered first, then John and Max, ensuring no one saw them all enter.

Bobby rested on the sink area and John got on his knees in front of him. Max stood to one side and watched as John placed his hands on Bobby's leather thighs.

"These look and feel so good, I knew you were gay and up for it when I saw the jeans," John said. Max winked at Bobby.

"Unzip me," said Bobby, "and get to it," he added forcefully.

John wasted no time and opened Bobby's fly, putting his face in. Bobby had chosen to not wear underwear as well, so John had access instantly to his cock and balls. Bobby was still limp but starting to get aroused as John handled his balls and took his cock in his mouth. John was stroking his own cock while he sucked on Bobby.

Bobby took control and said, "Look at me bitch. Watch me as you suck, pleasure me. What do you say?"

"Thank you, young sir," said John. "This tastes so good."

He was taking Bobby as far as he could, not as experienced as Bobby in sucking. Max had his cock out now and was stroking it, getting it nice and hard.

“Look at me!” said Bobby. “Suck him now.”

John looked over and saw Max’s hard on.

“Yes sir,” he said and shuffled to take him. The taste was different, but equally good, thought John.

Bobby came and stood next to Max and was jacking off at the sight. John moved from each cock in succession. Slurping each leather clad manhood.

“Open up,” said Bobby, as he jerked his cock and shot beautiful ropes of cum in John’s mouth and face and then forced his dick back in for a final clean and suck.

Max wasn’t far behind and said, “Me now cumslut,” and matched Bobby’s load, into John’s mouth and face.

John held Max’s load on his tongue for a while.

“Swallow bitch,” said Bobby, in a real command and master role. John did as he was told. Bobby grabbed a hand towel and wiped his cock and then zipped up. Discarding the towel on the floor and then Max did similar.

“Better clean up before the flight, you’ve got cum on your top,” said Max, as they both left the cubicle, checking no one saw them.

John got off his knees and looked in the mirror. His face was covered in cum and so was one shoulder. He smiled and scooped the cum off his face into his mouth.

"Fuck that was hot," he said, getting his own cock out and jerking himself off to his own reflection.

He pumped hard and shot a load onto the counter and mirror. Smiling to himself. He cleaned himself up as best he could, including the counter and mirror and then left. He looked for the two men who had cumdumped him, but they were nowhere to be seen.

Max and Bobby left the cubicle smiling. Max looked at his watch and said, "Let's go to the gate."

They gathered their things and left, leaving before John came out.

"That was fun," said Bobby.

"Yes, you were quite the dominant in there," replied Max.

"He wanted it. I could tell. He was cute, shame we couldn't have fucked him too," said Bobby

"Maybe another time. If we see him at the gate, I'll get his number for future, maybe something we could all play with in the new year. I'm sure Cole would like a go at him too," said Max

The flight was now being called and they headed towards the priority queue. Bobby was quite excited now. He had a permanent grin on his face. He'd only flown to Mexico on holiday, and never been to Europe, and never been business class. This was all so cool. He was also with his sexy daddy boss and already had his cock sucked. Damn this was all so good.

While they were waiting in the queue, John arrived and spotted them. He smiled but was in the queue further back. He leaned over with a piece of paper and gave it to Bobby. It had his number on it, and said, <call me if you wanna play again when back in

Chicago>, He signed the message off with a smiley face. Bobby winked back and smiled. Bobby showed the note to Max.

“That will be useful, if we have a dry patch in January,” he laughed and nodded at John across the people.

Max and Bobby went through the check-in desk and walked down to the plane. They entered to be greeted by two stewards, a lady called Tina and a handsome guy called Richard. Richard pointed to their seats and smiled.

“Welcome aboard, if you need anything, and I mean anything, let me know,” he smiled with a raised eyebrow.

“Jeez. Does everyone come onto you Max?” said Bobby.

“Not always, but I’m not always travelling with a sexy young cub like you either. You forget how handsome you are and I believe it was you he was more interested in,” Max replied.

“Ahh thanks Max. Since meeting you and Cole, I’ve never felt so sexy and confident. Before then, I was a bit reclusive and not positive. Being in a shit job with no prospects and no one close, living in a dump, really brings you down. You saved me from that, that evening. That fateful evening,” said Bobby as they took their places in the Club class duo seats.

“And to think, Cole and I just wanted to ruin and fuck you hard. You were just a piece of meat that night and I do feel a bit guilty about that sometimes,” said Max

“But hell, I wanted it! I’m mainly a sub and I was so turned on by the pair of you, being dominated by you two was one of the best and also scariest nights of my life, but it was amazing. And then getting to know Cole better and falling in love with him,” Bobby said.

“You’re in Love?” asked Max.

“Yes, I think I am and I’m sure he feels the same. We are so close, and we decided to have a similar open relationship to yours. We love playing with others and each other. I love living together with Cole. The apartment we have is awesome, not as plush as yours, but we love it. We partner in the gym downstairs and the apartment has two bedrooms. Ours and the fuck dungeon as we call it. We play with others there, but never in our room. That’s just for us,” Bobby expressed with great enthusiasm.

Richard, the steward, arrived with glasses of champagne, passing them to them both, but staring at Bobby.

“See, you’re in there,” said Max smiling. “You also have it well mapped out. I’m real happy for you and Cole, maybe one day you’ll invite me to the dungeon,” he smiled.

“Sure, you would always be welcome. If it wasn’t for you, none of what we have would have been possible, I can’t thank you enough and how grateful I am for that chance,” said Bobby

“You did it all by yourself, you had it in you. I gave you an opportunity, yes, but you grabbed it and worked hard at it. That’s what I loved about you both. Initially I wanted hard sex with you both and fuck did I get it, but when we got to talking after, I saw a different side to you come through. You took control and wanted what you wanted, even if it was piss. You took control and then with the session with Ollie. You really started to become a very interesting man to me and now look at you. Those gym sessions with Cole have really worked wonders.”

“Yes, Cole has helped me a lot. I’m not his size and doubt I will ever be, but he has really toned me up and I feel amazing. I’m real happy with my look which helps with the confidence,” said Bobby.

"You have been a real asset to the company and the team love you. You have also brought Troy out of his shell and his makeover was amazing. I assume you had a hand in that," said Max.

"Yes, he's a good lad and he's a dirty boy too. I shouldn't say this, but he loves being fisted. We have played a couple of times, but now he's got Jamie, who I have also fucked. God I sound such a slut. Troy is really happy now."

Max smiled, "You are a slut, but aren't we all. Enjoying your bodies and getting pleasure and sex is so important. So many don't get any and that's sad. Peter and I are the same, we have huge appetites for sex and wouldn't be able to contain it to just us two. Doesn't mean we don't love each other to the ends of the earth. Sex and love are different. I make love to Peter, I fuck others."

"Please fasten your seat belts and I'll take those glasses," said Richard, again only staring at Bobby.

Bobby and Max were in a duo seat which was at the back of the section. Which meant they had a certain amount of privacy, as they were not on an aisle. Bobby was looking at all the gadgets around him. He started to look at the films he could watch.

"You need to put that away for take-off," said Richard.

"Ok," said Bobby.

"Will you be looking after both of us this flight, or just Bobby?" laughed Max.

"I'm sorry. Sir of course, yes," he blushed.

"I'm playing with you young man, Bobby here is far more attractive than I. I can fully understand your interest, he's cute and bloody smart too," he smiled. Now Bobby was blushing.

"You're very handsome too sir. I will be on hand for both of you," Richard smiled and winked, then went to see to the other passengers.

Once in the air, they both settled into watching a film and eating and drinking. It was a night flight so they would be getting some sleep before the morning. The seats reclined to a bed position which made sleeping far easier. It would make them fresh for the morning.

"I need to pee, before I get some sleep," said Bobby and headed to the bathroom. It was locked, so he stood outside. Richard passed him and stroked his arse.

"Fuck that feels firm and nice in those jeans," Richard said.

"Are you allowed to molest the customers?" smiled Bobby.

"Only the sexy ones and fuck you are one of those," He smiled. "You and your colleague an item?"

"He's my senior Boss. He owns a business in Chicago and London, we are heading to London to sort some problems out, then I fly back on Thursday," said Bobby.

"Which flight? I'm on this route for the next week until Christmas," said Richard.

"I think it's the 11.10am. If I'm lucky I may be in First," said Bobby.

“That’s my route for Thursday. I’ll ensure you are in First sexy boy,” said Richard as the toilet door opened and a lady came out and stared at them.

Bobby moved towards the toilet.

Richard whispered, “If you need a hand in there let me know,” again squeezing Bobby’s arse, “Those jeans feel awesome,” he added.

“You should feel how hot they are up against your cock and balls,” said Bobby as he closed the door with a smile. “I’m such a tease,” giggled Bobby.

Once he got back to his seat the lights were out and it was quite dark. Max was lying fully out. Bobby got his seat in the same position and got under his blanket too. Max was quite restless.

“Never gonna get to sleep, I can’t seem to relax,” said Max, sipping his G&T. After a couple minutes, Bobby moved his hand under the blanket and felt Max’s crotch.

“I can help you relax sir,” he said in his best submissive voice, along with the dirtiest of grins.

Max looked over and around to see how out of sight they were. The plane was quiet now with little movement, with the exception of Bobby’s hand stroking his leather crotch. His stroking was getting Max aroused, and that pleased Bobby. He gently found the zip and unleashed Max’s cock. Still under the covers he felt around the shaft and stroked it gently, teasing the head, and running his fingers inside the foreskin. He ran his hand firmly up and down and pleasured his Boss, who was sighing gently.

"When you get close let me know. Don't want to mess up that shirt. I'll do my best to eat it all, never like to see waste," Bobby whispered.

"You're a good lad, keep going, this feels awesome," said Max and Bobby continued his strokes and then started to wank a bit harder. After a couple of minutes, Bobby decided enough was enough and he needed Max in his mouth. He dived under the blanket and took Max is one move. Christ, he tasted good. He still had cum around his head from the session in the airport. The taste of leather, cum and sweaty crotch was perfect. Bobby slurped and took Max's dick in and out and then worked his lips and tongue up and down the shaft. He caressed his balls and started to finger his arse hole.

Max opened his legs to allow easier access to his hole and whispered, "You're fucking good at this. You have such a magic touch lad. I'm getting close now, keep going, get ready for it."

Bobby took his cock to the hilt, licking Max's balls when at the bottom and then moved back and wanked the bottom of the shaft, which was all Max needed. Bobby felt the delicious nectar hitting the back of his throat, hot jets of cum, filling his mouth. He kept his mouth tight shut round Max's cock to ensure none leaked and more importantly wasted. Once Max's pulses stopped, Bobby pulled off and showed his cum filled mouth to Max, and then swallowed it in front of him grinning. It was then Max noticed that Richard was standing just behind them watching what was going on.

Rather than be embarrassed or shamed, Max looked at him and said, "I'd invite you to join us, but you appear to be busy. Can I worry you for a couple of napkins please and another G&T."

Richard grinned, "Of course sir." He was back within seconds passing the napkins.

"That was very sexy to watch and I apologise for spying, but I couldn't keep my eyes off the pair of you. You're lucky you have me on this section. If Doreen was on, she'd have reported you for indecency, frigid bitch."

"We will have to find ways to thank you," said Max, wiping his cock in front of Richard, and zipping it away.

"I'm hoping your employee will help with that on his journey home," Richard grinned, staring at Max's very handsome cock.

"Oh good. I have to say, he is amazing," said Max.

Richard left to get Max's G&T and returned. He then left them to rest and hopefully sleep. The remainder of the flight was less eventful and soon they were landing at Heathrow.

Part 4 – Passport to Leather Central

Chapter 8 - Sunday Sunday, a day of two halves

They got through security via fast track, which helped speed things up with Bobby's US passport. The non-EU passports queue was lengthy and slow. They picked up their luggage and were pleased to be met by Peter at the arrivals hall. He was grinning, holding a card saying "2 hotties."

"Wow!" said Max, "You don't usually come and pick me up personally. You normally send a car," he smiled and kissed his husband.

Bobby was pushing the trolley, loaded with the three cases and bags.

"Well you don't always bring sexy guests for Christmas and looking at you Bobby, my Christmas has come nice and early. My you look more handsome than I remember and you have filled out beautifully. Have you been working out?"

"Yes sir," he replied.

"Less of the sir. I can't abide it, unless it's in the bedroom," Peter laughed.

"Ok, then let's hope that happens later," said Bobby with an angelic smile.

"My, you have got bold too. I like him even more," Peter grabbed Bobby and gave him a hug and a peck on the cheek.

They turned and headed to the short stay car park, Peter said, "Anything interesting happen on the flight?"

"Well….." Max told what had happened, much to Peter's excitement and thrill.

"John and Richard sound adorable," said Peter as he pressed the button to open his car, a deep purple Porsche Panamera.

"Wow Peter, I love your car and the colour," said Bobby.

"Thanks, I love Purple."

They sped out of the car park and onto the motorway and then took the road into central London. They talked some more about the flight and then about the problem in the office.

Peter said, "Brian is in the office today and still working on stuff."

Bobby said, "If I can grab a shower, I'm happy to get to see Brian and start work on this today. I got some sleep on the plane and it would be good to get an idea of the issue. I can then think about it overnight and be ahead of the game for Monday."

"Good lad, thanks. That would be appreciated," said Peter pulling up in Chelsea outside a beautiful three story Georgian house. He parked in the resident's parking on the street and they mounted the steps to the front door and then headed up to the first floor apartment. The building had such beautiful character. Peter opened the heavy door of the apartment into short hallway, with wooden floors and rugs. The spacious hallway opened on to a large room either side. One side was a large lounge area looking over the street, with a huge Christmas tree, impeccably decorated, next to one of the three large sash windows. It had two sumptuous sofas facing a grand old open fireplace. On the other side, towards the back of the space, was a dining room and open kitchen. The dining area was traditional, but the kitchen chic and modern. The combination worked brilliantly.

Opposite the short hallway was another hallway leading to three doors. Two bedrooms and a large bathroom.

“This is your room,” Peter said opening the door.

Inside was beautifully furnished in a classical style. Lots of wood and rugs. A beautiful huge bed made up with white linen stood in contrast to the sex sling in the corner.

“Oh, jeez Peter, you might have put that away,” said Max with an annoyed tone.

“No worries,” said Bobby. “Maybe, you’ll find me in it later,” he laughed.

“I’m sorry it’s not ensuite. These old houses are difficult enough to convert, though the main bathroom is yours,” said Peter, carrying Bobby’s case in.

“Ok freshen up and shall we say forty five minutes I’ll take you to the office?” said Peter to Max and Bobby. They both entered their bedrooms.

Bobby opened his case and hung up his clothes and then stripped out of his flight clothes and walked to the bathroom with his wash bag. There he found fresh towels and a bath and shower. Peter caught a glimpse of Bobby naked from behind. He liked Bobby’s new body, still petite, but beautifully toned and that arse was wonderful he thought. He could hear the two showers start up. Bobby in the bathroom and Max in their ensuite.

Fifteen minutes later, Bobby appeared with a towel round his waist, with beautiful wet hair and damp body. Peter stared at the front view.

"My god you are a ridiculously handsome young man. Would you like tea or coffee when you are dressed?"

"Thanks, coffee please," Bobby smiled and strode into his room and shut the door.

He got dressed in smart denim jeans, a check shirt and some brown desert boots. He towel dried his hair and combed it to dry naturally. He then walked out of the room into the kitchen and found Peter with a coffee and some pastries.

"Perfect," he said, "Thank you. I feel so much better for the shower."

They sat and chatted and discussed how his and Cole's jobs had been progressing.

"I knew Cole would excel in Sales rather than Marketing. Glad we made that change and I understand he landed a great deal?" said Peter.

"Yes. He is so much happier, which makes me so much happier. He was going into a bad place when he felt he was failing you guys," said Bobby.

Max appeared at the door in casual clothes, jeans and a cashmere jumper and trainers.

"Wow that feels better. Any Coffee for me?"

"Yes sweetheart. Here you go," Peter poured him a cup. "Ok once you are done drinking, we shall head to the office. I've rung Brian and he's hanging on to see you."

"Ok, let's go. Don't want to keep him waiting, especially as it's a Sunday," said Max. They grabbed their jackets and headed to the car.

"Bobby, you go up front, then you can get a good view of the city," said Max.

"Thanks, if you're sure," It was great to see London by car, thought Bobby. The office was in the City of London, so they drove from Chelsea via Kings Road, then through Belgravia, and even went round Buckingham Palace and the Mall. Round Trafalgar Square, then partially down the Strand, before turning down along the Embankment towards the City. On Sunday traffic wasn't too bad and it took about forty minutes to get to the office.

"Thought I'd take you past some of the tourists spots," said Peter.

"It's great to see all the places I've only seen in films and pictures. I hope I get some time to explore the city before I leave," said Bobby.

"That depends on how good you are at trying to sort our system bugs," said Peter as they got out the car, which was now parked in the underground car park of a large block in the City.

They entered the offices of Bartholomew Steadman London division and it had a similar feel to Chicago. Smart and stylish, but not too grand, also with lots of plants. Again, all the desks were the same, the same as Chicago, no hierarchy in furniture. A man in his mid fifties, but who looked older, was in the office. He was sitting in the corner desk in front of his screen and he stood up.

"Brian," said Max, "good to see you. This is Bobby, who we hope will be able to help."

Brian smiled. He was balding at the back and in a tired set of clothing. Brian was an old school friend of Peter's and was instrumental in setting up the structure of the company at the beginning. Bobby sat down with Brian and started to look through the systems, deep in conversation with Brian. Peter sat by watching and trying to understand what was being said, but they may as well have been speaking mandarin, as he was clueless to what they were saying, but it was lovely to sit and watch Bobby in action. This beautiful young man, so intelligent, holding his own with someone Peter counted on and who had a wealth of experience.

Max decided he would be of better use getting refreshments.

"I'll head out and get some provisions. I may be some time, as the City of London is practically closed on weekends," he said to no one in particular. "I'll have to get closer to St Paul's before I get to find anything open. I'll bring back a selection of stuff."

Bobby opened his laptop and started comparing items with what was on Brian's screen. Overall they spent about three hours looking through stuff. Bobby was taking copious notes and making lists. He set up an access to the systems via his laptop.

"I'll be able to have a look at this overnight, I need to have some thinking time."

The system was based on an old IBM AS400 set up, which was starting to get a bit dated, and creaky thought Bobby, but he didn't want to say too much at this stage. An arrogant young man in Peter's domain, with an old friend at the helm was not a good way to win friends he thought. He'd keep quiet for now.

They all decided that was enough for today. It was now 4pm on Sunday.

"Let's all get home and make a fresh start tomorrow. We'll be back here at 8am. Would be great to meet up with the team," said Max.

Bobby collected his stuff and all his notes, shook hands with Brian and said, “I’m sure we can sort this. I just need to get my head around a few things beforehand. I’ll have a think tonight and we can start a fresh tomorrow.”

Brian smiled back, “I hope so, you will also meet Katrina, who works with me.”

“That will be great,” replied Bobby.

Bobby walked towards Max, and Peter and Brian carried on chatting.

Peter asked, “Are you happy with Bobby? He’s a bright lad.”

“Yes Peter, he was talking about some new ideas that I had read about. He has a sharp and quick mind. I hope he can help crack these errors. I’m just sorry I let this happen. I have to say, once we fix this, I will need to review the use of Jackson Technology who support us. To be honest they cost us a fortune and have been pretty useless with all of this.”

“Well, we can review all this once we get ourselves back into order,” said Peter.

They all headed to the car park. Brian headed off in his one series BMW. Rather modest car Bobby thought compared to Peter’s Porsche. They headed back to the apartment. It was getting dark and Bobby could see glimpses of Christmas decorations and lights on the main roads. It felt magical to be here in London.

“So, what do you reckon Bobby?” Peter asked. “Can you fix it?”

Bobby paused and was quiet for a while.

“Crikey Peter, give the boy a chance,” said Max, breaking the silence.

“Well, I need some time to look through the code and fully understand the system. It’s slightly different from Chicago. Is Berlin like London, or Chicago?” Bobby asked.

“London is the oldest. Berlin is the newest office and was built on the Chicago system,” said Max. “Not ideal I suppose. I feel we may have exposed ourselves with this glitch, we may need to review all areas at some point,” Max added.

“Brian won’t be keen I imagine,” Peter laughed.

“Well he might have to be,” said Max pointedly.

“Come on. Brian has so much knowledge, he built our business systems from nothing. Plus he’s a good friend,” said Peter.

“Ummm, let’s not discuss this now,” Max said trying to change the subject. He wasn’t comfortable with Brian and didn’t want to discuss that in front of Bobby. “I do hope you have got something good for dinner tonight Peter,” he added, definitely changing the subject.

“I have made a steak and ale pie for us, with baked potatoes and veg. It’s large so I hope you are hungry.” Peter said.

They got to the apartment and got into the warm.

“I need to finish the pie and prep the veggies. How about you get a fire started, and opening a nice bottle of red.” said Peter.

“Do you mind if I spend some time sitting here at the dining table? I want to go through some stuff while it’s still in my brain,” said Bobby.

"Of course," said Peter.

"Do you have the WIFI code so I can log in remotely, please," said Bobby.

Peter gave him a card with it on.

Bobby logged both his laptop and phone onto the WIFI and then messaged Cole to say he was there safely and it was all amazing. They exchanged a few messages and then Bobby cracked on with the notes all over the table. Max built the fire and started it and Peter prepped dinner, spending much of the time looking over at Bobby, studiously working trying to solve their problem. He looked adorable Peter thought. His left hand half way through that sexy blond hair as he leaned on the table, pen in the other hand and scanning papers and his screen.

Bobby noticed him staring, when he glanced up, and smiled, that awesome smile, and then winked. Peter looked away, cheeky lad, he thought. Cheeky, fucking sexy, and down right horny young man, he thought again. I hope he's up for playing while he is here. That would be the best Christmas present, Peter thought.

Peter and Max went and sat on the sofas with a glass of wine and left Bobby with a glass at the table. After another hour had passed, Peter announced dinner would be ready very soon so Bobby packed up his stuff and took it to his room. He left the notes and laptop all open on the dresser in his room. He got changed out of his jeans, the house was so warm now. He put on some gym shorts and a vest top with some white socks. He looked real cute he thought. The shorts were very short too. He grinned, he was a fucking tease. He looked at that sling in the corner. He went over and got in it. He imagined Peter and Max at either end, filling his holes. He smiled and swung a bit. He was getting a semi. He decided to stop thinking about it and struggled his way out of the sling, which was a lot harder than getting in it he giggled to himself. He checked his semi was not too visible and went out to join Max and Peter.

"Sorry for being so anti-social," Bobby said as he sat down next to Peter. Max was on the other sofa. "That fire is awesome and it's so warm in here. Hope I'm not too casual for dinner?" he suddenly thought and said.

"Not at all," said Peter, "You look truly wonderful. Your arms are so toned, and the shoulders…."

"Yes, Cole has been working with me on a programme to get me toned up. He's been a real inspiration. Seeing his body and him helping me. It's so much easier having a gym buddy who is also your boyfriend," said Bobby.

"Let's eat. I'm starving," said Max. "You're hungry Max, not starving, people in Africa are starving," Peter corrected.

Max raised his eyebrows to Bobby with a smile. "He always corrects me on that," he laughed as they went to the elegantly set table. The food was very welcome after a long day and the flight last night. The pie was perfect, and the accompanying second bottle of Gigondas wine was making them all relax.

After the food, they retired to the sofas again and chatted more about their up bringing's and how Peter and Max met in Berlin. The fire was roaring and there was lots of laughter from the story. Peter was sat next to Bobby, who had his feet up on the sofa clutching his wine. His firm powerful legs, showing a nice layer of fur on them, which were a turn on for Peter. The calves in his socks were so near to touch. Bobby moved and tried to get more comfortable.

"Do you want to put your feet on my lap?" Peter asked. "I'll give your feet a massage."

Bobby looked at Max, for the ok.

"Fine with me. You know Peter finds you wildly attractive and hell you gave me a hand job on the plane. That was greatly appreciated, so a foot massage from hubby and whatever else you want to do is fine with me."

Bobby smiled and put his calves on Peter's legs. Peter put down his glass of wine and started to stroke Bobby's calves. The feel of his warm firm leg was wonderful. He then massaged the feet through the thick socks. It felt good and was very relaxing. Peter put his face closer and sniffed his feet. They smelt pretty fresh, with a hint of feet. He pulled one of the socks off and got a closer sniff and then started to lick Bobby's toes. He giggled as it tickled, so Peter held more firmly to stop the tickle sensation.

"Not only do you look beautiful, you smell and taste beautiful too." He started running his hand up Bobby's calf and then onto his hard firm thigh. He massaged his thigh, each rubbing bringing his fingers closer to the opening of his shorts. The sensation was making Bobby hard and that was visible to see. Peter grinned at the sight. He got closer, nudging the end of Bobby's hard dick on purpose and then his balls. This made Bobby totally erect, his throbbing cock forcing itself out the bottom of the shorts.

"You enjoying this?" said Peter.

"Sure am. You want it, go for it?" replied Bobby. Peter liked this new confidence.

Peter put his full hand into one side of the shorts leg opening and grasped Bobby's fine specimen of a cock, kneading it between his thumb and fingers. Bobby moved his body down and closer giving Peter better access. Bobby looked over to smile at Max, only to see he had his own hard dick out his fly and was stroking it, watching his husband, caressing him. The smile turned to a grin and a wink. Peter changed position and pulled the shorts leg opening wide to allow him to fully go down on Bobby's beast. It had been too long since he had been able to play with this lad, Peter thought, as he took every inch of his handsome cock. It tasted good, even better than his feet, and they tasted awesome he thought.

Bobby leant forward and took his vest off revealing his brand new torso to Peter, who pulled up to view him closely.

"Oh my, Cole has been working you hard. That's beautiful, just the right amount of toning and I love that you have kept your light hair on your chest," said Peter as he then went back down on his cock and ran his hands over the newly revealed abs and chest.

Peter then started to take his own shirt off and unzipped his pants to reveal his own erection. He moved back onto Bobby's chest and started licking him; his nipples and chest. He edged down his treasure trail onto his cock and then back up to his neck, drinking in the smell of his soft skin and kissing him all over. Then he went into the armpit and smelt hard.

"God you smell amazing," Peter licked at his armpit and moved to the other, finally moved in for a kiss. This time Bobby took control and grabbed Peter's head and neck, kissing him, his tongue hard into Peter's mouth. Then he moved his left hand down and rubbed Peter's erection, causing him to moan deeply.

"Think it's about time I got fucked on British soil, who fancies joining me in the sling?" said Bobby.

"Fuck yes," said Peter.

"Come on Max, you too, I want both my holes filled. Fucking spit roast me. Take advantage of your employee. I fucking want it so bad from you two," he smirked pulling himself up from the sofa and walking to the bedroom in just his shorts and one droopy sock.

Max and Peter followed removing their clothing as they went. Bobby was being an alpha sub and it was an interesting role reversal for Peter and Max. He looked so hot too. Once in the room Bobby dropped the shorts to reveal that perfect high and firm arse. He yanked the other sock off and with one simple jump landed himself into the sling.

"Someone's been practicing," said Max with a laugh.

Now all three men had raging hard-ons. Bobby lay back and got his legs up in the stirrups. Peter moved in, grabbed a bottle of lube from the shelf nearby and lubed up his cock, fingering Bobby's hole with his free hand. As he positioned himself, with the head of his cock resting on Bobby's hole, Peter grabbed Bobby's firm legs and kissed his right calf, sucking at his flesh, smelling him and his ankles heading to the feet again, as he reached the arch of his foot. He drove his cock into Bobby's arse, sniffing deeply at the same time.

Bobby marvelled at the erotic spectacle. He couldn't believe someone would find his calves and feet so sexy, but the vision was turning him on and he was playing with his own cock now. As Peter thrust against his prostate it was making him harder with each pump.

Max was watching, excited to see his husband in such ecstasy. He moved round to Bobby's head and leant down to kiss him. That handsome face and beautiful cheek bones. He really could have been a model with those features. Cole was sexy in a filthy evil handsome chiselled look, but Bobby was angelic and beautiful. Almost pretty.

Max stood back up and adjusted the sling with a pulley and lowered Bobby's head position to waist height. He then gently unclipped the head rest, which allowed Bobby's head to drop back and full access to his throat. Looking backwards and up at Max's crotch and raging hard on, Bobby smiled at Max and said, "Give it to me boss, rape my throat. I fucking want you both to rape me hard. FUCKING DESTROY ME!" he shouted, grabbing the chains for extra bracing.

Max held his head and thrust his cock into his face hard. Bobby took it no trouble. He started pumping and then got into a rhythm with Peter at the other end. They both pumped into this beautiful young man at the same time. Bobby gurgled, and gripped harder, as he took his two bosses dicks. He could feel their power destroying his arse and throat. It felt so awesome. He was beating his own cock as they destroyed him. He loved that feeling of being dominated and controlled as much as the occasional desire to dominate himself.

Max and Peter watched each other and grinned, both looking at the beautiful boy they were fucking. God he was perfect. This drove them on harder and watching him beating his dick below them was an amazing sight. Bobby twisted and then shot a huge load over his abs and chest. The sight was enough for Peter and Max to do likewise. Filling his two holes with their loads. Bobby, swallowed all of Max's cum, ensuring he didn't spill a drop. Once he pulled out, he started scooping up his own cum and eating it with a smile.

Peter pulled out and Max moved around, kneeling into position underneath Bobby's tight arse.

"Give it to me boy," he said with his tongue on his hole. "Give me my husband's cum," Bobby obliged, pushing out a steady stream of Peter's hot load.

Meanwhile, Peter started licking Bobby's cum off his chest and abs. Max took the felched load, which was warm and tasty.

“Fuck that was awesome,” said Bobby, clearing his throat. “Christ, I love being fucked by you guys. Just fucking.....awesome.” He clambered out the sling, raising his face to Max, he kissed him hard eager to find any spare remnants of cum in his mouth.

“You’re an animal for cum boy,” said Max.

“Yeah, that’s what Cole says,” he laughed.

“Now I need a shower and some sleep. I think as the time difference is catching up now.” said Bobby heading out the door for the bathroom.

Max and Peter left him to it, found their clothes and sat back down, continuing their drink.

Not long after, Bobby appeared with a towel and said, “Cheers guys, see you in the morning. Goodnight,” and he returned to his room.

It was now 10.30 and after half an hour Max was feeling the effects of both the red wine and the jet lag. They both got up and decided to head to bed.

Part 4 – Passport to Leather Central

Chapter 9 - Manic Monday

At 4am Max woke up, the time zone always played havoc with him. He needed some water, so went out to the kitchen to get a glass. On his return, he saw a light on under Bobby's door. He gently knocked and opened it. He found Bobby at the desk naked working through more coding. Bobby looked round and smiled.

"Christ knows what time zone I'm on," he laughed, "I was awake and started thinking about the problem in hand and some ideas came to mind, so started looking."

"Ok, well I'm heading back to bed. We are up at six to beat the traffic," he said, and then Max left. He's a bloody good lad; really dedicated he thought. In more than one way he smiled.

They all got to the office at eight. Bobby worked hard on some of the ideas he had come up with the previous night and early that morning. Brian liked what he saw. Bobby also met Katrina, she was in her late thirties and quite bookish and plain. A nice lady but, like Brian, also quite set in her ways. It took a while before she was happy with Bobby's ideas. He had to use all his charm to get her on board. This took until lunchtime.

Bobby spent the whole day tweaking coding and retesting. Then he worked most of the evening in the spare room on more changes. The same happened on Tuesday. He finished pretty much all he could on Tuesday morning. It was now for Brian and Katrina to run tests all that afternoon, to be sure everything ran smoothly.

Bobby went to see Max.

"Is it possible you could point me in the direction of some good shops? I need to get Cole a Christmas present and I'm surplus to requirements until Brian has tested what I have changed."

"What you after for Cole?" Max asked.

"I would like to get him a new wallet. He has this battered old nylon thing. I want to get him a nice leather one, something very British."

"Let's go. I'll take you to a few places. I think a nice Dunhill wallet would be perfect. I also have my eye on a new jacket. You can tell me what you think?"

Max told Peter he was off Christmas shopping. They grabbed their coats and headed out the building.

Max hailed a taxi and they headed to Piccadilly. They arrived at the Dunhill shop. It looked very traditionally British to Bobby. The clothing and suits looked very smart Bobby thought. Inside he looked around and felt the fabrics and then got to the accessories counter. The wallets looked really nice, Bobby thought, but they were very expensive. He found a lovely brown one that he felt would be perfect. Cole deserved nice things, after his rotten upbringing Bobby thought. Hopefully, in January, he would be seeing a bonus appear. He understood the business had done quite well, so he bought it. It came beautifully boxed and gift wrapped.

"Perfect," said Bobby, as they left the store.

It was busy now, Max said, "Let's walk to the shop I want to go to. It will be quicker than finding a taxi."

They headed north into Mayfair, passing many high end shops, all looking beautifully Christmassy. They arrived at the Belstaff store just as it started to rain.

"Good timing," said Max, as they got into the warmth. "I'm looking for new jackets for Peter and I. I'm getting him the Panther Jacket in brown. It's a mid-length classic jacket, he's wanted one for a while." Max tried one on as he and Peter were similar sized.

"That looks cool," said Bobby.

"I'm also after something for me, I've had my eye on the Outlaw Jacket in brown too. He tried it on. "What do you think?" he asked again.

"That's real sexy. Love the shape and the padded shoulders," said Bobby.

"It also comes in black, but I like the brown. I have so many black ones. Cole would look good in the black wouldn't he? Real manly, hardcore look?" said Max.

"Yes. That would be awesome, but at £1350 he can buy it himself!" Bobby laughed.

"Yes, you are right," laughed Max. "You'd look great in the Maxford 2.0 I like the neater shoulders and smooth finish, suits your neat features and beauty my boy. Try it on in black." Bobby put it on.

"No, that's too small, I forget I am broader now."

Bobby tried the next size up. The smell of the jacket was beautiful. He stood in front of the mirror.

"Wow, that is real nice. I'll have to see if I can find something similar at a more affordable price, but I think I now know what style I want. This is perfect, but maybe when I'm as rich as you," he laughed.

Max stood behind him and felt his shoulders in the jacket. "It does look perfect on you," he said as he studied Bobby in the mirror.

Max checked his watch, "Right, we better get back. I'm gonna get Peter's present and my jacket. Why don't you check out some of the other stores along the street? I need to wait for them to gift wrap his," said Max carrying both jackets to the counter.

"Ok," said Bobby, leaving the store.

As soon as he was gone, Max picked up the jacket Bobby had tried on and then looked at the Outlaw one in black. He needed to consider Cole's size. He was broad, he decided on the next size up from his own size. He took all four jackets to the counter. He had Bobby and Cole's specially gift wrapped and boxed, Peter's too. His own, he took as it came.

He asked the shop to have his purchases taxied over to the office this afternoon, in unmarked outer packaging. They agreed, considering he was spending over £5k on four jackets. He paid for the jackets by card, headed for the door and went to find Bobby.

He spotted the sexy young man with a shock of blond hair looking in a window further up the road. It was now about 3.30pm. He called Bobby and they met up and headed to find a taxi.

"Where are your jackets?"

"I'm having them sent to the office, they were being slow and also to save carrying them," he lied.

They headed back to the office, to find out how Brian had been getting on.

Brian and Peter were grinning like Cheshire cats. "You did it young man," said Brian. "Bugs are fixed and it's running smoothly. The modifications you added appear to be great additions too. You're a genius."

Bobby stood there slightly blushing.

"Well done Bobby and thank you for getting us out of this mess," said Peter.

"Yes, thank you Bobby for coming over and helping us out, it's really appreciated," said Brian rather sheepishly.

"I'm so happy I could help, but I…" Bobby paused. "Oh nothing."

"What is it?" said Max.

"Nothing really, I'm not thinking straight. Must be jet lag," he lied.

Max looked at him, smiled and said, "Ok." I'll talk with him later, he thought.

The office buzzer went. Max answered, it was the taxi from Belstaff.

"I'm coming down."

Max grabbed Peter's keys from him and went down and collected the jackets. He then put them in the trunk of Peter's car. Out of sight.

Within the hour they were all in the car heading home.

"Thank you Bobby, we really owe you. We must go out for dinner tonight and celebrate. You can use tomorrow to do your sightseeing before the flight home on Thursday," said Peter.

As they went into the house, Max held back. "You guys go in before me. No peeking as I'm bringing in presents Peter." He rushed in with the packages and dashed into their bedroom with them. He put his and Peter's jackets away in the cupboard and pulled out his spare suitcase from the rack and placed Bobby and Cole's gifts in it. He packed some jumpers over the top to hide them, put it to one side and then joined them both in the lounge.

"Done your secret squirrel stuff?" said Peter.

"Yes, my lovely husband, I have," Max replied. "Let's get showered and head out for a drink and some food."

They wrapped up and headed out to the King's Road. Over dinner Max asked, "Bobby, what were you going to say to Brian? You seemed to have second thoughts."

"I don't feel it's my place. Sorry," said Bobby.

"No, please. You really helped us today and am interested in your thoughts and ideas," said Max

"Well, I really think you need to look at the IT set up. Across all three businesses. London is quite an old system based on twenty year old technology. You are finding it more and more expensive to get support on it and it's clunky," said Bobby.

"Well I'm sure Brian would be keeping us up to date," said Peter.

"I'm sorry Peter, I think you might be wrong there. Brian is a good man, but we do need to perhaps look at this across all businesses. It is a bit mad we have three different systems," said Max.

"No disrespect to Brian, but the thinking is continually changing and I'm not saying I know what's best, but I think you would be wise to consider a review of all three systems, maybe looking at some cloud based technology. I think Freddie would agree that even Chicago needs updating. So, wouldn't it be best to look at all systems and work together on it? Brian needs to be a part of this, with all his knowledge and history of the present set up," said Bobby

"Ummm, ok you are probably right. This is not my area and I have somehow let Brian run it as he wishes. Maybe a three way review would be worth planning. I'll discuss it with Brian in January and get Kurt involved from Berlin," said Peter. "Thanks Bobby for your honesty and for your delicacy in handling this in front of Brian and Katrina. I can see why you paused in front of them. They are good people, but maybe they are a little set in their ways."

"Ok let's eat," said Max.

Part 4 – Passport to Leather Central

Chapter 10 – Play Time

Cole had been missing having Bobby around and it had only been a couple of days. They tried to grab some time on Skype, but the time difference made it difficult. They sent texts regularly and he was excited for Bobby, who said London was amazing and that they both must plan a visit very soon. That would be great, Cole thought and he already downloaded the passport application online and was getting that ready to be sent off. He needed some photos and was going to ask Bobby to help with getting a good one for his passport.

Monday he went into the office. It was quiet as it was the week before Christmas and no one was interested in buying property at this time, so it was a good time to catch up on admin and start planning workloads for the new year. Brad was in the office on Monday. Cole kept looking at his boss. He was a handsome, manly man. Cole kept thinking about how, at the Christmas party, Brad wanted sex with the piano player and he got it. So easy.

Towards the end of the day, Brad asked Cole if he wanted to go for a drink after work. Brad was on his own and he knew Cole was, with Bobby in the UK. So, Cole thought about it. Yeah, why not. They went for a drink and a bite and it wasn't long before they were talking about sex and Brad was coming onto Cole quite hard.

"You up for some fun, sexy boy?" asked Brad.

"Well I'm always up for some fun, but I wanna be clear that if we do anything, this doesn't mess up our work relationship. I can't afford to lose my job and fuck this all up, through casual sex that starts to get messy. If we play around, it's no strings and no connections to work. We remain professional in the office and we keep this separate," said Cole being quite forthright.

"Sure Cole. I don't want any commitments, just hot sex, nothing more. If you said no, that would be a shame, but wouldn't change anything at work. You are one of my star salesmen. You make sales that make me look good, so wouldn't want to change that," said Brad. "Anyway, I don't think I wanna fuck you. I wanna watch you fuck someone else you handsome stud. I wanna fuck someone with you, together. You up for that?"

"One of my favs. A three way. Perfect. You like it rough?" asked Cole.

"Fuck yeah. We need to find a guy to play with then. I wonder if piano man is up for some fun? Shall I give him a call? He was into you too," replied Brad.

Cole nodded and Brad picked up his phone. "Invite him to my apartment. We can meet and fuck there," said Cole.

Brad called the number he had.

"Hi Josh, remember me, cleaning cupboard, last Thursday? I was filling your throat with my cock," Brad laughed. "You busy tonight? Wondered if you were up for a three way with that cute guy in the leather jeans you were checking out. He's up for it, if you are?" There was a pause on the line. Brad smiled and nodded to Cole. "Great, I'll text you the address, get there for 9pm. Great. See you then," Brad hung up and passed the phone to Cole to text the address to. "We better get over to yours," said Brad, getting out his seat and waving to the waiters signalling the universal language of getting the check; wriggling an invisible pen on his hand with a smile.

They paid up and headed to Cole's and Bobby's apartment. Cole was racking his brain thinking how tidy it might be or not. When they got there, he opened up, and sighed relief. It wasn't as bad as he remembered.

"I'm gonna get changed. Do you wanna borrow some joggers or something while we wait?"

They were both in suits.

"Ok," said Brad. "I suggest you get those leather pants on, as I and he would love to see you throat fucking him in those."

Cole smiled and went in his bedroom, returned in nothing but the leather pants and threw Brad some joggers. He then went and checked the state of the spare room. It hadn't been used for a few weeks. Good old Bobby had tidied it and put clean bedding on the bed.

"What would I do without you Bobby Wilson?" Cole said out loud.

He was feeling slightly guilty at what he was planning without him, but then he remembered the story Bobby shared from the airport and his session with Peter and Max. They always agreed it was ok to play with others. But this was the first time in the apartment without Bobby as his partner in crime.

He came out the room to find Brad in just his underwear. Tighty whitey briefs. He had a good body and nice level of fur.

"Come her my sexy top salesman," said Brad. Brad studies this awesome boy's torso and arms in perfect balance to that small waist and those sexy leather jeans encasing his powerful thighs and calves. Even his feet were handsome, in proportion and no calluses or ugly bits. He was a beautiful man. Cole stood in front of him, at least three inches taller than Brad. Brad reached up and kissed him, his hand holding his square jaw. He entered Cole's mouth with his tongue. Cole's cock stirred in his leathers. He reached down and stroked Brad's bulge in his pants, which responded to the touch. As they kissed, the buzzer went. They stopped.

"Our victim has arrived," said Cole. Brad looked surprised, by the use of the term 'victim'.

"Victim?" he said.

"Yes. I wanna ruin this man tonight," said Cole very directly to Brad's surprise. Cole walked to the door phone and buzzed Josh in and opened the apartment door. He stood with the door open. His arm and hand reaching up and holding the door frame, creating a sexy pose, as he waited.

Josh arrived from the elevator and was surprised to see Cole at the door. Fuck he was a beautiful man. More sexy that he remembered from Howl at the Moon. And he was wearing those jeans again. Fuck, he looked hard already. Josh smiled as he approached.

Cole said, "Hello again, come in," and he swung the door closed behind him.

"You want a drink Josh? You as well Brad?"

Cole got some beers out the fridge. He then went over to Josh and grabbed him and kissed him hard. He started to undress him, pulling at his shirt and fly.

"Steady Tiger," said Josh.

"Fuck steady. I need to be inside you man," said Cole, with a level of venom.

Brad approached and assisted with the de-clothing of Josh, who was now quite excited by the rough treatment.

"You ready to be fucked hard?" said Cole, "Real hard!"

"Fuck yeah, let's get to it." Josh said, grabbing for Cole's fly. Cole pushed his hand away.

"I'm in charge. I'll say when you get a piece of that, cumdump," he said, dragging Josh, by the hand into the spare bedroom. He threw him on the bed. "Fucking strip the bitch," Cole said to Brad. Who was both surprised and turned on by Cole's personality change. He did as he was told. Josh helped get himself naked as Cole stood above them at the end of the bed.

"Ok, position him with his head over the edge of the bed, I wanna enter that throat," he said, slowly unzipping his fly, and letting loose his beautiful nine inch cock.

"Fuck!" said Josh, "Go easy with that."

"Not a chance," said Cole. "Open the fuck up."

Josh opened wide and watched upside down as Cole pushed his warm cock into his throat. Josh gagged a little at first, but then started to take the shaft dutifully.

"Knew you could take it," said Cole smirking as he pumped into Josh's throat.

Brad watched on his knees on the bed. Josh's cock was getting harder with every pump of Cole's dick in his throat. Brad grabbed it and stroked it and his balls.

"Don't pleasure him Brad! Take his other hole. Fucking breed this bitch," Cole ordered. Brad looked at Cole. Fuck he was sexy with that evil streak. He looked around for some lube.

"No lube, use spit. He can take it dry I reckon," said Cole with snarl.

Brad pulled off his briefs and stroked his boner and spat on it. He lifted Josh's legs and spat on his hole.

Cole paused, balls deep in Josh's throat, both hands on either side of his neck and chin, controlling his head.

"Fucking drive in. No fucking mercy Brad," said Cole. He did as he was told, and Josh yelled but didn't bite, dribble coming out the sides of his mouth.

"Good lad," said Cole, "I knew you were a cumdump. Ok destroy it Brad. Rape that arse."

Brad smiled for the first time, when he realised that Josh was enjoying it and he finally was appreciating Cole's control and dominance. He was formidable. Cole and Brad got into a rhythm and pumped Josh's holes for a few minutes, then Cole ordered him to flip on his front and turn round. He wanted to fuck him now deep in his gut. He got into doggy position and then Cole drove into his hole. Cole pulled him up by his throat and held him as he thrust.

"You're fucking owned boy," said Cole.

"Yes sir, I'm yours," said Josh. This made Brad so excited. He was kneeling on the bed stroking his cock.

"Fucking service him, and eat his load," Cole pushed Josh forward towards Brad's cock, still holding his waist and arse on his own cock.

Josh downed Brad's cock and sucked him hard, like he did in that cleaning cupboard a week previously. It was only a minute before both Brad and Cole flooded Josh's holes with cum. Both ends pumped with shot after shot of cum, coating his inner gut and throat. Josh retained all the loads. He wasn't wasting a drop. Once finished. Cole pulled out and pushed him to one side, like casting him off. He even spat on his back for good measure.

That last action, excited Brad to do similar. He pulled Josh's cum filled face up to his. "Open wide slut," he sneered and then spat twice in his mouth, once in his face, then threw him down. Brad lay back on the bed.

Josh moved up beside him and was really hard now. He smelt Brad's pits and nipples. Cole joined them still in his jeans and sandwiched Josh between them. Cole started to run his hands over Josh's body,

"You want me to edge you?"

"Please sir. Yes sir," said Josh, now fully embracing the submissive role. Cole rubbed his leather thighs against Josh's. They felt amazing. Cole, then caressed his cock and gently wanked him, stopping, then starting again. Tormenting him over and over. He also instructed Brad to hold his torso and put one hand over his mouth as he edged him. Being controlled by these two handsome masters was amazing. The smell and taste of Brad's hand over his mouth was awesome, added with him teasing his nipples with his other hand. Cole wanked him again, stop, start, stop, start, finally he kept going and wanked him until Josh blew his load all over his chest. Cole kept wanking and Josh squirmed as his cock got sensitive from the hard touch, but Cole continued and rubbed the head to make the sensation worse, laughing as he did so.

"Stop, stop, stop!" said Josh muffled under Brad's hand, as the load kept coming. Cole had fully milked him and looked at the huge load all over his belly and chest and up Brad's arms. Brad released his hold and looked at Cole with amazement.

"Man, you're intense," he said with a smile.

"Fuck that was the best," said Josh panting. He fell back on the bed. "You're an evil bastard, but that was so hot and sexy," he said to Cole, who was grinning back.

"I've been told that many times," he smirked.

"Jeez Cole, you even scared me in places. I've never seen that side of you at work," said Brad. "Thank Christ," he added.

"And you never will. There's a place for everything," said Cole. "Let's go finish those beers. They moved to the lounge pulling on their underpants, chatted more about various topics. Cole, mainly talking about Bobby and how much he cared for him, which surprised Brad and Josh.

Chapter 11 - A Thank You

Bobby had a free day on Wednesday and was left to his own devices by Max and Peter, who went to the office. As they left, he volunteered to cook for the two of them for their return home. While Bobby had his back turned, Peter grimaced to Max at the thought, but accepted his guest's generosity.

"Wonderful, how kind."

In the empty apartment, Bobby got dressed and was out and on the street by 9am. He spent the day visiting all the sights. Tower Bridge, the Tower of London, Piccadilly Circus and Oxford street. He bought some Christmas presents for his Mom, a small bag and scarf from Liberty's. He also bought a further small item for Cole. He then went to the Mall and saw Buckingham Palace from the outside, Westminster Abbey and the Houses of Parliament. The sights were amazing to see up close. By mid afternoon he headed back to the King's Road and went into a wine shop and decided to buy Peter and Max a Christmas present. Two bottles of Montrachet. It was hard to buy something for people who seemed to have everything, but he knew this wine would be good. He got one gift wrapped by the shop, and one for tonight. He then went to a supermarket and bought the food for this evening. He walked back to the apartment and decided to get himself organised and packed his bags ready for his flight home. He would be heading out at 9am tomorrow and flying at 12.30pm.

Once packed, he prepped his food for the evening. Cole was the main cook, but he studied his recipes and decided to make a large piece of salmon he would cook in a bag with wine and herbs. Baby potatoes and salad. He bought a lemon tart for dessert. He set the table like Peter had done the previous times and he finalised it all. He looked at his watch. It was 5pm. They would be leaving soon. It would take about hour before they were home. He placed the wrapped bottle of wine under the tree, tucked away at the back.

Bobby had a shower and washed London off his body. He then had a thought in the shower with a huge grin. He would dress as a leather house boy for them when they arrived. Christ he was a tease, but he was sure that Max wouldn't mind him borrowing some gear.

He dried himself and ventured into Max and Peter's room. He felt a bit guilty being in there but still opened the wardrobes. Mainly normal clothes, and then he found the leather section. He smiled. He found some chaps, a harness, some cuffs and a muscle arm band. He opened a drawer and found a leather jock to wear under the chaps. He lifted it to his face and smelt it. It smelt of leather and Max. It also had cloudy marks on it.

"Umm previous loads," he smiled and licked the inside. He loved cum and knowing it was Max's was just too much to resist. He put the jock on, then the chaps. He struggled with the harness. The fit was good on his new body. He clipped on the cuffs, the armband, closed up the cupboards and went back to his room. He was going to put his gloves in the back pocket, but feeling his own arse, he realised there was no back pocket on chaps.

"Fool," he said.

He then tucked them in the strap of his jock. He decided to stay bare foot, especially as Peter liked his feet. Like Cole, Bobby had nice feet. Some feet are real ugly but his and Cole's were in good shape and handsome. His nails were neat too. They had not mistreated their feet having mainly worn trainers, which helped.

He walked around the apartment and checked it was nice and tidy. He adjusted the blinds in the windows. He wasn't putting on a leather show for the neighbours, just Max and Peter. He started finalising the food, when he heard the key in the door and laughter on the other side. He rushed to the door to greet them.

Peter and Max came through the door, to be greeted by a beautiful vision. A handsome young man in leather. His arms crossed and his crotch pushed forward.

“Good evening gentlemen,” said Bobby with a smile. “Can I take your coats?”

They handed them to him. “Please go and make yourself comfortable. Dinner will be about an hour.”

Peter said, “My god, you can stay forever if you want to be my house boy dressed like that. He grabbed Bobby’s bare arse and kissed him, and then licked his nipple. They moved into the main rooms and didn’t want to sit. They just watched Bobby, this blond young God, moving around their kitchen. He was standing at the counter, prepping the salmon. Max came up behind him to see what was being prepped, and then couldn’t resist. He knelt down and opened Bobby’s buttocks and shoved his face and tongue into his crack and rimmed him for about thirty seconds.

“Steady now, I’m trying to cook and I don’t want your ruining your appetite,” Bobby said in a matter of fact way. “I suggest you go and dress for dinner,” he smiled over his shoulder.

Max stood up and both he and Peter went into the bedroom. Bobby could hear the shower. Half an hour later, they both came out there room. Both head to toe in leather.

“We dressed for dinner,” said Peter with a grin.

Both were bare chested but in biker jackets and leather jeans. Max had the zip round ones that excited Bobby so much on their first meeting. Both had Muir caps on too, looking like two official officers.

"Please be seated," said Bobby and opened the bottle of Montrachet.

"Wow you remembered," said Max.

"I remember everything you tell me," said Bobby, "and I learn so much from you both."

He poured the wine and served the salmon dinner. They ate and chatted, casually in their leathers. They were all comfortable in them, but it would look an unusual sight to an outsider.

Max said, "Thanks for this. The meal is delicious and the chef looks even more delicious. I have a favour to ask you Bobby. Would you take an extra case home for me tomorrow? I need to take some extra winter clothes back home. Would you take that extra case home with you? Business class allows two cases. It's just got woollens and winter stuff. It would save me trying to take three cases back in January."

"No problem," said Bobby.

"You can keep it in your apartment and I'll pick it up when I get back in January. Would that be ok?" Max added.

"Sure Max. I'd do anything for you guys. You have helped me beyond my dreams. No problem," Bobby smiled.

"It's been both our pleasures. You have brought so much to our company," added Peter.

After dinner they retired to the sofa. Max and Peter on one and Bobby sat on the other. Legs wide apart revealing his crotch and package. He had his gloves on now.

"I know you've had dessert. I want to thank you for my job and this amazing trip to London. Also to give you a Christmas present," said Bobby.

"You earned everything yourself. Thank you for saving the IT over here," said Peter with a smile.

"My present to you," confirmed Bobby, "is me. Now. This night you can have and play with me however you want. No limits. Whatever you both desire."

Max leaned forward, "That's very kind, are you sure of this?"

Bobby leaned back, spread his legs further and put his hands behind his head, thus showing off his new torso and toned guns to their best.

"Come and get it boys," he said and kissed his own guns.

Peter and Max both moved over and caressed Bobby. Peter went for his arm pit with his tongue while Max dived and smelt Bobby's crotch licking at the flesh he had on show, tasting under his balls. He lifted his legs to reveal his arsehole and he went in with his tongue, his hands on his leather chap smothered thighs. Max's leather chaps looked great on this lad he thought. Peter moved between Bobby's armpits, nipples and neck, then kissed him hard. Max pulled him down the sofa to ensure his arse was hanging over the edge. He undid his zip-round-fly and released his now hard cock. He moved up on Bobby and kissed him, pushing Peter to one side.

"My turn," and put his full body weight on Bobby, rubbed his cock against Bobby's hole. Peter moved down and stroked Max's cock and licked his arse. He fingered both Max and Bobby, smelling them both, licking anything he could get access to.

Bobby was smiling and groaning with all the attention. He was straining in his jock, stretching the leather.

"Release my cock, please," he sighed.

Peter put his hand in and un-popped the leather pouch on one side and Bobby's cock burst out. Peter dived in under Max and took as much as he could in his mouth. This beautiful boy was so perfect he thought.

"Let's take him to our room," said Peter. Max stopped what he was doing grabbed Bobby into a fireman's lift over his shoulder and carried him into the bedroom.

"Woah," said Bobby laughing. "Fuck you are real strong Max."

Max stroked Bobby's arse as he walked to the bedroom. He then threw him on the bed.

"Careful," said Peter. "He's a valuable boy."

Peter was tugging at his now hard cock, seeing Max manhandle Bobby.

"I need to be inside him Max, move over."

Peter reached for some lube, prepping his cock. Max moved off and lay beside Bobby, smiling and playing with Bobby's nipples. All three were still in all their leather. Peter raised Bobby's legs and positioned to enter. He looked down and started to ease in, then watched Bobby's face as his cock slid in.

Peter leaned forward and grabbed Bobby's chest harness to get purchase as he pumped him hard. Bobby held his own legs up and watched Peter enjoying his hole, admiring his body.

"Fuck, you are so beautiful young man," said Peter.

"He sure is," said Max rubbing Bobby's abs and then moving to his cock and working that in his hand. Peter, after a couple of minutes, pulled out and lay down beside Bobby on the other side and then rolled him towards Max. Max got to see that pretty face, which was grinning at him, those lovely white straight teeth. Peter put his arms round him and then entered again and pumped him on his side, kissing his neck and back, while playing with his nipples and stroking all over Bobby's body.

Max moved in and started kissing Bobby and they both battled their dicks together. Max grabbed both together and wanked them in one hand together. The intensity of kissing and stroking was awesome. These two wonderful handsome, older men were so strong encasing Bobby's smaller but perfectly formed frame. The heat from their bodies was intensified by their smell. A smell of experienced men, the smell of warm leather. Bobby was so hard now holding Max's strong arms and shoulders through his leather jacket. Peter was still pumping him from behind and kissing, biting his neck, grunting and groaning, his leather thighs against his own. Max was stroking and kissing him. It was all way too much. He couldn't help himself and shot his load up Max's chest, his jacket and up the bed sheets, with a cry of pleasure.

The load took Max by surprise, "Woah Mister!" he laughed, kissing him harder. He used the cum on his hand to lube his cock and scooped up some cum from his jacket and fed it to Bobby, who ate it with relish.

"Both cum on me please. Stand over me, my masters, stand over me in your gear and cover me with cum, please," he begged.

Peter stopped fucking him and nodded to Max. He pulled out and the two men stood on the bed over Bobby. Thank God for Georgian houses with high ceilings. The two handsome British men stood over their cute American lad and wanked at the sight of his beautiful body in leather below them. Bobby watched and rubbed his soft cock and balls.

“Give it me. Give me your fucking juicy English loads,” he urged as he sat up, mouth open.

Peter came first shooting a reasonable load on Bobby’s face and chest. Max wasn’t far behind, grunting as he pumped four good loads straight into Bobby’s mouth, crossing his cheek and eye. He had cum hanging off his lashes and his huge smiling lips.

“Fuck yes,” he said. Licking and feeding the two loads into his mouth. He was a dirty little animal, but so pretty with it.

Max and Peter got down and knelt on the bed and kissed Bobby’s cum filled face.

“You are a fucking adorable boy,” said Peter. “Sleep with us tonight. I’d like that. You ok with that Max?”

“Sure, but let’s get this gear off, I wanna sleep naked and feel our bodies together now,” Max replied.

“I’d like that too,” said Bobby.

They got undressed and took a pee, then all got into bed. Bobby in the middle.

“You get the wet patch, seeing as you made the mess,” said Max.

“Err, I’d say that was your fault. You two shouldn’t turn me on so much,” Bobby laughed.

Peter turned the lights off and they all snuggled in and wrapped their limbs around each other. Bobby was encased between his two strong furry bosses. Life was good. They fell into a deep satisfied sleep.

Part 4 – Passport to Leather Central

Chapter 12 - Homeward Bound

6am, Bobby woke to find himself in between Peter and Max. Max was on his back asleep, Peter was asleep but had morning wood resting on Bobby's buttocks. Bobby turned round, gently moved down and took his cock in his mouth under the duvet and pleasured him. Peter slowly woke to the wonderful sensation.

"Christ, you are insatiable, I wish you were staying all Christmas," Peter laughed. "Yeah take it boy. Yeah take my morning load, that's what you want isn't it. You dirty boy. Yeah fucking take it."

Peter now had his hands on Bobby's head and controlled the motion and finally letting his load flood Bobby's mouth.

"Yeah, fucking take it all, take my fucking load," he added as Bobby gurgled taking every drop.

Max had woken to see what was going on and watched his husband getting off with movement of Bobby under the duvet. He was stroking his morning glory now too. He looked under the duvet to see Bobby, cleaning up Peter's dick and said, "My turn boy. Come back up here now."

He turned Bobby around to face Peter and spat on his hand and lubed his dick and very gently entered Bobby. He caressed his body and tenderly made love to him. A feeling Bobby had so rarely enjoyed. So often sex was a rough affair, mainly requested by his own doing. He liked it rough, but he was also finding a gentler session with Max, and occasionally Cole, a more fulfilling experience. The feeling of hands on skin and gentle kissing and tender licking was very erotic. A different experience.

Max put his arms fully around Bobby and gradually moved his body so he was lying on his back on top of Max's chest. Slowly, he kept on moving in and out of his hole, Max's hands caressing his chest and neck, kissing the back of his neck. Max was also smelling Bobby's hair, which was awesome. Having the weight of this lad on him felt good and he was enjoying the sex. Bobby was getting harder in this position and started to stroke his own cock as Max pumped inside him.

Peter was watching the motions next to him and decided to join in. He went down on Bobby's cock. He tasted of yesterday's sweat and cum, a perfect taste and he worked that cock hard. The combination of both men working his body, was too much again for Bobby. He blew his load instantly into Peter's mouth. Peter drew back and wanked the remaining spunk from Bobby's cock, then fed it to him. At which point, Max shot his load deep into Bobby's gut. Deep, deep pumps into his hole.

Max withdrew, moved Bobby back on the bed and both him and Peter kissed him.

"Thank you for the perfect Christmas gift," said Max.

"You're welcome sirs," said Bobby.

Today, Bobby was heading home. He got his stuff together and dressed in his leather jeans, sweatshirt, high tops and his denim jacket. Pretty much what he wore coming out, but with a clean sweatshirt. Max brought out the case he needed him to take back. He opened it to show the woollens inside neatly packed and then he shut the case.

"Thanks for taking this for me. We are heading to the office now. I have arranged for a car to pick you up at nine, to take you to Heathrow. And remind them of that upgrade," he smiled.

Peter gave him a hug and said, "Thanks so much for sorting us all out. You have been a wonderful guest and the work you did at the office is priceless. We will be sure it is reflected in the bonuses in January, once we have confirmed all our numbers. Thanks again and hope to see you again soon young man," he kissed him on the forehead.

Max gave him a hug and said, "See you next year!" grinning at his stupid joke. "I'm back on the 5th January. Safe travels and have a wonderful Christmas. Just you and Cole?" Max asked.

"Yes, though my mom is coming over."

Max and Peter then left and Bobby watched them drive away. He'd forgotten about the bonus scheme. I bet Cole hadn't. His sales commissions would be key to his earning ability. He may get a real big pay out after helping clinch that deal he thought. It was just before nine. He checked his room and ensured it was tidy, he took some photos of the apartment, so he could share them with Cole, who would be interested to see the place Peter lived. Then he took the two bags down the stairs and decided to wait in the downstairs hall for the car.

A silver BMW arrived and he assumed it was his car. He opened the door and the driver, Carl, helped put the cases in the car. As they exchanged smiles and pleasantries, Bobby got in the car and looked back at the house and hoped he would be back some other time.

Traffic wasn't too bad and they arrived at Heathrow with plenty of time. He thanked Carl and found a trolley to put his luggage on. He found the baggage drop and thought he'd chance it in the priority lane. He wasn't sure without having confident Max with him.

The lady on the desk, smiled widely at him. He was easy on the eye, she liked what she saw and his smell was very attractive.

"Hello Mr Wilson, I can see you are travelling First today with us."

Phew the booking was secure. He checked his bags and took his boarding pass and access to the First lounge. He thanked her and smiled and she checked out his cute arse in his leather jeans. She looked at her colleague, a young man.

"How cute was he? And that arse! Obviously loaded. He smelt gorgeous too," she said.

Her colleague replied, "Yes and definitely not your type darling," he winked.

"Drat, all the good looking ones are bloody gay."

Bobby went straight through security and to the BA Executive lounge and sat down with a drink and some snacks. He seemed to be the only person in the First lounge under the age of forty. Many people stared at him. So young to be in first and alone. He felt like some kind of young billionaire tycoon. He laughed to himself. He couldn't see anyone he would be interested in fooling around with and to be honest he'd had so much sex these last few days, it was the last thing on his mind. He was just glad to be going home and would be with his lovely Cole. He had missed him and would have loved him to have been able to come. However, it was 23rd of December and he would be with him for Christmas very soon.

Before he knew it, the flight was being called, so he headed for the gate. He was whisked through the gate and onto the plane, via another door even. Wow this is the life. He arrived at the door and was greeted by Richard, the steward who witnessed him giving Max a blowjob on the flight coming out. Richard smiled.

"Welcome back sir. Great to have you on board. Your seat is here," he pointed. The space for one person was huge. A seat/bed with space around you for your stuff. A large table and much bigger video screen. Wow.

"Champagne sir?" said Richard passing him a glass.

"Oh thank you," said Bobby.

"I'll be back later to give you a hand with anything or everything," he said with a wink.

Bobby was feeling frisky, being hit on by Richard. That didn't last long Bobby thought, thinking back to the lounge where he wasn't interested in more sex, but now he had a stirring with Richard.

"I'm gonna get blown this flight. That's for sure," he said out loud. Not realising the woman next to him was in earshot. She was in her seventies easily.

"Lucky you," she smiled.

"Oh sorry," said Bobby blushing.

"Don't be sorry, you're young and both handsome. If you can't have fun and take risks in your youth, you may as well be dead," she smiled and then went back to her magazine.

"Err ok," he said. He put his bag away and settled into his chair. Once in the chair he was out of anyone's line of view, which he was happy about.

He was fed and watered throughout the flight with a selection of wines and gourmet food and the latest movies. He decided he needed to pee and got up and went through the curtain only to bump into Richard.

"It's occupied at the minute. Anything I can help you with in there?" he said look at Bobby's nice bulge in his leather jeans.

"Maybe, what you got in mind?" said Bobby smiling.

"When they come out, let me help you pee and give you some inflight relief. I've got fifteen minutes 'til I do my next rounds," said Richard.

The door opened and the old lady came out the toilet. She smiled at them both.

She then said to Richard, "Remember this is First Class," Richard was scared she had heard and was annoyed. She added, "It's first class, which means first class service. You blow him good," she laughed with a wicked smile and went back to her seat. Bobby and Richard looked shocked to hear the old lady say what she said and then giggled.

Richard checked the coast was clear and bundled Bobby into the First class cubical. Which fortunately bigger than standard class.

"I need to pee," said Bobby.

"I'll help you sir," said Richard, unzipping Bobby's leather fly. "Wow they feel so soft," he said grappling with the leather. "No undies? Dirty boy," he smiled.

He then pulled out Bobby's cock.

"Impressive. Shower or grower? If a grower I'm gonna be in for some fun."

He turned Bobby around to face the toilet and held his cock for him as Bobby started to pee. Richard could feel the piss running through his dick as Bobby peed. He stood close behind and smelt Bobby's neck and hair and pushed his own crotch against his arse as he pissed.

"Stop moving or you're gonna need to clean up after," said Bobby, who was finishing and giving his dick a shake. Richard started to stroke it, and Bobby soon got hard and showed that he was also a grower and turned round for Richard, to present to him eight inches of hard cock poking skyward.

"Now service me like a good little Cabin Boy. As the old lady said, I expect a first class blow job and if it is less than that I'll have to raise it on the customer feedback," Bobby laughed.

"Yes sir," said Richard and he took Bobby as deep as he could, which was only half way. He used his hand to compensate for his inadequate abilities. Most guys he sucked would be about around five or six inches and he still struggled with gagging. Bobby tasted nice. Young cock, tasting of leather and warm crotch. This boy was clean. Some of the guys Richard blew had cheesy filthy dicks, or stale bodies, not noticeable at first for the aftershave, and so he often regretted his unwise choices.

Not today, this boy was beautiful, smelt great and tasted awesome. He worked Bobby hard.

"Come on dream boy. Is that all you got? Let me show you how it's done," he knelt down and unzipped Richard and pulled out his already hard cock. Six inches was a generous estimate Bobby thought, but thick. He took it down in one, to the hilt and then licked his balls right under the sack, to demonstrate how far he could go.

"Fuck, that's amazing. How do you do that?" Richard said with surprise.

Bobby kept going and didn't take long to make Richard cum, not with his skills. Richard blew in Bobby's mouth and as usual he didn't spill a drop, taking Richard's thick salty load down in one and swallowed with relish. He came up for air.

“Now your turn. It’s all in the breathing and relaxing the throat. I used to practice on cucumbers. It is a control thing, breathing through the nose.”

Richard took him as well as he could, but he preferred to wank him, which wasn’t ideal, but Bobby accepted it. Bobby took over and wanked looking down at Richard’s handsome face. He knew how to get off with his hand and soon he was close. He then grabbed Richard’s head and shoved his cock in partially so not to choke the lad. He shot his load into his mouth. Bobby didn’t want to get any on his uniform.

Richard took the load into his mouth. He smiled with it open showing his cum covered tongue. Bobby pulled him up to his face and kissed him hard with his tongue and sucked as much of his own cum out of Richard’s mouth and then grinned with a wide cum filled mouth, before swallowing.

“You sir, are an animal,” said Richard with a smile, “And I should get back to work.”

They zipped up their pants and Richard listened at the door. He opened the door, someone was outside waiting, he opened the door a jar and said, “You don’t want to use this sir, still cleaning up. It’s like a car crash in here. I suggest you use the one in Club, while I clean this mess up. Really sorry sir.”

The man said, “Ok. You have been in there a while. I’m glad I don’t have to do your job. You must see some sights. Thanks for the warning,” and he moved off into Club.

“Go!” said Richard to Bobby.

“The messes YOU have to clean up? I think I deserve the medal for the clean up,” Bobby winked and he then returned to his seat.

The old lady leaned out of her seat, "You were a while, was he any good," she giggled.

"I have no idea what you are talking about?" replied Bobby with a wink, and a lick of his lips.

She was insatiable that woman. I wish she was my nan he thought, she'd be a hoot.

"What's your name son?" she asked.

"Bobby, Bobby Wilson. And you?" he replied.

"Barbara Jackson. What you do for a living Bobby?" asked Barbara.

"I'm an IT programmer and analysts for a realtor," he replied.

"Oh which one? In Chicago?"

"Bartholomew Steadman, my boyfriend works there in Sales," said Bobby.

"How sweet, pays well then judging by first class," she stated.

"I should be in Club, I got an upgrade 'cos of my Boss. We came out together but he's staying in London for Christmas. What do you do?"

"I'm retired now, but I was a clothes designer back in the day, mainly the sixties and seventies. I invested well. Worked all over, I'm half British half Canadian and settled in Chicago. Love it, crazy town, but love it. Well it was lovely to make your acquaintance young man. Maybe I'll bump into you in a Trader Joe's or something?" she laughed and leaned back in her seat.

The rest of the flight was uneventful. More food and drink from Richard and then it was time to land.

He landed to a bright and cold Chicago at about 4pm. He gave Barbara some assistance with her hand luggage, before she was greeted by an attendant. She smiled and thanked Bobby as they went their separate ways.

He found a taxi after getting his luggage and going through security with ease. He told Max he didn't need the expense of a car. A taxi would be fine. He texted Cole and said he was on his way from the airport. The journey would be around forty minutes to an hour, depending on traffic. Cole said he would try and knock off now as it was quiet. It was two days before Christmas the office was really winding down. Bobby would need to go in next day still and debrief Freddie and his team on the London trip though.

Cole got the text and was excited to know Bobby was back in Chicago, he looked across the desk to Brad.

"Brad, can I knock off a little early? Bobby is on his way back and I would like to greet him on his arrival," he grinned.

"Sure," said Brad, "You know you can go when you like here, as long as the job gets done. It's real quiet now anyway. Nothing will be happening 'til January. Work from home tomorrow if you like. Just give me your final numbers by close tomorrow and then we can all have a good rest over Christmas," said Brad.

"Cheers," said Cole, grabbing his coat and heading for the door. He said goodbye to the few people in the office and wished them a Happy Holidays in case he didn't see them tomorrow. He decided to get an Uber. He wanted to be home before Bobby and out of his suit.

He managed it. He got in the apartment and quickly cleaned up the dishes. It wasn't as tidy as Bobby made it and now with all the added decorations he had attempted to do, it was a bit cluttered. He raced around and tried to make it look neater. He had bought a real Christmas tree and some tacky decorations, plus he put some garlands around the place, to give it a warm feel. He felt he should do this as Bobby's mom was coming and Bobby wouldn't have the time.

He then got out of his suit and into something more comfortable, and a little tighter. He wanted to remind Bobby what he had been missing. He'd heard about all the sex he'd had and he wanted to remind him that he was his best fuck, his boyfriend, his true love. Bobby knew he'd had a session with Brad and Josh, and Cole felt it was good, but it wasn't the same without Bobby he thought.

He texted, Bobby <Hi sweet cheeks. I'm in the apartment. Got home early. Txt me when you arrive, I'll come down and help with your bags xx.> Cole paused and thought. Blimey he was getting soppy. It must be the season.

Bobby received the text and smiled. He had really missed Cole. His hunky love. They were a unit, he smiled to himself. As he turned the last block, he messaged, <I'm cumming!> he grinned as he sent it. Then followed with <Just arriving>.

Cole got the messages and rolled his eyes. He put on some sneakers and ran for the elevator and headed to the lobby. He waited at the window, then he saw a Chicago cab heading towards the building. It was bloody icy outside, so he waited until it fully pulled up and the doors opened. Bobby got out the back and struggled with his luggage.

Cole raced out when he saw there were two cases and greeted his Bobby with a huge hug.

“Christ I’ve missed you. And damn it’s cold!” Cole said, grabbing both cases and rushing towards the door of the building. They got inside and in the elevator, and as soon as the doors closed, Cole kissed Bobby tenderly and hugged him again. Almost like he didn’t want to let go.

“God, it’s just not the same without you around,” Cole stated.

“Ahhh thanks. I’ve missed you too and I have so much to tell you. And you must tell me what you’ve been up to,” Bobby replied.

They entered the apartment and Bobby smiled and grinned at the decorations and the lovely tree.

“You’ve been busy. It looks great,” he lied. It wasn’t done how he would have done it but at least Cole had tried and that’s what counted. “I was thinking about this on the flight and wondering when the heck we were going to get time to do this. It looks awesome,” said Bobby on reflection.

“You like it? Really? I was worried it wouldn’t be done to your taste,” said Cole.

“I love it. And It’s so good to be back. London was awesome, but I wanted to be with you. Next time, we both must go.”

“So, what’s in the second case?” asked Cole.

“Oh, Max wanted me to bring some extra winter clothing back as I had space in my allowance. He said he’ll pick it up in January. Let’s shove it in the cupboard in the spare room for now,” said Bobby

They spent the rest of the evening talking about what they both did while apart, to much laughter and excitement. They got pizza delivered and drank beer. That night, they went to bed, and instead of having their usual hot rough sex, Cole and Bobby just held each other and kissed tenderly. They just spent the time touching and feeling their bodies and looking at each other. Cole looked so happy holding Bobby and Bobby loved being encased by his strong boyfriend.

Their prolonged tenderness and touching released a deeper connection between the two and the resulting erections felt amazing. The two edged each other, one at a time, and the final ejaculation was far more intense than either of them had ever experienced. The sensation stemmed from their inner core. A hot rush swept through their bodies from their stomach to their toes. Considering the slowness of movement, they both felt exhausted by the experience.

"God, I love you Cole," said Bobby. "You mean the world to me."

"I'm so sorry I was cruel to you at school. I can't believe that now, you are my world. How could I have been so fucking horrible to you," said Cole.

"You must stop bringing this up Cole. It was all part of growing up and finding ourselves. I still fancied the pants off you then and now I have you it's even better. Can this be the last time you bring this up with sadness. The fact is, if you hadn't behaved like that, I may not have been as obsessed with you. I then wouldn't have wanked for many nights thinking of you, and that fateful day in the bar with Max may not have gone the way it did. If you had been a different person then that amazing evening would never have happened. We wouldn't have got to know Max and now have these incredible jobs. So, in fact, you bullying me, all those years ago, led us to all we have now. So embrace it fella. Now shut the fuck up and give me a kiss," instructed Bobby.

The following day, Christmas Eve, Cole was going to work from home but decided to go in, as Bobby needed to. He didn't want to spend any more time away from him.

They went to the office and a few were in. Bobby sat down with Freddie and Troy. He detailed what had gone on in London and showed them the changes he had made. He also discussed, that he suggested to Max and Peter that a review of all three systems would be advisable, as they are so out of sync, and starting to get expensive to support. Freddie agreed, and had wanted to do this for years but Peter had always been opposed. Brian was also part of the old guard, which Freddie was always conscious of.

Bobby said, "I think they are all open to it now, but we would need to involved all three cities and be very inclusive. Brian is ok, once he feels you are not pushing him out. I think he realises he is getting older and new ideas are coming in faster than he would like. He knows he needs to move forward and Peter is on board now. Brian has so much knowledge that we must not lose either."

Cole was watching Bobby in action from a couple of desks away. Not the place he would usually sit but the space was empty and he wanted to watch Bobby. He studied him and thought to himself, he's changed in the last four days. He's more confident, self assured and seems even taller, which couldn't be true. Bobby was holding himself more confidently and taking more control of situations and conversations, not in an arrogant way, just more self assured.

Cole watched and thought how much sexier Bobby was as well like this. The sex they had last night had been driven by Bobby, who slowed it down and took control, something normally Cole was in charge of. But he liked it and the sensations were electric. That boy has hidden depths Cole thought.

They finished at lunchtime and everyone left for home at this point. Bobby and Cole got an Uber to Bobby's mom's house and collected her and her stuff for Christmas. She was staying overnight, as Bobby didn't see her that much and missed that. So, some time would be nice and they had the room. He wanted to look after her this Christmas after the many times she did it for him. Since earning more money, he was able to get his mom on a healthcare insurance programme and help far more with her rent, so she could start to get back on her feet and live a little.

Cole hadn't seen his mom for over ten years and she had his number but never tried to call. He'd tried calling a couple of times and she just ignored or screamed down the phone. Bobby's mom liked Cole and gave him a huge hug. Though Bobby hadn't really shared their full history at school. Cole felt sheepish again thinking of how nasty he was, then he remembered what Bobby said again last night and snapped out of it. Man, he really was the best guy, Cole thought.

They got back to the apartment and Bobby's Mom, Marg, settled into the spare room. This morning, the boys completely cleaned, changed the bedding and checked for any offending articles. This was after all called 'The Dungeon', and where all action happened with others. They were glad they did check, there were a few stains and stuff under the bed that had to be squirrelled away out of sight.

Christmas Eve was a magical evening and the boys treated Marg like a queen, cooking and giving her small presents before the big day. It was great for her to be with her son and to see him so happy and doing so well. She asked all about London and what he did and saw. That required a lot of editing! Bobby showed her photos on his phone of Max and Peter and the places he had been. Just before midnight they all went to bed to be ready for the big day.

The following morning, Cole woke first and gave his sleeping beauty a kiss on the nose and gently on the mouth. As Bobby stirred Cole gently whispered, "Happy Christmas boyfriend," holding a small bag over his face.

Bobby woke up with a smile. He sat up and looked at the bag.

"Open it," said Cole.

"What now? I thought we were opening all presents with mom?" said Bobby.

"Not this one. This is for us only," said Cole.

Bobby looked in the bag and found a small box. He fished it out and opened it. Inside were two titanium rings. Simple clean design. One slightly smaller than the other.

"They are friendship rings. Yours has my name engraved on it and mine has yours. I wanted something to show how special you are to me and that I see you as my true friend and soulmate Bobby," said Cole.

Bobby pulled the smaller one out and looked at the engraving on the inside. It simply said 'Cole'. He put it on and Cole put his on.

"That's adorable Cole. I love it. I love them. I love you." He then grabbed Cole's face and gave him a huge kiss.

"Now I would like to play around with you, but we have stuff to do." Bobby laughed. "I need to get those presents under the tree and sort out that turkey. What time is it?"

"7.30," Cole replied.

"Shit. Come on. You jump in the shower and I'm get mom a coffee and get those presents out, so she thinks Santa has delivered"

Cole did as instructed and walked out to the bathroom naked, forgetting they had a guest.

"Hi handsome," said Marg with a laugh.

Cole jumped, "Oh shoot Mrs Wilson. Sorry, force of habit," he ran to the bathroom grabbing his tackle.

"Mom you're up. I was going to surprise you with coffee and I haven't got the presents under the tree yet," said Bobby coming out the room in only his shorts.

"Well I was excited to be here with you and..... my my you have developed young man," Marg was looking at her son's nicely toned body. Not something she had seen before.

"Yeah Cole helped me with a programme at the gym," replied Bobby.

"Cole is a feast for the eyes I have to say Bobby. How did you snag him?" she said with a cheeky smile.

"Mom please. I'm gonna put more clothes on. This is totes awks," he laughed.

"I'm only playing with you son. You and Cole make a very handsome couple. I'm really happy for you."

Bobby made coffee and got started on prepping stuff for lunch.

"Can I help?" said Marg.

"No, you're our guest," said Bobby.

Cole came out the bathroom with a towel around his waist, smiling that gorgeous smile.

"Give me two ticks and I'll be out and can sort that Bobby, while you get showered. Or Mrs Wilson, do you want to go now?" said Cole.

"Please call me Marg, and yes I'll go now."

Cole went into the bedroom and Marg looked back at Bobby.

"My, if I was twenty years younger," she smiled.

"And a gay man!" Bobby shot back with an eye roll and a grin.

Cole came back into the main room dressed in casual clothes and Marg went into the bathroom. They both put presents under the tree and then started prepping vegetables. Marg came out of the shower and Bobby went in. It was like musical chairs in the apartment. Cole put some cheesy Christmas music on and got the turkey prepped and in the oven. He enjoyed cooking. Wasn't sure how he got the bug, but since having a proper kitchen he started to self-teach from good recipes. He was great at following them and achieved good results.

Bobby got dressed and came out of the bedroom, singing along to Wham!'s 'Last Christmas'. Bobby's phone started to ring. He looked around to find it. He got to it.

"It's Max?" he said. "Hi Max. You ok?"

"Hi Bobby, Merry Christmas to you and Cole. Hope it's not too early," said Max. "Peter and I wanted to wish you both a Happy Christmas and to ask you a favour."

"What's that?" said Bobby.

Cole was looking perplexed. Bobby put the phone on loud speaker.

"Can you do me a favour and check something in my suitcase for me?" Max asked.

Bobby walked to his Mom's room and went to the closet at the back and pulled out the suitcase.

"Sorry Mom, just gotta check something," said Bobby.

"Hi Mrs Wilson. Merry Christmas, you have an extraordinarily talented son by the way," said Max hearing the conversation.

"Thanks," she replied. "Who's that?" she whispered.

"My Boss," Bobby mouthed back.

Bobby pulled the case into the lounge and shut the door, so his Mom could get ready in peace.

"Ok got it. What am I looking for?" said Bobby. Cole came over to the suitcase.

"Open it up. Now under the jumpers are two parcels. Presents to you and Cole from Peter and I. Thank you both for this last year. Merry Christmas and see you in January," he hung up instantly.

Bobby looked at the phone surprised at being cut off. He lifted the jumpers to find two large flat boxes beautifully wrapped with Christmas monogrammed paper and ribbon, with tiny leaf shaped design, that Bobby seemed to recognise. Marg came out the room.

"He sounds nice. Lovely accent. He's not looking for a wife is he?" she laughed. "What's all this then?" looking at the case.

"Presents for Cole and me," said Bobby.

Marg said, "They look expensive. Go on open them."

Bobby checked the labels and passed Cole's to him and he held his.

"Reasonably heavy," said Cole.

They undid the ribbon and then the realisation came over Bobby.

"Fucking hell. Really?" said Bobby.

"Language," said Marg.

"What is it?" said Cole.

"Open and you'll see, I can't believe it," said Bobby, realising what the emblem on the paper was. It was the Belstaff logo. They both opened the boxes and the smell of leather filled the room.

"Wow," said Cole, picking up the black Outlaw design jacket and looking at it closely, feeling the quality. Cole had the Outlaw design with the padded quilted shoulders.

"Put it on," said Marg. Cole stood up and unzipped it. Bobby stopped opening his and watched Cole, he wanted to see him putting it on. Cole put it on, and it fit perfectly. It felt great, it smelt great and the sizing was just right for him.

"This feels amazing, trying to see his reflection in the window.

"Have you got the same?" said Cole.

"Don't know," said Bobby, he then opened and pulled his jacket out the cotton bag. His was black but slightly different

"This is the Maxford 2. This is the one Max got me to try on in the shop. He's mad our Boss. You know how much these were?" said Bobby.

"Try it on," said Marg all excited for the boys.

"How much?" said Cole, having not looked at the label.

"Fifteen hundred bucks equivalent," said Bobby trying on his jacket. The Maxford was a similar cut to Cole's Outlaw jacket but with smooth shoulder detailing and angled zip pockets. Bobby's fitted perfectly too.

"Fifteen hundred bucks!!!!" screamed Cole.

"What did you get them?" laughed Marg. Bobby looked at them both

"A hundred dollar bottle of wine."

Cole stared at Bobby, and Bobby stared back. Then they looked at each other's jackets. Cole said, "You look awesome in that. Fits so well."

"Yours is perfect on you and Max so got the designs right to each of us. He had me try this one on. He was buying a different one for Peter and your jacket in tan brown colour. He must have sneaked the other two on the order while I was out of the shop. He must have spent about six thousand bucks that day in that shop!" said Bobby.

"Let's check them out in the mirror," said Bobby.

The both ran to the bedroom like school kids. Marg followed loving seeing the excitement on the boys' faces. They looked like young teenagers rather than young men, she thought, as they jostled for position in front of the mirror.

"I love them," said Cole grinning. He then whispered in Bobby's ear "I'm gonna fuck you in these very soon."

Bobby whispered back, "It may be me fucking you handsome,"

"What you whispering about? Anyway, those are gonna make my presents look rubbish now," she smiled.

"No, they will not Mrs Wilson. We will love them 'cos they are from you, and besides, Max has so much money this would be a drop in the ocean for him, not that I'm belittling their kindness and thought. It's not the money, it's the thought and I can see he also took some time choosing these for us," said Cole.

"We should ring him back to say thank you. Quick Mom, take a picture to send him."

Marg took the phone and photographed them together. Bobby examined it and then sent it to Max with couple of kisses. He then rang him back.

"Hi Max, Peter. We love them but they are too expensive. You really shouldn't have," said Bobby.

Max replied, "You look awesome in them. You still on speaker?"

"No," said Bobby.

"Then when I get back you can repay me by both fucking me wearing them," Max laughed and said, "I'm so glad Cole's fitted perfectly, I had to guess a little. You have been real assets to our business, just don't tell the other staff we bought them or they will all want one! Have a wonderful day lads. And thank you for the wine. It's chilling as we speak. Too kind. Take Care."

Max then hung up.

About five minutes later Max sent a text of him and Peter in their new jackets, both in brown. They looked great.

The rest of the day was opening presents, eating and drinking and singing. Cole loved his wallet. Most of the presents Bobby and Cole bought each other were clothes. Grinder boots for Cole, CAT boots for Bobby, jeans and shirts. Marg bought them some kitchen items and wine glasses, to add to the new apartment. She loved her scarf and bag from London.

Christmas was a truly magical end to an amazing year for them both and with a new year on the way, what could possibly go wrong.....?

by Nick Christie

TRAGÖDIE IN DER STADT
(Part 5 in 'The Misfits' Series)
NICK CHRISTIE

Tragödie in der Stadt

(Tragedy in the City)

(Part 5 in 'The Misfits' Series)

(Erotic Gay Fiction)

Nick Christie

Chapter 1 - Back to Reality

Max was greeted by his driver at Chicago Airport. He was tired after his flight and was now heading back into the city to his apartment. He was thinking about how good it was being with Peter in London: the extended trip had been wonderful. First, with Bobby in the house adding a bit of spice and then driving up to Leicester to collect his parents and bringing them down to London to spend Christmas with him and Peter. His parents were getting older now, but were still full of life and laughter and they stayed a couple of nights with them. They also took them to see a musical in the West End on Boxing Day, best seats of course, and took them to a great restaurant. Max always liked to spoil his parents, because they had given up so much for him during his childhood.

They worked hard and didn't have much money, but anything they had spare was spent on Max. They were great when he came out to them at the age of fifteen. Peter adored them too, he wished his parents had 10% of their compassion. He rarely spoke them and knew he had been cut out the will many years ago. He saw Max's parents now almost as his own and would pretty much do anything for them.

They had a great Christmas and on the twenty ninth of December both Max and Peter drove them back up to Leicester, with a car full of presents. Max smiled at how lucky he was, but he also how sad it was he didn't see them more often.

He smiled at the thought of the cosy New Year he had with Peter. Just the two of them in the apartment, nice and quiet. The days of going to New Year parties was well over. Both were tired of them, often seeming to last an eternity and then it was a huge arse ache trying to get a taxi home after. They'd much rather stay in with a couple of great bottles of wine, a good meal and a roaring fire.

He arrived at his apartment and unpacked. He liked to get everything back in order. He cranked up the heating too. Chicago was now bitterly cold and the apartment felt cooler than he liked. It was late afternoon. He called Peter to say he was 'home'. Strange to say this was home he thought after. Peter's apartment was nearer to home, in reality, but these last few years Chicago was his main home. It was too late to be bothered to go to the office, so he would call Gina for an update on everything and start afresh tomorrow.

Bobby and Cole had also enjoyed a wonderful Christmas and the extra time off spent together had been very special. From the day after Boxing day until New Year's Eve, they spent the time totally together, barely speaking to other people.

They went to the cinema twice, the gym at least once a day and for a couple of nice meals out. They went to the two restaurants that Max took them to, to see what it was like without his presence, to see if the staff were as attentive. They were happy to say they had a great time. The rest of the holiday, they were in the apartment. It was too cold to be out for long and not having a car, meant getting around was a cold existence. But Cole had loved the time in the apartment so much. Just being able to hold and cuddle his Bobby.

He loved being out with Bobby and spent most of the time during the meals staring at his boyfriend. He loved being so close to someone, being close to Bobby. His own childhood had been without a great deal of love or affection and now he had Bobby it was like he was making up for lost time.

In bed Cole would always want to be holding Bobby and in and around the apartment, he would be forever cuddling, kissing or touching him. He was totally in love with that man and Bobby knew it.

Bobby was amazed at how much Cole had changed. From when they first met, he was an arrogant, nasty lad who treated him badly. Cole was the total alpha male. Bobby loved that side of Cole, it was exciting and sexy, but he also loved the attention of the softer side, the way Cole cared and looked out for, almost protected, him now. In the week over Christmas time Bobby saw real love in Cole's eyes for him and it made his own heart melt.

Fortunately for Bobby, Cole occasionally switched on the alpha role with Bobby in bed, or wherever sex was happening, which satisfied Bobby's desires. But Bobby was changing too. He was becoming more confident. The fact that he was dating a man like Cole, made him feel about ten feet tall and boosted his confidence. It was like seeing two alpha males, both madly in love with each other, taking on the world.

For New Year they went out with Troy and Jamie to a restaurant and then to a late-night gay club to see the New Year in. Both were wearing their new leather jackets from Max and Peter and fuck did they look hot in them. These four handsome guys in the club were getting hit on continually, which they all found hilarious. But amazingly they weren't interested in any of the guys hitting on them, they just wanted to dance and have fun, drink and be with their respective partners. Troy and Jamie had also been going from strength to strength.

To save on the crazy taxi prices, not to mention the fact it was impossible to get one at New Year, it was decided that they would stay at Bobby and Cole's apartment.

They arrived, back at the apartment in the early hours, had a final drink and then both couples crashed in their respective rooms. Troy had expected the invite to mean a four-way sexathon and was surprised, and a little disappointed, it didn't. It had been a while since he had been man handled by Cole. But he understood why. Cole only really had eyes for Bobby.

Troy also knew how much Jamie meant to him, and their sex life was every more satisfying. Troy's deviant side was taking Jamie into new areas, which he was thoroughly enjoying. In the spare room Jamie fucked Troy hard, making quite a bit of noise.

Bobby and Cole could hear them as soon as they got through their door. They got undressed but started to get aroused at the sound.

"Put your jacket back on Cole. Just you and your jacket and fuck me like the bad bad leather boy you are," said Bobby.

"You do the same and I'll fuck you even harder," responded Cole.

They both stripped off their clothes and put their jackets back on. By this point they both had huge hard-ons. The pair looked so damn sexy in their jackets. Just them and their erections. Cole moved in and kissed Bobby hard. He then grabbed him and threw him on the bed. Bobby was face down. He raised his arse.

"Take me now, fucking destroy my hole," he urged.

Cole spat on his cock and climbed on top of Bobby, reaching his hand around his head and over his mouth with his other hand fingered his hole, guiding his engorged cock in. He muffled the yell with his hand as he drove into Bobby's hole.

"Yeah, that's it. Scream for your Master, leather boy. Take my dick you little bitch boy."

Cole pounded Bobby's arse with relish and enjoyed the feel and the smell of the two leather jackets warming up with their body heat. His Bobby looked so hot in his jacket and he was growing stronger now and more difficult to control.

“Oh, fighting back now are we?” he said, as Bobby struggled to get out his grasp.

Cole put both hands on Bobby’s shoulders and back, pinned him down and kept pounding.

“Yeah, fuck me Cole and when you’re done, you’re gonna fucking get it back ten times over. There are two leather boys here and I gotta fuck too,” Bobby gasped aggressively.

Cole eased off and moved over.

“Go for it sexy. Plough me hard.”

Cole was on his back now, his jacket open, framing his beautiful abs. He raised his legs, ready for Bobby, who stood up and took position.

“Fuck you are so fucking hot and you fucking know it, which makes you even hotter,” said Bobby as he prepped Cole’s twitching hole.

“Yeah I fucking do. Now breed me,” ordered Cole smirking.

Bobby gently entered Cole and then started pumping him. Bobby was looking down on his handsome man, in his sexy jacket, the smell of leather rising from both their warm bodies. Bobby moved forward and Cole raised his arse, allowing Bobby to come down face to face with him, gently fucking his man, while also kissing that handsome mouth and jaw.

The noise next door was getting louder from Troy and Jamie.

“Let’s go join them,” said Bobby. “Let’s offer to fuck them, you and I as tops, together.”

“Hell yeah,” said Cole. “Which you want?”

“I know Troy will want you, but I want to fuck him. It’s about time I fucked my work mate,” Bobby laughed.

They got up, still in their jackets both with raging hard ons and burst into the spare room.

“What the fuck’s happening in here?” Cole shouted.

They found Jamie naked, kneeling at the end of the bed, driving a huge dildo into Troy’s arse. Troy was squealing with delight. They stopped and looked round at the sudden door opening. Bobby and Cole standing there in their leathers with boners.

“Come join the party and see in the New Year,” said Troy.

“This is our apartment and our rules. You boys are going to be fucked by us leather bad boys and you’re gonna fucking take it,” said Cole.

“Fine with me. Bring it on!” said Jamie.

“Your hole is what I want,” said Cole back to him.

“Which means you Troy is gonna get some Bobby punishment.”

The two men walked in grabbed their naked guys and pushed them back on the bed. Bobby pulled that dildo out roughly, grabbed Troy’s neck, pushed him on the bed, lifted his legs and entered him in three swift moves. Troy was mesmerized by how agile and strong Bobby was and how he manipulated his body into the correct position to fuck. He looked real sexy in that jacket. He’d noticed both of them all night. Bobby pumped Troy hard and Troy played with his cock watching his work mate ploughing him, reaching zones in his arse, that he hadn’t felt before. This boy was a master, he thought.

Standing at the end of the bed with Jamie sitting, Cole grabbed Jamie's head and fed him his cock, inching impatiently into his throat. Jamie was struggling with his size.

"Fuck you need more training boy," said Cole. "You need some lessons from Bobby," he added.

Jamie was only managing four inches of Cole's nine. Cole wasn't satisfied, so pulled out. He pushed Jamie back, grabbed his legs and twisted him over onto his front.

"Present that arse soldier!" Cole commanded.

Jamie raised his hairy arse and pushed his back down. Cole entered, straight up to the hilt. Jamie yelled at first and then started to moan as Cole got into rhythm. Troy watched both Bobby and Cole in action. It was awesome. Bobby and Cole looked at each other, Cole raised his hand and they then high-fived as they both thrust into the lads.

After a few minutes of hole destruction, Bobby said, "Get ready bitch. I'm gonna flood you," and he then delivered his load deep into Troy's gut.

Cole wasn't far behind and grabbed Jamie's hips as he pushed in hard a few more times. He pulled out and decided to jack off, giving his familiar roar as he pumped five ropes of cum over Jamie's arse and back. He stood back to watch Troy and Bobby, jump in to clean up that load, fighting each other for the nectar.

Bobby and Cole then stood up and headed for the door. "Now keep it down. It's 3.30 in the morning. Breakfast at the diner on the corner at ten."

They then both left Jamie and Troy to finish each other off. Bobby and Cole giggled as they went to their bedroom, hanging their jackets over the back of the sofa on the way.

That was quite a Christmas and New Year.

Chapter 2 - Bonus

Everyone was back in the office and at work by the 6th January. It was back to business and very soon the festive season was a dim and distant memory. The new contract they won last year with Trinity Enterprises was going to take some planning work. Brad and Max spent the best part of the first week back nose-deep in planning to be sure to give their projects the highest priority. Brad's right hand person, Sheri Dennis, was ensuring the rest of the projects didn't slip while this was happening.

Sheri was a strong minded extremely intelligent black woman, who knew sales and managing people very well. She had been at Bartholomew Steadman for three years and had worked her way up to second in command in sales within that time. Originally from Boston, she transferred to Chicago when she met Brad at a trade event. He was impressed with her skills in selling, as well as her sexy arse. He tried it on with her, but she was having none of it, which intrigued him even more.

The chase was on and she knew it. She took advantage of Brad's advances and finally landed a job with Bartholomew Steadman two months later. To this day Brad hadn't managed to get in her pants. To be honest Brad gave up once she started at the office. He felt it wasn't right to with a colleague. In fact, Cole was the only member of the team Brad had fooled around with, but he felt with that guy, no strings meant no strings. Ladies can be harder understanding that, he had found.

Bobby, Troy and Freddie started mapping out a plan for a group system upgrade. They were working on scoping the project to share with Max and Peter and then Brian in London and Kurt in Berlin. The idea was to create a proposition for all the areas to discuss and amend. The project would probably take six months to implement so they thought it best to start now.

Cole was working on another housing development, working hard on getting as many sales in as possible during January, which is usually a very sluggish month.

Gina was finalising the year end accounts with the finance team and the auditors. Overall the year had been very good. The Trinity Enterprise deal had yet to start, so no profit yet from that. The benefits from that would show in next year's figures. This year the profits would show a healthy bonus for all and by late January everyone would get their letters detailing what they could expect to receive.

Each area, London, Chicago and Berlin were run individually. Successes and failures were kept in those profit centres. But in each, Max and Peter were the 80% shareholders, and the employees in each centre shared 20% of the profits after reinvestment. So, in Chicago, this would be split based on years of service, pay grade, and type of job.

The letters were out, but everyone was very discreet to not share what they got. Max made it clear that everyone was paid handsomely for their work against market rates and he would not tolerate any bitching about bonuses. While there was room for individual queries around their bonus, comparisons were discouraged. Max said that was vulgar and would be like comparing apples and pears. He would never consider it. To be fair everyone was normally more than happy. They loved their jobs and were paid well, with great perks. The bonus always seemed more than fair. The letters were sent in the post, to avoid being opened in the office.

Bobby and Cole received theirs in late January. They opened them quickly.

"Wow," said Bobby.

Bobby had received $6,524 bonus for his five months' work for that year. But in addition, he received a staggering $7,000 for solving the problem in London.

"Jesus Cole, I got sixty five hundred dollars as bonus and an extra seventy hundred for sorting the fuck up in London. My God that's amazing. What did you get?"

Cole was staring at his letter, his mouth gaping open like a fish.

"Well?" said Bobby.

"I don't believe it!" he passed the letter to Bobby. Bobby read it. Cole had received commissions of $28,355 partly due to his incredible margin retention and the sheer number of sales in two months, plus he got $2,000 for helping clinch the Trinity Enterprise deal and then at the end of the letter it said, he was to be given a personal company car for his own use, which he would be issued with this coming Friday.

"Fucking hell Cole. That's amazing," said Bobby, who crossed the table to him and planted a huge kiss on is open mouth.

These amounts would be before tax of course, but these numbers seemed ridiculous for five months' work, and Cole felt he'd only really added value these last two months. The next day, then both went to Max's desk.

They asked, "Can we have a word please?"

"Yes, let's go to the conference room," Max said. Gina looked at them as they went to the room. She saw they were holding their letters.

Once inside Cole asked, "Are these numbers correct Max?" passing him the letter. Max didn't need to look he knew he had already checked every letter thoroughly.

"Yes, they are. Why, were you expecting more?" Max asked.

"Good God no. I wasn't expecting anything like this," said Cole.

Bobby added showing his letter, "Me neither. Are you sure they are right?"

"Yes, I'm sure. I check each letter individually," said Max.

"But we have only been here five months, plus the jackets at Christmas and everything else you have done for us. Getting us the jobs in the first place," said Bobby.

"Yes, I gave you a chance at first, the jackets were a gift, and I still hope to see you in them at some point," he smiled. "But the rest after that was your doing. Cole, I told you when you moved to sales, that the basic pay was lower but the commissions from Sales will more than make up for that. The Trinity Enterprises, was an extra for now, even though we haven't made any money yet from them, but we will. The car is a must for a sales person of your calibre. It also helps poke the others who are under performing," he laughed.

"You Bobby, have excelled in your role and the amount of overall money you have saved the business counted for a lot. The work you did sorting the fuck up in London, was priceless. I wanted to give you more, but I have to look impartial. I can't have favourites," he smiled. "So yes, the numbers are right. One more thing. You were told not to share with colleagues, I know you are a couple, but please be sure to not share those letters and numbers with anyone else," he added.

"We won't," said Cole. "And thanks again Max. You and Peter are legends and I can't thank you enough."

"Me too," smiled Bobby, and with that they all left the office and went to their desks.

Gina whispered to Max, "Not enough in their bonus?" with an eye roll.

"On the contrary, Gina. The complete opposite. They thought we got it wrong and it was too much," Max replied.

"Ahh how sweet," she smiled and carried on with her work.

Friday afternoon, back in the office, Brad asked Cole, "You wanna see your new car then mister?" in front of all the other sales people. Bobby watched from across the office, seeing what Brad was doing. He liked a small level of rivalry within sales, to spur them all on to sell more and better. A little competition. But Cole had sold way more houses than anyone else in the residential team: almost 50% of the last two months sales were his and he was one of a team of five! So, they couldn't begrudge him and he was a popular member of the team, always willing to help others, without claiming their sales.

"Come on then," said Brad, swinging a set of keys in the air. He took Cole to the underground car park. Max went too, followed by the sales colleagues, Bobby decided he wanted to go too.

They all got to the car park and Brad walked along the row of the silver Audi S3s that were the pool cars. Cole was full of anticipation of which one of these he would be able to have as his own company car. Brad gave Cole the key fob. Cole pressed it and heard a click of a car and saw some flashing lights but on the far side of the car park, not from the silver S3s.

"Which one is it?" he said, trying the key again, then seeing on the next row a flash of lights again.

Cole stood with his mouth wide open for the second time this week. Bobby saw his face and grinned at the car that had flashed. Cole moved so fast through the parked cars towards the car. In front of him was jet black Audi RS5 coupé with tinted glass and grey alloys. It looked awesome. He opened the door and the smell of new car hit him. Inside it had a black and red leather seats and an amazing sports interior. Cole sat in the driver's seat and Bobby stood at the door.

"Wow this is awesome!" said Bobby.

"My God Bobby! We are going driving this weekend," he smiled back.

"We need to get Jamie to sort a car park space in the apartment building," said Bobby practically.

The rest of the team were admiring the car and muttering. Cole smiled at them, got out the car and went to Brad and Max.

"Thank you so much for this, it's amazing," he said.

"You earned it dude," said Brad. "Ok let's get back to the office," and Brad and they all circled back and went upstairs again.

Bobby got on the phone to Jamie straight away about the parking spot. As a special favour he got a space sorted at a discounted rate for them which would be added to the rent. They just need to register the car on their website now, which Bobby sorted for Cole in less than fifteen minutes.

That evening they drove home together in Cole's new car and took the extremely long way home. In fact, it took almost an hour.

That weekend Bobby and Cole seemed to spend it entirely in the new car. They took Bobby's mom out for a spin as well. Then on the Sunday they went out of town and far up north and spent the day by Lake Michigan in the country park. It was still extremely cold, but the views of the icy trees and lake were amazing.

They parked up and Bobby looked at Cole sitting at the wheel of this beautiful car. His large manly hands on the steering wheel, his powerful thighs in tight jeans below the wheel. His boyfriend was so fucking hot in his eyes, as hot as the day he first saw him by the lockers when he started high school. Bobby started to massage Cole's thigh.

"What ya doing?" asked Cole.

"Do I need to explain? I think we need to christen this car with at least a blowjob," said Bobby. "Recline your seat, handsome."

Cole found the controls. He moved the seat the wrong way at first, then corrected himself and slowly moved the seat back. Bobby started to unzip Cole's jeans and undid his belt.

"Now relax and enjoy," said Bobby.

He took Cole's limp cock out and took it in his mouth, massaging it with his tongue and lips. Cole was getting erect and Bobby continued taking his shaft deep in his throat. Working it back and forth. Cole was moaning with pleasure. Bobby was the master of sucking dick and he had so many ways he did it, that it was rarely ever the same twice. The different ways Bobby approached sucking dick made it so exciting for the recipient and, with that largely being Cole, it meant each time almost felt like the first.

Bobby's talents were working their magic now and Cole was ready to blow.

"I'm close Bobby," said Cole.

A few seconds later Cole blew his load into the back of Bobby's throat. The hot cum filling Bobby's mouth and tongue. Bobby's lips tight around the shaft ensuring no cum was lost or messed up those hot jeans or the jock Cole was wearing.

"Fuck that tasted good. The cock of my man, in his hot new car that smells of new leather. Fuck that was exciting," said Bobby.

They sat for a while admiring the view and discussing how they were planning to spend their bonuses. New clothes was a start, they even considered getting a bigger apartment, but they did like the location of the one they had. Maybe a bigger one with another bathroom would be available. They would check with Jamie on Monday. Vacations too. Weekends away in Vegas or San Francisco. But then Europe was a big idea. A couple of weeks, in London, Paris, Rome, all those places. They now had the funds and the holiday time to do it as well. They would have to start planning very soon.

They drove home the long winding route and Cole enjoyed the car's performance. The four wheel drive was awesome on the icy roads.

"Do you think I could be allowed to drive your car?" asked Bobby.

"I'll check on Monday. As my partner I don't see why not. Plus you are also an employee. I'll speak to Brad and Gina on Monday," Cole smiled, wanting to share his new toy with his boyfriend.

Chapter 3 - Tight leather

The following Monday was an exciting day in the office. Bobby and Cole arrived to a lot of commotion and excitement. Whatever was happening, most of it was centred around Gemma, who was grinning and laughing and showing people her hand. Then the penny dropped.

"Hi boys, I have some news," she said as they arrived at her desk. "Vince decided to make an honest woman of me," grinning and beaming.

Cole stepped forward and gave her a huge hug.

"That's awesome news," he added.

"Congratulations to you both," said Bobby. "I'm very pleased for you. Let's see that rock then."

Gemma showed them both an interesting two stone diamond ring, probably almost a carat each, set in a rose gold ring.

"Beautiful," said Bobby. "Interesting style. Don't see many two stone rings. I like it. Did you choose or was that Vince's choice?" Bobby asked, knowing the answer before she volunteered it. Bobby recalled the bad fitting suit Vince wore and how stylish Gemma was.

"I chose it. Got it this weekend. Vince proposed on Christmas Day with a hula hoop in a box. He said I should choose my ring, he knew he'd get it wrong. I felt a bit sorry when he said that, but he was probably right. I really do need to take him in hand style wise," she added. "Maybe you could take him shopping, you both always look so cool," she laughed.

"Did you eat the hula hoop?" asked Cole.

"No!!! I couldn't. Gonna keep it. Did eat the rest of the bag though," she grinned.

Finally, people settled down and Bobby emailed Jamie about whether there was a bigger and better apartment in their block available. He replied immediately and said he would look into it.

Cole spoke to Gina about the car. She said it should be ok, she'd check with Brad and Max and if ok she'd need a copy of Bobby's licence for the files. Cole then got on with his planning for the week. The managers had their usual Monday morning meeting.

When they came out, Gina gave Cole the thumbs up regarding the car. She grinned across the office doing a thumbs up and a steering wheel motion which made Cole laugh, it looked particularly cute as Gina was in a wheelchair. Cole spoke to Bobby with the news and told him to give a copy of his licence to Gina. Bobby was so excited.

"Can I drive home tonight?" he asked.

"Course you can sexy. Just don't destroy it," he laughed.

The following few weeks carried on as usual. Cole was excelling in sales and Brad started to move him onto some bigger deals and bigger properties to see how he worked on the high end exec market. As he expected, he excelled at that. The boy's charm was perfect and so subtle. Never arrogant when selling, which is perfect for selling to the public. In a month's time, he would try him on commercial selling, which does need to be a bit more bullish as your opponent is normally much harder at negotiating.

Gemma sent out wedding invites to the majority of people at the office. The budget couldn't cover all but she invited everyone she worked directly with on a daily basis. Bobby and Cole, Troy and

Jamie were invited along with Gina, Max, Freddie, Dimitri and Brad. The wedding was planned for June.

Jamie came up trumps with a larger apartment and did them a sweet deal on it. The new apartment had a master room with ensuite and a second central bathroom, plus a walk in closet for the boys' ever growing clothes and shoes.

The weeks passed on. Peter was hoping to visit again but was too busy, so Max took a long weekend in early March to go see him in London and catch up with his parents, who needed some assistance with repairs on their house.

Max liked to help them out and support them. They never liked to take his money and he often had to insist, saying he had too much, and that it made him happy knowing they were ok. In the past five years, he had paid for better access to the house, an extension, new TV and bed. This time when he visited, he noticed the kitchen was really falling apart. He took his mother to a kitchen shop local to them and had her choose a new design. He then spoke to the owner and arranged a full planning session to happen once he was gone back to the USA and to ensure that all correspondence on the project regarding money was with him. His mother could decide on final finishes, but no mention of cost to her. Max was paying for the whole kitchen and appliances.

His parents weren't stupid and knew what things cost, but they also knew their son loved them so much. He always reminded them that it was because of their love and support that he got a great education and managed to achieve what he had done; that he and Peter wanted them to share in their success. Max wanted his parents to be happy and comfortable. Neither had great pensions. He had tried to buy them a new house, but they liked living with their friends and neighbours, which he understood. So, they stayed in the original family home, though Max did clear their mortgage for them.

Bobby and the IT team were finalising the new tenders for the IT infrastructure with Brian in the UK and Kurt in Berlin. After a number of Skype calls and variations to the proposal a final plan was agreed, which Peter and Max signed off while he was in London. Three companies would tender for the work. Two in the UK and one in Chicago. All of the meetings would be done over Skype to keep costs to a minimum. Bobby was really enjoying being in the thick of the project and thanked Freddie for allowing that.

Cole finally started on some corporate sales and found it a challenge at first. These people weren't as nice to deal with and saw through some of his charm or just ignored it. He had to learn some new tricks. He shadowed Brad in a couple of meetings and learnt a great deal and changed his approach drastically. The results started to pay dividends, after he built some relationships and trust with the people he was dealing with. After a few weeks he was back on form and getting some good results again, which was a great relief to him. Though Brad was less worried: he knew he could do it, he just had to find a new direction to take, and he knew he would find it.

Chicago was starting to warm up, spring had sprung, and it was now early April. The warmer climate was a great welcome after a very cold winter. On a particularly sunny Monday, Max arrived at the office in his black two piece Dainese leather bike suit, with helmet and gloves in hand. Bobby instantly noticed him. The leather was tight and showed off his great physique. Bobby knew he liked the gear but didn't know he actually rode a bike. How fucking hot was that? Bobby felt his cock getting hard as he watched Max arrive and put his gloves and helmet on his desk.

"Morning all," he said to the team, as he took his jacket off and revealed a tight black T-shirt underneath. Bobby expected he was going to get changed for work, but Max kept the leather bike pants on and the boots and carried on working. Nobody else seemed to care. They had seen it all before. Many times, Max came into work by bike, especially if it was good weather. Max had a passion for the gear and guys in the gear, but also the feel and exhilaration of riding a powerful bike.

Bobby walked over to him at his desk and said quietly.

"I knew you liked the gear, but I didn't know you rode? Well, a motorbike I mean," grinning at the double meaning and staring at Max's leather crotch.

"Oh yeah, I'll show you my bike at lunchtime, if you're interested," said Max.

"Oh yeah, I'm interested. Can't you tell?" said Bobby, massaging his boner right in front of Max.

"Yes I can. We'll have to take a look at that and the bike at lunchtime," he winked.

Fortunately no one was in ear shot or particularly interested in their conversation and Cole was out selling, so Bobby knew he had Max to himself.

At just after 1pm Max got out his seat and put his jacket on and picked up his gloves. He winked at Bobby and then walked out of the office. Bobby followed about a minute later to look less obvious. He followed Max to the car park in the basement in a separate elevator. He was getting excited about what would be greeting him and what would the bike be like. He came out of the lift and looked around. At first he saw nothing, then Max appeared from behind a wall of a corner parking space. His jacket zipped up and gloves on, but no helmet. He beckoned Bobby over. Bobby jogged over quickly, Max then smiled and turned to reveal the bike. And my God what a bike.

“Shit what kind is that? Looks like something that Batman would ride. You’re not actually Batman are you Max? You know and live in a cave?” he giggled.

“She’s a Ducati Diavel Carbon, 1200cc and 152 brake horsepower, goes like shit off a shovel. You want a ride?” said Max with a smile.

“I haven’t a helmet,” said Bobby.

“We could go for a spin around the car park, I’ll be careful. Also, there isn’t much space on the seat, so you’ll need to sit in close behind, pressed hard against my arse,” said Max, with a filthy look.

“Fucking will be hard up against your ass. That’s for sure,” said Bobby already feeling a boner coming on.

Max climbed on and took the bike off its stand. He manoeuvred it into position and fired her up. The roar and growl was awesome. He beckoned Bobby to get on behind him, moving himself as far forward as possible. He own bulge now resting hard against the fuel tank. Bobby climbed on and pushed himself into the small seat behind adjusting his hardening cock into a better position. It was now pressed up against Max’s arse inside his pants and Bobby put his arms around Max’s lovely leather waist. Bobby buried his nose into Max’s leathers and his neck.

“I’m so fucking hard now, sir,” he said, “Take me.”

With that Max pulled away. Bobby grabbed him harder and held him tight. The feel of his leathers in his hand made Bobby harder. Max sped around the car park, accelerating and slowing, making Bobby hold tighter and tighter. Bobby’s hands moved down to Max’s crotch and he could feel Max’s own erection pressed against the fuel tank. He rubbed him through his leathers.

“This is awesome he shouted, I have to blow you, sir.”

After a couple of more laps, Max pulled back into the bike space. Max turned off the engine and put his hand behind him on Bobby's crotch and started to rub it.

"I could feel your cock against my arse the whole time," said Max.

"I need to blow you now. I want you so bad in those leathers," said Bobby pleading.

"Not here. Too many cameras. The stairwell is fine. No cameras there, and everyone uses the lift. Climb off," instructed Max.

He then got off and looked at Bobby. He could see his boner, and then looked down at his own.

"Come on. Not something I would encourage at work but as it's you and I'm horny as fuck too..." they headed to the stairwell.

The got through the door and ventured to the bottom corner of the stairwell where there was a dead space. Smelt like someone had taken a leak in it, a lingering smell of piss. Max pushed Bobby against the wall and kissed him hard and put a leather thigh against him to pin him in place. The memory of that first encounter in the elevator came back to Bobby. That first brutal meeting. That fucking hot night. Bobby reached for Max's zip fly and tugged at it. He slid down the wall and was face level with Max's tight leather clad crotch. He pushed his face into the zipper and smelt the beautiful aroma of Max. Leather, sweat and cock. He pulled out Max's cock and took it whole to the hilt. Max moaned at the feeling. Max used the wall to his advantage and pushed his cock in and out of Bobby's skull. He put his bike-gloved hands behind his head to protect it from the wall and he drove his cock in and out, skull fucking Bobby, who was taking it with ease.

Bobby was grabbing at Max's leather arse and thighs trying to get more in. It tasted and felt so good. Fuck he loved this older man and taking his dick. Max was moaning and was close. He decided he wasn't going to warn him, he just kept pumping until he flooded Bobby's mouth with cum. The load was a surprise, but Bobby quickly adjusted to ensure he took it all. Licking up and down the shaft and grabbing the squeezing the bottom pipe, pushing out the last drops of spunk into his mouth.

Bobby was then, wanking his own dick, through his fly. He stood up and kissed Max.

"So good. So nice to taste," he said smiling that beautiful face at Max. "Jerk me off with that gloved hand, from behind. Wrap me in your leather sir."

Max turned him around and opened his fly to free his large cock. He put his leather gauntlet glove onto Bobby's dick and gently worked it. He moved up close behind and brought his left hand around him to cover Bobby's mouth. He pushed his crotch and dick up close behind him.

"Smell the leather boy. Feel the control, the power I have over you," said Max as he wanked Bobby with his gloved hand.

Bobby moaned at the dominant words. He was right, he loved being dominated and overpowered. It was his default position, to submit to alpha men. He loved it. Cole and Max were the best he'd had. Peter was sexy, but not a true alpha. Max had it with spades and the experience of an older man was wonderful. The power he had over Bobby at this time, his tight grip over his mouth and the jerking of his cock was too much. Bobby could feel himself about to unload. He jolted and buckled as the gloved hand jerked him hard and then released a huge load. Bobby sent several belts of cum across the concrete floor and up the wall of the stairwell.

"Fuck boy. You had a big one stored," said Max as he continued to jerk Bobby past the sensitive stage, forcing every drop out.

Max stopped and released his grip and turned him around and kissed him. Bobby smiled, with watery eyes.

"That was beautiful. I fucking loved that," said Bobby, shaking his dick and wiping the final drips of cum onto his fingers, then licking them.

They both zipped up and walked back to the elevator and back to the office, checking each other for any stray bits of cum.

"Can't give the game away," said Max with a smile.

"I love that bike," said Bobby.

"I hear you have been driving Cole's car?" Max asked. "Yeah, is that ok, I understood you agreed it," Bobby replied.

"Yes of course, the team's partners are allowed to drive personal company cars and all employees have access to the pool cars if they need them, but they are mainly for sales," Max said as he held the door of the office open to let Bobby through.

Troy walked over to them both.

"Where have you been together?" he asked inquisitively.

"Oh Max was showing me his fantastic motorbike. It's amazing," said Bobby, who technically wasn't lying.

That afternoon, Max's mobile rang, it was Peter.

"Hi darlin'. How's it going?" answered Max.

His smile soon disappeared and his face went white.

“Oh my God, that’s terrible...”

Chapter 4 - Project Berlin

Max stood up and went to the conference room for some privacy. He was in there for at least ten minutes. Bobby and Troy both watched, as did Gina.

Max came to the door and beckoned Gina, Dimitri and Freddie into the office.

“Is Brad here?” he asked.

“No he’s out in the road,” said Gina.

“Ok we’ll call him,” replied Max.

They all entered the conference room and sat.

Max was still on the phone, “Thanks Peter, I’ll call you back once I’ve spoken to the team.”

On the conference phone, Max called Brad.

“Hi Max, how’s you?” he answered, obviously in the car.

“You alone?” said Max.

“Yes just little old me,” he replied.

“Can you pull over? I have Freddie, Dimitri and Gina with me and I need to tell you guys something, but best you aren’t driving.”

“Woah ok, pulling into a side street now,” said Brad and turned the engine off.

Max began, “Ok, I have some very said news to share with you all. Kurt and Rolf in Berlin have been killed in a motor accident. It happened just this morning, on their way to work. They were together on Kurt's motorbike and were wiped out by a truck. Both were killed instantly. This is terrible terrible news."

Kurt was the Head of IT at the office in Berlin and Rolf was the Head of Sales. Berlin is a smaller set up than both London and Chicago, with a much smaller team. They were two of three main heads in a team of twelve. Only Claudia, the Marketing Manager, was left in a senior position in the office and she reported to Kurt who ran the overall set up.

"My God that's terrible," said Dimitri.

"Those poor guys and their partners. Hasn't Rolf got children?" said Gina.

"Yes he has," replied Brad. "They will all be devastated."

"This is terrible news," Max interjected, "But as you all know Berlin is a small set up and with two key heads taken so cruelly away from us, the junior team left is pretty rudderless. Peter is flying over tomorrow to meet with Claudia and see what he can do, but we need a few of us over there to help get the situation back on its feet. As most of the systems mirror ours we need to help."

"My suggestion is Gina, Freddie, Bobby, Brad and Cole all need to go to Berlin. Gina, Kurt managed the office structure, so you may be starting from scratch there and Freddie we need to ensure all is clear IT wise, especially with the planned system review. Sales will be rudderless now with Rolf gone. Brad, you and Cole will go to help the junior sales team pick up any outstanding sales calls. You will need to leave Sheri here in charge. Freddie, brief Troy on managing the systems here and let Bobby know. I suspect you may be required over there for a week at least or maybe two. Is that going to be a problem for anyone? Check with your partners. We can support with any childcare issues."

"And pets?" said Gina.

"Yes, pets too," said Max.

"I was joking, trying to lighten the mood. Sorry in bad taste," she replied.

"No, not at all, it's going to be a strange trip. We need to organise flights for all as soon as possible, can you get on it Gina please. I think you will have to go via London, or via New York."

"Are you coming too?" asked Freddie, "I know it's a lot of us, but I think Peter might need your help on this."

"Yes you may be right. Peter and Kurt were good friends and he sounded in a right state when he called. Ok, as long as we are not leaving the team here too light. I may come back sooner, once you guys are settled in. Ok let's speak to Bobby, Sheri, Cole and Troy. Once they know I'll speak to the whole office," said Max.

After fifteen minutes, Bobby and Cole knew of the plan and called each other, slightly excited, but also sad for the people involved. Cole hadn't met either of them but Bobby had been on many Skype calls with Kurt. He was a great guy and had a strange German sense of humour, which Bobby enjoyed.

Sheri was happy to take on the challenge, another chance to show her management skills. Troy was a bit concerned, but once he knew they would both be on the end of a phone he was happier. Gemma and Dimitri agreed to help support in Gina's absence and would manage the office calls. Gina would still manage other issues online remotely.

Once they were all briefed Max called the office to order.

"Afternoon everyone. I have some very sad new to announce from our Berlin office. Some of you may know Kurt and Rolf. This morning they tragically lost their lives in a motor accident. This is a very sad day for Bartholomew Steadman. They were good colleagues and I personally counted them as friends. Some of you may know that Berlin is a smaller office and Kurt and Rolf were pivotal to the running of the section. We are planning to send a small team from here to assist. Gina, Freddie, Bobby, Brad, Cole and I will all be going to help get the office back on its feet. I know this is a large out take, but we need to act fast and effectively. Dimitri and Gemma will be your go to people for Gina's role and Sheri is taking on Brad's responsibilities. We will, of course, all be still available on the phone. No question of that. Oh and Troy will deal with any IT queries. The aim is to fly out tomorrow evening, so the rest of today and tomorrow is to manage handovers and get prepared for the trip. Thank you for listening."

Max then walked around the office to see that each of his team were ok with the news. Some knew Kurt and Rolf so he focussed on them the most.

That afternoon those who were directly affected work wise were working hard on planning for Berlin and contingency for the Chicago office. Fortunately those going to Berlin, didn't need the evening to check if all was ok with home. They rang their partners, those that had them, and sorted it. This was what was so great about Bartholomew Steadman: they treated their staff so well that they were also willing to help out and this included their partners. Dimitri and his wife had previously been given lots of paid time off to look after their sick child. So with all people available to go, Gina was able to look at the flights and accommodation for the following day. They would be flying out Tuesday evening to London, an overnight flight and then the following morning onto Berlin. They should be there for mid-afternoon Wednesday.

That evening Bobby and Cole discussed the trip and how exciting it was. They also needed to get the mountain of laundry done, so they had clean clothes ready. They were packing for at least a week. The plan was to go to the office in the day and be picked up at 4pm from there together.

Part 5 - Tragödie in der Stadt

Chapter 5 - Ich bin Berliner

The following day the team all arrived and carried on working through final plans and handovers. Those travelling were casually attired. Bobby and Cole were wearing their leather jackets that Max and Peter bought but no leather jeans, well not wearing them. They were safely in their cases. Max was also just in a leather jacket, not leather jeans. Bobby and he smiled at each other. Both knowing that travelling with a group meant no funny business at the airport this time.

At 4pm the car arrived and those leaving said their goodbyes and headed for the elevators. Gina had booked a small mini bus which she could wheel into. Cole, carried her case and helped push her up into the vehicle. They all got inside and they headed off. Max in the front with the driver and rest in the back. Cole leaned in and spoke to Gina.

"Please don't take this the wrong way, but would you like me to assist you with the wheelchair throughout the journey? Be on hand to help? I don't mean to think you aren't capable, you most definitely are, but as a colleague, I would like to help and make anything easier for you," he smiled.

"Yes that would be lovely Cole. Thank you," replied Gina. "I can manage, but it is useful to have someone help and if I know I can count on you I don't have to do the embarrassing ask," she smiled back.

"That's good, just let me know what you want me to do and when. I'm happy to push you through the airport for speed and stuff," he replied.

"That will be great. We have a deal and I'll buy you a beer in Berlin," she grinned.

"Deal," he replied and set back in his seat.

"You are sweet sometimes Cole," said Bobby.

"Only sometimes," Cole whispered back, "I'm planning on being real nasty with you in some Berlin club if we get any free time."

"Awesome, I hope Max knows some real seedy sex clubs. I wanna see some real leather filth while we are there," he replied and kissed him on the mouth.

Brad and Freddie sniggered at them both.

"Get a room!" said Brad.

"Leave them alone you two," laughed Gina.

At the airport Bobby and Brad grabbed two trollies and the team loaded them up with their six cases and hand luggage. Max walked ahead with Freddie while Brad and Bobby pushed the bags.

"We know our place," said Brad joking.

Cole pushed Gina at the back and then sped up past the bag boys so not to be left behind. Max lead them to the BA priority check in.

"Passports," he commanded to all. "Six seats to Berlin via London, Business," he said to the attendant.

"Yes sir," she replied. "How many bags are checking in?"

"Six, one each," said Max. Not being his usual friendly self. The whole Berlin event was distracting him.

After weighing and checking documents she said, “Thank you. That’s all done for you.”

They all then moved onto security. Gina spoke to Cole.

“At security they will probably need to move me to one of their wheelchairs to go through. Can you help me with that? Mine will need to be checked in the scanners. I’ll need lifting.”

“That’s fine, I’m strong, I can ask Bobby to assist too,” he smiled.

They went through priority security and as Gina had stated they needed to transfer her to check her wheelchair. The staff assisted her and Cole was on hand. Before they knew it, they were all through and drinking G&Ts in the Exec Lounge.

“Was this where that guy blew you both?” asked Cole sipping his drink.

“Yeah, just through there,” Bobby pointed at the toilets. “And no we are not doing a repeat performance,” he laughed.

Cole pulled a sad face.

“We have to be careful. We are not just with Max.”

Boarding was easy. They got priority and once on the plane, Cole lifted Gina from her chair and placed her gently in her seat. She was petite, weighing much less than Bobby and he had no trouble wrestling and lifting him he thought.

“Thank you,” she said, “Always nice to have a strong guy around, especially one that looks and smells as good as you,” she winked.

“Cheeky. I’m taken I’ll have you know,” he grinned back.

"Yeah, stop hitting on my boyfriend," laughed Bobby.

They all took their seats. Gina was with Max, Bobby and Cole sat together. Freddie and Brad had to have separate seats as that was all that was left at such short notice.

Cole was very excited to be in club class. As excited as Bobby was when he went to London.

"This is awesome. Exec Lounges and big old seats. Cabin crew are easy on the eye too," he said.

"I know, that blond guy is pretty cute," said Bobby.

"Not as cute as my blond guy," said Cole and gave him a kiss, grabbing his cheeks.

"Champagne sir?" the blond steward interrupted, giving Cole a very long stare.

"Yes please," Cole answered, "and one for my boyfriend please."

"And what a handsome couple you make," he smiled and winked at them both.

"I know, I know," said Cole. "I know what you think I'm thinking. I'll keep my hose secure for the flight," he grinned, chinking his glass against Bobby's.

The flight was pretty uneventful and they watched films and then slept. In London, they transferred through the airport and then caught another BA flight to Berlin. The smaller plane and available seats meant that only two could be in Business. Gina and Max sat there and the others took Economy.

Part 5 - Tragödie in der Stadt

Berlin was a short flight and they arrived just after 1pm. By the time they had got their luggage it was an hour later. Cole wheeled Gina through the airport and the group picked up the pace. Gina had pre-arranged transport and after another forty five minute drive in the rain, they were pulling up at the hotel. As they were staying a while, no big glamorous hotels. They checked into the Motel One in Tiergarten. A business hotel chain, but modern and new, and wheelchair friendly. Peter was already in the lobby. He greeted them and gave them all a hug, a slightly longer one for Bobby and Cole.

It was 3pm and they were all pretty knackered from the travel. They decided to start a fresh at the office in the morning, rather than head in now.

"You guys get rested and washed up. I took the liberty to book us in for dinner at 7.30pm at a lovely Italian restaurant, Ristorante Il Sorriso. It's about a five minute walk from here, so no hassles with taxis," Peter smiled at Gina.

"Perfect Peter," said Max. "Shall we meet in the bar for a drink just before seven everyone?"

They all agreed and headed for the check in desk.

"Gina, I know you booked standard rooms for the guys but, as we booked for the week, I managed to persuade the very handsome young man on the desk to upgrade us all to superior rooms," Peter smiled and winked at Max.

Once they had their room cards they headed to the elevator.

"Do you want a hand getting to your room?" Cole asked Gina.

"No that's ok I'm sorted. I've got a room with extra wide and automated doors, so all good and the bellboy is bringing my bag up," she replied.

Max and Peter went to their room, the best they could get in the hotel. Gina had a large room with good access and Bobby and Cole were in one room and Brad and Freddie were in their own superior rooms.

Cole threw himself on the large bed and did starfish shapes. Bobby jumped on top of him and kissed the back of his head, tickling him. They got up and started checking the room equipment, putting the TV on and looking out the windows at the view. They were reasonably high and had a terrace. It was still raining so they didn't venture outside. Cole turned round to find Bobby undressed apart from his socks, which he was ungracefully tugging at. He studied the spectacle and smiled. Bobby, was really developing his body nicely Cole thought. Walking over to him from behind, he gave Bobby a huge hug and kissed his neck.

"Jeez your jackets cold against my skin," jumped Bobby.

"I thought you liked my leather against your skin?" Cole said sleazily, reaching for Bobby's cock.

"I do, but I stink of airplane and need to wash that off," Bobby wriggled trying to get away.

"I like the way you smell, all dirty and stuff. Bet that cock tastes real ripe. Nice and pissy," Cole pulled him close again rubbing his hand on Bobby's bell end and bringing it up to his nose and mouth to smell. "Umm yeah, fucking ripe and tasty."

Cole turned Bobby round and dropped to his knees and took Bobby's limp cock in his mouth and started to suck. He was fully clothed still in his leather jacket. Bobby looked down at the sight of his handsome man. He was getting harder and decided to give into Cole's advances. He grabbed Cole's head and started pumping his cock in his throat. Cole was loving it.

He pulled out and said, "I wanted to do this all the flight. You taste so good." He then got back on it. Cole's large hands were now around Bobby's buttocks, fingering his hole. Those strong hands were all he needed, Bobby blew his load without warning.

"Fuck Cole, take my shit," he said grabbing his head harder.

Once the last pump of cum was shot, Cole got up and gave Bobby what he always wanted, a cum kiss. It was a long kiss and real messy.

Bobby swallowed his load with relish, then bent down and pulled off his last sock.

"Let's get in the shower lover boy. I think it's time you fucked me as well."

Part 5 - Tragödie in der Stadt

Chapter 6 - Late Nights

They all gathered in the bar for dinner. Gina laughed at her boys.

"Is this a leather convention? Am I your chaperone?"

All but Freddie were wearing leather jackets. Freddie was in denim.

"At least we spared your blushes. I didn't wear my arseless chaps," said Max.

"Don't mind me Big Boss, you wear the trousers at work, if they happen to be arseless, suits me fine. You have a very nice arse," she replied. Bobby and Cole laughed at the banter. Gina was a real cool lady.

After a drink in the hotel bar, they all headed to the restaurant. Cole offered to push Gina again and she was happy for the help. The food was good and the wine was flowing. Once finished they all headed back and decided on an early night. They were all pretty tired and needed to be fresh for tomorrow.

Next morning, Peter and Max were down for breakfast first, followed by Brad and Freddie. Bobby and Cole arrived with Gina a short while later. The continental breakfast choice was average, but ok. The coffee was good at least. Once done, they headed to the Berlin office. Two taxis took them there. The Berlin set up was on the ground floor of a small two story block and occupied about a third of the space of Chicago or London.

When they arrived they were greeted by Claudia, who looked stressed and tired. Peter greeted her with a hug and a kiss. The rest of the team were also present. Five sales people, one marketing assistant and two admin/finance assistants. They all had looks of loss on their faces. They looked so all at sea. Max greeted them all personally, as he had met them many times on his visits over. He then introduced the team.

"So sad we have to meet under these circumstances. Let me introduce the team. Gina is our Office manager in Chicago and basically runs our office, she will be key to helping you all get the office back on its feet. Claudia I suggest you work with Gina and the admin team to ascertain what is the best course of action. Freddie and Bobby are from our IT section. They will work closely with Gina in the initial stages. Brad and Cole are in our sales team. I suggest they sit down with all you sales people and work out what has been happening. We need to ensure we don't leave any clients hanging. Peter and I will be on hand to work with you all and will speak to any customers who have any concerns. We will get Berlin back on its feet and we will all get through this dark time."

The teams set to work on discussing what needed to be done. Max and Peter looked through some recent sales figures and overall numbers.

"I think at some point this week, maybe in a couple of days we should visit Kurt and Rolf's family," said Peter. "To see if they need any support. We need to ensure their death in service payments are triggered correctly."

"Yes that sounds like a good plan. Though I think we should ring first today and then see them when it is convenient. Can I leave that with you, as you know them better than I? But we can visit them together," said Max.

Fortunately for the teams, both Rolf and Kurt were pretty organised and had left most planning and client reports up to date. Max and Peter spent the next couple of days calling any key clients that dealt with Rolf directly and assured them of their service. This was very much appreciated by all. Brad spent most of his time studying the sales team, to see if there was a likely internal successor to Rolf.

That would be easier than recruiting outside, or at least someone who could step in for an interim period. Two people were showing promise, Angela and Klaus. He would monitor them closely over the coming week and then discuss with Max and Peter.

Each evening the visiting team would go out for dinner and, where possible, take members of the Berlin office with them. But only if convenient. The aim was to hopefully give them all confidence in their futures. The evenings were fun and it was good to make new friends. Surprisingly, all the Berlin team were straight. Bobby and Cole tried to check all the guys out and came to the same conclusion. Klaus was very handsome, but straight. Bobby leaned over to Peter.

“How come you employed only straight guys in Berlin?” he laughed.

“Yes, well they are employed for their talents not their looks and sexual preference. Not all of us employ hot gay boys,” he winked. “But you fortunately have all three. I have missed you since you last came to London.”

On the Friday evening, the dinner finished quite late and they all headed back to the Hotel. The team would have the weekend off to relax and see the sights. Bobby and Cole had decided to take Gina around the sites with them. That evening they all went to their rooms. Max and Peter got in their room.

“I need some dirty sex Peter, I need the thrill of a hunt, and I need it now,” said Max.

“It’s gone eleven and I’m knackered Max. But you go and find some fun, I really haven’t the energy, not tonight. But if you find somewhere good, I’ll join you another night,” said Peter.

“Ok, I’m gonna gear up. I need to feel leather on my cock.”

Max went to the wardrobe, took out his zip round crotch leather jeans, a harness, bike boots and a black biker jacket. Once dressed, he smiled at Peter, who was climbing into bed.

"Fuck I'm hard already. You sure you don't wanna come?"

"I'm sure. Maybe that young concierge will come and service me for a few euros," he laughed. "Be safe Max."

Max left the room, and was in the elevator, when he had an idea. The doors opened at reception but he went back up. He knocked on Bobby and Cole's door.

They opened the door in their underpants.

"Oh hello sir. What you planning?" said Cole.

Max walked in and shut the door.

"Are you up for some real sleazy fun? I'm as horny as fuck and I'm planning to go to a sex club. Peter's too tired and I have a raging desire," said Max

"What and where is it?" said Bobby.

"There's a hotel with a club below it. We normally stay their 'cos the men are on tap there. Downstairs club is like a dungeon and full of dirty men who like just about everything. Wanna come and join me? I need to stalk some guys. I'm missing the thrill of the chase."

"What do you say Bobby? Sounds like some fun," said Cole.

"Hell yeah. I'm assuming it's a leather place. Shall we gear up too?" said Bobby.

They moved swiftly and got their gear on. Both put on leather jeans, no shirt, just their Belstaff jackets. Cole in grinder boots and Bobby in hi tops.

“Fuck this is exciting,” said Cole.

“Leave your phones or valuables. Where we are going there are some real thieving cunts,” said Max.

They zipped up their jackets to cover their bare chests and headed for the elevator.

It was just before midnight as they went through the lobby. Max could see the cute concierge, packing up to leave. He saw them as they came out the elevator and gave them all a knowing smile.

“Well hello, you all going out?” he said to them all. “I’m just knocking off now too, you guys enjoy yourselves,” he smiled.

Max went over to him and said quietly. “You met my husband didn’t you?”

The concierge looked worried.

“Err yes sir.”

“Don’t worry. I know he blew you. I’m cool. You wanna earn two hundred euros? If yes, go upstairs and give him some personal relief. He was well into you young man.”

“Three hundred?” he smiled.

“Two hundred, that’s all I got,” he lied.

“Ok, two hundred.”

Max gave him the money.

"Room three four four. Say Max sent you as a gift. And be real dirty with him. He'll like that."

"Thanks."

The Concierge headed for the elevator and the three went into the night.

"What was that all about?" asked Bobby.

"Oh I was just setting Peter up," Max laughed.

"Where are we going?" asked Cole.

"Tom's Bar. Two blocks down this road. It's where we usually stay. A gay hotel, but downstairs is a bar and private room. It's all leather and denim. There will be some filthy cunts down there and when they see you two handsome fellas, you'll be beating them off with clubs."

They walked down the road. Three knights on the prowl.

"Ideally we need to find a real cum pig. Someone who we can really mess with. There will be a few. You can tell them. They usually don't wear much except cum stained jocks. A piss pig would be excellent, want something that can take a good pounding."

Bobby and Cole looked at each other. The look they gave each other was of excitement, but also nerves, as Max was obviously after something specific. Tonight was going to be very, very interesting.

Chapter 7 - Room Service

Peter was checking through his phone. He was looking at porn, a nice little wank would help him off to sleep he thought. He jumped when he heard a knock on the door.

"Forgot your key?" he shouted to Max.

"Room service sir," said the voice on the other side.

Peter hadn't ordered anything. He grabbed a robe and walked to the door and opened it. He smiled at the handsome concierge. The same guy he had given a blow job too only two days before.

"I didn't order room service young man," said Peter.

"No sir, your husband did," he replied.

"How sweet. Bring whatever it is in then please," said Peter. The tall black haired guy walked in and shut the door.

"It's me, I'm the gift. Shall we have a drink and then fuck?" he asked bluntly.

"Oh now that is a nice gift. Better than a bedtime wank, which is what I was just about to do before you knocked," said Peter taking off his robe to reveal his slim and toned body.

"Umm nice. Don't stop because of me, I'd like to see you jerk that cock. I'm Helmut by the way" he said as he started to undress.

"I'm Peter."

Helmut stripped. He was dark haired and slender, he revealed a good body, not perfectly toned but good, and he was hairy. Dark black hair around his balls and cock, and a nice cock too.

"You have a nice helmet, Helmut. I enjoyed it before and I will again. Come over here."

Peter was lying on the bed and Helmut joined him. Peter was jerking his own dick and beckoned Helmut to take care of it. Helmut grasped the shaft and started to pull on it and massage it. Peter lay back on the bed and moaned. Helmut then took Peter's cock in his mouth and took it deep. Peter groaned some more.

"Oh that's good young man."

Helmut licked at his shaft and balls, running his hands up Peter's chest. Peter held his hands and pulled him up to his face.

"Come here you handsome young man. Your blue eyes are amazing. So unusual on a guy with black hair," Peter then kissed him and held him, running his hands all over Helmut's body and through his chest hair. He also felt round Helmut's buttocks and ran his fingers down his arse crack, feeling the delights he was soon to enter.

"You are fantastic to feel," said Peter.

"You're pretty hot for an older guy. You'll be my first guy in his forties," he said.

"You flatter me young man. I'm fifty four but I'll show you how real men fuck."

With that, he grabbed Helmut and he got on his knees on the bed and turned him around. Peter held Helmut's back to his chest and put one arm around his waist and the other across his chest, holding his neck, as he kissed the back of Helmut's neck and pressed his hard cock between his arse cheeks. The thrill was intense for Helmut. It was the first time he'd really been with an experienced man. Most of the guys he fucked were young, inexperienced and just wanted a wank or a blow job. Most wanted to be fucked, so finding an experienced top was getting harder and harder. Helmut was thirty one and hadn't been in a serious relationship. His work hours at the hotel didn't help either. But here he was, his first time with a guy actually older than him and he was surprised to hear someone a lot older than him but he felt good.

Peter was now stoking Helmut's nice bushy cock and balls and groping his throat gently. The combinations of his neck, cock and throat being given attention, along with a hairy cock resting in his arse crack was wonderful. He was becoming overcome by all the sensations.

"You like me being in control blue eyed boy?" said Peter.

"Yes sir."

"You want me inside you Helmut? You want me to fuck you tonight, like you've never been fucked? You want me to breed you boy?" said Peter giving his instructions deep into Helmut's ear and neck.

"Breed me sir. Breed me good and hard."

Peter pushed Helmut forward onto the bed.

"Stay still boy," Peter grabbed for some lube and prepped his cock and Helmut's hole. Peter then snatched him up and back in position as he was and fingered his hole. He then circled his cock around Helmut's arse hole and gently started to enter, an inch at a time. Helmut moaned at the feeling of Peter's rock hard cock entering his arse. It felt good, and Peter held him tight, and he drove his cock into his arse.

"Ooo you feel good boy. Nice and tight. Love a nice tight hole."

Peter drove his dick in and out thrusting upwards into Helmut's gut. He kissed his neck and stroked his chest and nipples as he pumped.

"Fuck sir, this feels so good, don't stop. I fucking love that dick in me. Fuck I needed this. Fucking hard English dick. Breed me sir."

Peter kept driving his dick up his rectum, then he pushed Helmut down on the bed and put his hand on his back to lower him down.

"Don't arch. Down," said Peter and he spread his own legs wide and kept driving his dick into Helmut's hole. "Down I said," Peter pushed Helmut's back down. "I wanna get in deeper."

Peter then moved down and lay on Helmut. He spread Helmut's legs with his and put his arms under Helmut's and grabbed his shoulders and rutted the boy hard. He put one hand over Helmut's mouth and kept fucking.

"You're mine you little bitch. Take my English dick. Fucking take it."

Peter bred Helmut for a good couple of minutes, driving deep inside him. Helmut could taste Peter's fingers on his lips. He started to lick them. This man was a God. This was the best fuck he'd had in years. And he was being paid. Seemed wrong to be taking cash for something so good. In fact he should have been paying for it he thought. The strange things you think when you have cock in your hole, he though even more.

Peter then rolled on his side and pulled Helmut with him and kept pumping the lad, moving the other hand to Helmut's throat and holding him by the mouth and throat as he pounded his hole.

"Fuck I'm close. We are going to make beautiful babies," said Peter stabbing at his hole a few more times, before letting out a deep moan as he pumped his load into Helmut's cunt. Fuck that was a big one too. Peter hadn't cum in a week and he delivered his spunk deep inside Helmut, coating his gut with cum. Helmut felt Peter's cock throb at every shot he delivered and squirmed at the feeling. Hot cum up his arse. The load of a true master. His first real alpha. It was good. Peter withdrew and moved down to lick Helmut's arse.

"Fuck you're amazing," said Helmut as Peter felched his load from his hole. Helmut's hole tasted of a day's work. Sweaty, hot and now with a nice load. Peter enjoyed the young arse. Helmut moaned at the tongue and stubble around his hole.

"Jeez, you're a God sir," said Helmut.

Once finished, Peter put Helmut on his back and started to kiss his thighs and then up under his balls and again took his cock in his mouth. He sucked that man and played with his nipples with one hand and his balls with the other, taking the shaft fully, up and down. All these sensations were too much. Helmut blew a creamy thick load into Peter's throat. Another big load too. Rope after rope hitting Peter's tongue and teeth. Some of it dribbled from the corner of his mouth. Peter's hand retrieved it and pushed it into his mouth. Helmut tasted good, good thick salty load, the best type.

They both lay on their backs and rested. After a few moments Helmut took Peters cock in his mouth and cleaned him up. He tasted of cum and his dirty arse, but he didn't care, he'd just had the best sex of his life.

"Fuck. Sir, you are amazing. That was the best fuck ever. Wow!"

Peter moved in and held Helmut close. Helmut moved in closer still and rested his head on Peter's chest. A feeling of closeness he hadn't experienced before overwhelmed him. Amazing he thought. Why hadn't he found such a feeling with other guys his age? He closed his eyes and held onto Peter, enjoying the warmth of this strong man.

After around ten minutes, Peter moved and kissed Helmut's dark hair.

"I'm sorry to wake you young man, but I have an early start."

Helmut looked up and smiled. Peter moved down to his face and kissed him hard and deeply. Again Helmut felt a sense of excitement from the kiss.

"You are amazing. The best lover ever," he repeated.

"You think I'm good, you need to be fucked by my husband. He's far better," he laughed.

Helmut put on his clothes and smiled at a naked Peter who was lying on the bed watching him get dressed, admiring the sight.

Peter stood up and saw him to the door and kissed him again before he left. Helmut smiled back with watery eyes. "Thank you. See you tomorrow sir," he said and then left.

Chapter 8 - Avenues and Alleyways

Max, Cole and Bobby approached a crossroads and turned into a tree lined street, which had some small shops and bars on it. Most were now closed but opposite them they were greeted by an unusually shaped corner building with TOM'S written over the door.

"Here we are boys," said Max.

They headed to the door and a face appeared at a small window. Max spoke in German to the man, who seemed pretty grumpy. After a bit of interaction and some raised voices, he finally opened the door and let them all in. The bar area was pretty busy, but there was space. Lots of guys standing against the wall in differing levels of clothing. The bar smelt of men, sweat, stale beer and cigarettes. The music was reasonably loud, but you could just about hold a conversation.

"What the fuck was the doorman's problem?" asked Cole.

"He's an arsehole. Said you guys could come in but not me. Ageist cunt. I told him we were all together and we had money to spend," said Max.

"What an asshole," replied Bobby.

They headed to the bar and found three stools on the corner.

"Right boys, tonight we are three alphas. Only topping tonight. Fuck knows what diseases these boys have. Max handed them two condoms each. If you feel you need to fuck someone, I suggest rubbering up in here. I know it's not ideal, but wise. If we are three alphas and ready to dominate we will have our pick. This bar mainly has lots of bottoms eager for manly cock. There is a dark room down stairs too, we can go there a little later. Let's get some beers."

Max ordered some beers from an equally grumpy barman, who couldn't keep his eyes off Cole. Max unzipped his jacket to reveal his chest and harness. Cole and Bobby did the same. Fuck, the three of them looked amazing. Three perfect doms. They were getting a lot of eye contact from the subs in the bar. Guys in Muir caps and jocks, some in leather chaps and some in footie gear. One guy was already on his knees with his face in a young blond guy's crotch, sniffing and licking while the blond ignored him, drinking his beer with a friend.

The three drank their beers and chatted.

"Don't look around to obvious. We want the cunts to come to us and with you two good looking boys, they will," said Max.

Within a couple of minutes, one guy walked up to Bobby and said something in German.

"Sorry, I don't speak German," Bobby stammered.

The man, in chaps and a harness, was probably mid 30s. He eyed Bobby appreciatively.

"Oh you're American. Handsome blond American. Are you all American?"

"No, one of us is British. Can you guess which?" Bobby replied.

"Your father. Is he British?" he replied with a bitchy smile. Bobby grabbed the man's harness and shoved him away.

"Fucking asshole."

The man moved away.

Another older guy in a denim jacket, tight jeans and boots walked up to Max and Cole and put his arms around each of their shoulders.

“You two wanna fuck me downstairs?”

Both Cole and Max shrugged him off their shoulders and turned to face him. The man’s denims were covered in stains and he stank of piss and grime. Fuck he was ripe. He knelt down and started licking Cole’s thigh, his grubby hands on the other and on Max’s. He worked his way to Cole’s crotch. Cole looked at Max with a look of distaste.

Max pushed the guy back.

“I think we’ll pass,” he said.

He wasn’t happy with the push back and headed for the basement.

“I know you said this was sleazy, but fuck some of these guys are downright filthy and not in a good way,” Cole laughed.

“I know,” said Max. “We just need to bide our time. At the moment we are getting the attention of the real desperate guys. We are the nectar and they are swarming for our attention. I’ll get more beers.”

Once the beers arrived Max said, “Let’s see what’s happening downstairs.”

They got up and all eyes followed them to the doorway and they ventured down the stairs to the dark room below. A man stood at the bottom by the doorway and pulled a curtain back to let them through. It took a while for their eyes to adjust. There was a red light giving some light in the room. The music was quieter and you could hear the sound of guys fucking, but it was hard to see. The room smelt of sweat and sex, a heady cocktail.

A few guys brushed by them. Max grabbed one guy who was standing by the wall. He was bare chested and in jeans. He grabbed him and pushed him to his knees and Max pushed his face into his crotch. The man obliged and grabbed Max's thighs, smelling his leather zipped crotch. Max pulled the zip round and release his boner. The man started to suck him. Swallowing his engorged cock enthusiastically.

Bobby and Cole watched, stroking their cocks in their leather jeans. They both decided to unzip and stroke each other's dicks until they were fully hard. Max beckoned them to join him. They moved over and he put his arms around their shoulders and moved them closer, surrounding the man on his knees. He's eyes lit up when he saw the two young cocks joining the party. Three of the best cocks he'd seen and two were huge. Max kissed Bobby and Cole in turn, while the man worked all three cocks, one in his mouth and one in each hand.

Max surveyed the scene for a couple of minutes. He then pulled back.

"I'm thirsty," he said and walked to the door.

Bobby and Cole followed, leaving the guy on his knees. They walked up the stairs like three total alpha studs. Cocks still on show. Hard as hell as they walked into the bar. As they walked into the bar, Max zipped himself up, teasing the watching crowd with a glimpse of what is on offer. Bobby and Cole wrestled their cocks back into their leather jeans, which was easier said than done. Cole's nine inches took a lot of force. They sat at the bar with the boners finally under control but obviously straining against the leather.

"Now if that doesn't raise the interest stakes, I don't know what will," Max laughed and then ordered more beer. "I have to say boys, the talent tonight is disappointing. We could have had more fun in our hotel room to be honest. This bar has gone downhill. Full of bitches and run by ageist cunts. It comes to something when a gay guy is prejudiced against in a gay bar. You guys are the sexiest men in here by far," Max added, looking around.

"Max you are the sexiest guy in here. You have shit loads more sex appeal than us. Handsome, experienced and my God you have authority. I'm turned on every time you come in the office, honest," said Bobby. "I'd be more than happy to fuck off and go back to the hotel with you and Cole. The fucking dream team for me," he added.

"Yeah I agree. Being young has some advantages, but you have it all Max. You're the man," said Cole.

"Well you are both very kind, but I wanted us all to play with something this evening. The guy downstairs was the worst cocksucker. Christ you're a sub, then learn to suck cock is what I say," Max laughed.

They chatted some more and then Cole felt something on his foot. He looked down to find a guy wearing nothing but a dirty jock and knee pads, licking his grinder boots. Cole pointed it out to Max and Bobby.

"Turn to him, and kick him away," said Max, "not too hard, this is a test."

Cole moved his chair round and looked down at the guy. Probably late twenties. Cole kept a stern face, lifted his boot away, put it on the man's shoulder and pushed him back. The guy fell back and Cole swirled back to face Max. Within a few seconds, the man was back on his boot, stroking his tight leather calf.

"Push him away again," said Max.

Cole did so, a little rougher this time, with his evil smirk.

Others were now taking an interest in the activity. A few were stroking their dicks witnessing the authority of Cole. He was a handsome, well-built young guy. Head to toe in leather and confident. With two other equally handsome men. They were strangers to the locals, which made them all the more inviting.

The man on the floor decided to take his chances with Bobby and crawled around and started to lick his hi tops and feeling his lower leg. Bobby decided to take control. He swivelled round and looked down on the guy.

"Thirsty?" he said.

"Yes sir," the guy said, opening his mouth.

Bobby took a swig of his beer, held it in his mouth and then beckoned to the guy to move closer. Bobby then fed him the beer from his mouth. Most went down the guy's chin and chest. Bobby then pushed him away and swivelled round with a laugh and clinked bottled with Max in celebration.

"Nice touch," said Max. "He could be the one, but I don't want it here. Too much of an audience. Let's drink up and leave, we can see if he'll follow."

The three of them downed their beers and got to their feet. Bobby winked at the man and then they headed to the door. The room almost parted, like the red sea, as they walked towards the door. Max said something to the doorman on the way out with a sneer.

Part 5 - Tragödie in der Stadt

"What did you say?" asked Cole, as they stood outside on the corner.

"I said, to think you weren't going to let me in and we had the whole bar eating out our hands. The best event you're ever likely to host."

They crossed the road and then heard the noise of the bar door open again. All three turned around to see the young man who had been licking their feet, leaving the club. He looked towards them.

"We are on!" said Max. "Keep walking slowly. There is an alleyway up here, we'll go down there."

The three walked ahead and the man crossed the road quickly and followed them, closing the gap slowly. He was still just in a jock, boots, knee pads and an alpha industries bomber jacket. Fortunately it was a mild night. Max, Bobby and Cole turned right down the alleyway and stopped just out of sight of the street lighting. Max kissed Cole and then Bobby. Feeling both lads crotches.

"I've missed fucking with you guys. I know Peter wants to play again soon."

The conversation was interrupted, by a break in the light and they looked around to see the young man standing at the end of the alleyway.

"Come here, come join us," said Max to the man.

He slowly walked towards them. All three moved into the light and stood side by side.

"Who do you want first?" asked Max. The man dropped to his knees and crawled to Cole's crotch.

"Fucking knew it. The bitch wants some Cole loving."

Cole laughed. He grabbed the man's head and pushed it into his leather clad groin.

"Smell it! Lick it!" he ordered.

The man did as he was told. He was about Bobby's size but lighter. Nice and easy to play with they all thought. Cole was getting hard now and wanted to get a bit rough. He threw the man to the ground with a two handed shove.

"Lick my boots cunt!" he demanded, and the man moved to his feet.

Cole then unzipped his leather jeans and opened his fly. Max and Bobby followed his lead, admiring Cole in action.

Cole grabbed him by the jacket and pushed him against the wall, one hand on his throat and the other on the man's dirty jock, that was showing signs of a hard on.

"Down and suck me."

The man dropped down the wall and at Cole's crotch level, he found the reward he wanted the whole night. Cole's hard on was huge. His cock and balls pushed out of the fly. He then held the man's head.

"Open cunt."

He then forced his cock into the man's skull, with his head against the wall and Cole holding it in place. He had no option but to take all nine inches. He choked and gagged, but Cole pressed on, laughing at the man struggling.

"Fuck Cole, leave some for us," laughed Bobby, stroking his meat at the sight.

"Ok," said Cole.

He pulled out and stood to one side and held the man's arm against the wall.

"Max you take the other," said Cole. "Now Bobby, your turn."

"You want it cunt?" said Bobby, swinging his cock side to side in front of the man's face. Cole and Max holding his arms.

"Yes sir, give it me please."

Bobby grabbed his head and forced his cock in his throat. After a minute, Max let go of the man's arm and watched Bobby in action. Cole then manoeuvred the man so he was standing behind him and the back of the man's head pushing against his cock. This allowed Cole to face his Bobby, who was grinning and enjoying deep throating this bitch below them. Bobby continued driving into the man's throat, when Cole moved closer and started kissing Bobby over the man's head. Thrusting his groin into the back of man's head as they kissed, forcing Bobby's cock in deeper.

"Fucking nice," said Max, beating his own cock at the beautiful sight.

Max got a rubber out and put it on his cock and then got out some old leather gloves. They looked like they had seen some action. Tight, the cuffs were curling back on themselves. These were Max's cruising gloves. They got washed after sessions with real street strangers and so we're getting tighter and harder, but it also made them more abrasive which had additional advantages.

Sheathed and gloved up Max said, "Ok love birds, let's have a go at its hole. Stand it up," Max said. Using the 'it' word again for the first time since that first night when Bobby was their bitch.

"Ok cunt, bend over let's see what your offering," said Max.

The man bent over and Bobby held him tightly in a head lock. The man could smell and feel the softness of the Belstaff jacket. These men were awesome he thought. Three handsome guys, hard and tough and meaning business.

Max spread open the man's buttocks to reveal his rose bud, which was huge, gaping and swollen.

"Fuck he's been around. This guy could take all three of us," Max laughed. "Hold him tight."

Max inserted his gloved fingers and punched the hole a few times. Pulling out quickly.

"Fuck he is loose," Max spat on his rubbered cock, not that he needed it, and pushed his cock in the man's hole. It was loose and easy, like fucking a whore he thought. The cunt moaned at the feeling.

"Fuck he is so loose, I'm barely touching the sides."

Max pumped back and forth, holding the sluts hips to get purchase.

Bobby decided to loosen his grip on their victim, moving his cock back around into position for fucking his throat. He was being spit roasted now by Bobby and Max, stroking his own boner as he was being punched at both ends. He was groaning and gurgling with pleasure. Cole, was beating his cock at the sight.

"Rubber up. You're next," said Max.

Cole took the condom from his pocket and tore it open with his teeth, spitting the wrapper at the cunt being pounded in front of him. He rolled it on his huge cock. It barely reached the end.

Max pulled out and allowed Cole to get in position. Cole went in dry and with ease.

"Fuck this hole could take a train," Cole said.

He fucked the man roughly. No mercy as usual. Cole fucked him hard, watching Bobby destroying the man's throat. Max pulled off his condom and threw it to the ground and started beating his cock at the sight of the man being impaled by his two young alpha comrades.

Bobby was watching Cole in action. Nasty Cole in action was always a hot sight to see. It was too much for him and Bobby blew his load hard into the man's mouth. The man wasn't like Bobby, the load fell out of his mouth onto the concrete below and onto Bobby's trainer. Seeing Bobby cum was all it took for Cole. He flooded the condom up this man's arse and thrust all the harder as he came. Cole pulled out with the condom still on and holding a huge load in the end.

"Take that off carefully, I have an idea," said Max.

Cole gently pulled the rubber off and ensured the contents were safe.

Bobby pushed the man to the floor.

"Clean my sneaks you cunt. How dare you not swallow my load."

The man did as he was told and cleaned the trainers. Max was still wanking his cock.

"Lay on your back cunt," Max ordered.

He did as he was told and Max put a booted foot on his belly and wanked over him. The man watched and stroked his own dick. Max finally cum and threw ropes of came over the man's chest and face.

"Cole, feed him your cum," said Max, wiping his cock on his glove.

"Open wide," Cole grinned, leaning down and tipping the contents of his rubber into the man's mouth. Cole squeezed the last drops out and discarded the rubber. The man ate it all.

"I need to pee now. Shall we?" said Cole.

"Me too," said Bobby.

"Fuck yeah," said the man and be beat his cock as the three men stood around him and pissed all over him.

They aimed at his wanking hand and cock, his face and mouth, and after three beers they were flowing nicely. The feel of the hot piss was beautiful for the cunt. He was hard as hell with these three leather Gods abusing him and now pissing on him. It was all too much and he shot his load all over his chest and stomach. He smeared the cum and piss together and grinned at the three of them, as they finished and zipped up.

Cole spat on him and Max and Bobby followed suit and then the three left the alleyway, without looking back at the guy on ground, covered in cum and piss. They walked down the street towards their hotel, initially in silence. Then Max cleared his throat.

"That was fun, but that bar was a real dive. I won't be going there again," said Max.

"It was interesting," said Bobby. He paused. "But the reality is I would have preferred to just be with you guys. Don't get me wrong it was worth trying it, but ok I like man smell, but some of these guys fucking stank. A day's sweat or day old cock is nice, but that one in the denim was fucking gross," he laughed.

"I know what you mean. Some do take personal hygiene to a new low, which is why I suggested the condom. It's not just HIV you have to watch out for with these guys. I'd enjoy a session in the hotel at some point, with Peter, he's missed you since London," Max replied.

Cole walked holding Bobby's hand as they headed back to the hotel. They said goodnight went to their separate rooms. Bobby and Cole took a shower straight away.

"I need to wash that guy off me," said Cole, "If I'm honest I didn't enjoy it that much. I got into it for sure and in the moment I was rocking, but that bar and those guys. It's like a meat market. I'm glad you were there."

They finished showering and got into bed.

"I'm starting to feel like I don't want sex with others without you Bobby." Cole continued, "I'm happy to play with others while you are there, but while you were in London, I had a session with Brad and that piano playing guy. It was ok, but I didn't enjoy it as much and I kept thinking of you. How do you feel?"

"I know what you mean, I do prefer it with you there. Maybe we should tone it down with others. But what about Max and Peter and Troy and Jamie?" Bobby asked.

They had had sessions with all of them, but Cole had only had them with Bobby present. Bobby meanwhile had been with Peter and Max in London and also in the stairwell of the office.

"My suggestion," Cole began, "is we agree to only play with others together. Max and Peter, I'm less concerned about, if you want a cheeky play with either of them, that's cool, but let's keep everyone else a together thing. We can see how that works and if either of us have concerns we must speak up. The more I think about tonight, the more I would have hated it if you hadn't been there. If it was just me, or even me and Max, it would have felt wrong. It really was a dump wasn't it?" Cole said putting his arm around Bobby and cuddling him close under the bedding. Bobby put his head on Cole's chest.

"It was exciting at first and I did like the attention we got, but then that ageist asshole said Max was my Dad and the guy that stank of piss. Jeez. The best bit was seeing you in nasty mode. I fucking love seeing you like that. Gets me hard every time."

"Why you like that so much?" Cole quizzed.

"Ultimately I'm a sub, and I love dominant strong guys. Seeing you like that turns my crank. I always loved that about you. At school you were so hard. I fucking worshiped you and used to watch you from afar. Wank myself stupid every night thinking of you fucking me," Bobby replied.

"I suppose it's no different for me. I used to get such a thrill from being a nasty bastard, though I feel bad about it now."

"Ah Ah, now stop right there," interrupted Bobby, "we ain't going down that path again."

"No I wasn't. I do feel bad about it, but I blame a lot of my anger and behaviour on my parents. I took a lot of my anger for them out on you guys, which wasn't right. But domination and control in sex is great, especially if both sides like it. And you obviously do," said Cole

"Umm, so not sure why I love being a sub. I was small and a weak boy and looked up to you guys. You were all muscular and powerful, I would have loved to be like that but wasn't. I wanted that feeling of power, and also I fancied you all like mad. Remember Dex, he was hot too. Mean fucker, but not as handsome as you. You had the nasty side and beauty with it. A toxic combination. Fuck I'm hard Cole, talking about all this," Bobby said as he adjusted himself.

"Fill my hole, I'm done with being an alpha male, that's your job. Fuck me hard, no flaming mercy!"

Cole's gentle arm around him suddenly gripped Bobby in a head lock, his other hand reached for Bobby's cock.

"You are hard, you dirty cunt. Right, time you got the full nine inches from your school bully."

"Fuck yeah. Do it!" Bobby pleaded.

Cole flipped Bobby over and fingered Bobby's hole, putting his full weight on his back. He then massaged his growing boner and moved Bobby on his side. Spat on his hand and lubed up his hole, Cole then put his hand over Bobby's mouth, and drove his cock deep into Bobby's arse, pumping him mercilessly. He gripped Bobby with both arms and fucked him hard. Bobby moved his legs to open his hole further. Breathing heavily now is mouth was free.

"Deeper bad boy. Fucking deeper!" said Bobby and Cole rutted harder. Finally Cole slowed down and pulled out.

He then positioned Bobby gently on his back and moved Bobby's legs onto his shoulders. He entered Bobby, gently this time, face to face, and then kissed Bobby sensually and tenderly, using the slower rhythm that Max had taught him months back. He was now making love to his boyfriend, not fucking, or breeding him, he was making love to the most wonderful person he knew. His Bobby, his happy, sexy little Bobby, who Cole couldn't imagine life without.

"I really love you Bobby. I can't imagine being without you. You are just the most amazing guy," and he kissed him again, tenderly, as he gently moved in and out.

Bobby was in ecstasy. The sensitive Cole was even sexier, a wonder he hadn't expected. His words and tender love making, felt so good, better than ever.

"I love you too Cole. I've loved you since I was fourteen, it's always been you. No one else compared," Bobby held Cole's head and ran his hands through his wavy hair and pulled him in to kiss him.

"I so fucking love you mister," he said as their tongues met.

Suddenly Cole felt a rush through his body and a huge jolt as he shot his load into Bobby. The spasms shook them both and he could feel it through his legs and neck, an orgasm like no other.

"Fuck!" said Cole, taken aback by the rush. He dropped onto Bobby and held him tight in his arms. "I know this sounds corny, but I want to spend the rest of my life with you Bobby Wilson," Cole whispered into Bobby's neck, exhausted.

"Well that's good, 'cos I'm not intending on letting you go Mr Peterson," Bobby whispered back. Cole squeezed him event tighter. Gently he pulled out of Bobby and they rested beside each other.

Part 5 - Tragödie in der Stadt

The lovers spooned and fell asleep. It was now 4am in the morning.

Part 5 - Tragödie in der Stadt

Chapter 9 - Auf Wiedersehen

The next morning the team met for breakfast.

"You guys look shot," said Brad to Cole and Bobby. "Late one?" he winked.

"Something like that," yawned Cole.

Peter and Max turned up last and greeted them all. Max saw the concierge trying to catch his eye, so he walked over to Helmut.

"Christ you work some shifts," said Max. "How can I help?"

Helmut gave him an envelope.

"What's this?" asked Max.

"It the money you gave me yesterday, I wanted to give it back," said Helmut.

"Why?"

"I took your money and went and saw your wonderful husband. He fucked me in ways I've never experienced. I found the whole experience amazing. You husband is so great. He made me feel good too and was very kind with me, something I've never felt with another man. For that I felt I cannot take your money. You have a special husband sir."

"I do, and thank you, but no please keep the money. Buy yourself something nice, maybe a leather jacket?" he laughed. "You can tell I like to see a young man in leather."

"No sir surely," Helmut protested.

"No I insist," replied Max.

"Ok. Your husband said how wonderful you were. He even said you were better than him. You guys are very lucky," Helmut smiled, putting the envelope inside his jacket pocket.

"We are very lucky and one day you will find your special one. They will be where you least expect them. And yes, I am a good fuck, or so I'm told. Maybe, if we have some time, you could play with both of us?" Max winked, turning away to head back to the group. God he was such a tart Max thought. But he also thought Helmut was very handsome.

When he got back to the table Peter whispered, "What did he want? I know it was you that sent him last night."

"He was singing your praises. Said that you were the best sex he'd ever had," laughed Max.

"What's so funny about that?" Peter protested. "And there I was telling him you were even better than me, I wish I hadn't now."

Peter and Max loved a bit of banter between each other.

"Maybe later in the week we can both play with him, he is cute," said Max with a wink.

"Now that's a thought," grinned Peter.

After breakfast the team decided to do some sight-seeing as it was Saturday. Brad, Dimitri, Gina, Cole and Bobby all went off together. They wanted to do the touristy stuff and it felt best to do it together. Peter and Max decided to stay back. They had other things that needed to be done.

That afternoon, Max and Peter visited Rolf's wife. They arrived at her home to be greeted by her at the door. She was holding up reasonably well, but Peter could tell from the length of the hug she gave, she was struggling inside. He held her tight. They discussed the good times they all had together and then Peter enquired about her finances. He wanted to ensure she was ok, and that money wasn't locked away in probate. She said Rolf had been very organised and everything was in shared access, so she was fine. Peter informed her of the 'death in service' insurance payment that she would be receiving. It would probably come through in about two weeks' time. Four times his annual salary, tax free. She was a little surprised.

It was an emotional afternoon and she informed them of the planned date of the funeral. It was about a week away. Max said he would stay until then and would be attending, which she was pleased about.

The following day Peter and Max did the same with Kurt's long term girlfriend. Not being married it wasn't as straightforward. She was equally very cut up. Fortunately there was a will, but the death in service had not been allocated directly, so it would have to go into the estate, which would slow access. Peter offered her an interest free loan until that came through. He would get paperwork drawn up, so she had access to some money now. Kurt's funeral would be the day before Rolf's.

"Christ what a week next week is going to be," said Max as they left her apartment. "We are going to have to keep an eye on both those two."

The rest of the team made the most of the weekend visiting the sites and doing some shopping. Berlin was an amazing city and to see the old Eastern part as well as the West was very interesting. The team did the obligatory photo at Check Point Charlie and at the Brandenburg Gate. The weather was good for sight-seeing and

Gina really enjoyed having the team to support her getting around. Being in a wheelchair normally meant she had to plan trips with military precision, but being with four strapping young men, made getting around real easy. Even steps and stairs Bobby and Cole picked the chair up with ease and saved the issue of finding ramps and alternative access. Gina was happy for the help, when it was done with dignity and respect. These boys were all being kind, but not doing it with any pity, which she hated.

Each evening the team met up for dinner and had a real good laugh. The trip was a great opportunity to build relationships and to get to know each other far better. But the trip would soon be over. It was decided that the team would fly back Tuesday, having been there for just under a week. Max and Peter would stay back for the funerals and ensure the office was ok.

On the Monday before they were planning to leave, the team headed to the office and carried on restructuring and finalising the teams. Brad had decided that Angela should head up the sales team in the interim and discussed this with Peter and Max. They agreed based on his reasoning. Klaus the other candidate was a little annoyed at missing out, but accepted the decision and shook hands with Angela.

Freddie structured a plan that the IT could be supported remotely from London with him as back up, but office management did need someone. Peter decided that he needed to recruit a new team head/Office manager for the Berlin office. The remaining team, were too specialist and didn't have the overall experience. Max and Peter discussed that the best option may be to advertise the role internally across all three group offices, as someone may be interested in a move from London, or even Chicago, then look outside. Peter would need to visit every fortnight in the interim and co-ordinate interviews. That was reasonably easy for him, and London pretty much ran itself these days. Peter's main role was acquiring new business and meeting influential people. He was very good at that, especially in the UK and USA.

On the Monday evening, Peter had organised a full team meal as a thank you the Chicago team and a motivation for the Berlin team. They took over a small restaurant and as it was a Monday, they were the only ones in. They all raised a glass to their missing colleagues and friends.

"To Rolf and Kurt," said Peter as the team chinked glasses.

The whole motorbike incident really got Max thinking about his own. He only rode his in fine weather, but he knew it was a dangerous toy. Peter loved seeing him on the bike and especially in the gear, but also hated him having it. Many times, he asked him to give it up.

"I love you too much to lose you. I know you are careful, but the other drivers are the ones I worry about," he would often say.

Kurt had been an experienced rider for many years. He often took Rolf out on it. They were wiped out by a lorry who just didn't see them. 'All the experience can't save you from that' thought Max. He'd think some more on it when he got back to the USA.

At about 10pm the USA team said their goodbyes to the Berlin guys as they had a very early start on Tuesday. Peter and Max hung back with the local team. Peter said goodbyes to them all. He went over to Bobby and Cole.

"Real shame we didn't get to spend more time together. I've missed you both. And thanks again for everything you have done for the business. You have been a real asset," he smiled.

"When you are next back in Chicago, you will have to come to our new apartment and Cole will cook for you. He's getting real good," said Bobby.

"Yeah, I'm loving cooking," piped up Cole.

"Sounds like we have a date then," replied Peter hugging them both.

Back at the hotel, Bobby and Cole packed their bags that evening, leaving out their clothes for travel tomorrow. They needed to be up at 5am. They had an 8.10am flight to London. The Chicago flight was at 1.05pm, so turnaround would be tight.

The young men snuggled together in bed. Both quite tired from the weekend and the last day's work. They knew they needed to get some sleep before the early alarm. Cole wrapped his arms around Bobby in their usual spoon position. Bobby loved the feeling of Cole's cock resting within his arse crack and feeling of his firm thighs on the back of his own and those strong guns wrapped around him and across his chest. Bobby felt so secure in this position.

"I love you," Bobby said.

"I love you too," said Cole kissing the back of his head.

They fell asleep, both smiling.

Chapter 10 - Homeward Bound

The following morning the alarm on Bobby's phone rang and they woke with a start. It was still pitch black in the room. They both groaned at the ungodly hour.

"Come on lover boy, in the shower. We gotta be in reception in half an hour," said Cole.

He turned on the light and ripped the covers off Bobby, exposing him to the light and cool room air. Bobby was in the foetal position, with his hands over his eyes.

"You bastard," he replied.

Bobby turned over and changed to a starfish position on the bed, squinting at Cole. Cole looked at his boyfriend, his body was very impressive he thought. All that gym time was really paying off. The toning and proportions were beautiful and all framing his lovely hairy cock and balls.

"You really are fucking sexy," Cole said standing over him.

Bobby was admiring his own view. Cole was perfect to him, that lovely hairy chest and treasure trail to his groin, and that beautiful cock.

"You ain't half bad yourself, but we have no time for sexy shenanigans. We have a plane to catch," said Bobby jumping out of bed and heading for the bathroom to take a pee.

They were all waiting for them in reception. No breakfast, to early, so they headed straight to the taxis. Gina had sorted the cheque out the night before and they were on their way. Driving through Berlin at dawn was equally interesting. To see only marginal movement was quite eerie thought Cole. The closer they got to the airport the busier it got.

The flights home ran reasonably smoothly with little delay which was fortunate. The transfer in London was a short window, so they didn't have time to hang around, before they were on their final leg of the journey. No upgrades this time, thought Bobby, but Business was amazing. They all relaxed into the flight and settled into watching the in-flight entertainment and tucking into the food. Bobby hoped he would see Richard, the cabin crew member he played with on the flight back home to Chicago last Christmas. He would have loved to see Cole he thought. But sadly he wasn't to be seen. In fact there was no real eye candy crew wise on the flight but he thought, he didn't need it, not when he was on the flight with Cole. He didn't need any more eye candy than him and leaned over and kissed him on the ear.

"What was that for?" said Cole smiling.

"Because I can," said Bobby with a huge grin.

Cole grabbed Bobby's nose between two fingers and gave it a gentle wiggle, smiling back. These new levels of affection were growing more and more between the pair and they both loved the deeper connection that was developing. They were feeling a new safety in the partnership. Bobby felt a physical safety while he was around Cole, just knowing he was safe when near him, and Cole felt a different form of safety. Bobby, brought a level head and stability he'd never really had. When he was with Bobby, he felt safe to be himself and be more adventurous. Cole looked up to Bobby. He was intellectual, clever and a great sounding board. Bobby gave Cole further confidence, because behind the macho bravado, was a small insecure boy, who had a loveless childhood. In Bobby he had found a little miracle.

Part 5 - Tragödie in der Stadt

It was late afternoon when they arrived back at the apartment. They said their goodbyes at the airport and everyone got separate taxis home. They would all be in the office tomorrow to check on what had been happening while they were away.

Bobby unpacked the bags and started loading the washing machine, while Cole went and got in the shower. He walked out the bedroom ten minutes later, wet hair and a white towel around his waist, just low enough to show he perfect cum gutters and treasure trail. Bobby watched him enter the lounge area.

"You really are so friggin' sexy Cole. What the fuck are you doing with me? You could have anyone," wondered Bobby.

"Stop right there," said Cole. "I don't want 'anyone', I want you. The shape you're in now, I could be asking you the same question. You are beautiful and I consider myself now to be punching above my weight. You need to take a look in the mirror. Now, no more of suggesting I'm too good for you. You mean the world to me and our unit completes me. Now go and get showered. I'll put the toiletries away and sort the bags."

"Ok boyfriend," said Bobby, feeling a little foolish asking the question. Why would he doubt it? But he remembered how popular Cole was at school and Bobby was in the geeks' group. Bobby got naked and headed to the bathroom. Before he got in the shower he looked in the mirror, at his new body. Cole was right, he would barely recognise his body to how it was a year ago. The slim untoned body had been replaced by a nice T-shaped torso, defined abs and good arms and shoulders. His legs are developed too. He wasn't like Cole, who was more defined and muscular, but he was well-toned and nicely in proportion. Bobby smiled and thought to himself, 'Yes Robert Wilson, you are a bit of a hottie actually.' He smiled at himself, then turned on the shower and lathered up his hot body.

They both got dressed in trackies and fell on the sofa, when there was a knock on the door. They both looked at each other.

“Who’s that?” said Cole.

Knowing that it must be an internal person to the apartments. Cole went to the door. He opened it to be greeted by Troy and Jamie.

“Surprise! Welcome home!” said Troy pushing his way in past Cole to give Bobby a hug.

“How did you get in?” said Cole to Jamie.

“Well we have some news. Troy and I have moved in together and we are in a new apartment four floors up. We liked it here and it’s great having the gym downstairs and of course you guys are nearby. Wanna come see it?” asked Jamie.

“Ok,” said Bobby, grabbing his keys as they all headed up to the apartment. Inside it was a similar layout to their old apartment but configured like a mirror image.

“I’m so pleased for you, and moving in, that’s nice,” said Cole.

Troy asked, “You guys hungry? We could get a takeaway delivered, and you can help us celebrate, like a mini housewarming.”

“Sounds great,” said Bobby

Pizza was ordered and the boys all settled down to food and some beers and Bobby and Cole told them all about their trip to Europe. They even talked about the hideous club night. It was gone 10pm before Bobby and Cole went back to their apartment. It was good to have friends nearby. Life was really good.

Chapter 11 - Back to Normality

It was Wednesday morning, the day after they got back from Europe. Everyone was in the office by nine. The jet lag was kicking in for some, but everyone was chatting and sharing the adventure they had experienced. It had been a fun trip, but under very sad circumstances. Gina was soon on top of any outstanding items thrown up by her absence while Brad's team provided him with a thorough update of sales. Fortunately, everything in Chicago had run pretty smoothly.

The team began to settle down to normality, getting back to business of selling space and properties.

Back in Berlin, Max and Peter spent as much time with the team as possible, supporting those who were in new roles and helping plan recruitment for their replacements. At the end of the working day on the Wednesday, they headed back to the hotel. Helmut was on reception as they arrived. He smiled at Peter and Max.

"He is rather handsome," said Max. "Was he a lot of fun? You up for a second helping?"

"Always," smiled Peter, heading to the elevator, leaving Max to do the negotiation.

"Evening young man. How are you? Peter was just singing your praises again. You interested in some more fun, with both of us?" Max enquired without any inhibitions.

"Sure would sir, if you are as good as Peter said you were I'm in for one hell of an evening. I finish at six this evening. Does that work for you? Or I could come back later?" said Helmut.

"Six will be perfect," said Max. Winking as he headed for the elevator.

“We are on, he’s coming up at six. Time for a shower me thinks.”

Max and Peter had a shower and waited in their bath robes. At just after six, there was a knock at the door. Max opened it, to find Helmut standing in casual clothes rather than his suit. Jeans, T-shirt, trainers and a black cafe racer leather jacket.

“Well hello young man, you got changed. Nice leather,” said Max.

“Thanks. You bought it! I showered in the staff area beforehand and wanted to be out of my suit, so I always have a change of clothes,” said Helmut.

“You look good in leather. As you know I have a real thing for it. So does Peter. A man, even the most perfect, will always look better and more sexy in some leather in my opinion,” said Max.

“And you Helmut, are very handsome. Now even more so,” said Peter across the room. “Sit on the bed. I want to slowly undress you,” he continued dropping his own robe to the floor.

Helmut smiled at the sight of Peter’s naked body. Helmut sat on the bed and Peter knelt down on the floor. He took Helmut’s right trainer off, raising it to his face, he inhaled. The smell of a man’s trainers, feet and socks was a real turn on for Peter. Helmut was wearing white, nylon sports socks. Peter raised his foot and smelt the arch and toes.

“Such sexy feet. A slight hint of sweat,” he said drinking in the aroma.

Helmut was getting hard at the sight of a man at his feet. Max noticed him adjusting his bulge.

Max dropped his robe and said, “Let me see if I can help you out with what’s troubling you down there.”

Max had a growing boner now too. He sat on the bed next to Helmut and unzipped his fly and put his hand in, stroking Helmut’s bulge through his soft white briefs. He then smelt the leather of Helmut’s jacket, inhaling the beautiful scent, and feeling its soft buttery lamb’s leather texture. He moved up to Helmut’s face, still with his hand caressing his bulge. Max kissed Helmut, tenderly at first, then after a few seconds, he pushed him back on the bed and held his jaw as he pushed his tongue in hard and deep.

Max pulled back and said, “Fuck boy, you taste good,” and then dived in for more of the lad.

Peter was now enjoying both feet and removing Helmut’s socks. He began licking his toes, which tickled Helmut, so Peter grabbed them firmly. Peter then moved up to the jeans and undid the belt and button and started to pull them down. He smelt Helmut’s bulge and crotch, getting his nose under his ball sack.

“Now that smells good, a day’s worth of sweat in those, even after a shower. You are a fine smelling young man.”

Peter then pulled the briefs down to reveal Helmut’s beautiful hard cock. He was longer than average with an impressive girth. Uncut too, which was very appealing to Peter. Peter took his cock into his mouth and ran his tongue around the foreskin, then down the shaft. He then drew it in whole and stroked his own cock as he blew this handsome boy.

Helmut was moaning at being pleasured by these two handsome older dominant men. Max told him to take the T-shirt off but put the leather jacket back on. He was now naked except for the jacket. Max instructed him onto his knees on the bed and positioned himself behind him, both upright. Max lubed up his hole and ran his cock around it for good measure. He then started to enter Helmut, holding his arms around his front, caressing his nipples. Helmut, whined a little as Max entered and thrust upwards.

“Oh fuck, das fühlt sich so gut an,” he said reverting to German in his state of ecstasy.

Peter moved in front of him and started to kiss him and held his own and Helmut’s cock together in one hand and wanked them gently as Max kept thrusting into his gut.

“Züchte mich, Papa,” Helmut pleaded.

Max took the instruction and grabbed his head back by his hair with his left hand and held his throat and mouth with his right, as he roughly started to rut Helmut. He moaned in rhythm with Max’s grunts as he pumped his hole.

Peter then moved down on the bed. Lying on his back and moving his head under Helmut’s and Max’s groins, he started to lick their balls and undercarriage. He was holding and stroking Helmut’s thighs as he watched the spectacle from below, licking whatever was on show.

“Oh God, Peter was right. You are fucking good sir,” said Helmut.

He was holding his own cock now and stroking himself. Peter was wanking himself too as he pressed his face into Helmut’s balls.

Max then pushed Helmet forwards and down, “Blow my husband bitch,” he ordered pressing his face onto Peter’s hard cock. Helmut took Peter’s cock and sucked him, as Max still pumped his own hole with increasing vigour. In this position, Peter was able to lick Helmut’s shaft, but not take it in. But being so close to his husband's cock, pounding Helmut's hole, was awesome. He could smell the aroma of arse, balls and cock.

The fucking and sucking continued for another couple of minutes until Max could feel his need to cum. He felt the rush and delivered his load deeply into Helmut's cunt, roughly roaring as he did. Peter knew that sound and moved up close to Helmut's hole, to await the withdrawal. He wasn't disappointed, as Max pulled out, Peter was greeted by a pushback of cum and Max's beautifully coated cock, which he lapped up. This exciting treat was enough to trigger Peter's load deep into the back of Helmut's throat. Helmut was a little surprised and choked a little at the load hitting his throat. He had received two awesome loads from two awesome sexy guys.

Helmut pulled himself off of Peter's cock, which gave Max the cue to pull him back up onto his knees. Max put his left hand over Helmut's mouth and brought his right and round hand grabbed his cock.

"Sit on Peter's face," Max ordered.

Peter received Helmut's arse crack. He smelt and licked at the hole, still dripping with his husband's cum. Max then started to wank Helmut hard. Max was smelling the aromas of leather coming from the man and he licked the back of Helmut's neck and licked the leather collar.

"You smell and taste so good," said Max, jerking at the young man. The feeling of Max wanking and Peter rimming him was truly amazing. Peter could sense his excitement and decided to move down the bed until he was now lying under the jerking cock, ready to receive the impending load.

Helmet could smell and taste Max's hand over his mouth. The hand of a domination expert, the hand of a real man, an Alpha God.

"Oh sir, take my load, take my load," said Helmut as he shot several ropes of cum into Peter's face and cross his chest. Shuddering as the cum pulsed out. Peter smeared his hands over his cum covered chest and tasted the lads warm load. He then leaned up and licked the end of Helmut's cock to get the last drips of cum.

"Such a beautiful young man," said Peter.

Max released his hold, and kissed Helmut on the ear.

"You were real fun to play with," he said.

"Sir, you are a God. That was awesome. Peter was right, you are an amazing fuck. You are both pretty amazing," said Helmut.

They all lay down on the bed and paused, basking in the feeling of all three cumming. Max was still stroking the smooth leather of Helmut's jacket.

"This is real nice, suits and fits you so well," he said.

"Thank you," said Helmut, "I've never had a leather jacket before, but I have liked having this on. Makes me feel sexy, never appreciated that before."

"I got my first leather jacket at fourteen. Second hand, off Leicester market. That's the city in England, where I was brought up. I saved my pocket money for it," said Max. "I was so excited. I had loved seeing men in leather from an early age. Always loved cowboy films and the bad guys always had black chaps, waist coats, and black leather gloves. Used to get a hard on and didn't know why because I was that young. I still remember the day I got that jacket. I put it straight on and put the one I was already wearing in the bag and walked home, constantly touching and smelling it. It was an old used biker jacket. It smelt great, dirty leather, but also the scent of another man on it, which was a real turn on. I had a boner all the way home. I walked through Bradgate Park, in Leicester, I was so horny, I went into the bushes and wanked a huge load while in that jacket."

"You still got it?" Helmut asked.

"No I grew out of it. I think I sold it on, whoever got it had a jacket with huge amounts of my DNA on it. I was always jacking off over it. I now do this to ever new piece of fetish leather I have and I have lots," Max smiled.

"Oh he does have lots, crazy amounts," said Peter. "Shall we wash up and if you are free, would you like to get some dinner with us?"

"Only if you don't mind. I've not got anything planned for this evening. Just a TV dinner," Helmut replied.

"Good we can go to that little Italian place again," said Max.

Part 5 - Tragödie in der Stadt

Chapter 12 - Ms Jackson

Gina was at her desk typing up her notes from the Berlin trip. She liked to document what was agreed, to ensure everyone had clear actions and there was no confusion. Her desk phone rang.

"Hello Bartholomew Steadman, how can I…." she was interrupted.

"Hello, I have a number of buildings in Chicago and I wanna sell them. You up for that?" said the lady.

"Yes, we can help you with that. May I ask what type of property and how many?" Gina asked.

"A block downtown, five houses on upper and few others," she replied. "Does Bobby Wilson still work for you?"

"Yes he does," said Gina. "We can come to you or you are more than welcome to have a meeting here, with one of our top salesmen, to discuss your needs in more detail."

"I want Bobby to be there," she said.

"Bobby is not a salesman, but I'm sure he'd be happy to attend and see you. Are you a relative?" asked Gina

"No just a friend. If I don't see him, I'll go elsewhere," she insisted.

"Of course you can, that's not a problem," replied Gina. "Let's get a date and time and I'll have our Head of Sales and Bobby meet with you. May I take some details?"

Gina wrote down the name, address and contact details of the lady and agreed a time for the meeting; in the office the following day at eleven. She wished her well and said goodbye.

"Hey Bobby, you know a Barbara Jackson?" Gina piped across the office. Bobby looked up.

"Who?"

"Barbara Jackson. Lady wants to sell some properties."

Bobby looked confused. "No, I....." he paused some more. "Hang on, I met a funny old lady on the plane back from London last December. She was a hoot. I think her name was Barbara."

"Well, whoever she is she remembers you and wants you in on a sales meeting. So I've booked you in with Brad tomorrow at eleven. Be smart," said Gina.

"I don't know about selling," said Bobby.

"Brad will do all that, but she wants you there. You obviously pushed some buttons on that plane," Gina raised an eyebrow.

Bobby smiled at the thought. He definitely pushed some buttons alright. She was the naughty old lady who knew Bobby had had a blowjob from the flight attendant. I hope she's discreet in the meeting he thought, while also thinking she's likely to be anything but.

Chapter 13 - An Idea

Max, Peter and Helmut headed out for dinner. Helmut left via the employee back exit.

"If I leave with you now, an hour after my shift, out the front door, people will put two and two together and know I have been with you. Fraternising with customers is sackable offence," said Helmut, as he headed to the rear of the hotel.

"Meet you on the corner in five," he added.

Max and Peter chatted in the elevator.

"He's cute isn't he. Bright too. I'd like to know more about him work wise," said Peter. "He said he'd been in the hotel management trade all his working life."

"What are you thinking Peter Bartholomew?" said Max, in an inquisitive tone.

"I want to find out more, that's all," Peter replied. They headed out of the hotel and met Helmut on the corner. He looked very sexy standing on the corner, with one leg resting against the wall, like a rent boy waiting for action. His dark hair with that leather jacket was a sexy combination and the cute smile and twinkly eyes were the icing on the cake.

They headed to the restaurant and were seated. Wine and water were ordered by Peter and the men started to chat. Peter asked, "So tell us some more about your career and what you've done?"

"I went to catering college in Cologne and specialised in hospitality. I then did Hotel management and got my first job in a small hotel as a receptionist. I have worked my way up to manage a hotel. But then nine months ago the Hotel group closed and I was made redundant. A new hotel opened up around the corner and we could not compete. The place needed an overhaul, but the top brass would not spend the money. So I lost my job when they shut it. Management jobs are difficult to come by, so I took the Concierge role at Motel One, hoping to find a better role within. There is a management role coming up soon, which I'm applying for," said Helmut.

Peter asked some more about his skill set and what current role involved.

"Is this an interview?" Helmut joked to them both.

"Sure sounds like it," Max rolled his eyes.

"Maybe," said Peter.

Peter then explained their business and what they did. He also explained about the tragedy that recently happened and the fact there was a role as Office Manager. Peter explained the role and Max added to it.

"Slightly different from managing a hotel, but the hours and pay are better," said Max. "We employ people we like. People with drive and people that have a spark."

"Give us your details and I will send you the job spec and package. If you're interested we can do a formal interview later this week. If not, we won't be offended, no obligations," said Peter

"Now let's stop talking about work. Let's also get another bottle of wine," said Max looking around for the waiter.

Part 5 - Tragödie in der Stadt

Chapter 14 - Commission

It was Thursday, 10.55am at the Chicago office when the buzzer on the office door rang. Bobby knew it would be Barbara and decided to go and greet her personally. He was looking very smart in his Hugo Boss charcoal suit, white shirt, shiny black brogue shoes and a green striped tie, like a private school tie. With his shock of blond hair, athletic body and handsome face, the whole outfit looked instantly cool. Bobby was transforming into a very sexy handsome young man.

He opened the door to Barbara with a huge smile. He shook her hand, but she reached out for a hug.

"Oh my, how handsome you look. Far more handsome than I remember. I'm so glad to see you again," she smiled.

"Mrs Jackson, it's great to see you too and thanks for choosing us," said Bobby leading her into the office and on the way to the conference room.

"Less of the Mrs Jackson. Call me Barb please," she giggled.

"This is Gina, who you spoke to on the phone," Bobby said as they passed Gina's desk. Gina smiled and shook Barbara's hand. In the conference room Brad was sitting. He was in a light grey suit, with a huge salesman smile on his face.

"I'd like to introduce you to Brad Regent, our Head of Sales," said Bobby.

"Nice to meet you Brad. I'm Barbara Jackson, you can call me Mrs Jackson," she smiled and winked at Bobby.

"Good Morning Mrs Jackson, it's great to have you here. I understand from Bobby you have some property you would like to sell," said Brad.

"Yes, I own a seventeen story block of offices on South Franklin Street. It's largely rented out to small business, with a few apartments on the top. Plus I have five houses in upper and seven in lower that I'm looking to liquidate. I'm shipping out and moving back to the UK," Barbara detailed. She then listed the addresses and handed a document containing all the properties to Bobby and Brad. Brad studied them.

"Bobby, would you mind getting Cole to come and join us?" said Brad. Bobby stood up.

"Who's Cole? I thought I was dealing with you two," said Barbara.

"Cole is one of our top sales men and specialising in selling houses. He's our best," said Brad.

"What do you think Bobby?" asked Barbara.

"Well Barb, I'm biased. Cole is my boyfriend and he is the best in *many* ways," he said with a dirty grin.

"Oh ok. Would be great to see what this boyfriend looks like. He better be a hottie otherwise he's gonna be punching, having a cute lad like you on his arm," she laughed.

Brad was perplexed at the conversation and how this crazy lady behaved about business. Bobby left the room to get Cole.

"So how did you meet Bobby?" Brad asked.

"He was on the same flight as me on the way back from the UK just before Christmas last year. He was so sweet and a real gentleman.

Basically he gave me the time of day, which doesn't happen very often," she replied.

The door opened and Barbara looked around to find Bobby and another handsome man. He was also impeccably suited, very broad and with a strong square jaw, piercing eyes and an awesome smile.

"Hello, I'm Cole."

"Jesus Bobby, he's a knock out. Is everyone in this office bloody beautiful? I'm including you here sweet cheeks," she smiled at Brad, who blushed slightly.

"Wow, I've not been in a room with so many handsome men before for a long time," she cackled.

"Ok sit down fellas. Let's get down to business and see if we can come to a deal. My opening deal breaker is the following, whatever personal sales commissions you make on this deal, Bobby gets 30%. He's the reason I'm here, so he gets a share," said Barbara.

"Well, we already have our sales commission structures and bonuses clearly laid out for employees and Bobby is not in sales," said Brad. Bobby was blushing now.

"Not really interested in that. This point is non-negotiable. Bobby gets 30% or I go elsewhere."

"I'm very handsomely paid Barbara," confirmed Bobby, "and Cole and Brad would be doing all the work. It was just a pleasure to meet you and for you to give us the chance to work on your portfolio."

"You see, kind hearted and humble. He's the reason I'm here, on those kind words alone, I feel like moving it to 40%. So do we have a deal on Bobby getting 30%? Answer now!" she barked.

"Yes we do," said Brad.

"Good, let's crack on with the rest of the details," Barb smiled at Bobby, who was looking a little shocked.

They worked through the portfolio and discussed the details. They agreed on a four percent commission on sales value for Bartholomew Steadman, which would be confirmed based on valuations to be done in the next week. From this, paperwork would be drawn up, which Barbara stipulated needed to include details of Bobby's 30%.

At the end of the meeting Brad got up and shook Barbara's hand and left her in the room with Bobby and Cole. Barbara smiled at them both.

"You two make such a gorgeous couple. I would love to take you both out to dinner at some point once the sales are done and before I head back to England. Cole you must remember you have a very special man here in Bobby. You treat him good," she smiled, getting up.

"Oh I know. He's the best and I love him very much," said Cole sweetly, making Bobby blush. That was the first time he'd heard Cole tell someone else that he loved him and it felt wonderful.

Barbara smiled and headed for the door. Bobby helped her with her coat and walked her to the elevator.

"Do you need transport anywhere?" he asked.

"No son, I'll enjoy a walk and then get a cab the rest of the way. Speak soon," she said as the elevator door closed.

"I'm sorry Brad," said Bobby when he got back in the office, "I had no idea about the commission, really I didn't. I only met her on a plane."

"It's ok. She's a bit mad, but I liked her. Got real fire in her belly and knows what she wants. We can live with that commission, and she wouldn't be here if it wasn't for you," he added. "You can earn that 30% by keeping Cole on his toes with the selling task he has ahead of him," he laughed.

Bobby whispered in Cole's ear, "Guess I'm gonna be the boss of you for a while. Would you like that?" grabbing Cole's chin with his hand roughly, like a dom does his sub.

"Later, Tiger," Cole replied with a wink.

"Put him down," said Brad, "Let's crack on and plan this sale."

Part 5 - Tragödie in der Stadt

Chapter 15 - Meeting an old acquaintance

Back in Berlin, Max and Peter attended both funerals for Rolf and Kurt. It was a tough two days, saying goodbye to two great work colleagues, cut off in their prime, people who had been instrumental in building their business. It was a truly sad period. Peter and Max spent as much time as was appropriate and always knew when to leave at the right time to give the family their time. On both days, they headed back into the Berlin office.

On the Friday afternoon, Helmut came in for a formal interview for the Office Manager's role. He was very smart in a slim fitting, dark suit. The colour of the suit really made his blue/grey eyes shine bright.

The interview went well and they offered him the role on the spot. The pay was twice what he was on at the hotel and would be reviewed after the first six months. The hours were better and it offered new challenges. He would start in three weeks.

The following morning Max flew back to Chicago via London. Peter flew back also but would be back in Berlin for when Helmut started. Peter would keep constant contact with the Berlin team during this transition period.

Max's flight home was pretty uneventful to London, but on the Chicago stretch, things took a more positive turn. He settled into club class and was greeted by Richard the cabin steward who he and Bobby had met on a previous flight. Richard had got off watching Bobby blow Max in his seat.

"Hello again, sir, if you need a 'hand' with anything, just let me know," he smiled.

"I might take you up on that," Max said, knowing this boy meant business. He was cute, and Max was starting to feel a bit horny. It had been at least four days since he had cum. The night with Helmut was the last deposit and his balls were now feeling full.

After the drinks were delivered and empties collected, Max nodded to Richard to come over.

"I need a hand," Max winked.

"I have two heavy balls full of cum that need relief and I'm in the mood to blow a handsome member of the crew. You got any ideas how this can be arranged?" he smiled.

Richard smiled. "Sure anything can be arranged for the most handsome gold card members and you sure fit the bill. Am I a handsome enough member of the crew to take that filthy load sir?"

"Hell yeah, I'd love to pump cum into a pretty face like yours," Max grinned, stroking his growing boner with all the dirty talk.

"Follow me sir," said Richard.

Richard walked up the aisle and through the curtain. Max followed. Richard and he were alone in the kitchen area, and Richard gently closed the curtain. Richard lead Max into the First Class toilet which was a little bigger. Similar to the one that he and Bobby used a few months back.

Once inside, Max took over control and held Richard's face with his hands. He pulled one back and reached in his back pocket for his pair of soft police gloves.

"I like it a bit kinky," said Max as he put the gloves on, flexing the fingers as they tightly entered the soft leather.

He then put one hand over Richard's mouth and nose. "Smell the leather boy. You like it? These gloves have held many cocks and subs. They are littered with filth and cum."

Richard groaned at the smell and the authority Max issued. Max then unzipped his own jeans and released his raging boner. He pushed Richard down by the shoulders to greet his waiting cock.

"Fucking take it," he instructed, shoving his hard cock deep into Richard's throat. Richard gagged and struggled with it. Not being very good at sucking cock, as Bobby had also found.

"Fuck boy! I thought you'd be better than this at taking cock," Max shoved it in deep, choking Richard, but he didn't care, he held Richard's head with his gloved hands and raped this lad's throat, roughly thrusting in and out.

Richard whimpered but Max continued, deeper and deeper.

"Look at me," he ordered.

Richard looked up, eyes all watery and vulnerable. That was the look Max enjoyed in his victims. He kept thrusting. The young man's wet throat felt awesome on his hard cock. Max watched his victim looking up at him, his head encased in his tight gloved hands, the last few whimpers were all he needed to flood this boy's mouth with his four day cum load and fuck it was a big load. Thick and creaming wads of cum hit the back of Richard's throat, dribbling out the sides of his mouth onto the floor below. Max pulled out and caught a few dribbles of cum from Richard's chin and pushed the cum back into Richard's mouth with his gloved fingers. He let the fingers linger inside his mouth a little longer so he could taste the leather also.

Max pulled him up to his face. "Fuck that was good, but you need to practice."

"I do sir," Richard struggled to say, his throat feeling very hoarse. Max felt Richard's crotch. He was hard.

"You did enjoy it. Now let me show you how it's done," Max ordered.

Max got on his knees and unzipped Richard and pulled out his tidy cock.

Max caressed Richard's cock and balls with his gloved hands. Richard thought it felt amazing. The leather was awesome to feel on his cock and balls. Then Max took his cock to the hilt, just like Bobby did, no trouble of gagging. Max even licked his balls.

"Wow sir," said Richard.

Max pulled down his pants so he could access Richard's arse. As he blew him, he massaged Richard's buttocks with his gloved hands, gripping and squeezing as he went up and down his shaft. He also fingered Richard's hole as he took his cock. The sensations of lips and tongue on cock and leather and fingers on his arse and hole were too much. He blew his load into Max's mouth. Max could feel the warm nectar hitting his tongue. The bitter salty taste of another man's cum, fucking awesome. Max noshed him until all the cum was sucked and he swallowed the whole load. No mess on the floor when he was blowing a guy.

Max stood up, and pulled Richard's pants up for him, as space was limited. Max kissed Richard tenderly and said, "Thanks. You scratched an itch."

Max zipped himself up, smeared the cum on the floor under his boot, to make it look less obvious and left the toilet.

Richard shut the door after him and sat down on the toilet. He looked in the mirror. He looked dishevelled and he had cum on his lapel.

“Fuck.”

He tidied himself up and cleaned the cum off his lapel and the floor and made sure there were no obvious signs of what had just happened in the toilet. He looked at himself again in the mirror and smiled.

“Fuck he was brutal, but wow was he hot. I think I have Daddy issues,” he said out loud to his reflection. He turned and put on ‘the smile’ and left the toilet.

Part 5 - Tragödie in der Stadt

Chapter 16 - True Love

Max was in the Chicago office the following Monday and heard about the Barbara Jackson story. He congratulated Bobby on the lead and also took time to speak to all the team, after being away for two weeks, finding out what was happening and how everyone had been.

The next few weeks went by quite quickly. Helmut started in Berlin under Peter's watchful eye and fitted in well with the team. Cole and Brad worked hard on finalising Barbara Jackson's portfolio sale and signed a contract, with Bobby by her side. In the coming weeks Cole sold all her properties, either to the tenants in situ or to new landlords. He did that in five weeks. Brad masterminded a lucrative sale of the office block, with a special deal; the penthouse apartment at the top, would remain in Mrs Jackson's name, so she had a place to stay when she came back. She liked that idea and thanked him for his thoughtfulness.

It was a busy few weeks, none more so than for Gemma. She was to marry Vince in the next few weeks and all she could talk about was wedding planning. After some changes with the guestlist, she managed to ensure the whole team were invited. It was another chance for the team to socialise together.

The wedding date was planned for early June at the River Roast rooms, with its beautiful views of the Chicago river. Gemma took the week off before the big day and all the team were looking forward to the event as it meant they could all get dressed up again.

Peter flew in from London to join Max. He arrived on the Thursday before the Saturday and spent time with the team on Friday. Max and Peter pulled into the office car park in Max's new toy, an Audi R8 Spider, in a deep purple colour. Bobby and Cole were pulling into the car park at the same time and spotted the car but couldn't see the occupants because of the tinted glass. After they parked up near each other and saw Max climb out.

Cole yelled, "Oh man, you're the man, love that fucking car."

Then Peter got out the passenger seat and then all four guys greeted and gave each other a hug. It was great to see each other again after over a month.

"What happened to batman's bike?" asked Bobby.

"It's gone. Batman wanted it back," said Peter sternly.

"Yes, it's gone, and this baby is the replacement. After seeing Ralf and Kurt, so easily snatched from us in a bike accident, I knew it was time for me to give it up. I loved it but they are so dangerous. Peter has been nagging me for years," said Max, "but I will be keeping my leathers," he laughed.

They all walked to the office and the team cheered to see Peter, who gave a small bow. Everyone was buzzed for the wedding tomorrow.

Bobby and Cole as usual had taken a lot of time choosing their wedding outfits. Well Bobby had. He masterminded their look. Bobby was always the style planner. Cole loved clothes but was more used to dressing for casual style and gym wear. He knew how to accentuate his assets, with tight clothes, but Bobby was the one to plan a wow factor with events.

That Friday evening Bobby and Cole went out with Jamie and Troy for drinks and dinner. These guys all got on so well, the night would always be filled with laughter and fun. In the past they had often fucked and played as a foursome but that started to happen less and less. Each couple were starting to get pretty serious in their relationships and both were finding it harder to be open sexually. So the friendship continued as just that, which made the company all the better.

Bobby and Cole were inseparable. Bobby still couldn't believe that he was in this wonderful relationship with the school jock. Cole still had the occasional nagging guilt about how he treated his wonderful man in the past, but the pair loved each other and loved each other's company twenty four seven.

The next day, they got up, had breakfast and then started getting ready. First thing was a shower and then a quick trip to the barbers for a tidy up. Both boys had their sides shaved tight and the tops tidied up. They also had highlights done to give the hair a fresh look.

Then, it was back to home to have another shower, it was a hot day already, and get dressed. They need to be at the venue for two. The boys got dressed in three piece suits in linen. Cole's was pale blue, and Bobby's was dusty pink. White shirts and the ties matched the suits' colours. The twist was the boys were wearing linen shorts rather than trousers and white Vans baseball boots. With perfectly manicured hair and the suits fitting their beautiful shaped bodies, the look was perfection. Smart meets casual, wedding meets street and with their looks and confidence they could carry it off.

They met Troy and Jamie in the lobby.

"Wow you guys," said Troy.

They were in deep blue, well fitted, tuxedos with different colour ties. They all looked sharp as they got a uber to the venue. When they got there most people had arrived and were waiting in the aisles laid out church style. Everyone noticed Bobby and Cole, their suits and shorts were a talking point. Bobby liked that, but suddenly felt conscious of upstaging the bride and groom. He ushered Cole to come and sit down and draw less attention away from them. Max and Peter were in fine tweed three piece suits. Brad looked sharp in a cream fitted suit. In fact all the gay men looked impeccable, you could spot them a mile off!

Vince was also looking sharp. With some help from Bobby via Gemma, he was in a Hugo Boss dark blue suit, with brown brogues. The suit was well-fitted, unlike the one he wore at the Christmas party. He had his hair nicely done and was looking very handsome, as was his best man, who was wearing similar.

"Vince is looking pretty hot. Do you think we could turn him?" Bobby whispered to Cole with a giggle.

"No," replied Cole. "But the best man has something going on."

Suddenly the casual music stopped and the wedding march piped up. The doors opened. Everyone turned around to see Gemma and her father walk in. She looked stunning. Her delicate oriental frame looked beautiful in a simple off-the-shoulder dress in ivory silk, with her hair up with a diamond tiara and a simple veil. She looked sweet and chic and was beaming from ear to ear. Vince looked like he was about to cry at the sight.

The wedding was amazing. A simple ceremony, then the guests moved to tables for wonderful food and drink. The outside doors to the terrace were opened and the warmth of the air and sight of the river was magical. A band played music and everyone had a great time. The bride and groom looked so happy and so did Bobby and Cole as they danced together for a slow dance. They looked so cute in their suits and shorts.

Everyone retired at midnight, tired and a little drunk.

Part 5 - Tragödie in der Stadt

Bobby and Cole took an uber home leaving Jamie and Troy. They decided to carry on the party and were spending a lot of time with the best man.

"Maybe he was up for fun," said Bobby to Cole as they headed for the exit.

"Yeah maybe, but not with us," he smiled giving Bobby a tug in at the waist as they went through the door.

They headed back to the apartment and pushed through the door. Cole pulled Bobby by the arm to his chest, caressed his face, and gently and tenderly kissed him. He then gently undid Bobby's tie and unbuttoned his shirt and waistcoat, stripping him of all of them gently. He walked the half-naked Bobby to the bedroom and then sat him on the bed. He knelt down and undid Bobby's vans and pull them off, lifting his feet to his face and sniffing his feet through the short white trainer socks. He then pulled the sock off with his teeth, stroking Bobby's calves as he did so. Cole ran his hands up Bobby's legs and inside his shorts, which were too tight to get any access to his crotch. So Cole opted for the more obvious access and unbuttoned and unzipped the shorts, pulling them off revealing Bobby's 'Pump!' branded jock. The whole time this was happening they both remained silent. Bobby was about to speak, but Cole put his finger on his lips to silence him.

Cole then stood up. Bobby watching from the bed, as his beautiful jock boyfriend seductively undressed in front of him. He first took his jacket and waistcoat off, then pulled his vans off with each foot. Standing upright at all times. No staggering or awkward balancing. This boy knew what he was doing. He then very slowly took his tie off and unbuttoned his shirt. Revealing his beautiful chest, and he played with his chest hair and nipples. He stepped closer as he took the shirt off. He unzipped his shorts and slipped them off and stood closer over Bobby's legs, wearing now only his socks and his matching 'Pump!' jock.

Bobby had a growing boner now and Cole was just starting his. Cole then moved down and pressed his body on Bobby, pushing him down on the bed and kissing him tenderly. He stroked Bobby's body and caressed his nipples and chest. He kissed him deeply and passionately. They lay kissing for at least several minutes, intensely absorbed in each other. Feeling each other's bodies and breathing in each other. Bobby could take no more and pushed Cole over and dived down to his crotch. He needed cock and he needed it now. They pulled off each other's jocks and Bobby sucked Cole's cock good and hard.

After about a minute, Cole pulled him off and lay him back down on his back. Bobby was about to speak, but Cole again, touched his lips with his finger. Cole raised Bobby's legs and rested them on his own shoulders, gently dripping some spit on Bobby's hole from a height and then leaned down to meet the face of his lover. He kissed his tenderly again and rested his moist cock, which was oozing precum, on Bobby's wet hole. He then gently inserted the head into Bobby, who received it with a moan, and then gently added an inch at a time. Just like Max showed him that first night of tender sex all those months ago.

Tonight Cole was going to make love to Bobby, not fuck him, make love. The feelings he had for this man had been growing stronger and stronger and he now knew what true love felt like. Cole tenderly pushed his hard cock deep into Bobby and started a gentle rhythm and pumped his hole carefully, kissing and stroking his body throughout the motions. Bobby was in heaven. This beautiful man he had yearned for, for so many years, was now making love to him. This beautiful sexy man, who he felt he couldn't live without was with him. His heavy warm, beautifully smelling body was pressing against his and filling his hole and massaging his prostate perfectly.

"I love you Cole," said Bobby.

Cole's hand touched his lips, "I know you do, and I love you, more than you will ever know."

Cole kissed him again and they made love for what seemed like forever. Then Cole, while kissing Bobby, climaxed deep inside him. Bobby could feel the warm load entering his body. The sensations and Cole's spasms were too much for him also and he came across his and Cole's beautifully sculpted abs. They both groaned and yelped as they came and collapsed.

Cole paused, and stared into Bobby's eyes. He smiled, the sweetest smile Bobby had ever seen. Cole rolled to one side and pulled out. He then wrapped his legs around Bobby and held him close in his arms. They lay there face to face. Nose to nose. Cole kissed Bobby's nose gently.

"Bobby, I'm so in love with you. Will you marry me and be my husband for the rest of our lives?"

Bobby's eyes lit up and were a little watery at the question. Here was the man he had always wanted. The boy who seemed to hate him, who he secretly yearned for. His alpha jock, his tough guy. He was now the most important person in his life, now asking him to marry him.

"Yes, in a heartbeat Cole, in a heartbeat."

Bobby took Cole's face in his hands and kissed him deeply.

Part 5 - Tragödie in der Stadt

by Nick Christie

Printed in Great Britain
by Amazon

41523687R00267